BLOOD SPRING

A BLACK AUTUMN SAGA

BLACK AUTUMN SERIES
BOOK 9

JEFF KIRKHAM

JASON ROSS

ReadyMan
PUBLISHING

THE BLACK AUTUMN SERIES

Series in order:
1. Black Autumn
2. Black Autumn Travelers
3. Black Autumn Conquistadors
4. The Last Air Force One
5. White Wasteland (same characters as Black Autumn)
6. Honor Road (same characters as Travelers)
7. America Invaded (same characters as Conquistadors)
8. President Partisan (same characters as The Last Air Force One.)
9. Blood Spring (all characters from all books.)
10. Fragments of America (short stories)

"Bryhtwold spoke out, heaving his shield (he was an old comrade), brandishing his spear;

very boldly he advised the warriors: 'Resolution should be the tougher, keener the heart,

the mind should be greater *when our power diminishes*."

— THE BATTLE OF MALDON, AUGUST 991 AD, ESSEX, ENGLAND

PREVIOUSLY

**The Homestead,
Oakwood, Utah**

Jason Ross sat on his dead daughter's bed, in her room, and cradled her plate carrier vest in his lap.

It held full magazines for her carbine, medical tape, a tourniquet and surgical shears. He ran his hand over them, one at a time, like talismans of her short life. The trauma kit, attached with MOLLE loops would hang at her hip, close-to-hand. The tourniquet was velcroed to Emily's shoulder strap where she could strip it off and save a life.

She'd saved many lives. She'd defended this place. She'd become the woman she'd dreamed of becoming, and now she was gone. She would rest forever in the soil of the bluff overlooking the Homestead.

Emily had died of the flu, allowed through the Homestead quarantine by his wife, Jenna, and by Emily herself. They'd been complicit in feeding and sheltering orphans—sick children who spread the disease of the wasting world into the safe haven that Jason had built.

Did this homestead even matter, when he couldn't even protect his children?

Emily had always been a passionate girl. To risk her life for orphans was fully within her; the beating heart at the center of her. She'd been drawn to study medicine by the orphan children of Africa. Jason should've known that his daughter wouldn't let orphans die in the refugee camp clumped around the gateway to their neighborhood.

Could he have protected her from herself?

Emily had been a passionate idealist, and they had all died in the winter of the collapse.

But *Jenna* should've done better. She should've known better. His wife was a middle-aged woman, well-versed in the serrated backside of life. *She* should've weighed the risks. *She* should've stopped Emily.

Jason lifted Emily's gun belt and hefted the weight of her Glock. It felt loaded, as were all guns these days. Firearm safety had taken a distant backseat to the burgeoning peril of the desperate winter.

"When did you become so cruel?" Jenna's voice startled him. She leaned on the door frame of Emily's room. She'd been watching Jason weep, his legs folded under each other on his daughter's bed. He spun toward the curtained windows and uncurled his legs. She'd seen him grieving and he couldn't brook it.

"My feelings are no longer your concern," he said. "Our marriage was over the moment you sided with Kirkham."

She stood up straight in the doorway. "Our marriage was over the moment you sentenced me to death."

"Right after you sentenced her to death." Jason held up their daughter's plate carrier vest. "Is that when you mean?"

It was a profoundly unfair thing to say, but he meant it. He meant to hurt her.

Jenna turned and fled down the freezing, stone-lined hallway.

Jason thought he heard her sob, but it might've been the cold mansion, creaking on its foundation.

Jeff had to go, had to get back to his troops. Tens of thousands of men were counting on him to lead.

"You're *not* leaving. Our son could *die*," Tara drew out that last word like a growl. She had never fought him about a deployment before, but this time, something was different. After almost thirty years as a Special Forces operator, his wife stood against him.

It wasn't only that their son had suffered an amputation. The war, and the air around their family, smelled like stomach cancer, like death lingering in the next room. What awaited Jeff in St. George wasn't a battle like any he had fought before, and despite Doc Eric's assurances, their son's injuries yo-yoed between healing and foul ruin.

"Leif has already lost his hand. Next, they'll take his arm to the shoulder." She choked, sobbed and faced away from Jeff, not toward him. Before, she had always gone toward him, no matter how angry. She had always cried into his chest, screamed into it, and even pummeled it. Turning away pained him more than ten thousand fists.

Last fall, their youngest son had been bitten by a rattlesnake in the woodpile, just another pointless price to a pointless apocalypse. If one collected enough wood, one ran afoul of snakes and spiders. No big deal. Except that everything was a big deal now that modern medicine had been obliterated: every scratch, a potential staff infection. Every broken bone was a lifelong deformity; every sniffle was a slow death from the flu.

Without antivenom, the boy barely recovered from the neurological effects of the snake bite, but he survived it. But the bite had been on the meat of his palm, and the flesh up-and-down the hand

and forearm curdled like bad cream. The weal erupted in blisters, bloody cankers and, finally, loose strips of flesh that peeled away like string cheese.

The Homestead doctors burned through their shaky supply of antibiotics with abandon. The wounds festered, healed over, and then festered again from within. They boiled and broke through where they should've cured and healed. The original snakebite became the least of their worries. Myriad infections colonized his son's flayed arm in a dozen grisly nooks and gouges. His immune system was laid low by the venom, and even with medicines, the open meat of Jeff's son was naked against every breeze-borne spore.

Leif's body reacted with a savage allergy to penicillin, struggled two days, recovered, and his sores exploded again. The doctors took off his little finger, which had rotted to the bone. Leif then caught the flu, weakened again, and a long, dark-red weal burst apart at his wrist. The doctors took a quarter-pound of flesh and packed the gash with honey and gauze.

But the arm still wouldn't heal, and when it did close up, infection wormed back in from below. In the deepest doldrums of ironclad winter, the doctors finally took off half of his arm. They left enough of a stump so that Jeff might someday fashion a prosthetic. It was all the solace he would get from this nightmare.

"You can't go. I forbid it," Tara said again. "The Homestead isn't safe. You can't know for sure nothing will happen here. You can't leave us like this."

Jeff would leave anyway. He was a warrior and fifty thousand men had pledged their lives to stopping the iron juggernauts of the narco army—eighty M1-Abrams tanks staged in St. George, Utah, poised to cauterize them all with psychotic tyranny. Jeff could fight them in the middle lands of Utah, or he could fight them within machine gun range of his family. But there was no doubt he would fight them. Tara knew better than to pretend he had a choice. But her shattered heart denied the stark peril.

The day before, their family stood around a tiny hole and laid the desiccated, six-year-old hand to rest where hungry dogs wouldn't dig it up, in the flower bed below the window of their family suite. Perhaps the echinacea flowers would root around the arm and derive small nourishment. Maybe the flowers would provide next year's medicine to heal another boy.

Jeff didn't know if he and Tara would survive this as a couple. Sinking despair settled around his thick shoulders. It seemed as though his family would fall to the apocalypse, one way or the other.

"If you go, I'll take the boys and I'll leave you, Jeff." Her eyes burned like obsidian near the fire.

He knew she wouldn't. There was nowhere to go. There was no one else to take her. This was the end of the road, at the last stand of humanity, at the fall of the world. There was nowhere from here but into the ground.

"I have to go," he said. "I gave my word."

"Damn you," she spat. "Go die, then."

It wasn't a curse. It was her greatest fear.

Jason crossed over into Wyoming in a driving snowstorm. He ran from the howling wind, into the hull of a dead Ford Prius, half-buried in a snow bank. He had only the clothes on his back and the gear inside his bug-out bag, having abandoned his BMW X5 where Interstate 80 cut through Chalk Creek on the Utah side of the border. The trackless snow, eighty miles from the surviving husk of Salt Lake City, had piled up against the bumper of the BMW and forced it to a stop.

He'd been prepared to walk. He knew his car wouldn't take him far in the shiftless world where snow plows no longer ran and fuel was like liquid gold. When he'd fled his home, Jason had grabbed snow shoes and an ultralight bug-out bag that he'd set up years before the collapse: a one pound tent, winter sleeping bag, water filtration, extra socks, med kit, and eight days of freeze dried food. It weighed twenty-five pounds and he should easily reach his cabin on Bear River, despite the holocaust of snow that entombed everything in nine feet of crystalline stupor.

He pried open the ice-gripped door of the Prius, popped the bindings on his snow shoes, shucked his backpack around to the front and tossed it into the passenger seat. He wormed through the door, scraping his chin, and settled behind the steering wheel. Jason glanced about. The car was perfectly clean, and free of dead bodies. He approved. Not only had the fastidious owner kept the car immaculate, but he'd refrained from fouling it with his corpse.

Jason slapped his gloved hands on the wheel and exhaled a plume of frost. The Prius was an instant snow cave. Bivouacking in the dead car made more sense than setting up a tent. He figured that he was still about five miles outside of Evanston, where he'd take a hard right turn and angle up the north slope of the Uinta Mountains toward the cabin. In just fifteen more miles, a single day of snowshoeing, he'd dig out the front door, slip inside, start a fire in the stove, and begin a few well-earned months of abject grief. As the agony of the loss of his children, and now his wife, abated, he would think and plan, plan and think. His mind would pivot to where his heart held fast, around dreams of black revenge.

When the spring broke the back of this hellish winter, he would return to his home and murder the man who had taken it from him. Jeff Kirkham.

Jason dug the tiny, titanium stove from his back and filled it gingerly with denatured alcohol from a small, plastic bottle. He'd once been a rich man, but the contents of the backpack, and the buried cabin along the frozen river, were everything he now owned. Still, the dainty perfection of the ultralight stove gave rise to that old feeling of superiority. Where other men burned oily-smoke car tires to warm their meal, he burned an invisible, clean flame. He flicked his Bic and the blue tell-tale of the alcohol flickered to life. Jason perched the puck-sized stove on the center console and carefully fished out a zip-locked meal, his titanium pot, and a spoon. He cracked the door open and scooped a heaping pot of snow, cradled it in his lap, stripped off the gloves and assembled the tiny pot stand. With a satisfying clink, he put the pot on the flame and began the multi-phase process of boiling water, then reconstituting the backpacker food.

The sun was going down hard now. The deep snow on the windshield turned from translucent white to gray. Soon, it would be black. The only sound in the cockpit of the dead vehicle was the shushing as the alcohol burned.

How could he have lost so much? It made no sense to him. He'd been the most-prepared person he had ever known. Like his perfect backpack, perfect stove, and perfectly-measured alcohol fuel, he had assiduously readied his property for just such an apocalypse. He'd spent a fortune, earned through a string of business start-ups, to surround his loved ones with layer upon layer of stored food and supplies. And those supplies had held, despite every vagary the dying world had thrown at his Homestead. He had been vindicated in his planning, proven prescient in his foresight and held aloft over Salt Lake City like a monument to his own good judgment. No one could argue that he was not, in every conceivable dimension, *right*.

Yet, those he loved, even those he had saved, hated him for it. They could not bind their envy. They took it all from him and, essentially, cast him out.

But he wasn't a man to wheedle and whine. He was, and would always be, a man of action. He who had stolen from him had signed his own death warrant. Jason didn't know how, but he was certain that he would once again walk his land, and harvest the fruit of his orchard.

The snow hissed as it boiled. He shook the Ziploc baggie and settled the dry meal to the bottom, some kind of noodle casserole.

The door of the Prius flew open. The night rushed in. Rough hands seized Jason's arm and yanked him into the yammering wind. The contents of the baggie flew into the night air.

"*Kito tih?*" a man shouted in Jason's face through the bristles of a brown scruffy beard. He wore a snow camouflage jumpsuit of a pattern Jason didn't recognize.

"Who the hell are you?" Jason sputtered.

"*Pri-hodit!*" A second man entered the halo of the flashlight of the first, grabbed a handful of Jason's coat and dragged him along the new tracks they had made in the snow.

Jason looked back as the strange, foreign men steered him, snowshoe-less and stumbling, toward a rumbling, tracked vehicle in the middle of the snowbound interstate. The cockpit of the Prius glowed with a slight blue flicker. His last, fine belongings, there remained.

By the time the slow-moving armored transport arrived in the town of Evanston, Jason gathered he'd been taken by Russian military. What they were doing in the United States, in the middle of winter, at the rim of the end of the world, he had no idea whatsoever.

They herded him out of the vehicle in front of a barely-lit building that must've been some kind of county courthouse or city hall. Jason had never tarried much in Evanston, so he didn't know. The men didn't treat him any more roughly than it required to keep him heading in the direction they wanted, up the steps and into the old government building.

Jason had contemplated an escape attempt while locked in the back of the transport, but the Russians' chuckling, easygoing manner belied concerns of rape, torture or cannibalism. They'd rolled him up without prejudice or fury. They'd searched him, but not cuffed him. His gut told him to just go with it.

They passed into the chill of the brick building, through the glass doors, and into a standard, drop-ceilinged conference room, previously home to ten thousand pointless county meetings. Lanterns exhaled on the tabletop, giving light to the otherwise dark room. Around the fringes of the yellow glow, six men murmured in Russian. They looked up at Jason and one barked a question at the soldiers. They discussed some matter concerning him, no doubt, and the Russian officer spoke to him in Cyrillic-dipped English.

"You come from Utah?"

"Correct," Jason said.

"From Salt Lake?"

"Yes." Jason didn't know how to read the man's rank on his shoulder, but he was obviously in command. And he was vulnerable. It was in his eyes, how he glanced to the side when he spoke, like a bird checking its broken wing. It was something Jason could work with.

"We have questions," the Russian officer circled the table to face him. "You answer, no?"

Jason considered those he'd loved and left behind. He weighed his loyalties, and his marriage—what fragment of it remained. He mulled over the injustices committed against him. He pictured Jeff Kirkham.

"I'll answer," he said. *And I'll wager we're going to be very good friends.*

1

Sinclair, Wyoming

A MONTH AFTER ARRIVING IN EVANSTON, AS WINTER LOOSENED ITS fingers 'round the throat of America, Jason Ross pursued his revenge.

Wyoming gave way before him like a chastened lad before the switch. Behind him, arrayed in their might and fury, two battalions of Russian Spetsnaz—lately abandoned by the Motherland—sought refuge or plunder. Ross promised them the Salt Lake Valley. They promised him retribution.

They paused where the interstate crossed the Utah state line, staring past the sign, down the narrow canyon that would funnel them through the mountains and into the Salt Lake Valley.

"The army won't chase you past Evanston," Jason explained to Colonel Zhukov. In the last month, the Spetsnaz commander had come to rely on him a great deal. The steel that'd once hardened Zhukov's eyes had dissipated since they first met in March after the apocalypse.

In Zhukov, Ross witnessed the decomposition of a man who'd lost his home. Ross wondered what his own eyes looked like to them. His hatred for Jeff Kirkham had annealed him, not diminished him. Jason's eyes were like burnished leather, he believed.

But Zhukov *was* diminished, as were his men. They looked over their shoulders back along Interstate 80, where the third Spetsnaz battalion had been exterminated in Denver by a ten thousand man horde of Native Americans and U.S. Special Forces.

"Why would they not chase us?" Zhukov asked. He'd picked up a habit of kneading his hands.

"Because the Rocky Mountains will make them reconsider. They'll marshal their forces rather than take the long way around. The mountains are impassable still. You gave up the missile bases. Why follow you now?"

It'd been easy to convince them to run from the fragment of the U.S. military and descend to lower elevations. At first the Russians had taken Ross prisoner—a source of intelligence about what lay ahead—but they soon came to rely on his counsel. He offered a path out of the windswept Wyoming plains. They would flee the snows and take warmth where the mountains lay down into desert. He would direct them west, where their fingers wouldn't freeze in their gloves.

The expeditionary force of Russians had arrived in America before the snows, across the Aleutians and down Alaska and Canada, to seize the greatest weapons system in human history: the American nuclear missile arsenal. But they had failed.

Taking control of three Air Force bases had been easy for the Russians, given the collapse of the American military. Gaining the ability to fire the ICBMs, however, had been impossible. They'd been confounded by the analog nature of the launch codes and the buried, mountain fortress of NORAD.

They'd wanted control of American missiles for a preemptive strike against their Chinese neighbors, but before the Spetsnaz could gain control of American missiles, the Chinese army had poured across the Russian frontier. Moscow turned their attention to the Chinese battlefront, and the fifteen hundred elite Russian commandos in America found themselves abandoned in the post-apocalyptic, American West, starved of resupply and pursued by a Native American army of irregulars.

That was how Jason Ross came upon the Spetsnaz in Evanston; angry, betrayed and bristling with a killer's disquietude. In that regard, he empathized with them. He'd been stripped of his home and cast to the winds of winter too.

Salt Lake City was ripe for the picking. Jason would return, but not as a fog-like version of his former self, but as the righteous storm.

Present day
Interstate I-15
Cedar City, Utah

"GO, GO, GO!" Jeff Kirkham shouted into his radio. He'd already lost three gun trucks that morning to the cannons of the M1 Abrams tanks. The cartel army advanced up the center of Utah, just three hundred miles from the refineries of Salt Lake City, and Jeff's force of a thousand pickup trucks could do little to stop them.

A wolf pack of six tanks crested the ridge between Harmony Mountain and Coffee Peak hovering over the tiny town of Kanarraville, Utah. A partisan Ford F-250 pickup truck maneuvered for a shot.

"Get the hell out of there," Jeff ordered over the radio. The truck crew still believed they were the hunters, not the hunted.

The TOW missile, bolted to the bed of the truck, burst with a white cloud of smoke out the back as the team fired the guided missile at an Abrams on the mountaintop. The boom of the launch took two seconds to reach Jeff's observation perch.

Ka-boom! The TOW lanced across the battlefield and struck the tank.

A chunk of its reactive armor blasted loose, and a cloud of smoke enveloped it. Jeff couldn't tell if it was disabled or not. If so, that'd be the third tank they'd killed out of the eighty the Hoodies fielded.

The Ford truck with the anti-tank crew punched the gas and roared away from the overpass where they'd made the shot. The TOW gunner almost flipped over the tailgate, as his driver fled the cannons of the Abrams.

Five tanks opened fire at once from the ridge. By the time the muzzle blast reached Jeff, the shells were already raining down on his fleeing gun truck. The Ford swerved in an "S-curve" between the two northbound lanes of I-15, but it made no difference. The arcing high explosive shells from the Abrams rained down on the ribbon of asphalt, bisecting the Utah desert. The Hood Rats had learned to shoot the Abrams during the long winter. They ravaged the strip of interstate like a kid dropping lady fingers on an anthill.

A shell blew a crater in front of the fleeing Ford. The front tire plunged into it and bounced the chassis four feet into the air. When the twisting truck slammed to the pavement, the TOW gunner flew out and the gun, lately bolted to the truck bed, broke free of its moorings and flipped out the side of the truck bed, plowing the asphalt like a wayward anchor.

The Ford spun to the side, pivoting around the dragging gun, then barrel-rolled down the length of the I-15. Two bodies pitched out the shattered windows as it tumbled. One disappeared under the churning metal. The F-250 came to rest on its contorted wheels in a sea of metal and plastic.

The HE rounds of the Abrams followed. Within seconds, the gunners doped the range and vaporized the crash site with a hail of cannon fire.

The TOW gunner who'd flown out of the truck crawled off the road and into the sagebrush.

"Send in two rescue buggies," Jeff ordered over his command radio. The tanks on the ridge had the crash site ranged, and the buggies would be at risk, but the drivers knew their stuff. They wouldn't stay in one place for more than five seconds.

Jeff couldn't leave injured men, not with the precarious nature of his partisan unit and the viciousness of the cartel. If he left wounded men to the enemy, they'd be tortured and their severed heads would be staked along the roadside with their penises stuffed in their mouths. Jeff's Mormon troops weren't hardened to that level of war. Jeff wasn't even sure he was any longer. With his family at risk, and Tara hating him, there was no safe haven, nothing "home," no solid backstop, and nowhere to regroup. If this was Afghanistan, then they were the out-gunned *mujahideen*.

Jeff's medevac dune buggies streaked across the sandy plain, dodging between cedar trees and tumbleweed clumps, sending up twin plumes of dust behind their tires.

The former drug lord, Gustavo Castillo, had wintered somewhere in the Nevada desert. Then, he advanced into Southern Utah, taking St. George and topping its storage tanks with Mexican fuel.

There'd been a cartel leadership shake up that Jeff's spies scarcely understood, but it ironed itself out as the winter snows abated from the ancient seabed of Lake Bonneville. The Great Basin, from the southern border of Utah to the rusting, white refineries of North Salt Lake, would be the final battlefield of the Rockies, and likely Jeff's last war. Spring had come to central Utah, and with it had come the Hood Rat menace—a brigade of Abrams tanks and ten thousand former drug soldiers. They rolled north from their base in St. George, intent on taking Salt Lake City and its gas refineries, the last in the West, and maybe the nation.

He'd always been on the side of might and right, the United

States of America, with high technology and an inexhaustible supply chain. He'd never battled the M1 Abrams tank, or any tank for that matter. This enemy even had drone reconnaissance. The Hood Rats, "Hoodies" to Jeff's men, had a massive advantage, and yet it fell on his shoulders to hold out against them.

He had the gasoline refineries at his back and fifty thousand pumped-up Mormons armed with hunting rifles. Lately, he'd cracked the concrete tombs of Dugway Proving Ground and Tooele Army Depot, and deployed moldering mounds of weapons and ammunition. His men fought with mostly Viet Nam era weapons against the apex of American military might—the M1 Abrams main battle tank.

They couldn't afford to trade a TOW missile truck and four men just for three armor plates blown off the cheek of a tank. Jeff needed solid kills to stop the Hood Rats in their steady march toward the Maverick Oil Refinery, and he wasn't getting those kills. Not even close.

As best he knew, his wife and three boys were huddled in the Homestead stronghold, within eyeshot of the spiraling smokestacks of the refinery. Unless Tara had actually taken the boys and left him, his family was at ground zero, dead in the crosshairs of the cartel war machine.

Tara wouldn't have left, Jeff reminded himself, not with his son's arm recently amputated. She wouldn't pull Leif away from his doctors. His family was safe, at least until the cartel made it past Jeff and his gadfly trucks. He could focus on the fight, sure in the knowledge that his maimed son would keep their marriage from flying apart.

With the fall of St. George, Jeff's army abandoned the twin towns of Pintura and Kanarraville. They took refuge in the next farming community between St. George and Salt Lake—Cedar City. There were only 250 miles between the Hoodies and Jeff's family.

He barked into his radio and redeployed the swarm of trucks

along the high ground to the south of Cedar City, almost a thousand of them. A few had bed-mounted TOW missiles, and all the rest ran with M-2 .50 caliber machine guns and 240D heavy machine guns. They were many, but only the TOWs had any chance of disabling a tank.

Jeff had hoped the gangsters were inept with the heavy weapon system, but they were not. They had obviously trained over the winter. The cartel soldiers hunted in coordinated wolf packs with half a dozen tanks accompanied by several solar-powered, fast-attack buggies, followed by passenger trucks brimming with infantrymen.

At the battle of St. George, Jeff lost twenty-seven trucks and a hundred men. He didn't have a reliable count of how many tanks they'd killed, but he suspected it was no more than three, and all of those thanks to the TOW.

If this battle was anything like the disaster at St. George, the Hoodie fuel trucks would consolidate in Kanarraville. They'd refuel their main battle tanks, and then lay out their portable solar fields to recharge the gun buggies. After that, they'd overtake the next town along the interstate. Then the next, and the next. Steadily, they'd chew up the road between St. George and the refinery.

As Jeff watched his medevac buggies dodge tank fire, a Polaris RZR roared from the north across the dry lake bed toward Jeff's elevated command post. He recognized the vehicle from the Homestead motor pool. It was Evan Hafer, and whatever he was coming to say might've been said over the radio. Instead, Evan came in person. A chill wormed down Jeff's spine.

Jeff returned to glassing the brave rescue. A medevac buggy scooped up the wounded man from beside the road and darted away as shells and machine gun fire fell around them. A second buggy checked the burst-apart Ford for survivors. There didn't appear to be any. Both buggies turned and sped for the cover of friendly forces.

Evan skidded to a stop in the OHV and leaped out of the driver's seat. He wore his "commando face" which didn't bode well. Evan usually greeted Jeff with a pithy insult. Not this time.

"The Homestead fell," Evan blurted. "Our families...our families were inside." His face could've been carved in stone. This was no joke.

"What does that mean?" Jeff demanded.

"It means exactly what it means. Our families are captured. Our home is occupied by the enemy." Evan's face tightened with rage.

"Who?" Jeff staggered.

"I don't fucking know who..." Evan choked.

Jeff doggy-paddled in a bog of confusion, the set piece battle before him forgotten. The Abrams tanks were meaningless, his dead and dying men, a fog.

His *wife*, Tara. Their boys. His wounded son. The other families.

How could the Homestead have fallen?

They were two hundred and fifty miles from the Homestead. How could the cartel have maneuvered around him? Jeff's surveillance network, and thousands of Utah ranchers, would've alerted him if the drug dealers had circled north. *And how would the cartel have known about the Homestead?*

"Tell me everything." Jeff wrestled with his rage behind professionalism. "Who, what, where, when, and why; tell me every detail."

Evan wiped his face with a gunpowder-stained glove. He inhaled through his nose and slowed himself down.

"Who:" he exhaled and held up five fingers to organize his thoughts. "I don't know, but they had armored vehicles." He ticked down one of the five fingers.

"Cartel!" Jeff interrupted.

"Just stop," Evan gathered himself again. "Not Abrams tanks. Some kind of armored troop transport, they said."

"Who is they?" Jeff interrupted again.

"Witnesses. The neighborhood people. Let me talk...next is

WHAT...They overran the Homestead defense and they're inside the walls."

"Who is they? Stop using pronouns." Jeff's feet rooted to the ground. His spine curved into a fused, angry arch. His shoulders were made of pig iron.

"*They* are the fighters with MRAPs, or whatever armor. *They* are the shit birds who have taken our families captive."

Jeff thought of Leif, his arm gone, the stump vulnerable and his doctors, captured.

"They have MRAPs?" Jeff said. "So they're cops?"

"No. Maybe. Light armor, dude. Maybe not MRAPs *per se*. Just shut up and listen." Evan looked at his four extended fingers and continued. "*WHERE?* The Homestead. They ran the neighborhood roadblocks to the north. I think they got through on the Oakwood side of the mountain." Evan inhaled and checked off another finger. "*WHEN?* First light this morning. *WHY?* I have no fucking clue. Maybe because the Homestead is the most kick-ass spread in the Western United States. It's Disneyland for survivors. It's a legendary piece of land now that everyone's eating lawn grass. I have no idea *why*. Could be anything."

Jeff's adrenaline peaked, and then fell hard. His shoulders slumped and his feet stutter-stepped. "Fuck. Fuck. Fuck," Jeff mumbled, looking at the ground, struggling to think.

He hoped Tara had left him, had taken the boys and found a cabin anywhere other than the Homestead. He hoped she'd been serious and had packed her bags the moment he went to war.

But he knew in his bones she hadn't. She would never pull the boys away from the Homestead because they'd had an argument. She'd been Army intelligence and she wasn't a rash woman, not when the boys' lives were on the line. She'd stayed in the Homestead. Whoever had seized it could be raping her right now.

BOOM! BOOM-BOOM-BOOM! Jeff looked up, focusing his eyes on the ragged mountaintops. The cartel tanks fired a final salvo then maneuvered back toward the interstate. All of Jeff's trucks and buggies had completed their retreat southward.

"Take over for me," he ordered Evan.

"What? No. That's crazy. You're in the middle of a battle."

"It's over. We're retreating. I can't do this right now. I have to go to them."

"Stop. Pull yourself together," Evan seized Jeff's forearm. "Stand still."

Jeff had been prowling in a circle like an alley cat with his tail nailed to a board.

"I can't do it. I bailed on her. I left her to come here. I shouldn't have left her. I should've conducted better long-range recon. I should've known about the other enemy—whoever was probing us to the north."

"Dude. You have to stop. *Just stop*," Evan said. He looked around them, and Jeff followed his glance. Men were watching. His staff had ceased orchestrating the army's retreat and looked on with faces of confusion. Evan whispered urgently: "Handle this battle now. You're a general. There's nothing outside of a five mile radius, not for the next hour. Get your men to safety."

Evan was right. *Fight the battle in front of you.* This fight was lost, but they could retreat, tend to their wounded, and live to fight another day.

"Get back to work," Jeff bellowed at his men. But mostly, he said it to himself.

2

"After the Black Autumn collapse, the first winter extinguished ninety-four percent of Americans and Canadians. Mexico fared better, losing only half her population. The North American continent drew into spring, unkempt and gun-shy. The slow decomposition of hundreds of millions, those who hadn't already been eaten by man or beast, hastened, warmed, and subsided. A trembling peace arose among the survivors. It was a peace of the tormented and infirm, too weary to do others harm. The violent people starved soon after the foodstuffs of modern society were gobbled up, or hoarded and lost. Like all predators, brigands perished soon after their prey. Those who survived the winter were cooperative souls, inclined to huddle together in thick-skinned clans, fortresses, and communities. They were the cheerful, the gracious, the hard-working, and ruby-cheeked. They were the kind who gave their lives for those they loved; and thus they bid death be patient."

— THE AMERICAN DARK AGES, BY WILLIAM BELLAHER, NORTH AMERICAN TEXTBOOKS, 2037

The Homestead

Oakwood, Utah

JENNA ROSS PLACED A DRIED FLOWER ON THE THINNING SNOW OVER her daughter's grave and said a prayer. Her husband, or ex-husband perhaps, was back, with all the sound and fury of a man betrayed. Jenna wondered how Emily felt about it, looking down from heaven with a god's-eye view of things. She must still love her father, despite his fall from grace. If Emily were alive, she might even counsel reconciliation. It wasn't beyond the realm of possibility, not in this world, where violence turned families under like dandelions before the plow. Jenna would do what she must. She had new children to protect and a home to preserve.

Jason harbored a dark, jealous heart, and now that he had overcome the Homestead by force, he would not be easily appeased. He had taken his portion like a man filled with scorn, the unrighteous victor. He had sent for her, and now she would face her fate.

It shouldn't have surprised her—Jason attacking the Homestead with a thousand Russian Special Forces soldiers. He'd raised a cadre of Special Forces before, to defend the Homestead during the collapse of society. This time, six months later, he'd retaken the walled Homestead with a thousand men and a dozen Russian tanks while the Homestead's defenders were south, fighting the cartel army.

Jason and his Russians came down the freeway, up the foothills, over the roadblocks, and through the shattered gates of the compound. From first warning to final assault, the Homestead fell in fifteen minutes. The few defenders left by Jeff Kirkham had been unwilling to waste their lives against commandos and tanks. They surrendered without firing a shot.

That'd been two days ago. The Russian commandos had since consolidated their grip on the Oakwood neighborhood and quartered in the surrounding homes, half of which were empty. What had once been the domain of Jeff Kirkham and the LDS Church was now in Jason's control, the entire Oakwood hillside. Jason's troops consumed what food they desired, but nobody had been hurt, imprisoned or exiled. Not yet, at least. Jenna feared she might be the first.

She stood up from Emily's grave and scraped the crumbly snow from her knees. She'd done her hair that morning and she wore a fur-lined jacket that set off her green eyes like emerald fire. Her hair was freshly touched up, the fringes of gray restored to auburn by a lost magic of modern life, the hair dye she kept tucked away in her boudoir. She'd added light makeup, perfected her lips, and pulled on snow pants that accentuated her long legs. An ancient instinct instructed her in the ways of the feudal pageant and the coming confrontation with her estranged husband and warlord. She was the queen, deposed yet royal. He was the victorious potentate with power over life and death. She would bow to him, for now.

If he was as smart as he thought he was, he would execute her immediately and endure the eternal hatred of his children. It was the only way she would not eventually win.

Jason held court in the great room of the main house. His soldiers had swept aside Jenna's custom-upholstered center couch and re-arranged the seating so no backs were turned to Jason's chair against the crackling fireplace. Russians in dirty snow camouflage stood about the room and sat on her floral sofas.

Jason greeted her with a sneer. "It's the Grand Dame of the Homestead, in the flesh." He didn't get up from his seat by the fire. "This is my former wife," he introduced her to a Russian, somewhat older than the other men. His eyes drifted over her legs, her breasts, and her face.

"A pleasure," the Russian said in a thick accent.

"It's good to see you, Jason," Jenna said, and she meant it, in a way. She'd worried that he might've died in the winter snows.

"Yeah, I'm sure it's just *wonderful* to see me. How're your orphans?" he asked with a raised eyebrow.

Together with her daughter Emily, now passed, and the other women of the Homestead, Jenna had organized a forbidden orphanage for lost infants and toddlers. It'd likely been the breach of quarantine that allowed the flu into the community, the sickness that took their Emily's life.

Jenna raised her chin. "The children are doing well. We're finding homes for them now that the refugee crisis has slowed."

The crisis hadn't "slowed." The refugees had all died. Over eighty percent of Salt Lake Valley had perished—either to starvation, the flu, dysentery, violence, or death by freezing.

"Did Kirkham take you as a second wife now that he's Mormon?" Jason asked. It hadn't taken long for his insecurity to bob to the surface.

Jeff Kirkham wasn't really a Mormon. Mormons north of the Oquirrh Mountains didn't practice polygamy anyway. Tara Kirkham would tear out Jeff's throat before she'd allow such a thing. It'd been a hollow jab, a placeholder for Jason's angst.

She knew how she looked, and she could see the hunger reflected in his eyes. Even in her fifties, Jenna Ross' long legs, slim figure and proud breasts drove middle-aged men to behave like much younger men. In a particular brand of dominant male, she could be the object of insatiable desire. Her aloof bearing, on top of her still-fresh femininity, agitated something primal, even in men who had aged out of garden-variety lust.

She ignored his jab. Silence on the matter of Kirkham would increase Jason's unease, and that was exactly what she intended. There was no chemistry between Jenna Ross and Jeff Kirkham, beside the tremendous affection she held for him as protector of her family, but Jason didn't need to know that. *Let his imagination run.*

Silence was a keen-edged weapon, and she wielded it deftly against the blunt force of masculinity. She waited while the soldiers in the room shifted their weight from foot to foot, and flicked glances between her heart-shaped ass and Jason Ross' face.

He waved away the question about Jeff Kirkham with a look of disgust. Jason often knew when she was manipulating him, but that didn't stop it from working.

"Kill a goat and have the women make stew for my friends," Jason ordered Jenna. "Bake plenty of bread."

"For how many?" she asked.

He seemed irritated by the question. "I don't know. Kill two goats."

"If we kill too many goats we won't have enough to breed. They're going into estrus now, and we're leaving them alone so they'll multiply over the summer."

Jason took a ragged breath. "Just do what I ask. Please."

With that last word, "please," she turned to leave, knowing she'd won the engagement. She wouldn't be executed or even exiled. He wanted her, and that cut deeper than any sword, penetrated more violently than any bullet. The day of man had passed, and he hadn't realized it. His power was on the wane. The womb of the earth was opening. The edge of the sword would rust quickly, now.

The dead had cleared the streets, left empty the buildings and enriched the soil with their corpses. A new dawn approached, where stability and peace would flow back into the low places. Seeds would be planted and protected. Trees would blossom, and then fruit. Animals would breed, multiply and replenish the quiet forests. The domain of the feminine would shimmer at first, over the mountain tops, and then gain in light and warmth. Genesis would nibble at the edges of war, but then bite down hard. Mankind would be compelled to begin again, and the compulsive gravity of peace would overcome the chaos of war.

Jenna yearned for the simple pleasure of seeing her children return to sow, then harvest the gardens and orchards of the Homestead. Three of her children were still missing. They were lost to her somewhere in the train wreck of post-apocalyptic America. She prayed for them. Tessa, Tristan and Sage.

Jason had set them up with survival supplies before the collapse, but fickle chance, as much as any preparation, had plucked the quick from the dead that past winter. She often found herself gazing, many times a day, at the long driveway up from the gate, hoping her children would appear.

Jenna had adopted three little ones from the starving refugee camps that hung around the perimeter of the Homestead, and brought them into her home. Elle, Sebastian, and Jude. When Jason discovered them, her personal vulnerability would multiply. A woman with children was as exposed as a flowering apple tree against the tempest.

Jacqueline Reynolds caught Jenna's arm as she withdrew from the great room. "How'd that go?"

Jenna glanced about to see who might be listening. "He didn't send me packing. At least not right away. I'm supposed to make them all dinner."

Jacqueline blanched. Food was growing scarce in the Homestead. "Someone needs to tell him that we can't feed an extra thousand men. We'll starve by June."

It was late April. The snows had abated in the valley, on the sunny patches in the hills. The rains rolled over Utah several times a week. Yet there would be a deadly season between planting and harvest. The Homestead had gone into the collapse with astounding riches: over a hundred and eighty thousand pounds of wheat, beans, and sugar, stored in Lego-block stacks of IBC totes racked like walls everywhere on the three-hundred acre property.

They had preserved starter families of goats, rabbits, bees, and egg-laying chickens. At the onset of the crash, the seed vault was fresh, topped up and perfectly matched to their altitude. The Homestead had planted an extraordinary garden every year for more than a decade. There was little they didn't know about growing food at 6,000 feet on the western exposure of the Wasatch Mountains.

The orchard bloomed with over a hundred and fifty fruit trees, a hundred elderberry bushes, a dozen berry patches and a half-acre of lavender to delight the hives of drowsy honeybees. The wild forest around the compound also provided—saskatoon, chokecherry, nodding onions, elderberry, and acorns in the fall. The well drew clear, cold water from six hundred feet below ground, pumped from the depths by twenty kilowatts of solar power. The Homestead was remarkably blessed, all thanks to the dark man, who sat on his throne in the great room of the "big house."

Despite being blessed with preparations far more elaborate than anything within a hundred miles, the Homestead hung precariously on the verge of starvation. Many of the fruit trees would bloom, but then be crushed by a late spring frost; new pests would invade the gardens, potatoes would fail to sprout, goats would be killed by mountain lions, bees would mysteriously vanish, and that would be just the beginning of their peril. It'd be just like any other year growing food, only *this year* their lives would depend on making perfect decisions, and getting very lucky.

Everyone was a gardener now. Every man, woman, and child in the Homestead not fighting a war tended plants. They wrestled with the vegetable starts in the greenhouses. Some of the seeds refused to germinate, for reasons known only to the fickle gods of gardening. Other tender starts had been touched by the withering hand of frost. Many, like the crookneck squash and bell peppers, had been replanted after the seeds failed, and now they ran late for the fall harvest.

The Homestead was nearly out of wheat, beans, and dried veggies. They'd planned to grow potatoes over the winter in greenhouses to supply the bulk of their carbohydrates, but the Ross family had been Whole Foods health nuts. They hadn't eaten potatoes, corn, or even bread, much, before the collapse. They ate mostly vegetables and proteins, which left them almost no experience growing potatoes, corn, or grains. They made many mistakes as they learned, in a rush, and their winter season harvest was paltry, despite the promise of lavish greenhouses.

They'd stocked and over-wintered seed potatoes in their root cellars. Jason had set aside hundreds of potato "grow bags" in which they were to sprout the potato eyes, but as a practical matter, they'd only ever piddled with the process. They had very little idea where, when, and how to grow starchy foods. If the slow-growing potato harvest failed as a result of some ignorant misstep, they would starve next winter. They were playing a slow-motion game of Russian roulette with potatoes, weather, and Mother Nature. Half the conversation in the Homestead circled around conjecture of potato husbandry.

Most vexing of all, they had almost no industrial inputs for their gardens and fields, no fertilizer, no herbicides, and no pesticides. Jason Ross had not thought to stock up on the lifeblood of modern gardening, manufactured crutches that guaranteed pest abatement and soil nutrition. The Homestead kept three concrete bins of seasoned compost, but the several cubic yards barely put a dent in the new demands of the potato grow bags and the waking planter beds. The compost had been scarcely enough for their hobby garden. They'd have to rob soil from the forest if they were to have any hope of supplying nutrition to the seedlings, and that wild soil would bring noxious weeds and unknown pathogens, like white leaf mold, squash bugs, and aphids.

Every eye turned to the declining totes of grain, and the precious promise of goat milk and meat, and looked forward to rabbit flesh, saskatoon berries, eggs, and honey. With the new demands of the quartering invaders, the survival of the Homestead tipped into doubt.

"Will Kirkham and the men come back?" Jacqueline asked

Jenna. In other words, *would the Homestead find itself at the center of yet another battle?*

It would be their third violent threat. The two women knew the cost of war on home ground. The delicate plants, not to mention the tender children, would pay a dire price.

"I hope they stay south," Jenna answered. "The surgery could be worse than the wound if they return."

Jacqueline nodded and considered. She was the community's therapist and erstwhile pastor, their advocate of peace. She was clear on the psychological pathologies of Jason Ross, once their benefactor and Jenna's husband, now their tyrant. He'd been changed by killing, racked by the death of his beloved daughter, addled by alcoholism, and obsessed with revenge against Jeff Kirkham.

Both Jenna and Jacquelyn were high on the list of Kirkham's allies. They would be the playthings of Jason's revenge, alongside Tara Kirkham and the Kirkham children. They'd also been caught inside the Homestead when the invaders stormed the gates.

"Yeah," Jacqueline agreed. "This is *our* war." She ran her fingers through her hair, then turned and faced the direction of the great room, her feet planted and her hands anchored on her solid hips.

Jenna shivered involuntarily. Motherhood had unfurled its fangs.

McKenzie, Tennessee

FOR ONCE IN HIS LIFE, Mat Best felt good about how he was leaving things with a girl. She was a dead girl, but all the more reason to whip out his weather-beaten honor and compare what he'd done against what she would've wanted.

Caroline's brother, William, stood with his own woman now.

William had barely turned thirteen and his girlfriend was just a year older. The kids had pointed weapons at evil men and stood their ground. They were adults now, at least by the standards of this tenuous world. Gladys Carter stood beside the young ones in all of her six-foot, four-inch glory. A couple of tears meandered down her face, and Mat would've loved to think they were being shed because the two of them had never hooked up and she was heartbroken over it. But she and Mat had become close friends, and they made an awkward, but good faith effort to co-parent the two orphan sweethearts, kids that would, much too soon, start their own family. Mat hugged Gladys hard.

In the apocalypse, when two people waved goodbye, they would likely never see one another again. The distances were too great, the fuel too precious, and the perils too severe. It was *see-you-later-alligator* like a grenade in the gut. Goodbye forever.

He loved these three, but they weren't his blood. As the deadly winter rolled from being a dance with death to a less-harrowing daily grind, Mat's mind turned to his birth family on the West Coast. He needed to know if they were dead or alive. He hoped to see his father's craggy, handsome face and his mother's bright eyes and lilting crow's feet. As the fight of his life to protect the town of McKenzie winnowed down to weekly schedules and security rotations, he knew he'd soon be leaving.

"If I'm back around this way when you're in your twenties, I'll put you through Ranger School. Sound good, Champ?" Mat said to William and clapped him on the shoulder. The boy nodded and clung to Candice. He couldn't speak. "Stay on top of your push-ups and pull-ups, 'cause I could show up any day and selection's going to kick your narrow ass."

The boy smiled around his snot and tears. He nodded, probably to make Mat feel less horrible.

Mat was going to Santa Barbara, California. He'd cross the mighty Mississippi, climb the Rockies, take a pit stop in Salt Lake

City, then descend to the California coast. He had enough gas, gifted from the townsfolk, to make it as far as Salt Lake.

Things were safer now. Violence had gone out of the region like a fart under a fat dog. All at once, it just dissipated. It hadn't gone down like The Walking Dead, where canned goods could be found in cupboards years later. With people scavenging as hard as they were, when the stuff ran out, it went away like the flicker of a mosquito's soul. Finding a can of chili was like finding a silver ingot.

Even the highway bandits starved between February and March. The "trick" to survival, it turns out, had been to group up in large clans or small towns and behave like family. Even cannibalism had only strung out the inevitable wipe out by a few weeks. It wasn't the lack of something in the belly that killed most folks; it was the disease and dysentery from drinking surface water, accelerated by their beat-up immune systems. Living outdoors in the elements took people down faster than anyone had thought it would. Camping was eventually a death sentence.

Mat and his friends in McKenzie survived, by eating metric tons of cattail and the hogs that ate the cattail. If Mat never ate pork stew with swamp 'taters again, it'd be too soon.

The town of McKenzie had worked out a system with Doc Hauser and his thousands of refugees that ringed the town, and that system had pulled them through the worst of winter. The refugees harvested cattail while the townsfolk herded pigs and brought them to slaughter. Now, the town would have a rough spring, without tractor fuel or fertilizer, while they figured out how to restart the feed crops. There wouldn't be loads of feed corn coming by rail to fatten the pigs. A whole team of senior citizens was researching in the library to figure out how they used to raise pigs without a global supply chain.

With McKenzie encircled by friendlies, and the HESCO wall complete, Mat was rendered obsolete. McKenzie needed gardeners more than gunmen. Young William had found himself a mate. The loss of so many people was being grown over by new love.

Mat climbed into his Ford Raptor with a final wave, cranked the ignition, and pulled away from the town he'd lately called home. His AR-15 lay across the passenger seat and he wore a chest rig bulging with mags.

He twiddled with the dial of the shortwave radio screwed to the dashboard, and found a guy in Kentucky yapping about a seed exchange forming between towns. The radio, these days, was full of people excitedly comparing notes about community and cooperation. Tales of roadside murder and mayhem were scarce. A few Mad Max gangs still persisted, but they were a shadow of their former leather-clad menace. They'd been beat down and forced into hiding by city/states of "regular folks."

Crossing the Big Muddy would be a trick. If any bandits still existed, they'd gravitate toward the best bottlenecks, like suspension bridges across the Mississippi. Mat would take a day or two and reconnoiter that "danger crossing" area.

A few towns still had roadblocks, all the towns that'd survived. He'd bypass the roadblocks he could, and talk his way through the rest. He hoped he wouldn't have to shoot his way through any. Things weren't like that anymore. People had had their fill of violence. Still, the drive to California that'd once taken two days would require weeks, if not months.

Gladys and the kids hadn't understood why Mat needed to go. When he said the part about seeing his parents, they didn't argue, but they didn't nod understandingly, either.

Gladys, in her southern drawl, said, "I hear the words, but I don't hear the music."

He wasn't sure what she'd meant by that. It seemed pretty clear to him: he wanted to make sure his family was okay on the West Coast. Usually, she was the one with the most common sense. This time, she served him a heaping dose of stink eye. They'd just have to agree to disagree.

Mat's Raptor growled west down the highway. The staticky radio bounced between tidbits of local news in faraway places. The hills over the home and family he had made for himself disappeared entirely from the rearview mirror.

Once again, he was alone.

———

Cedar City, Utah

BILLY MCCALLISTER KNELT on the man's chest as Filemon cut out his tongue. Bill had been waiting for this chance, the opportunity for his personal cadre to scare the hell out of the rest of the gangbangers.

The chucklehead under his knee had fired an insult at him and Filemon as they'd walked past with a cuffed prisoner. Mister Soon-To-Be-Licking-Ice-Cream-With-His-Nose had said, "Los niñeros! No les joden a los infantes!"

Bill understood the part about not having anal intercourse with the captives, and the opportunity met his needs. He'd grabbed the loudmouth by the long, black hair and dragged him back away from the miserly, plastic-fed campfire. Filemon's folding blade flashed out of his pocket like a snake. File's knee came down on the yelping man's throat and compressed the yelp to a gurgle.

Filemon plunged his hand in, yanked the tongue, and with a swift scoop of the razor-sharp blade, cut it off at the root. Blood overflowed from the coughing, gasping maw of the poor bastard. Bill shoved a dirty handkerchief into the mouth and stood up off of his chest.

"Tell them," Bill instructed Filemon, "that if they defile my prisoners again, they'll get worse than this ass-monkey got."

Filemon stood silent.

"Well, tell them," Bill ordered. "Translate."

Filemon shrugged, "I don't know what it means... *defile*."

"To beat them up, and slice off their dicks," Bill explained to his man, frustrated. Half the dramatic impact of the moment had been lost to translation. "You know, don't mess with our prisoners. We interrogate captives, not sacrifice them to these dipshits' psycho murder fantasies."

Filemon translated but Bill couldn't follow the Spanish. The cartel maniacs backed away from the campfire like someone had thrown a cobra in the middle. They stared, wide-eyed, at the severed tongue in the mud. The mewling man half-drowned in his own blood.

The impeccable war machine of Gustavo Castillo had, so far, wiped its ass with the Utah Militia, and Bill McCallister felt quite pleased. It appeared he'd backed the right horse. The spoiled brat that'd once been America was dead, and he'd been the first to embrace it.

The king is dead. Long live the king. From one tyrant to the next. At least this tyrant wasn't such a complainer. Every time he thought about how democracy had become the worst tyrant of all, Bill pictured armies of gender-confused hash-taggers milling the streets and crying into their Instagram phones. At least the current tyrant knew how to run a gun.

The backbone of the cartel fighting force was its tanks, consolidated in six rows, like an old black-and-white film of the NAZI *Wehrmacht*, occupying both the northbound and southbound lanes of the I-15 interstate—fifty of eighty surviving M1 Abrams tanks were there, followed by over a hundred electric OHVs, all mounted with 240D machines guns or Mk 19 automatic grenade launchers. They'd "liberated" semi truckloads of munitions from the Hawthorne Army Depot while winter had them bottled up in

Nevada, and now they were "cocked, locked and ready to rock," as the late, great Ted Nugent was known to say.

Billy assumed "the Nuge" was dead. Despite being the only rock star who didn't disgust him socio-politically, Billy couldn't picture the Nuge surviving, what with his guitar-player biceps and advancing years. Bill toyed with the idea of searching him out after all of this and getting him alone for a bottle of Kentucky rye and an all-night rap session where they'd deconstruct how the world had crapped out.

But Bill McCallister was the rock star now. He'd come from the edge of the apocalypse, out of the clean-swept deserts of Nevada, at the head of the hardest power in the region, an army that'd been funded by drug trade, but had become tougher and more-organized than most of the armies he'd fought in as a merc. It was going on six months, now, since America pitched face-first in a pool of it's own vomit and drowned, and it'd probably been four months since the last hit of cocaine had gone up anyone's nose. Gustavo Castillo, the mastermind of this war, had parlayed his expertise in criminal enterprise to land warfare, and it turned out to be a pretty good fit. *Hand-in-glove*, as they say.

Castillo had been forced to murder his hot-ass daughter and the lieutenant who'd been diddling her. That'd been a three month setback. The chick had head-tripped her own mother into putting a kitchen knife through her dad's throat. Castillo survived the assassination attempt and parlayed the recovery period into a reconsolidation of forces and a "streamlining" of his leadership corps. All that remained now were Castillo's two SOF-veteran business partners, Alejandro and Saúl, and Bill McCallister himself. There were no family ties left to tangle 'round their feet and trip them up. This was a balls-out campaign to take down the entire Rocky Mountain West, complete with Wyoming oil fields and Idaho amber waves of grain. By autumn, they'd hold the perfect mountain fortress—the Intermountain West—nestled between the California High Sierras and the Rocky Mountains.

Bill didn't have time to philosophize over the conquest of Cedar City. As Castillo's spymaster, he had captives to interrogate, including an interesting cat who claimed to be a former Navy SEAL. A picture was forming in Bill's mind of the Utah Militia: a combination of Mormons, rednecks and a central core of SOF operators led by Jeff Kirkham, a Green Beret, just like Bill.

He turned on his heels and headed back to his electric OHV. Bill climbed aboard and buzzed over to the Motel Six where his intel guys were shoving captives into the ransacked rooms. Bill whipped up under the lobby awning and levered his legs out of the off-road buggy. He hadn't done any actual fighting the day before, but his legs were sore from running back and forth, watching the show. He was in his mid-sixties, and it didn't take much running to stove him up.

Abuelo stood with a foot in the sliding door, holding it open for Bill to pass. The man was easily five years younger, probably in his late fifties. The men called him "Abuelo" anyway, "grandfather" in Spanish, because he was one of the oldest cartel fighters. Mexicans had neither mercy nor thin skin when it came to racist, or "ageist" nomenclature. If you had Asian-looking eyes, they called you "chino." If you were fat, they called you "gordo." If you were dark-skinned, then you were called "negro." Bill had caught them calling him "*Correoso*," and he asked Filemon what that meant.

"Like old leather," he said without flinching. "Skin like a saddlebag."

Excellent. Like Sean Connery. The call sign worked fine for Bill. *Correoso*.

"Abuelo!" He slapped him on the shoulder as he breezed through the glass doors. Like every other city in America, there was no electricity in Cedar City. Abuelo had pried the doors apart for

Bill's arrival. In the lobby, they'd broken out a couple of windows for ventilation and set up a place for Bill to "interview" captives.

Bill had hand-picked the ten craftiest gangbangers in the Castillo crew to be his intelligence cadre. He drilled them on the five "S's" of interrogation: secure, silence, segregate, safeguard, and speed to the rear. He equipped his guys with police zip ties and beat into their heads the need to protect captives from the rank-and-file sickos. Many of the cartel "army" were straight-up psychopaths. They got their rocks off carving up captives and arranging their bodies on altars of blood and guts. That kind of shit would make Bill's intelligence mission difficult. You couldn't get good intelligence out of captives if they thought that their next stop was the Aztec Emporium of Human Sacrifice.

He'd caught a couple of psychos hacking dead men's heads off their bodies, sticking their severed dicks in their mouths and plunking them on fence posts along the rangeland beside the freeway. Bill shut that shit down hard.

Aside from the torture, and all the Catholic mumbo-jumbo from the dozen priests that Castillo kept around the camp, Bill kind of liked this gig. The cartel was like the Devil's Boy Scout troop, Troop 666, and Bill was the Assistant Scoutmaster.

Abuelo brought in the Navy SEAL guy. They generally started interrogations with the highest ranking captive and worked their way down. Then they'd rinse and repeat from the top.

Bill didn't believe anything anyone told him, least of all captives. But if he had to guess, this fucker really *was* a Navy SEAL. He dropped into one of the upholstered lobby chairs and sprawled out like a house cat, despite his flex-cuffed hands. He had short, sandy-blond hair, good looks, and an insouciance that implied he'd gotten captured on purpose, like he was waiting to audition for Jack Reacher. He didn't shift in the chair as Bill approached. He was probably only five and a half feet tall. *Good luck playing Reacher.*

"Well lookie here," Bill trilled. "Seems like we caught ourselves a movie star. Didn't you play the boyfriend in that rom-com with the girl with nice boobies?" Bill didn't know any romantic comedies. He was just stirring shit up.

The SEAL sucked a chirp through his front teeth. "The one with your sister, you mean?" he said.

"Couldn't say." Bill sat down opposite him. "My dad got around a lot. I'm still adding to the list of prospective siblings. It's a big dick thing. Family curse, ya know. Hey, has anyone ever told you you're kinda pretty?"

The SEAL didn't bother responding.

Abuelo handed Bill a scrap of paper. It was a list of captive names. "Chad Wade." was at the top of the list.

"So you say you're a Navy SEAL?" Bill asked.

The man shrugged one shoulder. "How come you're white?"

Bill had already decided not to come down heavy on this guy. Not at first. Bill thought he might like it if he did, as though "resisting torture" would be another achievement in his list of combat bragging points. He could either kill this guy or befriend him, but it'd take way too much energy to torture past the razzmatazz and down to any reliable information.

Bill leveled with him. "I'm former Army Special Forces and these are my guys. I'm management."

"No you're not. These guys are drug dealers from South of the Border and you're some kind of merc."

"I work for them, *with* them, actually," Bill stared eyeball-to-eyeball. "I'm *senior* management."

Chad nodded. "All things being equal, the winning team is the best team," he said as much to himself as anyone.

Bill saw an angle that could work. "Sounds like we understand one another, then. What do you want to tell me about the enemy we're facing?"

The intel value wouldn't be in what the SEAL told him. Bill

would have to triple-confirm anything this guy said. The value was in *how he said it*. The guy's attitude *was* the intel.

"They're a bunch of do-gooders, bro. Between all the Mormons and the flag-waving patriots, you'll never pacify those guys, no matter how many Abrams you got. You might as well go back to Taco-landia. These Utah guys are true believers." The SEAL gave him the side-eye from behind a forelock of glowing, yellow hair.

Bill interpreted the bullshit: the SEAL thought the locals were naive, but he harbored a begrudging respect for them, probably even for the top dog—"General" Jeff Kirkham. This guy thought he was smarter than everyone else, which was standard-issue for a SEAL, but he gave the Utah soldiers props.

That didn't bode well. If the Utah militia had earned the respect of this Frogman egomaniac, then they weren't a petty band of fundamentalists, political zealots, or rednecks. The cartel army faced an ethical, committed army, with all the flag-waving, Bible-thumping strength that came with true religion. Bill's job was to sift out their weaknesses.

"What're they doing for gas?" Bill always began an interrogation with answers he already knew.

The SEAL thought about it and chuckled. He waved his flex-cuffed hands like it didn't matter. "You already know: they have a refinery. That's why you're here."

"Where is it?"

"You already know that too," the SEAL said.

"Humor me."

"It's north of Salt Lake City. Now I have a question for you."

Bill chortled. "That's not how this works."

Chad the SEAL ignored him. "How do you plan on getting to that refinery before they torch it? If you come within five miles… *poof*. It goes up like Hiroshima."

The SEAL was right. That was Bill's exact job description: to devise a way to get his hands on the Maverick Oil Refinery before the partisans blew it up. That worst-case scenario—*KA-BOOM!*—had happened to Castillo before. The Big Boss had the third-degree burns to prove it.

Sometimes the direct approach worked with people who had very high opinions of themselves. *It takes one to know one,* Bill thought. So he asked, "How would you do it?"

"Ha!" the SEAL barked. "I'd fast rope in from helos with Team Six and hit 'em like Bin Laden."

"No you wouldn't," Bill said.

"Obviously not." The SEAL made a lavish motion with his flex-cuffed hands. "You've got to make them *want* to give you the gas. You can't brawl your way into a whorehouse and still expect to get laid."

"How would you make them want to give you the gas?" Bill had been juggling ideas: he could threaten to destroy their families. He could trade them a few Abrams. Or form a fake alliance. If he captured enough hostages, he could trade them for fuel, and then use that fuel to surround the refinery. But what then?

"That's why I surrendered to your troops: to negotiate a deal," Chad the SEAL answered.

"You surrendered?"

"Yeah. You don't think a bunch of saggy-bottom drug slingers captured me without my permission. Come on." The SEAL offered a twisted grin. "Like that was ever going to happen."

That part was bullshit, but Bill would go along with it. "So you're here to broker a deal? Gasoline for goods and services?"

"Yeah. As soon as I see anything we need, I'll let you know." The SEAL slumped back in the lobby chair, like he was waiting to be shown a parade of options.

Bill's boss, Castillo, expected a plan to capture the refinery soon. Bill needed to produce actionable intelligence. Every day they chewed their way north, closer to the oil refineries, and every day the need for a plan to take the refinery rose up like cliff face on the horizon.

"Enough peacocking. Where do their families live?" Bill's voice picked up a saw's edge.

"Whose family? Kirkham's?" The SEAL waved the idea away like a gnat. "Forget about that. They live above the refinery. If you go for them, the refinery burns."

If that was true, if the families of the partisan leadership lived near the refinery, then they could scratch kidnapping off their list of options. The SEAL was right, they wouldn't be able to cut the families from the herd without blowing the mission objective.

"Fine. Then we'll burn their temples." The cartel already had possession of two Mormon temples, one in St. George and the other in Cedar City. They could destroy them at will.

"Won't work," Chad said. "Half of the partisan fighters aren't even Mormon. Kirkham isn't really Mormon. They won't care. Or it'll piss them off even more. That won't buy you a damn thing."

Bill refrained from nodding. That was almost exactly what he'd said when Castillo floated the idea. Bill hadn't known that General Kirkham wasn't one of the Bible-thumpers. He filed that bit of information away for further consideration. *Could he drive a wedge between Kirkham and the Mormons?*

"So what then? What's the deal you came here to propose?" Bill played along.

"You give us all your Abrams and we give you Nevada."

Bill laughed out loud. "So, we hand over our chip in the big game and you let us keep the desert state we already have? How long until you turn our own tanks against us?"

The SEAL smirked. "We're not dumb enough to drive fuel-guzzling dinosaurs two states away to seize territory we can't hold. This is your bucking bronco to screw, not mine. You turn around, leave us the tanks, and we'll give you the gasoline to get home."

Bill rubbed his face to hide the piece of his mind that agreed.

Castillo was gambling big by invading Utah, and civilians never understood the nightmare of logistics. They always underestimated the three hundred-pound tail that wagged the dog.

The one thing the cartel army should've had burned into their brain pans since pushing north of Nogales: the M1 Abrams main battle tank had a massive appetite for fuel, bullets and parts. Without Big Army backing them up, the tanks were *almost* more trouble than they were worth. A single Abrams tank could control a square mile of ground, and destroy virtually any weapon system or hard point defense, but it came at a pecker-puckering cost. Fuel. Parts. Ammo. Maintenance. Support personnel. Every tank in the U.S. Army required fifteen men just to keep it running, and that wasn't because the Army was stupid.

The cartel army had grown to over fifteen thousand men. New recruits had poured in from Vegas, Laughlin, and even from the desperate, starving fragments of the Arizona resistance. Scavenge within range of the cartel base in Nelson, Nevada had run out. Castillo needed a long-term breadbasket to feed his troops and solidify his empire. The cornfields of Utah and potato farms of Idaho fit the bill. With Salt Lake City under their control and plenty of fuel, they could push into Wyoming and command the oil fields, eventually restoring diesel production. It made sense on paper, and they were already kicking the shit out of the Utahns. But if the oil and gas refinery north of Salt Lake City was destroyed, they'd be left scrambling for a backup plan and Bill's ass would be in a sling. Castillo would pin the cocked-up mess on him.

They'd been here before. Bill's boy, Noah, had fisted Castillo by bringing the Vegas refinery down around his ears. If Noah could do it, so could Utah inbreds. Hell, a guy with a DeWalt drill and a Bic lighter could destroy a refinery. It wasn't hard—just drill a hole in a tank, pour fuel on the ground, and set it ablaze.

"Am I right or am I right?" the SEAL chirruped as Bill got lost thinking about his son. He hadn't seen Noah since that day in Flagstaff with the nuke.

"Let me get this straight." Bill took back control of the conversation. "You supposedly surrendered to me to offer us this deal: we hand you our tanks, turn around, give you back the farmlands and cities we've taken, and you'll pat us on the ass and wish us *good luck?* That's it?"

"It's a good deal," the SEAL said, but the truth was painted on his face. It was ludicrous, especially since they'd just finished their first major engagement where the cartel stomped the living shit out of the Utah Militia.

Bill chuckled and shook his head. "Leave it to a SEAL to call a turd a tuna fish sandwich. I give you high marks for audacity. Unfortunately, it'll cost you a finger. Pick one and say goodbye."

The SEAL didn't budge in the lobby chair. He was probably thinking about giving Bill "the finger," but he must've thought better of it, because he held out his left ring finger. "I'll give you this one. It'll fit perfectly up your ass."

Bill glanced at Abuelo standing by the glass doors of the lobby. "Cut it off and put it on a necklace around his neck. Let him smell it rot."

Bill stood up and walked into the still-chilly freshness of the coming evening. The SEAL didn't make a peep as Abuelo dragged him away to be maimed.

If Bill didn't figure out something quickly, he might end up losing a lot more than a finger. He'd already seen Castillo put a bullet through his own daughter and his closest partner. The boss wouldn't hesitate to make Bill pay if he couldn't unlock the puzzle of the refinery. He would find himself splayed and filleted on one of those Aztec altars, surrounded by candles and looking down at his own guts, strung around like Christmas lights.

Like the SEAL said, *all things being equal, the winning team is the best team.* Logistics problems aside, the eighty Abrams would give Castillo the win. One way or the other, this army would likely roll up Utah and Idaho. Bill was on the winning side of this war. Castillo would be in the champion's circle when it was all said and done. Bill just needed to figure out how to come out on top.

This was what he did, and he'd survived a lot worse. He rubbed his hands together in the brisk air and pumped himself up.

Time for a fresh round of shenanigans.

NOAH MILLER DROVE his Toyota Land Cruiser steadily along the backbone of Utah on a quest to save his father from himself.

Noah was convinced that he'd been honest with his militia comrades, that he'd told them everything they needed to know about his father's treachery. He'd laid out the whole spaghetti-shaped story to his commanding officer, Colonel Withers, formerly of the Arizona Air National Guard. Noah's duty was to tell the colonel the truth—that Noah's dad worked for the enemy. He gave up every scrap of information he had, and let the chips fall where they may.

Was it his fault that the trail of bread crumbs led the Arizona Freeman's Militia toward Noah's heart's desire?

He had misjudged his dad, despised him for abandoning him, only to find that his dad had been bending the chess board to save Noah's life all along.

Flagstaff, lately liberated from the cartel, vanished in the rearview mirror of the Toyota as Noah and Willie Lloyd drove up into the juniper-studded sandstone of Kanab. Willie Lloyd, Noah's brother-from-another-mother and fire team buddy, sat quietly in the passenger seat. The road through mountain hamlets sparkled wet and free of snow. The pink sands of the Utah/Arizona border thickened with juniper, then filled with ponderosa pines. The sun-baked desert surrendered to the turpentine aroma of evergreens and high mountain air.

The remnants of the Arizona Freeman's Militia had consolidated in Flagstaff for a spring offensive. Very few had come. Many had starved over the winter, but Noah's heart lifted when he set eyes on Willie Lloyd, back from the south and ready to deploy against the cartel.

After the Battle of Phoenix, Willie, his family and the scant survivors had gone south to cluster around the Gila River and grow food over the cold season. As temperatures rose and the winter crop ended, they packed up and moved north, back to Flagstaff for a spring planting.

Arizona had become a place of nomads, gardeners who wintered in desert wetlands, then moved north to escape the summer scorch. By nomading, they laid up two crops: winter corn in the southern deserts and summer vegetables in the mountain foothills.

"Did you ever learn how to grow a cucumber?" Noah asked Willie, to pass the time. It was meant to rib him: Willie, the black urbanite from Scranton, Pennsylvania, hadn't the faintest clue how to plant vegetables, but that was six long months ago in the past.

Do you plant a cucumber up-ways or sideways? Willie had once asked.

Willie gave Noah a hard glance that meant, *why are you jacking with me?* Then, he yawned and appeared to accept the question at face value.

"Naw. Noel took over all that gardening shit. She's got a knack for it, dawg. Who would've guessed? City girl like her?" Noah vaguely recalled that Willie's wife had done peoples' nails back in the old world. Now she was a gardener. Hell, everyone was a gardener. Everyone who'd survived.

When he and Willie left Flagstaff, the Lloyd family garden had been well-started, planted directly overtop of the golf course south of town. Noel Lloyd laid old cardboard over the turf, dumped three inches of topsoil on top of that, and then cut her seedlings into the dirt through the cardboard and sod. The cardboard snuffed out the sod and left it composting below.

"Does that 'instant oasis' thing really work, with the cardboard and the compost?"

"That's how she did the winter garden outside of Buckeye." Willie shrugged. "Looked like a damned dump with all that cardboard poking out, but we harvested a metric butt-ton of corn from it."

If they didn't put an end to the cartel that spring, the drug lords would flow back into Arizona and tyrannize them all. Flagstaff, Phoenix, and Tucson were all lined up in the cartel crosshairs; dots on the resupply route between the farms of Idaho and the cartel's home in northern Mexico. The cartel army moved north into Utah, but the Arizona Freeman's Militia still traded gunfire daily with their supply chain and support vehicles. Arizona's best chance was to push north, link up with whatever force was fighting the cartel in Utah, and defeat them together.

"Any word from your old man?" Willie broached a raw topic. It was a fresh wound for the Freeman Militia, the first real treachery they'd confronted.

"Not precisely. Not since Flagstaff. Not since I saw that mushroom cloud off on the horizon."

Bill McCallister, in an uncharacteristic act of community-mindedness, had wiped out every leftover nuclear warhead in the western United States in a single blast.

Noah and Willie drove into the southern highlands of Utah in a convoy of dozens of vehicles. It was slow going around the melting snow banks still crowding the road in the shadiest passes. There was plenty of time to catch up.

Billy McCallister, Noah's adopted father, had once served the patriot militias as an officer-without-portfolio, a trusted advisor and messenger between the fragmented units of Arizona partisans. The whole time, McCallister had been on the drug dealers' payroll. A wolf, wrapped in the red, white, and blue. In a moment of vulnerability, Noah had handed over a cruise missile warhead to his adopted father, and Bill McCallister had surprisingly done the right thing with it. He'd turned aside from the will of his master and detonated the nuke over the bunker complex of Nellis Air Force Base, destroying that warhead and all others. Then, he'd gone straight back to work for the Mexican warlord, the same man who terrorized their homeland with Abrams tanks. As much as Noah loved his father, he couldn't keep the truth from the militia. Bill was a traitor.

In his heart, Noah had made peace with Bill's choice, and Willie was probably the only man in the unit who understood Noah's dad, his cocked-up logic, runaway brilliance and high-octane bitterness.

Willie had been with them in Oklahoma. He'd fought beside Bill McCallister and watched the father and son dance the Resentment Rumba. That shit was complicated, and Willie "got it" about both of them.

And Bill was a hater, if ever there was one. He had no love for the United States government. He despised what the U.S. had become, yearned to see it burn. It wasn't entirely surprising when Bill folded in with a cartel warlord.

But Bill's treachery against the flag didn't mean they weren't still father and son. He'd come through for Noah, risked it all to take a suicidal trigger out of Noah's hands. Bill had put himself on the line to save his son.

Willie had seen it all. He loved them both, treacherous father and loyal son. He could be trusted with the truth.

Noah dug into his front pocket and passed a crumpled scrap to his friend. "I got a note from a refugee family passing through Phoenix two weeks ago."

"Noah. Mom and I are moving north up I-15 toward El Lago. Hope to see you in Idaho next harvest. Dad."

"What's that mean?" Willie asked.

"It's Bill's way of telling me the cartel's pushing north to Salt Lake City. Then they'll move on to Idaho."

"Why would he tell you that?" Willie scratched the back of his head. "Who is *Mom*?"

Noah chuckled. "There is no mom. He was just covering his ass in case the note got intercepted. He's letting me to know what the cartel is planning. He probably didn't want us wandering into anything we couldn't handle."

"Then why're we going north?" Willie asked.

Noah tapped the steering wheel. "I guess we gotta do what we can. It's our duty. We know there's a bunch of Mormons out of Salt Lake City who've organized, and we've heard rumors of a Navajo army that headed north up the middle of Colorado. Who knows what they're doing? If we hide out in Arizona, we're no good to anyone. If we link up with friendly forces, we might be able to make a stand."

"Against tanks?" Willie asked, flat-voiced.

"You never know." Noah shrugged. "Lots of squirrelly shit happens out here in the Wild West."

"So now we're like the Apple Dumpling gang?" Willie snorted. "What's with you white people and your delusions of grandeur? Tanks beat soldiers. End of story."

"Yeah?" Noah lifted his eyebrows. "Then why're you here?"

Willie shifted around in his seat. "I thought you and I were a team. *Compadre*."

"We are, but you have a family."

"And my job is to protect them. I figure you know how to do that. But that doesn't mean I'm going up against tanks, dawg."

Noah nodded. He didn't want to go up against tanks, either.

That was why they were taking the long road around. Bill's note implied that Highway 89 would be clear and the cartel force would be moving up the center of the state, Interstate 15. The Freeman's militia put a mountain range between them and the column of Abrams. There was a good chance they could scoot around the cartel and pop out of the mountains north of their advance. Hopefully, they'd make contact with the Utah patriot forces before Highway 89 folded back onto I-15 at the town of Levan. There was a long-ass way still to go—a two hundred mile string of mountain towns that would each require an explanation as to why they should let an Arizona militia pass.

Up ahead, the convoy ground to a stop. They'd reached the town of Mount Carmel Junction. It'd be the first test of their story: the battle-scarred patriot militia rolling north to support their brothers-in-arms. They'd probably have to explain about the cartel threat. These little towns might not have heard about the enemy fifty miles to their west, on the other side of the mountain range.

Every town would be a stop, a parlay, a flurry of handshakes and, hopefully, another pass through a rugged, starving cabin community. They might even pick up a few more fighters, but the passing could take weeks.

Unfortunately, there was no quick way to do this. If they didn't want to shoot it out with each small town, bristling with deer hunting rifles, they'd need to stop and explain themselves; at least nineteen times in nineteen different towns. That was the price of passage along the two hundred mile valley on the backside of the Wasatch. The alternative was to risk wading into Castillo's army on the flatlands to the west, where Utah descended from pine mountain into sagebrush plain.

Noah became agitated with the ponderous thought of it, mucking through one barricaded town after another while his dad's soul corroded away in the company of human trash. He could barely tolerate the thought of glad-handing mountain-town mayors.

Noah was ready to trade his life for victory, more than happy to reunite with his wife and daughter in heaven. But before he did, there was one debt to pay. One more asterisk in the balance sheet of karma. He and Bill were more than just father and son. God had torn them from the same bolt of cloth, and their ragged edges lined up perfectly.

Every time Noah misjudged his father, it'd drawn them closer. They were two courageous men, grown crusty on the same ranch, in the same Arizona dust bowl, raising the same tawny cattle.

If Noah could reach Bill, get a hand on his booze-soaked bag of guts, they wouldn't need to face Abrams tanks. They would slice up the cartel from the inside out. Together.

3

Shortwave Radio 7150kHz
3:00pm

> "Welcome People of Planet Shortwave. You are the last vestiges of technorati. The final podcast listeners on Planet Earth. This is your short wave radio show, and I am your less-inebriated host, JT Taylor. Former alcoholic of the apocalypse. Fellow Drinkin' Bro. Broadcasting from the frontline of the literal War on Drugs.
>
> "Drug pimp extraordinaire, Gustavo Castillo, got his hands on a tank brigade and he's laying hands on the farmers' daughters of the Intermountain West. The hoodie-wearing, drug dealer army just rolled up on Cedar City, Utah and kicked our trash back to Parowan. If you love America and you're near the 801, come give us a hand. If you got one, bring a squad of Apache helicopters, 'cause we're getting shellacked."

The Homestead
Oakwood, Utah

JASON ROSS HELD JEFF KIRKHAM'S FAMILY CAPTIVE. IT SHOULD'VE felt like a bigger victory, but it was more like winning at Monopoly when you picked up Boardwalk and Park Place in the first fifteen minutes. The outcome was assured, but there would still be a long, slow, unsatisfying process of crushing your opponent before you could claim total victory.

Jason was having a hard time getting out of bed. His temple throbbed and the tissues in his mouth stuck together like wet newsprint. He needed to offset last night's half-bottle of "trade whiskey" with a couple of liters of water. He'd passed out on top of his old bed without refilling his Camelbak, so he'd spent the dehydrated night going in and out of sleep set to the rhythm of the bongo drums in his cranium. He had formerly believed that laying waste to his enemies would be a lot more satisfying than this.

The Mormon prophet, Thayer, asked for a meeting today. It should be interesting. Jason debated whether or not to bathe.

To think: he'd once fantasized as a boy about rising through the ranks of the Mormon Church. Back in that day, he would've spent his life savings on a new suit if he'd had the chance to meet the prophet.

Jason used to say to his kids, "Life is long and strange." It was a minor family mantra.

Looking back now, lying sprawled on his once-marital bed with a half-bottle of Old Crow whiskey and a mouth full of cotton, Jason recognized that he'd had no damn idea just how strange life could be.

If his four children could see him now...the thought slowed, then got mired in the mud. His *three* children. His Emily had died. *They* had been responsible for that, Kirkham, the women, and Jenna.

If they could see him now, his *three* children would be disappointed in him. They might even despise him.

His victory against Kirkham turned sour in his mouth. It took on the flavor of his rank morning breath.

His children would be disappointed in him.

Jason sat up too quickly and the bongo drums became an artillery barrage. The thunder of sluggish blood, fighting its way into his brain, blotted out thought.

The *old* world despised winners. It loved to tear down the likes of Elon Musk and Jeff Bezos. The new world wasn't much better. He imagined Jenna telling their kids some soft, reasonable-sounding, bullshit version of events. He pictured her bending their minds to her victim story. He saw each of their faces as they believed her and turned against him.

He stumbled to the bathroom, her old bathroom, actually. Jenna's.

It still smelled of her. He closed his eyes, inhaled, and then shook his head. He turned the knob to run the sink, but nothing came out. He pulled the bowl of three-day-old wash water into the sink, splashed his face, and then rubbed his eyes.

He didn't know where his remaining children might be. When the collapse happened, his oldest daughter, Tessa, had been on an Air Force base with her husband in northern California. Jason's oldest son, Tristan, had been deployed in Iraq. His youngest son, Sage, had lost contact on his way back from his grandparents' house on the Olympic Peninsula. Odds increased every day that he'd never hear from them again, any of them.

"Screw it," Jason said, more as a commentary on his mood than anything.

Jenna's old bathroom was three times the size of his. A huge bay window wrapped around her enormous bathtub and took in the view of the Great Salt Lake. It was a faint mystery to him how she had scored the big bathroom with the astounding view, while his much smaller bathroom didn't even have natural light.

The old world despised winners, he reminded himself. *And the new world isn't much better.*

His roiling unease found nothing specific to blame, so he straightened up, jammed his hands on his hips and stretched, rolling at the waist. Somehow, he'd gained a bit of a paunch during the apocalypse. Maybe it was the lack of working out. Maybe it was the bread he ate, or the Russian-style Meals Ready to Eat. They really were outstanding.

Or maybe it was the booze, the lack of sleep, or the depression.

Yes, he admitted it: depression.

He was entitled to a little depression. His daughter had died. His three children were missing, probably dead too.

The belly paunch folded over his belt and scraped a raw spot as he did hip circles in the 5.11 tactical pants. He'd slept in them.

Kirkham would come for him. Jason held Tara and their boys behind the walls of the Homestead. It'd drive Kirkham mad. They said he had a thousand gun trucks at his command, around 50,000 men. But they weren't Kirkham's men, *really*. The Mormons wouldn't follow him just anywhere. They'd want Kirkham to put personal matters aside to lead. If Jason re-captured his own home, why would the Mormons care? Jason's name was on the deed. He held title to the place and everyone knew it. The church would probably ask him to release Jeff's family, but what more could they reasonably want?

Jason passed through a facsimile of his morning ablutions, toothbrush, shit, and sponge-bath, and left his room to find coffee. It was one of the few good things they still had in abundance. The cook shed behind the bunkhouse had become the go-to place for morning joe. It was, perhaps, the greatest luxury afforded the Homestead. Jeff and Evan had discovered a warehouse full of green coffee beans at the outset of the calamity, and they eventually transported it back to the Homestead where it could be properly defended. Jeff and Evan would want that back too, but they probably wouldn't get much help from the Mormons. They took a dim view of coffee.

Jason stopped in his tracks. His ex-wife stood with Colonel Zhukov, enjoying a cup and each other's company. The Colonel laughed and clinked his coffee mug against hers, affirming some pleasant comment she'd just made.

Jason took half a step backward, and then retreated behind the gamble's oak that hemmed the path to the cook shed.

That bitch. Were they sleeping together already?

Jealousy. Worry. Concern. *Rage*. The emotional cascade ran from primal to tactical and back to primal again. *Could Jenna yank the Russians right out from under him?* They'd only been at the Homestead a week. Was that long enough for her to woo Zhukov?

Jason replayed in his mind the clinking mugs. Her smile. Her lilting cheeks. Her long legs. Her perfect hair. Her slim, feminine hands. He hated her, and he despised her deliberate, elegant way. He wanted her more than he'd ever wanted any woman before.

Of course, a week was long enough to woo Zhukov. She could get it done in an hour, if she put her mind to it. For a man in his fifties, she was sex on a popsicle stick.

Jason's legs went weak. A cluster of people mumbled as they passed, heading toward coffee. He'd known them for years, yet nobody wished him good morning as they passed. The ungrateful assholes.

Jenna and Zhukov weren't sleeping together. Not yet. She wasn't "that kind of girl," he knew. He hoped. She'd make Zhukov pay for the good stuff. She'd make him pursue her, prove his devotion, and commit. It could mean only one thing. *Damn it.*

People thought of "slutty" women as the ones who used sex to get what they wanted. No. Slutty women were the ones who made it affordable. It was "respectable" women like Jenna Ross who made a man *really pay*, kids, mortgage, embarrassing family vehicles, and trips to Disneyworld. A "respectable" woman, one as adept as Jenna Ross, could trade sex for control of a hard point military asset, a compound with towering, rock walls and stores of grain.

By comparison to that, Jason had no real hold on Zhukov. He'd promised the Russians entree into the Salt Lake Valley and a place at the Homestead table, and he'd delivered on that promise. But that was *last week* and this was *today*. Today had legs that wouldn't stop and a laugh that could thaw frozen stone.

Jason turned and headed for high ground. His tactical sense, when he found himself in the midst of unknown threats, was to assume overwatch. Coffee forgotten, he plowed through the drifting knots of waking Homestead members and climbed onto the colonnade outside his office. From there he could see the encampments that'd formed within the Homestead walls.

Almost immediately his eyes rested on a couple meandering the slatted boardwalk between the tents on the great lawn. Zhukov's second-in-command, Major Kvashnin, walked and talked with Jacqueline Reynolds.

Jason backed up so he wouldn't be seen.

He was being encircled. It was deliberate, an ambush in the making. His mind shuffled through his options: kill the Russians, kill the women, rally support from old Homestead members. None of the options had even a whiff of probable success. He could flee now, and take with him all the trade goods he could carry.

He had failed to read the threatening signs and perceive the tactical choke points. He'd walked his Russian allies directly into an ambush, redolent of a woman's musk and home cooking. With their Russian families seven thousand miles away, the Spetsnaz would gravitate toward new mates and new families. They would *want* to be ambushed.

Jason should've sensed the threat, but he didn't think in these dimensions of power and influence. He hadn't considered women as an encircling force. It would be more than just Jenna and Jacqueline. Other women would have been conscripted into the maneuver, women who had lost husbands in the Homestead battles and single women who were coming of age. This was no accident, no "nature taking its course." This was a planned attack, and he'd waltzed right into the middle of it. If they hadn't already, the women would assume control of the Spetsnaz by the end of the day, and there was nothing he could do to stop them.

Jason could grab what supplies he could and make a run for it. It was probably his best chance, but he was loathe to lose the Homestead a second time. He would lose Kirkham's family too, but now, from his view atop the office colonnade, he realized that he never really had them. They hadn't even been locked up.

Jason rubbed his face with the meat of his palms and caught the dollop of sleep sand still in the corner of his eye. He was a smart man. A genius, really. Yet he'd never been so completely and utterly out-maneuvered. What was worse, he had no clue when it'd happened. Maybe he'd been defeated the moment he walked through the Homestead gates. Maybe he lost when he first took a stand against the illegal orphanage. Heck, maybe he'd been underwater since he married Jenna thirty years ago. He didn't feel like a genius at all. He felt like a rube.

Two could play at that game, he hoped more than thought. This was a different kind of tactical map, nothing more. Once upon a time as a businessman, he'd been good at getting people productive and motivated. He could do it again. This was a challenge of organizational jiu-jitsu. He could redirect the women's energy and use their weapons to achieve his aims.

Jenna wasn't the only one with sex appeal. He'd let himself slide a little, but his salt-and-pepper good looks hadn't been hurt by outdoor living. When he saw himself in the mirror, he pictured a barrel-chested William Shatner. He could still get it done. She'd loved him once-upon-a-time, six months and an apocalypse before, and that carried its own gravity. Women like Jenna tended to mate for life, and the bond left an indelible impression.

He would set his own ambush by using the weapons of history and nostalgia. He'd deploy the draw of a good, old-fashion redemption story.

Jason rested his hand on the Glock on his battle belt, but the plastic solidity of it didn't deliver the sensation of confidence it had the day before.

He and Jenna Ross had "a song." They'd given birth to children. They had photo albums brimming with memories. They'd built the Homestead together—his architectural mind and her stylistic eye. Literally everything around them spoke to their lifelong love affair, and to the decades of investment in each other and their family.

Time to cash that motherfucker in.

———

Interstate I-15
Parowan, Utah

CEDAR CITY HAD FALLEN, and Jeff harbored a rage he hadn't felt since the Panjshir. He'd been up all night coordinating the retreat, and then lying on his cot, staring at the ceiling of an abandoned child's room in a farmhouse six miles outside of Paragonah. He fixated on each glow-in-the-dark star, stickered to the ceiling for a child, lately fled before the coming cartel, and Jeff burned a hole through each one with his hatred.

He'd sworn it would never come to this, that the United States would never slide into the hell of Afghanistan. Yet here it was, and here he was. His homeland was being overtaken by an unstoppable criminal. His friends were cut down by cannon fire. Tara and his boys were being held captive by the enemy. It felt like he'd dragged Afghanistan to America, to Utah.

The bacterial filth of combat had hung in his cloths, his hair, his skin, and had returned in his duffle bags to infect the United States. Once upon a time, America had been a ruby-cheeked child of hope. Now it was a rotting sack of flesh.

He had accepted Tara's civilizing influence, even during the months of apocalypse. But he'd been wrong to do that. He shouldn't have believed her. He shouldn't have hoped for better. Evil men could only be stopped by blood-soaked fury. Men like Jeff must become the black beasts, the malevolent storms, the fused-spine warriors of vengeance. Only by sacrificing his humanity could evil men be annihilated.

The first blush of dawn colored the black glass windows of the child's room, and the glowing stars on the ceiling vanished one at a time as the gray rose. He swung his feet to the floor and blood stampeded into his head. He rubbed his scalp, got up, searched the small pocket of his assault pack, found his toothbrush and a water bottle, and stumbled into the tiny farmhouse bathroom.

He'd been a fool to think he could return home to family and hearth. Weeks before the collapse, he'd come back from his final deployment. He believed in the new life Tara wanted for him. He'd even convinced himself that he'd never again smell the reek of burst guts. The watery bowel-stench of Afghanistan would remain half-a-world away, and he could return to the familiar scent of wet asphalt and dewy grass, to America.

But war had followed him home. Death accompanied him. It spread under the rotting crops, flourished, and ruined everything Jeff had fought to protect.

There was a freedom to it, to finally turning his back on God and goodness. Forfeiting himself to mayhem-soaked Hades bought him freedom, and he could fully justify the transaction with visions of his wife and boys suffering at the hands of evil men. With his black-dipped blade, he would cut down his enemies. Jason Ross would be cleaved in two. Castillo's skull would be crushed beneath the blade of his tomahawk. Every man who had laid a finger on Tara would have his arm hacked out of its socket. There was no evil too dark, no malice too wide for him to bring against those men. Bullets, rockets, fire; concussive, brain-mulching oblivion; spine-twisting chemical death. His soul be damned.

Jeff had wandered outside onto the road in front of the farmhouse as his heart darkened. He despised the rising sun, and cursed the cool, morning mist.

"Dude. Are you even listening to me?" Evan Hafer had approached while Jeff wandered in the ghosts of Afghanistan, Iraq, Dante's Hell, and St. John's apocalypse.

"We're pulling out, bro," Evan said. He tried to tug Jeff's shoulder around to face him but Jeff's frame had become rooted to the earth. He barely shifted a millimeter.

"I'm leaving" Jeff said. "Get me a four man team. One man with a .50 BMG rifle, a spotter, a driver, and one security guy. I need a 240D and a belt of tracers. I'm the machine-gunner. You're in command until I return."

"Want to tell me what you're thinking about, General?" Evan asked.

"No time. Send the warning order now. Get the rest of our brigade to pull back to the town of Beaver. I'll be back in a few days."

"You're going after the logistics train?" Evan shaded his eyes into the morning glare that crested the mountains to the east. "There'll be civilians in their convoys. Even the Hood Rats have civilians with them." Evan knew this version of Jeff. He'd met him in Afghanistan.

Jeff ignored the warning. "Call me on our command channel when Thayer checks in about the Homestead." Jeff couldn't bring himself to say Tara's name. He and Evan had agreed not to overreact to the Homestead's capture. Tara and the boys would be in even greater danger if they rolled in heavy with gun trucks. Evan had family there too, a wife and children who were going about life in the Homestead in peace. President Thayer, the Mormon prophet, had offered to personally talk to Ross and his Russian consorts, and to attempt to free Tara and the boys.

Jeff begrudgingly agreed to the plan, for now. There were too many wild cards still in play to bring the violence of action he yearned to rain down on Ross and the Homestead.

What the hell were Russian commandos doing in Utah? What did Ross want? And most of all, *were Tara and the boys inside, alive?*

Tara wouldn't sit on her hands and wait for him to ride in like Sir Galahad. She'd go straight to war if she felt the boys were threatened. She might already have escaped, but to do so with three boys would be perilous in the extreme. The Homestead was a fortress, one that Jeff had personally built. It had a lot in common with a prison.

Communications were slow and irregular across the ham radio nets, even inside the borders of Utah. Jeff hadn't had the luxury of building high power radio towers yet. The cartel advance had been too swift.

So, he had only old news about Salt Lake City and the Homestead. President Thayer had gone to meet with Ross days ago, and Jeff still hadn't heard back.

As much as he wanted to rush home to his wife and boys, it'd leave them in greater peril if he pulled back from the Hood Rat surge. He needed to be in two places at once, had to protect his family on two fronts, but this was the front where he'd do the most damage.

Ross was an enemy. He'd cast a cloak of fear over Jeff's family, and that could never be forgiven. Jeff hoped Ross knew better than to lay a finger on his wife and boys. Still, against even a one percent chance that Ross had completely lost his mind, Jeff twisted in the wind, unsure and possessed with demons of violence.

He pictured Tara being waterboarded. He thought of his boys being forced to watch. He imagined Ross taking a drill to her arms, her legs, or her face.

"Get me that fucking 240!" Jeff roared, to nobody in particular.

His blood boiled and he hungered to kill.

It took Jeff two days to plan the counter-attack against the Hoodies. He was angry, not stupid. Planning came before violence, whenever humanly possible.

Jeff bounced in the back of a truck, standing behind the belt-fed machine gun as he and his recon team wormed slowly along the dirt roads of central Utah, roughly paralleling the interstate, seeking the enemy. With night drawing around them, and the desert as silent as the inside of a casket, Jeff's anger finally had a real target. It wasn't the target he wanted most of all, but it would do for now. His meaty fists clamped around the stock of the machine gun and he nursed the violence churning in his gut. Soon they would encounter the cartel and he would hurt them.

The Mormon prophet, Thayer, had finally reached Jeff with news. Tara and the boys hadn't been harmed, though Thayer hadn't seen them with his own eyes. Jason Ross told the Mormon president that he was "their host," which was probably meant to sound ominous. Everything about this setup smacked of medieval war—the hostages, the mercenary Russians, the taking of a castle. Jeff would have to adjust his thinking to this new/old reality. It wasn't the Global War On Terror. It was Game of fucking Thrones.

At the Homestead, there'd been no executions, nor exiling of old enemies. Not yet. Ross occupied the refuge, he fed his Russian friends, and he likely organized a defense behind the walls. The Homestead would be a hard target. Jeff stewed on that question while he searched for the soft underbelly of the Hoodie army.

The Homestead compound was surrounded by a twin wall, and it perched on steep ground. There was no vehicle, including a bulldozer, which could approach the wall without flipping on its back.

Jeff's motto, that winter, had been "never stop fortifying," and the process had been driven by the Homestead's inexhaustible supply of diesel fuel from the refinery they'd captured at the beginning of the collapse. Jeff had put backhoe crews to work, twenty-four hours a day, cutting a ten foot-wide road perpendicular to the slope of the hill around fifteen acres of the Homestead. Front-end loaders followed with fencing, stone, debris, and soil to form a HESCO-style castle wall. Once the heavy wall was done, another crew constructed the outer wall from chain-link, barbed wire, and curling razor wire. It was a nasty rampart: impossible to defeat with armor and very difficult for infantry to take.

The Homestead had been built by Ross on a pinnacle in the mountains overlooking Oakwood. Not only did it provide stunning views back when that shit mattered, but the slope made it ludicrously defensible. The pitch leading up to the twin wall would force men to clamber on hands and feet toward, climb a razor wire fence, then scale, a HESCO barrier, all into withering rifle and machine gun fire. Jeff frankly had no idea how to defeat it other than to send waves of thousands of men. Not even his gun trucks would have much luck suppressing defenders on top of the wall. The wide cap of the HESCO had been built with crenellated stone shooting positions with a walkway behind them. Snipers between the gaps would maul his crew-served gunners. Jeff would need dozens of mortars to put even a dent in the defensive wall.

The gate into the Homestead was even harder to kill than the wall. With months of time, thousands of hungry laborers and limitless fuel, Jeff had built layer upon layer of staggered barriers, gates, overlapping fields of machine gun fire, stone machine gun emplacements, and shaped charges built into the walls and hidden under the asphalt. The fortified entry point was almost two hundred feet thick and riddled with peril for an attacker.

Jeff pictured Ross and the Russians admiring his handiwork. Those smug bastards were undoubtedly laughing it up over how profoundly Jeff had screwed himself.

With enough time, he could breach any defense, even one he'd designed. But hammering at the perimeter of the Homestead with mortars put the civilians inside at grave risk. Nobody could guarantee where a mortar would land. Some mortar rounds would overshoot and hit structures. Ross might even use Jeff's family and friends as human shields inside the perimeter wall.

A direct attack was simply not feasible. Jeff would have to come up with something Ross wouldn't consider, which meant Jeff would have to come up with something *he* hadn't considered. Everything Jeff knew about the Homestead, Ross knew too. It was like playing chess against himself.

Jeff considered using fire to drive them out. But mountain wildfire, natural and man-made, had been the subject of hundreds of hours of consideration. The Homestead had layer upon layer of defense against fire, plus the wilderness around it was too green to burn in all but the two driest months of the year. It certainly wouldn't catch fire now, in early spring.

Jeff would have to mount a commando raid. He would attack on foot from the steep, wooded mountains to the east. The massive wall extended even there, but the overwatch and interlocking machine gun fire was thinner on the back side. The assault would require weeks of recon, then days of planning and practice. A thousand Spetsnaz commandos could hold the fortified Homestead against even ten thousand of Jeff's own. And, unless Ross started committing atrocities, Jeff didn't see the Mormons cooperating with such a costly venture.

He'd learned more about the Russian Spetsnaz in Utah: they were a remnant force from a failed Russian attempt to take over the American nuclear missile silos in Montana, Wyoming, and South Dakota. They were stranded men, not mercenaries, but Ross had bought them. If Jeff could drive the cartel back, and get some breathing room, he could approach the Russians and take Jason's legs out from under him. Any warrior who'd been purchased once could be purchased again.

Jeff imagined his family terrified. He pictured his boys with worry hanging on their tender brows. He pictured Tara soothing their fears. The thought of it was like an afterburner roasting the back of Jeff's bald head. Anger pulsed through his veins like molten steel against the coming cold of night. The wind whipped away the heat coming off of his head, and he thought about digging out his skull-cap beanie from his pack, but the bouncy road didn't permit him to release his vice-like grip on the machine gun. Also, he was the man on the main gun, responsible to bring covering fire if they encountered cartel scouts.

His long, frayed string of thought returned right where he'd begun: that he must defeat the cartel. Grinding Ross' face into the gravel would have to wait. Jeff could not turn his mind toward Ross until he destroyed Castillo. If he took down Ross only to lose the region to a drug lord, what had he really gained?

Tanks required fuel to maneuver. They threw tracks and often needed repair. Tank drivers had to be fed. Ammunition needed to be topped off. For every combat soldier, the Hoodies would have to field four support personnel. It was the indelible truth of war: without ironclad logistics, an army was nothing more than a wandering band of impulsive thieves, incapable of making serious war. This was no band of thieves, and their logistics train would be their weak underbelly, and that was what Jeff hunted that night with his band of reconnaissance men, the soft spot in the cartel's flank.

Since February, when the Hoodies first rolled into St. George and garrisoned there, Jeff's militia forces had scoured the highways and byways from Las Vegas to Salt Lake City and out two hundred miles, capturing or destroying every fuel tanker truck in existence. They couldn't dig the cartel out of St. George, but they could pull fuel trucks off the chess board. Jeff couldn't know how many trucks the cartel already possessed, but he could make it hard to replace them.

At the moment, the Hoodies were consolidating in Cedar City and preparing to refuel south of town. Jeff's recon truck crossed the interstate at night, deep into cartel territory at Kanarraville.

The Hoodies were economizing the movement of the Abrams. They ran them as little as possible, choosing to protect their logistics train mostly with the electric gun buggies. It made sense, since the buggies could hypothetically run forever on solar.

To protect their umbilicus back to St. George, the Hoodies placed one Abrams tank every two miles. Twenty-five of their eighty tanks were tied up covering the supply chain. The farther they stretched from the hard point defense in St. George, the more strung out they would become.

Cedar City was the cartel's next supply depot. The cartel was leap-frogging their way to Salt Lake City, one fuel storage yard to another. But their next jump after Cedar City would be a long one, all the way to Spanish Fork. That was two hundred miles, the hairy edge of the Abrams range.

Jeff and his team pulled off the road on a rise in the valley floor. Their spies had reported two tanker trucks coming north from St. George. The security guy dashed forward with a pair of binoculars and a magnified night vision scope. The sniper with the Barrett .50 and his spotter went looking for a hide. Jeff stayed with the machine gun and the driver.

This would give Jeff a chance to see how the Hoodies reacted—and he'd get his hands bloody and *do something*. The molded, plastic stock of the 240D machine gun took him back to Afghanistan. The cold plastic against his cheek reminded him of a time when war was simpler. When his family was safe, tucked away in America, surrounded by a vast ocean. If he couldn't be a father right now, at least he could be a soldier. He wrapped himself around the gun stock so tightly that it groaned.

Jeff's forward security man advised them over the radio: the twin tanker trucks were incoming, flanked by three electric gun buggies.

"Two minute warning. Prepare to execute." Jeff spoke into his radio.

"Acknowledged." The sniper team radioed back.

Jeff's gun truck crawled forward through the black night up a dirt road onto a juniper-studded peak. From that vantage point, they could see the four-lane strip of asphalt cutting across the range.

The Abrams had thermal imaging. If the Hoodies had figured out the system, as soon as the Abrams tank, on station in the next valley, responded to the ambush, they'd pinpoint his truck and send them to Valhalla. But the fuel tankers weren't shadowed by tanks, and that'd give Jeff and his men a few minutes before the Abrams raced into the fight—when they'd be up against just the electric gun buggies. He could do a helluva lot of damage in a few minutes.

The dim running lights of the cartel convoy flickered into view through Jeff's night vision goggles as they crested a rolling ribbon of interstate. They were still two kilometers out, double the distance Jeff preferred for this "far ambush."

"Hold for my signal," Jeff reminded the sniper over the radio.

He could hear the little convoy now. Just the rumble of the fuel tankers. Of course, their headlights and taillights were blacked out, but even the tiny dash LEDs inside the buggies and trucks glared like fog lights in Jeff's NVGs.

Jeff aimed the 240D at the trucks, visible in his night vision goggles, clicked the push-to-talk on his plate carrier vest and said, "Execute, execute, execute."

Boom! Boom!...Boom!

Jeff's snipers went to town. As planned, they went after the fuel trucks.

Thunk, thunk...thunk.

The .50 caliber sniper rifle rattled off four shots, two each, low into the fuel bowsers. The convoy screeched to a halt and the gun buggies flared out, circling the wagons in a defensive posture. Their machine guns opened up for a second then stopped. They had no targets, only the shadows of sleeping mountains. The big sniper rifle had punched holes in the tankers and they were undoubtedly gushing precious gasoline onto the interstate, but nobody wanted to climb down from the trucks, into the dark, and repair the gushing holes.

Jeff counted down sixty seconds in his head. The longer he waited, the bigger the pool beneath the tanker trucks would grow.

The closest Abrams roared to life. The angry grumble silenced the crickets. Jeff glanced at his glow-in-the-dark G-Shock watch. The Abrams had taken forty-five seconds to get the alert and fire up its engines. It'd take them another two minutes to cross over into Jeff's valley.

If the Abrams team was any good, they'd scan the hills for thermal targets and instantly begin obliterating anything with a heat signature. But this was inhabited land. Farmhouses and barns dotted the landscape for miles. Pickup trucks and tractors had barely cooled after the spring day's work. There would be dozens of heat signatures for the Abrams to tease apart. Could they distinguish Jeff's truck among the twenty or thirty other thermal signatures?

As planned, Jeff made it easy for them. He opened up with his tracer-packed Ma Deuce at the gushing fuel trucks. Every round in the belt sizzled with scorching heat, less accurate than ball ammo but burning with white-hot phosphorous. Jeff made small adjustments to the scorching arc of gunfire and within two seconds, he walked the burning bullets into the helpless forms of the tanker trucks. He ran the gleaming rope up and down the convoy, once, twice, three times... The tracers burned a streak in his night vision. But tracers went *both* ways. They lit up their target but they exposed the source too. The electric gun buggies opened up on Jeff's truck, but by then he was done. His belt was exhausted, and down on the interstate, hungry flames licked around the trucks, pooling, growing, and seeking more fuel.

Jeff's driver gunned it and lurched forward, putting the knob of the hill between them and the gun buggies. Jeff almost spilled out the back, but hooked his arm around the welded-in tripod before he could fly over the tailgate.

"Whoa!" Jeff shouted, unsure if anyone could hear him. "Go easy," he shouted. His driver, Hector, had never taken fire before.

Jeff looked back in time to see a mountain of flame on the interstate—a towering tongue licking the sky. The rat-a-tat-tat of the electric gun buggies wavered as they fled from the growing inferno. Jeff felt the explosion in his inner ear a split-second before he heard it. Then another. Then another. A flame, half the size of a city block, rolled into the sky.

Boom! The Abrams thundered.

The shrieking shell streaked over Jeff's truck, now rumbly-crunching down a sandy wash.

Ka-thung! the air clapped as the shell exploded into something. The Abrams had probably blown up a goat barn. They couldn't target the truck with the thermal imaging now that they were behind the string of low hills.

Jeff checked his watch again. It'd taken three minutes for the first cannon shot from the Abrams.

That was good, enough time for a hit-and-run campaign up and down the interstate between Cedar City and St. George. They would bleed the Hoodie convoys, and drain off their ability to make war. They'd nip at them like hyenas and make Salt Lake City seem as hospitable as the dark side of the moon.

The Ford bounced down the dirt road to the rally point where they'd planned to pick up the sniper team.

"Take it easy, Hoss," Jeff radioed the driver. "Smooth is fast."

The truck cut its speed in half without tapping the brakes. *Men almost never went too slow in combat,* Jeff recalled and smiled.

It felt good to blow some shit up, he admitted. War chewed up lives like breakfast cereal and that was his job. His trade, his craft, was destroying men and machines. Every Hoodie he killed and tanker he wasted put him one step closer to going after the real enemy: the man who held his family captive.

The Ford crunched to a stop in the black of night. Jeff's NVGs were tilted up and out of the way on his bump helmet, so he couldn't see anything beyond the cocoon of the red headlamp hanging around his neck.

Out of the gloom, the sniper and the spotter appeared, lifted the Barrett rifle into the bed, jumped into the truck bed then patted the side. The Ford continued on its way. Jeff clapped the spotter on the shoulder. The mission had gone precisely as-planned, and they now had the makings of a strategy that'd slow the beasts of war in their march toward home.

Hitting the supply convoys was the obvious play, but hitting them from an offset sniper position in the blind, then sending tracers to ignite fuel from a secondary position would make the enemy scratch their heads, at least for a week or two.

They'd vaporized 3,000 gallons of gas, which roughly equated to six Abrams tanks making it from this place to Salt Lake City. With every tanker truck they burned, a handful of Abrams would drop out of the fight. It wasn't sexy, as strategies went, but it would work.

BILL MCCALLISTER WOULD'VE THOUGHT by now that Gustavo Castillo, his boss and champion, would get it about war. The enemy always got a vote, and that's what made the enterprise so darned interesting. Even with scores of clanking, invincible heavyweights, a clever enemy could make life hell.

Bill, Castillo, Alejandro, and Saúl stood at the oil slick grave of the burned out tanker trucks. The asphalt had cooked down to a shiny pond of tar. It was early morning, and the enemy had slipped away hours before. Still, the thought of it made the hairs prickle on the back of Bill's neck. He hated snipers. A sniper had been there just hours before. He'd set off the ambush that killed the trucks and rendered the drivers down to grease stains.

Castillo roiled and Bill worried about how much of this would land in his lap. Castillo had a habit of choosing one of his three lieutenants to take the blame when something went wrong: Bill McCallister, Alejandro Muñoz, or Saúl Ortega. *Spin the wheel of fortune. Take your chances.* Would Bill eat the Big Enchilada today?

The other two lieutenants were Latin American SOF vets. Bill had once been an American Special Forces commando, but he was the latecomer to the crew, and much older than the others. Plus, he was a gringo. He got extra spins at the wheel.

Months before, the cartel had scooped Bill up by threatening his home town if he didn't comply. That'd been Bill's motive at first: to keep Patagonia, Arizona from being wiped off the map. Since that time, he'd come to realize that this new form of government made sense to him. One guy, one set of opinions, with everyone facing in the same direction. In now-dead America, it'd been a system of *follow whoever bitched the loudest on TV.* He couldn't remember why monarchy, historically, had been considered such a bad thing.

Bill frankly liked Castillo's style: smart, ruthless and organized. The handsome kingpin thought of everything. Months after the collapse, Bill had proven his worth to the Big Boss, and was offered a grass-painted valley in northern Utah for his services: A hundred and twenty thousand acres of waving grass and a lazy river right down the middle. It beat the shit out of Bill's gravel-caked, cattle refugee camp in Arizona. If he was going to fight a war, he might as well get paid for it. So Bill went from being a hostage to being a merc. It wasn't the first time he'd been paid to fight, and it probably wouldn't be the last.

The cartel plan to take Utah was simple: get within twenty miles of the Salt Lake fuel refinery, blockade every avenue of approach into the city, and starve the Utah Militia out. When the perfect window of opportunity presented itself, they'd rush in and seize the refinery. That would require a touch of providence, but once they had the refinery surrounded, they could just wait.

Obviously, Kirkham would set fire to the fuel the moment conquest felt inevitable, but with a blockade in place, and with the Abrams tanks in a ring of death around the refinery, time would be on the cartel's side. Castillo could send expeditionary units north into Idaho while they starved out the locals. The region would be theirs. Defeat for the Utah Militia was inevitable. The insurgents would eventually sue for the best peace they could negotiate.

Bill warned Castillo a dozen times of the hit-and-run strikes on their supply convoys. Progress toward Salt Lake would be no Nazi *blitzkrieg*. It was too far for one tank of gas, and any sudden advance on the refinery would trigger its destruction.

Nobody wanted to destroy the irreplaceable fuel in those tanks. Not Castillo, not Kirkham and not the Mormons. The Salt Lake refinery was a liquid bridge back to modern civilization. Without that gas, it'd take years to restore power, pump crude oil, refine fuels, and jump-start the industrial capabilities of the region. If they couldn't power generators, or fuel heavy equipment, how would they repair a damaged pipeline? How would they rebuild a refinery?

The Utahns hadn't destroyed the refineries yet, which meant they weren't crazy. They didn't want a dark age, either. But they would destroy them if the cartel got too close, too fast. Bill wanted to dance, not fistfight. Their army needed to come off as unstoppable, but judicious. Less of a threat and more of a foregone conclusion. Patience would deliver the refinery.

Gustavo Castillo was many things, but patient wasn't one of them. He preferred action to siege. Just months before, he'd killed his own daughter to simplify the chain of command—which reminded Bill just how mercurial *El Canoso* could be.

Castillo's veiled eyes dwelt on the dinosaur hulk of the burned out fuel tankers, then flicked across Alejandro, Saúl, and Bill. They returned to Alejandro. The supply chain was his command.

"Alejandro," Castillo said in a half-growl. "How are you going to make absolutely sure this doesn't happen again?"

Bill was very curious to hear the answer, since the cartel's fuel trucks and fuel depots had been getting the shit shot out of them by snipers since the beginning of the collapse.

"I need more tanks," Alejandro complained. "I can't cover fifty miles of open country with just twenty-five tanks. There are thousands of farmers in this valley and a *puta-madre* lot of cows. We've got heat signatures everywhere. Detecting snipers against that background is like plucking a pubic hair out of a bowl of *frijoles*. It only takes one tracer round to light a fuel truck on fire. *Just one.*" He held up a finger to make his point.

"So kill them all, then," Castillo said.

Bill hoped to hell he meant the cows and not the farmers. There were hushed rumors among the men that Castillo had killed an entire town in New Mexico. Bill chalked it up to exaggeration, but he wasn't entirely sure. When Castillo got angry, virtually anything was possible.

"Kill who?" Alejandro asked. Bill wondered the same thing.

"The cattle, *cabrón*. Run the farmers out. Kill the cattle. Clear this whole valley, from here to St. George," Castillo said.

Bill released a breath he didn't know he was holding. He loved a genius warlord as much as the next guy, but there were limits. Mass murder was one.

Castillo shot Bill a glance that gave him chills. Like he'd read his mind.

"What've you learned from your interrogations?" Castillo turned to Bill. "I heard you cut a finger off that SEAL we captured," Castillo said, a pointed reminder to Bill that no one's hands were clean.

"Just what I told you before," Bill said. "They're set to blow the Maverick refinery if we push into Salt Lake City too hard."

"Yeah, and how do you propose we iron out that wrinkle?" Castillo asked.

Bill really needed Castillo to hear this, so he straightened up and looked him in the eyes. "We move in *slow* and *steady*, we stop at least twenty miles short. Make them think they ran us out of fuel. We secretly top off the tanks and wait for a window of opportunity. They want to believe that we can be stopped. Give them evidence that they're right. Lay a quiet siege. Lull them into what looks like a long war, then *strike* at the perfect moment."

Castillo didn't look convinced. "Sounds like Stalingrad to me."

"Don't believe everything you see on the History Channel," Bill argued. "That's revisionist history. The Germans won Stalingrad."

"*Mierda*," Castillo swore. "You listen to too much QAnon."

"I don't get that channel where I live," Bill said. "But hear me on this: if we charge into that refinery, it'll go up in flames just like Las Vegas did."

Castillo fingered his ruined ear, like reminding himself what happened when he jumped the gun. Bill's son, Noah, and his gang of merry freedom fighters had nearly blown Castillo up in that escapade. The reminder of the Vegas refinery pushed the boss' attention on to Saúl.

"What's your report?" Castillo asked.

Saúl nodded. "We're good, *jefe*. Even with these two tankers gone, we have plenty of gas in St. George to top off the Cedar City fuel depot. The Utah Militia was kind enough to leave the big fuel tanks in Cedar half-full. Looks like they're sharing the wealth with southern Utah, keeping them supplied with gas so they can plow their fields. Their mistake is our gain."

"I wouldn't get to sucking on each others' *chorizos* just yet," Bill interrupted. "The fact that they're keeping Cedar City in gas means they're organized. Damned organized. It means they're trading between towns and maybe obeying a central authority, like a government or the Mormon prophet dude. If Cedar City wasn't bone dry on gas, it means we're facing a military that's a shit-ton more squared away than we faced in Arizona."

Saúl nodded. "*Correoso* might be right. Cedar City got a fuel resupply from Salt Lake. Recently."

Castillo tended to listen to Saúl. Saúl was the only lieutenant who'd stayed by Castillo's side from the beginning. He'd dragged his half-drained body out of his kitchen, out the front door and away into hiding after Castillo's wife buried a butcher's knife in his throat. Bill sometimes wondered if the kid didn't have a boner for the boss. He'd stayed loyal like a Labrador retriever, no matter how FUBARed the situation got. Bill wondered what the boss had promised him. If Bill was getting a ranch, Saúl was probably getting a state.

"That also means the people of Cedar City are communicating our every move to the enemy," Bill added.

Castillo glanced around. They were alone on the interstate.

"If they're distributing gas and governing a state," Alejandro asked, "is this still the apocalypse?"

Alejandro tended to bitch more than was seemly, but he made a good point. Could the apocalypse be wrapping up now that it was springtime? Had they missed their window to conquer the West?

Castillo shook his head. "Don't get the yips," he said. "We're still the only ones with Abrams."

"For now," Alejandro said. "There are tens of thousands of main battle tanks in Northern California."

"And maybe twenty-five thousand Chinese too," Bill said. They'd been hearing reports over shortwave radio of Chinese troops occupying west coast ports: San Diego, Los Angeles, San Francisco, Portland, and Seattle.

"Let's not get carried away with paranoid fantasies," Castillo said. "We just wiped the floor with the Utah Militia, and we have a clean shot at taking the refinery in Salt Lake. There's nothing anyone can do to stop us."

"Except to burn down the refinery," Alejandro added. "Again."

Bill thought he could read the look in Castillo's eyes as he regarded Alejandro's bitching. *Disdain.* Castillo foresaw a region of electric vehicles, modern industry, and efficient, central authority. He'd proven he could do it in Nevada. Now he'd do it in the green fields of the Intermountain West. Despite the fact that Castillo was a prick, Bill believed in his vision. He admired his ruthless will. Castillo was the furthest thing from a gold-chain-wearing drug lord.

But here in Utah, shadows of the old Mormon order still flickered over the towns. The city councils still met. The churches held services. Salt Lake shared the fuel. The farming communities suffered, but they suffered *together*.

"Kill the cows," Castillo reiterated. "Run off the ranchers and farmers. Empty this corridor of every warm body. Nothing else to remain but our fuel trucks and the jackrabbits."

Bill genuflected; just a nod of his head, but also submission. In his mind's eye, he pictured a cattle ranch in Star Valley by the Wyoming border, with grass deep as a man's thigh. He saw himself on a porch, enjoying his morning smoke, considering what fence to build, what trout pond to dig, what outbuilding to construct that day. He saw his noble cattle, fat-necked, ranging along the winding river and wading through the shushing grass. He saw a reward equal to the labors of war.

4

"The Rocky Mountains might as well have been the Great Wall of China, that first year after the collapse. There was a regional war on either side, and neither army knew of the existence of the other. Rumors of skirmishes, battles and invasions peppered ham radio —Chinese, Mexicans, Russians, Mormons, Native Americans, California Lutherans—and even the most ludicrous of all those rumors turned out to be true, though not quite as apocalyptic as they might sound."

— THE AMERICAN DARK AGES, BY WILLIAM BELLAHER, NORTH AMERICAN TEXTBOOKS, 2037

Endicott, Nebraska

MAT BEST DROVE THE FORD RAPTOR NORTH OUT OF TENNESSEE, weaving through the small towns of the American Midwest. Most towns granted him safe passage. Some turned him away. Many appeared abandoned. All had suffered great loss.

Mat wrote them down on the back of an Applebee's menu, like a mass obituary along a stripe bisecting Tennessee, Missouri, Kansas, and Nebraska. Dead towns on one side, and a picture of mozzarella sticks on the other.

Cape Girardeau, Missouri: most dead from violence and dysentery. A gang from St. Louis took everything.
Reynolds, Missouri: lumber town. Most starved.
Vienna, Missouri: half survived. Ate grass root. Most children dead from dysentery.
Macon, Missouri: abandoned, except for the bodies.

All the fight had gone out of the farmlands. Mat was shocked to see livestock running wild, goats, cows, horses and pigs. People must've lost the energy to chase them, or bullets to shoot and eat them.

He'd never driven across the Midwest before. The few Midwesterners he saw at town blockades, or skulking down river bottoms, were probably one in five of the original population, and that didn't count the devastation in the big cities. From what Mat could tell, the cities had been wiped out.

With his heart in a grave funk, he took chances he wouldn't normally have taken, and spoke to people at roadblocks he would've bypassed at a distance. The survivors were laid low, in the mud, and Mat felt drawn to them. Wrapped in McKenzie, he'd been more fortunate than he deserved. None of the towns he passed had piggeries or defensive walls. Not one town had the providence and planning of his home for the apocalypse. The towns he passed had been overrun by the desperate, picked poor by starvation, then forgotten, moldering on the numb soil.

At Macon, Missouri, Mat abandoned his northward push and angled west on a straight trajectory toward Salt Lake City. There, he hoped to refuel for a final push into Southern California. At the tiny, silent town of Endicott, Nebraska, he pulled over to rest his eyes. It was late afternoon, and Mat drove only during daylight hours. He'd find a bolthole for the night.

Usually, locating an abandoned homestead wasn't a problem. More than half were empty. Mat rubbed his eyes to relieve the road-weariness, then blinked a dozen times. For a moment, the blurred town reminded him of McKenzie, out by Elwood Drive where the shanty town had sprung up among the now-ravaged starter homes.

It wasn't Mat's way to overnight in a house too near a town. It would be an invitation for desperate people to raid his truck. So far, he'd avoided gunfights. He would likely win, but that came with the knowledge that the best gunfight was the one avoided.

Mat looked to the distant edges of town for shelter. He'd had bad luck with remote farms, many of the solitary farm families had survived. Approaching their homesteads was hazardous. The homes a little way outside of a town didn't normally belong to the kind of folk who grew their own food, and they weren't the kind of people who stuck tight and organized, either. They were the ones who had mostly vanished, and their homes were usually empty for overnight squatting.

Mat rubbed his eyes again. He couldn't get them right. It was time to call it a night.

He flipped a U-turn and headed back up Nebraska Route 8. A mile later, he found a house with a dozen rusty vehicles up on blocks. There was no vegetable garden, a sure sign of abandonment. If a family survived the winter, they planted. There was no other way.

Mat pulled up the gravel drive and slammed his truck door with a loud clap, then waited with his rifle low, behind the engine block, for three full minutes. No dogs barked. No screen doors creaked. No floorboards moaned.

Mat approached, entered through the open door, cleared the house, then returned to the Raptor and prepared his vehicle for emergency departure, if it came to that. He backed across the lawn, almost touched the porch, slipped one shoulder into his go-bag, the other into his plate carrier vest, closed the door and set the car alarm with the fob. He climbed the creaky stairs to the second story and made himself at home in a kid's room with a view out front, over the Raptor.

Like most homes he'd squatted in, this one told him nothing about what had become of the residents. The cupboards were bare. Anything useful, like gas, batteries or camping gear had been scavenged, and Mat knew right where it'd all gone. Across the belly of America, the woods were chock-a-block full of abandoned camping gear. Ten million tents were being blown to rags by the elements in every forest patch from here to Annapolis, Maryland.

Mat's eyes still bugged him. He struggled to focus. That was normal when he was tired. It was nothing a little sleep wouldn't cure.

He'd been away from McKenzie, Will, and Gladys for eight days. The ragged isolation of the heartland gnawed at his resolve. Was there really anything he could do for his parents and his brothers at this point? Why had he left McKenzie? Why, really?

Now that he'd seen the magnitude of the winter kill with his own eyes, hope for his family darkened. Santa Barbara seemed like a remote beach village, but it lay just ninety-five miles from Los Angeles and only forty miles from Oxnard. There weren't many directions for Los Angelinos to flee: east toward Las Vegas or north toward Santa Barbara. Some would run into the desert of Palmdale or Hesperia, but those places offered little in the way of cover, food, or water. Santa Barbara had been overrun by millions. He couldn't deny it.

He had told himself that checking on his folks was his duty. In reality, his brothers had been with his parents since the first moment of the crash. His bros could handle themselves and so could his dad. Anything that could be done for his family had already been done. Or it hadn't. In any case, the die was cast. Like the heartland, things in Southern California had settled into a new normal, which likely meant millions dead and just a handful surviving. Los Angeles was the same as St. Louis or Kansas City, a black hole on the map—pasted over in asphalt and populated by the vicious and the dead. Without access to clean water, and without garden soil, the cities had little to offer survivors.

Santa Barbara stood in the way of the worst of the California exodus, and because of the nuclear blast in Los Angeles harbor, his family had likely been overrun. Chances were slim Mat would even locate them, if they were alive.

So why had he left Will and Gladys in McKenzie? And the sheriff and his wife? He'd made real friends there, almost as good as his brothers in the Ranger Regiment. He'd fought side-by-side with the people of McKenzie and shared victories and horrors. They knew him. They accepted him.

But the job had ended, and the town already had a good sheriff. With peace, came the end of Mat's usefulness.

They would've *acted* happy to keep him, and to feed him. They would've waved away his concerns. No matter how useful Mat wasn't, the town of McKenzie would've cared for him, like a three-legged dog that had, once upon a time, been hell on wheels against the pheasants.

Mat could've dragged it out and stayed. He could've traded on past deeds and kept his belly full of warm food, telling war stories and getting drunk on stale glory.

But that wasn't him. That wasn't the code. He'd moved on, because that's who he was: a gun fighter, not a storyteller.

———

TURKEY HUNTING in the woods served double-duty for Jason. It got him away from the Homestead, where he could breathe fresh air and not suffocate between looming threats. It also gave him a chance to get *her* back.

He hated the way that sounded: *to get her back*. It was so needy, like that limp-dick seventies song.

Baby come back. Any kind of fool could see
There was something, in everything about you.
Baby come back, you can blame it all on me
I was wrong, and I just can't live without you.

Jason laughed at the memory. He despised whiny love ballads. He pictured long-haired, seventies crooners banging roadies on tour, then going home to their supermodel wives to weep when they got busted.

He'd always been the kind of husband who stuck, who kept his word.

Did that change with the apocalypse?

Everything and everyone had changed. It was like COVID-19. After those two years, everyone became someone different. The Black Autumn collapse was like COVID-19, but after Fate slams a twelve-pack of Monster Energy and does donuts in the parking lot until she hits a light post. After that shit, every survivor became someone different.

Jason stepped off the dirt road, his Ruger 10-22 over his shoulder, under the canopy of maples, and tread lightly into the duff. He inhaled the aroma of his forest in spring. It was wet and woody, like a stream bank brushed in moss. A footfall raised the tang of young nodding onions beneath his boot. The next swirled breeze carried forest mint. Then, the scent of sweet decay, last year's leaves becoming the black soil that cycled nitrogen to the web of roots beneath, the fungus holding it all together.

He carried the suppressed Ruger in his hands and his ultra-light AR-15 across his back on a two-point sling. The Ruger might as well have been on the Ross family crest. His father owned one. Each of his brothers owned one. Jason's sons each got one for their fifteenth birthday. Jason's 10-22 was suppressed, for gliding through the spring-sprouted canopy, seeking plump Rio Grande turkeys for the feast. If he got lucky, he'd shoot one, then another, in their clucking, bobbing heads.

He'd been hearing turkeys under the trees for the last twenty minutes. Their soft chirrups sprinkled the silence like forest fairies beckoning. The birds stayed a few paces out of sight, just aware enough of his ghosting presence to keep their distance, but not enough to bolt.

Jason smiled at a memory of Emily, the daughter he'd lost to the flu. When she was five years old, he used to take her into this forest and tell her tales of forest fairies. The kind Fairy Queen. The cruel Coyote Lord. The clever Fox Soldiers. Emily had imagined that she saw them as they disappeared between budding oak limbs. She squealed with delight as the flying pixies dodged just outside the frank, uninteresting world of man.

He paused his slow step and listened as a turkey bat it wings against the morning chill. The flock was nearby, just as it'd been for the last thirty minutes. Nearby, but cautious.

He was far outside the double stone wall of the Homestead, deep in the back acreage that nobody thought of as his, except the now-dead county tax man. The original property boundaries cut merciless lines north and south, east and west. They left clefts and corners of ridges and valleys in awkward wedges between his land and his neighbors—mostly U.S. Forest Service, whatever that still meant. This corner of his quarter-section fell outside the defensive perimeter Jeff Kirkham had demarcated around the Homestead. The defensible boundaries ignored title or survey. Jeff had encircled the high ridges he thought best, set the listening post/observation posts where he pleased and left the rest to fallow.

Jason heard the turkeys scratching in the layers of leaf, and used the sound cover for another soft step. The scratching came fortuitously nearer. Turkey hunting in this way, on the slow prowl, required the flock to make a mistake, and it appeared they would. Jason leaned against a mossy, old oak and waited.

If he killed a few turkeys, he would give them to Jenna. He would stride into the Homestead with a brace of birds on his belt and hand them to her. No explanation. It was an exchange between man and woman as old as time.

Woman. I give you this fat and this protein. I have hunted. You are mine.

The shushed scratching neared. The cadence seemed off. Every creature of the forest had its own rhythm. The turkey went *scratch-scratch-peck*—silence—*scratch-scratch-peck*. A deer went *swish-swish*—pause—*swishswishswishswish*—pause. A man went *thunk-thunk-thunk-thunk*. This was none of those. A coyote? A porcupine? They were less ordinary. He didn't know their rhythm.

He waited and listened. The turkeys went silent.

Scrape-scrape-scrape-scrape-scrape. Exhale.

His blood chilled. It was human. Not a hunter. Something else. He raised the little rifle. There was no time to unsling the AR-15. If he must, he would shoot the entire banana magazine of thirty, tiny rounds at the intruder. He scanned the forest through the 3 x 9 Leupold scope, seeking movement in the tangle of maple and oak, saskatoon, and chokecherry.

There.

A strange color bobbed across a triangle window between trees. Blonde hair. A girl. Her face was filthy. Her hair was matted, yet flyaway in the back. Someone had trimmed the hair haphazardly with a knife, maybe. Her face twisted with the effort of the climb up the canyon, exacerbated by hunger. This was no child of the Homestead.

The girl came into full view. She stalked up the rise, twenty yards from Jason, then dumped herself to rest at the foot of a tangle of downed chokecherry. Jason scanned the forest for other threats. Humans never traveled alone. But he'd only heard the girl scrabbling through the forest. Nobody else.

Satisfied that she was alone, Jason stepped around the oak and lowered the rifle.

The girl's head jerked up and she coiled to bolt.

Jason raised the rifle. "Stay down. I'll shoot."

It was a lie, but everyone now understood the threat of a rifle. Guns were so much a part of life now that even children fathomed their utter menace. She uncoiled inside the nest of branches, her eyes terrified. He needed her to stay put, or she could become a true threat to him, raising the alarm and spoiling his stealth. He was safe out here, alone beyond the wall, only if undetected.

She settled back down, her eyes a miasma of fear. Jason held one finger to his lips. He stalked closer so they could whisper.

He ordered her in his dad voice, "Get up and walk. Quietly. Walk the direction you were going." He needed distance from whatever adult was covering her, tending her. The girl appeared to be eight years old. She wouldn't be far from an adult, and the adult would be a serious threat. Jason needed to get away from this spot, and he couldn't allow her to raise the alarm before he was within cover of the Homestead wall. "Keep moving and stay very quiet."

The girl nodded and resumed her walk. They were heading back to the northeast corner of the Homestead perimeter, directly toward the inner wall. The girl seemed strangely comfortable in the forest. There was no meandering or second-guessing. She knew the ground. She'd been here many times. His curiosity mounted the farther they ranged from where he'd caught her.

After negotiating two more folds in the mountainside, Jason felt safer. An adult would've had to bust brush to keep up with them, and Jason had paused occasionally to listen. It was impossible to move through the forest without sound, no matter how skilled, and he'd heard nothing but the girl. The turkeys were gone. They'd heard the whispered interaction with the girl and moved on to haunt another canyon.

He was abducting a child, but in this world that wasn't as bad as it sounded. It was necessary for survival. He had no designs on her other than his own safety.

They passed the security perimeter that ran the length of the long ridge. Jason pulled a blaze-orange square of nylon cloth from his hip pocket and held it over his head as he and the girl emerged from the tree line. He couldn't see the guard in the LP/OP watching him, but he assumed he was under the steady aim of a rifle. Re-entering the perimeter was always a risky moment, but the men and women of the Homestead had many months of practice. There was no crackle of rifle fire.

To Jason's amusement, the girl wormed between tall sage clumps. This was her "track," her regular route. She knew that the LP/OP hovered on the high ground above, on Middle Ridge, and she'd made a path to evade their sight lines. Jason followed her, the flag over his head, overtaken by curiosity.

A half-mile later, they reached the HESCO wall. The girl looked back at him, suddenly and with trepidation, like she'd been caught sneaking into the cookie cupboard. Her shoulders drooped, and she reluctantly led him to a spot in the wall where the chain-link had been pried up off the ground. The soil beneath it was scraped away, as though raccoons had been using it for entry. Light showed through the tangle of logs and stones that filled the HESCO. Jason approached and crouched. He could see a winding path where a small child could snake through the ten-foot thickness of rubble held together by the chain-link HESCO basket.

"I'll be damned," he said to himself. He regarded the girl. Her face had collapsed in regret. She knew she was busted.

"How long have you been sneaking through here?" he asked her.

Blood Spring 77

She blanched at the question and said nothing. Her blue eyes flared.

"Come on," he said, and guided her by the blonde head around to a proper entry point, the aluminum ladder Jason had used to climb down the HESCO in the pre-dawn dark. "Are you at least going to tell me your name?" he asked.

"Piper," she whispered. "Are you going to shoot me?"

"No, Piper. I'm not going to shoot you." He herded her up the ladder, over the HESCO, and into the Homestead.

"Show me where you go after you get in," Jason said. They were inside the wall, but the forest remained in heavy patches.

He could tell by the look in Piper's eyes, she'd surrendered to the gravity of an adult in charge. Piper did exactly as she was told, her shoulders slumped and her pace a defeated slog. Instead of walking down the dirt road that followed the bottom of North Fork canyon, she slipped into the trees and joined a deer trail along a wooded bench through the tallest, greenest part of the inside forest. They walked by Jason's family adventure course with rope swings, zip lines, and tightropes. Her trail took them under an old archery stand where he'd killed many mule deer with his compound bow. They passed around the large goat enclosure as goats bleated their many complaints. They circled the wetlands in the bottom of the canyon and slipped through the sliding doors into the motor pool.

Piper sulked. She stopped at one of the IBC totes, filled with grain. It was their deepest food storage—a retaining wall of wheat —and the Homestead still hadn't tapped into that final reserve. It was the furthest storage from the cook shed and it would require more work to reach it than the bucketed stuff. She pointed at the spigot.

"You steal wheat?" he asked.

The little girl nodded.

"How did you get it back to camp?"

She turned on her heels and displayed the Paw Patrol backpack she'd been wearing.

"I'll be damned if you're not the biggest little mouse I've ever seen," he said with a chuckle. "And you're all alone?"

Her eyes flashed, and he knew she wasn't. Even at her tender age, she understood that telling about her family would put them in danger.

"Where are your parents?"

Her face was slack, but her eyes hardened. She wasn't going to tell him anything else. Not today.

Jason surrendered to her will. "Let's get you a meal."

It was nearly lunch at the Homestead. The homesteaders would gather as they did three times a day, around the cook shed and on benches. He'd see Jenna there.

Maybe he had something for her even more "redemptive" than a brace of turkeys. He had a lot of making up to do for slamming the door on her orphanage. Little Piper seemed like a good place to start.

———

WHEN HE FOUND JENNA, she was with Zhukov again, pouring over some piece of paper on the capstone of the office colonnade; it was likely the quartering plan for the two hundred Spetsnaz at his command HQ.

Jenna swept a lock of hair back and laughed at something he'd said. She noticed Jason approaching and her eye darted to the little girl.

"Who is this?" Jenna Ross dropped to a knee and looked Piper in the eyes.

"I found her in the woods while I was hunting. She's been sneaking inside the wall and stealing our wheat," Jason said.

Jenna ignored the petty crime. "Where are your parents, precious?"

"My daddy's dead." The girl didn't have a problem speaking to the pretty lady. "My mama's in camp."

Jenna shot a glance at Jason. The camp must be close. Any nearby camp was a threat.

"How many are in your camp?" Jenna asked.

The girl quieted and shuffled her feet. Even at a young age and talking to a nice lady, she understood something of OPSEC—operational security.

"We're not going to hurt your family," Jenna assured her. "Don't worry about that." She pulled the girl into her arms and hugged her, but the girl's back stayed straight.

Jason wasn't so sure about not hurting the girl's family. They'd encroached close to the Homestead, and they'd been stealing food.

"Ross to Zhukov," Jason spoke into his Baofeng radio. "Please send a QRF to the cook shed. We're going outside."

Jenna scowled, but said nothing.

———

THEY LEFT the girl with Jenna and went outside the wall with overwhelming force; a QRF unit of over a hundred men, geared for a fight. They spread out and moved slowly through the folds of the forest. They made their way northeast along the girl's route in a tight line of scrimmage with only a handful of meters between each squad.

If he mishandled this recon and deconfliction, it'd set him back with Jenna. She already thought of him as a despot and she had Zhukov nibbling out of the palm of her hand. If she slept with

Zhukov, Jason might as well pack up and go. His days at home would be numbered in the single digits.

"All stations. This is Ross. Consider everyone a friendly unless fired upon." He hoped that translated well over radio. The squad leaders all spoke passable English.

Something about the terrain tugged at Jason's memory. He and Chad Wade had built the foundation of a cabin nearby. They'd spent half a summer building a stone fireplace with only local stone and without mortar.

"All stations, hold." he said into his radio. "Set security and wait for me to come back. I'm going out."

Jason waved one of the Spetsnaz to come with him. His name was Yuri and Jason knew him from the road. The other commandos drifted to security positions in the small clearing and made themselves comfortable. They still wore the same snow camouflage as they had in Wyoming. It was filthier than before, dingy and blotched gray by mud and miles. At some point, soon, they'd begin wearing street clothes, and that'd mark the final transition from being an invading army to becoming residents of Utah.

These professional commandos knew there was no going home. They were no longer Russian army, and little more than the uniform and their poor English skills tied them together. They'd find companions in Utah, maybe even join shattered families, and they'd weave into the fabric of the new Wasatch Front. Many would end up converting to Mormonism.

To men from the Old World, women and family were like a slow, steady tide. They intruded, gently, into everything they touched, and raised the water level with a silent force that could be stopped by neither stone nor steel.

The Spetsnaz would be happy again, someday. They had lost their families in Russia, but they would gain families here, and ultimately be welcomed as strong men in a rugged world. They would become a bold footnote in the history of Utah. Surnames like

Petrov, Sokolov, and Fyodorov would be chiseled over rosy-cheeked Utahns for a thousand years.

Jason had brought them here, like a modern day Moses. He hadn't done it to lead them out of bondage. He'd done it for revenge. But the morning sun ate away at that. Revenge had a way of becoming gusty angst, breezy unease... then quiet regret.

Still, the footpaths of Jason's landhold drew him toward a reckoning with Kirkham. The tectonic conflict could not be ignored. He could either face it or run. Even as hot revenge cooled, there was no way to avoid it and keep his home.

After re-taking the Homestead, and returning to its forest havens, Jason had to focus a bit to drum up his former fury with Jeff Kirkham. When he thought of that moment in the board room, when Jeff took possession of his land and family, he felt a surge in his belly. But that bile was no longer labeled "Jeff Kirkham." It didn't quite have another name yet, the new name was a whisper still, not discernible. But the memory was more than just a man, and more than just Jenna's betrayal.

His daughter was buried in the soil he trod, and her soul lightened every footfall. As he made his way through the oaks and maples, she brushed at him and calmed him. Emily had been part of the betrayal, and she'd given her life for it. A sense grew in him, now that he was home: if she'd known she would give her life for those children, it wouldn't have changed a thing. To reconcile with Jenna meant reconciling with Emily's truth, and every whiff of the forest swore to it.

Jason pulled his attention back to the tactical situation. He and Yuri patrolled closer to where he believed the interloper campsite would be. Turkey Springs trickled out of a cleft in a fold in the forest and surface water would draw anyone camped in these woods.

Jason had left the QRF a few hundred yards back so they didn't overwhelm the scene, or risk a blue-on-blue shooting incident. He didn't want to return to the Homestead having killed the little girl's family, either. It would mean another disapproving glare from Jenna.

He and Yuri passed through the hollow above the spring and encountered no one, nor any sign of passing. They dropped to the spring itself, and the handiwork of man became clear. The base of the seep had been dug out and lined with rock. The water pooled, deep and wide for a five gallon bucket to be dipped and filled. A muddy footpath led away into the bog of watercress and mint.

Yuri stepped onto the path and Jason swung wide of it. There was no reason for two men to walk on the same path when they could have two shooting angles instead of one, two sets of eyes instead of one. Their rifle barrels sought targets within the green, wet wall ahead.

The footpath snaked through the underbrush, visible only from right on top of it. It angled away from the bottom rut of the canyon and ran along a small escarpment. The trail dead-ended in a cluster of elderberry and log fall. Yuri looked over and shrugged.

Jason circled quietly and slowly around the woody tangle. Before the snow melted off, it would've been a thirty-foot hill of snow. With the snow gone, it'd be written off as a bramble. He completed his circuit and returned alongside Yuri.

"Come out. We have you surrounded," Jason shouted. He and Yuri lowered into a crouch. They didn't call the QRF forward. No more than a couple of people could be hiding inside and it was no defensive fortification. No hard cover.

Under the tangle, something shuffled. One woman emerged, then another.

"Everyone out!" Jason ordered.

The second woman herded children forward with insistent sweeps of her hand. Two children appeared through a burrow hole, both younger than five years old, a boy and a girl.

"Is that everyone?" Jason asked.

The two women nodded.

"We have your daughter," Jason said. Their heads sagged in surrender.

"Please don't hurt her. Don't hurt us. We're just hungry," one said.

"How long have you been stealing from us?" Jason asked.

Neither answered.

"All winter?" he asked.

They nodded.

"You ate boiled wheat berries all winter?" There was no possible way they'd baked bread under these austere conditions.

"That and dried elderberry," the pretty one said.

They looked remarkably clean for living under a log pile. The little girl, Piper, had been the dirtiest, probably from her forest runs.

"Who are you?" Jason asked.

"Molly and Susan Beringer. This is Paul Jr. and Samantha."

"Where's Paul Senior?" Jason asked.

Yuri took a few steps away, stepped behind a maple and set up security.

"He died. You killed him."

"I killed him?" Jason pressed his hand to his chest.

"Your people did. You shot him." She looked at Jason directly, but not defiantly. He understood: the winter had scrubbed away their revenge too.

"Beringer..." he whispered, struggling to remember the name. "You're the people with the prepper camp in the creek bottom. The one made out of pallets."

They nodded.

"And the men..."

"They died, either fighting you or from the flu. The other women and kids too. It's just us, now."

There'd been a fight with the Beringers before the big battle with the gangbangers, back in October. The Homestead killed a pack of raiders in the east forest. Jeff had ordered the bodies of the dead and wounded thrown in OHVs and dumped over the ridge as a warning to others. These women were what was left of that clan. They hadn't left the woods after all. They'd stayed and raided Homestead stores, one little backpack at a time.

There'd been a time, during the apocalypse, when intruders or thieves were seen as dangerous. Now, with the majority of Utahns dead, eighty or ninety percent, survivors didn't regard one another through the eyes of fear. Most of the evil men were gone. Now it was only the desperate and the lucky, clinging to survival and hope. Malice had largely gone out of man. Hunger and disease had drummed it from them. Their scant numbers gave each human life a new preciousness. Neither Jason nor Yuri had raised a gun at the women and kids.

"You're from there?" the pretty one pointed toward the Homestead.

Jason and Yuri had full cheeks and relatively clean clothes. There was no doubt they were from the Homestead.

"I'm Jason Ross and this is Yuri…I can't say his last name."

"Arsenyev," Yuri said from behind his maple tree.

Jason could see in their eyes that they knew his name. He was the lord of the land to them, and perhaps the murderer of their family.

"We're sorry for trespassing. And for stealing," the brown-haired one said.

Jason knew they weren't, but that was the past. They were dependents of the Homestead now. With workmen and hired guns, his dependents numbered around five hundred, not counting the Russians. If they were going to feed these cave dwellers anyway, they should at least pay for it.

"They already filled the hole you made in the wall. You should move your camp closer and we'll give you work," Jason said.

The women misunderstood. "Okay. We can be your friends," the pretty one said. Her eyes dimmed with the sad implications of her offer. She glanced at her friend, who nodded with slow-dawning resignation.

Jason looked at Yuri, still behind the trunk of the maple. Yuri shrugged.

The women were suggesting they become consorts. They'd live closer and serve Jason's *other* needs. Maybe Yuri's too. The men would bring them food a few times a week, then stay for a while. Then they'd go back home, until food ran out again.

Nothing about the offer was shocking. Jason had seen it hundreds of times before in Africa and Guatemala. It was an ancient and common arrangement, come back to America after one very bad winter. Only notions of Christian monogamy stood in the way, and in the dark corners of the woods, they too had gone feeble.

Men brought food. Women provided a warm softness. Children were fed, and even a modicum of a family began in the shadow and chill of the secondary households. The visiting men treated the children as favored nieces and nephews. Fats, proteins and the occasional sugars amended the boiled wheat. Health and vitality returned. The women would garnish their hovel with bedclothes and lumber. The children would play with greater gusto. The men would be more fulfilled, and happier too. The shame of it would scarcely matter. And in the thicket of the glistening wood, it could almost be forgotten how they'd all fallen to the disgrace of prostitution and polygamy. The life they made would seem almost idyllic.

"We can be your friends," she'd said.

Being restored to his land had not just lifted Jason's heart, it'd awoken his libido. Pursuing Jenna, thinking about her in *that way*, relit a flame. With the implications of the woman's offer, a warming rolled over him. He shuffled his feet, and took a full step back. It'd been a salvo his rifle could not defeat.

Why not? he wanted to say.

Yuri would not condemn him. Russian commandos weren't concerned with Christian monogamy. Quite the contrary.

"Stay here," Jason said to the women. "I'll come back to show you where to move, and I'll bring some better materials for your new shelter." He could see the tattered remains of their rain tarp, suspended underneath the log pile in a clever, concealed modicum of a tent roof.

Jason scratched the stubble on his cheek. Her eyes had settled, as though a bargain had been struck, as though he'd accepted.

Perhaps he had.

5

Shortwave Radio 7150kHz
3:00pm

"JT Taylor on the rickety shortwave freqs, and I want to talk about biblical apocalypse. I was just chatting up a young lady transmitting from the 'American Redoubt' in east Washington State. They're legit holy rollers up there, gettin' down with a Christian Constitutional Democracy, whatever that is...

"Any-who, this young lass tells me how the apocalypse of Saint John is upon us. I was like 'Yeah? So y'all seen Jesus come down outta the sky in a white Cadillac with a troop of angels, playin' saxophones on Harleys?' She said, 'Don't be sacrilegious' and she had a point there.

"Planet Shortwave, if this is the Apocalypse with a capital "A," then where do we go to see the lambs lying down with the lions, and peace reigning 'cross the nations of man, and God plunking down His phat finger on Las Vegas? That last part might've been something I saw in a movie, but you get my point. When's all the good stuff happening now that the bad stuff has had its way?"

The Ranchettes

Powderhouse Rd,
Outside Cheyenne, Wyoming

MAT BEST HAD BEEN HOLED UP IN THE STIFLING HOUSE IN WYOMING for three days. He could not get his eyes right, no matter how much he rested them.

"Hello!" somebody hailed outside, too near Mat's Ford Raptor. "Anyone in there?" the man called.

Mat pulled the blinds aside from the second-story bedroom and peered hopelessly through the slats. He could make out the black, solid form of his truck but the person standing in the street was a blurred scarecrow.

"Get back," Mat yelled. "Get the hell away from my truck."

"It's all good," the dark ghost on the street answered as he slung a rifle around to his back and raised his hands, as far as Mat could see. "Don't shoot. I'm just stopping by to say 'hi.' I can leave if you want."

By the voice, he sounded like a younger man, probably in his twenties.

"What do you want?" Mat shouted out the window.

"Nothing. I've got everything I need. I'm just a traveler passing through and thought I'd share a campfire."

Mat needed help. He'd spent the last three days rummaging around the cupboards of the surrounding, empty homes. He'd taken more naps than ever before in his life, and still his eyes were fogged over like a mirror after a hot shower. At night, he was functionally blind. He couldn't read. He could barely decipher the labels on the few cans he'd found in the cupboards. He operated a can opener, more-or-less by feel and memory.

"Okay," Mat yelled. "Set your rifle on the hood of the truck, along with your handgun." He was guessing about the handgun. "Then come in. Hands up."

He heard a thunk on the metal hood, then another thunk. Mat

descended the stairs, unlocked the deadbolt on the front door, and backed into the kitchen with his rifle at the ready. A moment later, the young man came through the door with his hands held high.

"I'm unarmed," he said.

"Who are you?"

"Gabriel Peña. From Rose Park, Utah."

Mat lowered the barrel to aim at the man's feet. "What're you doing in Wyoming?"

"Can I put my hands down?" he asked. Mat nodded. "I'm here on reconnaissance for the Utah Militia to see the operational status of the oil fields in eastern Wyoming. We need to know what it'll take to get the pipelines flowing again into Salt Lake City."

"They sent you alone?" Mat asked. No kind of military unit would send a man alone on a recon mission.

"My fire team buddy bailed on me outside of Evanston. I kept going."

"So Utah government's still around?"

The blurry kid shrugged. "Sort of. Between General Kirkham, the Ross Homestead and the new Mormon Church, they field 50,000 men. It's enough to put up a fight against the Hoodies."

"Who're the Hoodies?"

"The cartel."

"The cartel still exists? Who buys their drugs?" Mat asked.

"They don't sell drugs. They have Abrams tanks. They want to take over the Rocky Mountains. They want fuel. Gasoline." The kid might've been pointing at the Wyoming dirt beneath their feet or scratching his balls. Mat couldn't tell.

"Did you say 'Ross Homestead?' " Mat asked. He had a lot of questions about the cartel and their tanks, but before he'd gotten stuck on Blind Man Island, he'd been heading to meet an acquaintance in Utah named Jason Ross.

"Yeah. Jason and Jenna Ross. They own a compound north of Salt Lake City."

That sounded about right, though it was a strange coincidence. Utah's population was a couple million and there were probably hundreds with the last name "Ross." That number would be cut down significantly when filtered for "millionaire preppers who'd survived the last eight months of hell."

"I'm on my way there," Mat said. "To Salt Lake to link up with Jason Ross."

"Small world." The young man said. "But I don't think he's there."

"What's that?"

"Last time I was at the Homestead, a month ago, Jason Ross had disappeared. They think he bailed after Kirkham took control of the place. Nobody really knows. He didn't leave a note or anything."

Mat didn't know who Kirkham was, but he understood. Some asshole had taken Ross' millionaire bunker away. "Millionaire" meant nothing now.

What have you done for me lately, was a thing they said, and it meant more now than ever. If you weren't pulling your weight, you were gone.

You eat what you hunt and kill. That was another thing they said. It made Mat think about his eyes. If he didn't get right soon, he was dead meat. Nobody was going to feed a blind gunman.

Mat cleared and then safetied his AR. When he peeked into the chamber to confirm the condition, he saw blurred, blue metal. There might've been a Vienna sausage in the breach for all he could tell. The center of his vision was a mushy, gray hole. When he focused on something, that thing vanished. He could see things a little better in his peripheral vision. The kid, apparently, noticed it.

"Are you okay?" the kid asked. "Is something wrong with your neck?"

Mat wanted to talk about it, with as many people as possible, actually. He knew nothing about eyesight problems except what he'd seen on daytime television commercials.

"Macular degeneration, blah, blah, blah," was all he could remember. He was so discombobulated that he would've discussed his problem with a poodle. He didn't know if there was a pill, an operation, or if this was just a passing thing, or if he was blind for life.

...*blind for life...*

"It's not my neck. A few days ago, my vision started going blurry in the middle. It's worse in one eye than the other. I've been stuck here for three days trying to rest, but it's not getting any better."

The kid tilted his head in a way that might've been brotherly concern. "We need to get you to a doctor."

"Yeah. That'd be great. How the hell do we find an eye doctor?"

"We could start with a regular doctor," the kid said. "Ya know. Get a referral."

"And he'll refer me to an eye specialist?" Both men chuckled. It was a screwed up world in so many ways.

"Cheyenne's a mess, but a couple of doctors must have survived," the kid said. He would've passed through the ruins of Cheyenne. "There was some kind of fight between Russians trying to land planes and the locals. The Russians leveled Cheyenne for a mile around the airfield."

"Russians?" Mat shook his head. "Mexicans too? In America?"

Gabriel laughed. "I know. It's weird. It's like a potluck, except everyone brought tanks instead of potato casseroles."

Mat used to be an actual threat to the enemies of his country. Now, he didn't know what he was.

Gabriel continued. "I don't know why the Russians are here, but I saw a jet airplane and a couple of big helicopters, all black and burned out. The locals gave as good as they got."

"But you didn't come across any soldiers?" Mat asked.

"No. Whatever happened in Cheyenne, it's over. But I didn't see any people. None, actually. I'll take you back there and we can look around. I don't know anything about vision problems. Maybe it's an easy fix."

Mat hadn't vetted this kid as a travel companion, but the selection process would have to be streamlined given the circumstances. The kid seemed smart enough, and he knew where to find the Ross homestead.

"I don't want to pull you off orders," Mat said.

"Just a one day side-trip back to Cheyenne, then we can finish my recon of the oil fields. You mind if we take your truck? Mine ran out of gas thirty miles back."

Mat had enough fuel in the back of the Raptor for a loop around eastern Wyoming and a trip to Salt Lake.

"We can do that. I'm afraid I'm not much help as a shooter," Mat said. "But I do have gas and a good truck."

"It's a deal," the kid, Gabriel, said as he held out his hand. Mat shook on it.

KD Fuels Storage Yard
Cedar City, Utah

JEFF AND EVAN stalked through a church parking lot in Cedar City, toward the EZ-Store self-storage where local partisans had left them a suppressed AR-15 on the roof.

The cartel tanks assembled on the interstate, refueled and rearmed. Today they'd likely gobble up most of the distance between Cedar City and Salt Lake. It was time for Jeff to switch up the batting order and bring on the home run hitters.

"This is a dumb idea. I'm glad I didn't tell Tanya about this. She'd kill me," Evan said.

Jeff felt ridiculous wearing a cowboy shirt and jeans, and it made him even more irritable. "Only a douchebag talks to his wife about missions." Jeff didn't know why he said it. It wasn't even true.

"Oh really? Back in the sandbox, you yapped to Tara about missions all the time, dude."

The mention of her name stoked his anger. "Never happened," Jeff said flatly.

"Are you having your period today?" Evan asked.

Jeff shifted his concealed carry Glock around from behind the giant belt buckle and climbed the fence behind the church.

"And I still think this is a bad idea," Evan continued. "You're supposed be a general. Why are you hitting targets with a two-man team in hostile territory?"

"Did you see the tanks lined up on I-15? That's why." Jeff jumped the last three feet off the back side of the fence and grunted when he hit the ground. "Also, I don't trust anyone to manage the explosive devices," Jeff said, and that part was mostly true. "The Hoodies are ready to roll. If we don't stop them now, they'll be within cannon range of our refineries by Tuesday."

The bang-bang Jeff had given to the Cedar City partisans to place was a pasted-together combination of Tannerite, dynamite, and fuse. Jeff was the only man on his operator crew who'd been to demo school, other than Chad Wade, who had apparently gotten himself captured or killed. Jeff built the Franken-bomb and he insisted on triggering it.

Cedar City Mormon militia reported that the Hood Rats stored their reserve fuel at the KD Fuels storage site at the northern margins of the town. With twenty pounds of well-placed explosives straight out of the Anarchist's Cookbook, Jeff might be able to stop the advance and set them back a couple of weeks.

There were five, ten thousand gallon tanks lined up on the east side of the KD Fuels yard against a chain-link fence, facing the backside of a powder coating shop. Across the lot, two hundred yards from the above-ground tanks, there was another thirty thousand gallon tank underground. Jeff and Evan would need to blow the above-ground tanks and the thirty thousand gallon below-ground tank at about the same time. Most of the Hood Rat army was on the interstate preparing for the advance. There were no fuel trucks in the KD Fuels yard, just a small security force.

The local partisans had pre-positioned a suppressed AR-15 on the roof of the EZ-Store, sighted, loaded and ready to rock.

Jeff had written himself into this op from the get-go. Since he was the only general, there was no one else to stop him. He'd been in a black mood for weeks now, murderously angry that he couldn't storm the Homestead and kick the shit out of Ross and his Russians. All that tar-flavored hate pointed straight at the Hood Rats, also guilty of pissing in his cornflakes. Why couldn't they just stay on their side of the desert?

When Jeff built the explosive device, he didn't bother making it grunt-proof. He was always going to be the guy to clack off the mayhem. He *needed* to blow up some shit—send flaming frag through their war machine and burn them in their juices.

The Franken-bomb was essentially a fifty pound claymore. He'd built it to take out the above-ground tanks, and for that purpose, it was a work of art. Jeff was in a torrid love affair with Tannerite, the two-part, consumer-legal explosive that detonated when shot with a rifle. Jeff had "liberated" over two hundred pounds of the yellow stuff from Cabela's.

He had packed a cake of Tannerite over a fourteen-inch manhole cover, then wrapped it in dozens of layers of Saran Wrap. The Tannerite would serve as his remote detonator.

There'd been a dynamite factory at the mouth of Spanish Fork Canyon, and the locals had presented the Utah Militia with a limitless supply of old fashion sticks of dynamite, the red kind with an actual fuse sticking out of it. Jeff carefully sliced dynamite into quarter-sticks, then cut sixty short lengths of one inch galvanized pipe in a farmer's workshop. He packed them around a four-inch piece of PVC, bundle-strapped the pipes together with pallet bands, then gently shimmed them to face out at an angle, like a galvanized chrysanthemum of destruction. It even looked pretty, in a steam punk kind of way.

Jeff slid a quarter-stick of dynamite to the bottom of each pipe, then packed the top of the sixty "barrels" with Vaseline-slathered ball bearings. The Vaseline would behave like napalm. It'd catch fire and transport the flame from the claymore to the diesel tanks.

He spray-painted the center PVC tube blaze orange, then wrapped the whole shebang in more Saran Wrap to keep anything from jiggling loose.

The local partisans were asked to set it against the wall of the powder coating shop, and aim it at the above-ground fuel tanks. At the right time, they'd shoot the target from across the fuel yard, the Tannerite would detonate, trigger the dynamite and send the flaming ball bearings into the fuel tanks.

Ka-boom.

Jeff was *mostly* sure it'd work. If it did, in the chaos that followed, he and Evan would climb down off the roof of the EZ-Store, and drop dynamite down the hatch into the buried tank. Jeff gave that part a fifty-fifty chance of success. Sometimes, a distraction made the enemy more focused. It was hard to say. The plan had like six parts, which was probably four parts too many, but you didn't make an omelet without breaking a few eggs.

Jeff and Evan hopped another fence, crossed a defunct railroad track, and cut a line toward the EZ-Store. As claimed by the locals, the KD Fuels yard was nearly empty. There were only a couple of old, rusty trucks in the yard, probably in for repairs. A couple of men dawdled with rifles inside the fence.

Cedar City was a town in hiding. The town had a small university, and a population of thirty thousand, despite being in the middle of the desert halfway between Salt Lake and Vegas. Many of the residents had fled before the cartel arrived, but about half had stayed, choosing to protect their homes and resist the occupation. The Hoodies occupied thousands of residences, some with the owners still in them. Rape and murder had been rampant, according to the partisans. Theft wasn't even worth mentioning. The town was being pillaged down to the rootstock.

Jeff slipped through a slit in the fence around the EZ-Storage and Evan followed. The cut in the fence bode well; it was evidence that the locals were serious about helping. It'd been right where they said it'd be. Likewise, an aluminum ladder leaned against the "D Building" of the storage facility, as planned. Jeff scampered up and quietly levered himself onto the gravel roof of the building. The scoped and suppressed AR-15 waited for them on its bipod, tucked under the lip of the flat roof.

"Damn, dude," Evan whispered. "That's a Silencerco can. I thought it'd be an old oil filter. Utah's legit." The private weapons the state allowed its citizens were remarkable. There was next-to-nothing Jeff couldn't find in the way of exotic firearms if he put the word out.

Jeff lifted the AR and checked the breach. High-quality ball ammo glinted back at him from the mag. He ran the bolt. "Let's see where they put the claymore," he said.

Jeff and Evan crawled to the edge of the roof. They both carried small binoculars. Jeff looked first while Evan waited.

"You're clear," he said after a quick scan of the yard. "No dedicated security looking this way. Two guys at the front gate."

Evan peeked over the edge and scanned the far side of the yard. "Looks like they placed Big Bertha right where you asked them to."

Jeff grunted in agreement. The claymore with the blaze-orange center target was leaning against a cinder block wall. There was rusty junk scattered around it so the claymore only stood out if a searcher knew what he was looking for. A dude with a thousand hours searching for IEDs in hostile territory might notice it, but these Hoodie guards looked like the bottom of the barrel, guys wearing trucker hats and baggy pants. The Hood Rats with military experience would be on the interstate with the tanks and gun buggies, not cooling their jets on sentry duty.

The claymore was perfectly positioned to tag all five aboveground tanks—assuming it worked.

"There's no reason to wait, right?" Evan asked. It was almost ten in the morning and the tanks would begin their push north at any moment. Today was the day to kick them in their beanbags.

Jeff took the seated shooting position he'd learned in Boy Scouts, lifted the AR-15, settled it on the lip of the roof, squared the crosshairs on the orange-painted circle in the middle of the claymore, flicked off the safety and squeezed the trigger.

BOOM!

BOOM! BA-BOOM!

The building beneath them shivered, swayed, and then settled. Both men dropped below the little wall around the roof. The world flashed yellow, like a new sun had sprouted from across the lot. The fuel tanks exploded in rapid succession. Jeff hazarded a peek over the lip.

"Yep," he shouted over the din. "They're going up."

DA-BOOM! Another tank exploded. A chunk of something whistled past overhead.

Evan turkey-peeked. "Security guys are coming out of the woodworks and running to the other side of the yard. I count seven guards and five locals. All with small arms. One technical, one of those electric jobbers is coming in the gate. It's now or never, boss."

"Hold up." Jeff popped the mag out of the AR and checked it. It was almost full. "You go. I'll overwatch."

"You sure?" Evan asked. It wasn't in the plan. Evan shrugged. "Gimme the dy-no-mite." His furrowed brow said, *"You're in charge, I guess..."*

Jeff shucked off the assault pack and slung it to Evan. "Go," he said.

Overwatch was a good idea, generally, but in this case, it'd draw the eyeballs back their way, away from the flaming pyres of diesel and across the underground tank. Jeff went for it anyway. There were dudes to be killed, running around in the open, and he had a hard-on for war.

Evan ran in a crouch for the ladder and Jeff settled the rifle across the parapet.

The scope panned across the running men. Jeff couldn't identify who was in charge, so he picked out the gunner in back of the electric OHV. He sent a round through his chest and dumped the dude over the tailgate. The suppressed rifle barely barked.

At two hundred yards, he didn't worry about the hold-over, just point and shoot. With a snap-crack from the AR, Jeff sent two rounds into the driver. The guy flopped out of the driver's seat and writhed on the ground like a fish that'd jumped the tank.

Nobody on the sea of asphalt tried to take cover because there *was* no cover. The KD Fuels yard was almost entirely open ground, except for the two dead trucks and the mile-high plumes of smoke from the burning fuel tanks.

Jeff worked his way from the electric gun buggy out, picking off gunmen like the shooting gallery at the county fair. He dropped four guys before they dialed in his position. The suppressor made finding him difficult, but after enough shots, the supersonic crack gave him away. Jeff knew he should reposition. Trading fire with multiple gunmen was a good way to get domed, but his anger got the best of him.

The locals, in jeans and Carhartts, had enough sense to run away from the flames and the gunfire. Jeff focused his hate on the remainder of the Hoodies.

He popped the top off a gangbanger who was hip-shooting from a crouch. Then, as a bullet howled past Jeff's ear, he center-punched a guy shooting an AR off-hand. Several rounds of return fire gnawed pieces off Jeff's wall. Frag smashed his face. He ignored it.

Jeff lost count. *How many Hoodies had Evan said? Was he counting the dudes in the OHV? The locals?*

He dipped back behind the parapet and let the incoming fire rage. Evan would be on the tarmac now, and running toward the below-ground tank, but the shitbags were shooting at Jeff. There were probably still three or four that were combat-effective, judging by the incoming fire that whistled overhead and chewed at the wall.

Jeff scrambled to the far corner, redeploying a bit. It'd buy him a couple of "freebie" shots before the incoming fire came at him. He popped up, saw two guys, shot one, and then was forced back down by withering return fire.

Shit. He needed to cover Evan.

His angry dick had driven him into a mess he couldn't quite clean up. The enemy, no matter how schlocky, eventually got a vote.

He heard Evan open up with his handgun below. The 9mm Glock was a desperate gamble. Evan must've been pitching 9mm at guys over a hundred yards away. Evan was hell-on-wheels with a Glock, but Jeff had seen him lose bets at a hundred yards. If Evan was shooting his Glock, that meant he was returning fire, which meant they'd seen him. Shit was officially out-of-control.

The belt-fed on the back of the Hoodie gun buggy opened fire. Someone must've taken brave pills and got on the big gun.

Jeff ducked and ran to the opposite corner of the building again, and popped up, just in time to see *another* OHV barrel through the gate of the yard. He dumped ten rounds into it. The OHV skidded to a stop and the second belt-fed went to town on Jeff's rooftop.

Jeff had no choice but to bail off the back side of the roof. The technical was going to eat the roof down to a nub. Overwatch was no longer an option. Hopefully, Evan would just run.

KA-BOOM!

The blast was a LOT closer. Evan had gone for the underground tank, stayed on mission, despite a shit-ton of incoming fire.

More shouting voices wafted on the winds between fire-fueled gusts from the infernos. More Hoodies were arriving, probably the Hood Rat quick reaction force. The QRF wouldn't be fence monkeys like the security guys. They'd be their best shooters.

Jeff ditched the AR-15 onto the roof and slid down the aluminum ladder. He ran full-throttle in the general direction of the secondary ORP he and Evan had established in case shit went sideways. Jeff drew his Glock on the run and scanned for Evan and for hostiles.

BOOM!

Another tank blew up. Jeff couldn't tell if it was a secondary explosion or if Evan had gone for a second buried tank.

Damn Evan, Jeff urged. *Get out of there.*

His guilt was already starting to bubble up. *Please, God, let Evan be at the ORP,* Jeff prayed as he ran his guts out. He ducked through another cut in the fence and bolted between industrial buildings, junkyards, and a derelict MMA gym.

Jeff banked hard right and ran across undulating folds of an abandoned lot, choked with sagebrush and tumbleweeds. From there, he could see the interstate. A long line of Hoodie tanks had come to a halt outside the city limits. The black-on-blue column of smoke from KD Fuels had, indeed, stopped them in their tracks.

Jeff scaled the white sandy bank of Coal Creek Road and dropped down the other side just in time to see a convoy of speeding, whirring OHVs fly past toward KD Fuels. No one in the OHVs paid him any mind, probably because of the pearl-button cowboy shirt and the cowboy hat he'd clamped onto his head. For the first time, Jeff wondered what the repercussions of the raid might be on the locals. It was war, and the citizens of Cedar City were willing to fight. Maybe there were no civilians in this war, only combatants.

Jeff scrambled down the embankment and into the concrete channel of Coal Creek. He ducked into the underground box tunnel of a culvert. This was the secondary objective rally point where he was supposed to meet Evan. He wasn't there.

Jeff slid down the wall of the culvert, sat down low and sorted through his EDC, everyday carry. They'd run this mission "slick," meaning they had no plate carrier vests, bump helmets, or body armor. Jeff drew his Glock, dropped the magazine and checked it. Full. He slid back the slide and saw brass, then reloaded. The backup magazine was also full. He checked his Cold Steel Vaquero knife, still clipped to his right pocket. It hadn't fallen out.

His micro first aid kit and butane lighter, check. His Baofeng radio was still in his back pocket—apparently unbroken. The extended antenna poked out of the long pocket of his jeans. He slid the antenna out and screwed it into the radio. It was too soon to call the exfil force over an open channel. He needed to give Evan time.

Another convoy, this one with two tanks, rumbled down Coal Creek Road, almost directly above the culvert where Jeff hid.

He and Evan had kicked over a hornet's nest. It was enough to stop the Hoodie advance, at least for today. Hopefully, Evan had made it out alive. Jeff held the radio in one thick hand, the Glock in the other. He waited and worried.

BILL MCCALLISTER'S boss raged like a bull with a cocklebur up its dick. They'd circled their command Humvees in the church parking lot, a few blocks from where the fuel depot burned. They were all there except Saúl. He was too smart to leave his battalion of tanks, lest something happened to them while the focus was on the fuel yard.

In war, there was the map, and there was the terrain. No matter how long you stared at the map, you didn't know the terrain until you were physically on it.

On the map, Cedar City looked like a perfect jumping-off point for the push to Salt Lake. Cedar City shaved fifty miles off of their objective, putting them within 250 miles of the Salt Lake refineries.

250 miles was the exact maximum range of an M1 Abrams fuel tank, measured at optimal speed, on a smooth surface, without maneuvering to fight. On paper, Cedar City looked ideal.

The massive column of smoke told a *fucking different story*. St. George had been at the far, southern point of Utah, full of college kids and golden-years retirees escaping the cold of Salt Lake winter. Cedar City, on the other hand, was full of farmers, ranchers and country folk. One city had hunkered down while the cartel army quartered in their midst. The other had risen up and kicked them in the chicken tenders.

The two towns looked very similar on the map, St. George and Cedar City, but Bill and his boss should've noticed: one city had twelve golf courses; the other had a rodeo.

With the KD Fuels yard totally engulfed in flames, the cartel's fifty tanks could still reach Salt Lake City, but they'd arrive on "empty." There was no way to refuel them now, en-route. All the gasoline within fifty miles was going up in smoke, and they'd lost all but three fuel tanker trucks, and they were the little kind for filling up farm equipment.

The cartel plan had been to cross the vast gap between Cedar City and the outlying towns of Salt Lake—Payson, Spanish Fork, Provo—then refuel. Then they planned to roll slowly into Salt Lake Valley and set a slow-motion siege around the Maverick refinery. The gas for that was, right now, coloring the sky a filthy brown.

The enemy had penetrated their security perimeter in the middle of the stark light of morning and blew their fuel halfway to the moon.

Would the next town be a senior citizens' paradise or a cowboy hometown? Apparently, it mattered a great deal. As a cattleman himself, Bill McCallister wasn't sure which team he was rooting for.

"I want the locals lined up and shot!" Gustavo Castillo screamed at his lieutenants. There was little doubt this time who was to blame. Alejandro was supposed to have secured the fuel yard.

"We don't know for sure the saboteurs were locals," Bill disagreed.

"And Bill, you inept piece of shit," Castillo screamed. "You were supposed to have a finger on the pulse of this town. You should've known we were vulnerable to sabotage."

"We're vulnerable to sabotage everywhere," Bill risked his life by speaking up. "We're in enemy territory. We need full security, all-the-damn-time. Monday through Sunday."

Alejandro mounted his defense. "You're not giving me enough armor to cover our supply chain and our fuel reserves. I get the shittiest fighters, a handful of gun trucks and not enough tanks to cover the fifty miles to St. George. I don't have the resources to protect this big of an exposed flank," Alejandro argued. "Not when I have to defend against ten thousand locals, too."

"I don't think the locals did this," Bill repeated. "This attack was probably militia. We caught a wounded soldier escaping and I don't think he's from around here. He smells like U.S. Army to me. Give me time to interrogate him and I'll know for sure."

Castillo's hazel eyes burned with fury. Bill guessed he was hungry to take it out on Bill's prisoner. But angry or not, Castillo wasn't stupid. He'd let Bill bleed the man for information first.

But, in point of fact, Bill was straight-up lying to his boss. He didn't really believe that Kirkham's militia was solely to blame for this sabotage. The locals had done their part. Blowing up a secured fuel yard wasn't a by-the-seat-of-the-pants operation. It required intel, plus pre-placement of ordnance. It wasn't as easy as lighting a match and throwing it at a fuel tank. Generating this level of mayhem required planning, and planning relied upon local intel. The saboteurs had blown every one of the seven fuel tanks in the KD yard, and they'd ignited them within a minute of one another. That was like breaking into a man's house in the dead of night, impregnating his three daughters, and his wife, and only waking him when the old gal got off next to him in bed. Other than the wounded prisoner, the destruction of KD Fuels had been a perfect op. It'd set the cartel back at least a week, assuming they didn't get ambushed again. Assuming they could even find fuel tanker trucks.

To Bill's expert eye, the cartel still looked like the winning side, hands down. They had tanks, soldiers and a hundred gun buggies, powered by the almighty sun. The cartel had access to limitless ordnance and ammo from the Hawthorne Army Depot in northern Nevada. They could bring up fuel from northern Mexico, though the trip was long, ponderous and full of danger. Given enough time, they would take Utah, Idaho and Montana. Bill's promised cattle ranch was all but certain. Star Valley would be his, if he could just keep his boss' impatience in check. It was the end of April and they would have good weather from here on out. Even without the Salt Lake refinery, they might manage, if they were methodical and patient.

Castillo de-escalated a little with each breath. He'd apparently had his heart set on making the big push today, and now it was too risky, even for him.

"When can we advance to Nephi?" the boss asked Alejandro. He should've been asking Saúl, but Saúl wasn't there.

Alejandro hazarded a guess. "I'd suggest we hold here until first light tomorrow. Then, we should move up to the town of Beaver. We can use their underground tanks to stockpile gas and top off. From there, we'll be two hundred miles from Salt Lake City. That'd give us the ability to make a push if we still want to, or take another small jump, maybe to the town of Nephi."

It was the smart play. They'd nibble at Utah instead of taking it in one, giant bite. But Castillo wasn't a man to nibble. Bill nodded his head emphatically at Ale's plan, hoping the boss would accept wise counsel.

"Fine. That's it, then," Castillo relented. "We bump up to Beaver tomorrow and carve off another fifty miles."

"So, are we done here?" Bill asked.

"Yes. I want information from your prisoner by nightfall. Report to me directly," Castillo said. "I'll have a surprise for you."

Bill nodded and turned back to his Land Cruiser. He didn't know what the surprise would be, but he doubted he'd like it. Hopefully, he'd get good intel from this new captive and it'd mellow out the boss. Bill's men had the wounded prisoner on ice at the La Quinta Inn in downtown Cedar City. So far, they'd only gotten his name out of him, but they hadn't put the wood to him yet.

The dude's name was Evan Hafer, and he was in for a rough evening.

6

"In retrospect, democracy did not flourish in the apocalypse. It gave way to simpler forms of human organization , such as tribes, autocracies, theocracies, loose federations, and family clans. Usually, one person or a small committee made decisions for all. Rarely did people vote. Only when nostalgia was employed to inspire unity, as with the government in Colorado Springs, did old forms of republicanism and democracy reappear. In the final analysis, democracy was a luxury survivors couldn't afford."

— THE AMERICAN DARK AGES, BY WILLIAM BELLAHER, NORTH AMERICAN TEXTBOOKS, 2037

Monroe, Utah

NOAH MILLER AND THE ARIZONA FREEMAN MILITIA FINALLY EMERGED from the pine canyons of Highway 89 into the dry farms of Sevier River Valley. They'd passed through dozens of towns, one arduous roadblock at a time.

Very few townsfolk had perished to the apocalypse along the old Utah highway. They were hardy people, of a hardy religion, carving their existence out of cold valleys under arbors of pine. Surviving the apocalypse had been quite like every other winter. Lay up hay. Feed the animals. Chop wood. Go to church.

The militia informed the towns along Highway 89 of the looming threat of cartel invasion. The towns were almost all white, Euro-farmer stock so that a dark, foreign menace wasn't difficult for them to imagine. The Mexican drug cartel was an evil they believed, hook, line, and sinker. It wasn't racism, per se, but the farm communities didn't go out of their way to give Mexicans the benefit of the doubt, either. When they were told about a drug lord, *coming soon to a town near you,* their eyes grew wide and their heads bobbed up and down. *Yes siree. Time to fight.*

They were some of the oldest-style Mormons, and they were also patriots and Constitutionalists, maybe the last of a dying breed. The tiny towns along the 89 contributed men and machines to the war effort, and the Arizona Freeman Militia dropped the "Arizona" from their name, their ranks bulging with Utahns. The Freemen went from two hundred men to almost three hundred in three weeks of travel. With that success, the Colonel ordered Noah and Willie to range far and wide to enlist more.

"The locals say there's a prepper compound up yonder," Willie said to Noah as he returned to the Land Cruiser from the town gathering in Monroe City Park. "They say the compound's already soldiered-up."

Noah squinted into the morning sun just rising over Monroe Mountain. "The locals gave you the time o' day? Bet they've never even seen a black man before."

"I'm half black," Willie corrected. "I don't think there's another person of color in the whole place. This might be the whitest town I've ever seen."

"Will they contribute some young sons to the campaign?"

"Dunno," Willie said. "They said they were going to talk to the bishop about it, whoever that is."

"He's the local church leader. This town will kick in. I'll send Hofstetter to find the town's stake president and explain our mission. When they hear that Salt Lake City church is fighting, they'll fight too."

Monroe, Utah was a postage stamp of a town, but it was the largest town they'd entered since crossing the state line, with a population of maybe two thousand people, judging from the twenty square blocks of ancient, brick homes.

The Freemen would move on to Richfield next, and that town was big enough for serious troubles, and probably a lot of death. Any town over ten thousand souls suffered in the apocalypse. People were good together, until there were too many. Then they were really bad. That tipping point of self-destruction seemed to be a town of ten thousand. It depended on foodstuffs and water, to some degree, but politics got going in earnest after a population of a thousand or so. By ten thousand, corruption was almost guaranteed. With corruption came drama enough to sink them all.

Noah had seen it across Arizona, Nevada, Oklahoma, Texas and New Mexico. If he survived this, he'd never live in a place with more than a thousand people. There probably weren't too many of those left, now that he thought about it, places with more than a thousand souls. He needn't worry.

Noah and Willie's orders were to hit up pockets of likely recruits. The Freeman Militia would leave the town of Monroe in their rearview mirror by nightfall. They'd go have a look-see in Richfield tomorrow, then Salina. After a few more towns, they'd cut over to the interstate and meet up, hopefully, with the Utah Militia. Their scouts said the big militia numbered in the tens of thousands and they were making a fighting retreat up the middle of the state.

"Should we check out this prepper compound?" Willie asked.

"Sure. I'll radio Hofstetter."

The word "prepper" didn't mean the same thing it'd meant the year before. Before Black Autumn and COVID, it meant "tinfoil-hat wingnut," a fanatic. Now, it meant "someone who saw this coming and wasn't part of the problem." In the apocalypse, preppers didn't scavenge. They didn't compete for resources. They kept to themselves. Still, some preppers were weird before and were even weirder now. They didn't play well with towns.

Willie guided the Land Cruiser south, into the hinterlands of the Sevier valley, where the sagebrush plains reduced to hard grass and where the gravel sprouted turquoise and quartz. When they spotted the prepper compound, jutting out of the gray, mirage-layered desert, they hadn't crossed a creek in five miles.

Willie gave a long whistle under his breath. "That don't look too inviting."

The perimeter fence around the acreage was punctuated with three-story guard towers. If Noah were to guess, the preppers hadn't shot anything other than coyotes since the collapse. The compound was buried in the butt crack of nowhere. It would've required a parachute drop for marauders to get in there.

Noah hadn't seen any sign of marauders in over a month. Their lawless lifestyle got them in trouble with dysentery, disease, and ultimately, lead poisoning at the end of a hunting rifle. In a country with over two hundred million loose guns, a life of thievery was like playing the roulette table, where every time you rolled "black," you died. Most marauders didn't survive more than a couple of months. The violent lifestyle, á la Mad Max, came with a hard expiration date.

As the cluster of buildings came into focus at the foot of the mountain, Noah saw men in at least half the towers. A low wail issued from the compound and more men scrambled into shooting positions. They'd seen Noah and Willie's dust trail, probably the most interesting thing that'd happened in months.

"Hold up, dawg. Go in slow," Willie said. "Those white boys got itchy trigger fingers. I can feel it from here."

"White boys and their guns. Am I right?" Noah joked. Half of their kidding involved racism. Noah was the standard white guy, and Willie, the handsome black dude.

Half black, Willie liked to remind Noah. His mom was white as a fence post.

"Why doncha park here and we'll walk the last couple hundred yards," Willie suggested with a nervous laugh. "This place reminds me of the guys with bad teeth in The Postman."

"The Postman?" Noah slowed the Land Cruiser.

"Yeah, with Kevin Costner?"

"Gotcha," Noah yanked on the parking break, slung his rifle around to his back and hopped to the ground. "That's the one where the preppers are slave masters. I think you're doing what shrinks call *transference*. Just because we haven't seen another black man in two weeks doesn't mean you're gonna get lynched."

"Easy for you to say."

"I got your back. I'll make sure and tell 'em you're only half black."

"Thanks. What a pal."

The two walked forward, hands held high. Their guns were slung or holstered. Nobody walked around without a firearm these days. There was plenty of ammo too, now that the Army depots had been cracked open like bullet piñatas.

"Should we play a joke? Maybe pretend to quick draw?" Noah said as they approached the high chain-link fence and the shadow of their rifles.

"You go ahead," Willie said. "I'll run back to the Cruiser and watch."

Noah was in a mood. He couldn't help himself. "We come in peace." he shouted. "We are from the United Federation of Planets."

"What's that you say?" someone from the tower yelled back.

"We're from the U.S.S. Enterprise," Noah replied.

"You're an idiot," Willie mumbled. "Did you notice the guns?"

"You say you're from the government?" the man in the tower asked. "Hold on." He climbed down the tower, one rung at a time, then disappeared into the earthworks that were bulldozed up behind the fence. The tops of what looked like camper/trailers jutted above the berms. A few dozen sharpened sticks pointed outward from the dirt. It looked like the planners meant to porcupine the whole thing with pointy sticks, but ran out of wood. There weren't any trees for miles. The most noteworthy landscape feature was white-and-red-stained rocks.

"What's that smell?" Willie asked.

"I think it's sulfur. Maybe they have a hot springs or something," Noah guessed.

The fence jangled. The road they were on disappeared behind the bulldozed mounds in an S-curve. Somewhere inside, their must be a gate in the fence. Noah and Willie were standing back too far to see over the mounds.

A heavy-set man appeared from within the gap. Other men came over the earthworks with AR-15 rifles, covering their spokesman.

"I'm Burgmeyer," the man said without extending a hand. "You're from the government?" He squinted.

He sported a scruffy beard, wore old-school desert camouflage with a boonie hat, and was at least seventy pounds overweight. He looked to be in his early sixties.

Noah scratched his beard. Almost nobody was overweight these days. Nobody peering over the berm, or glowering from the towers looked skinny, either.

"No. We're not from the government. I was joking. We're with the Freeman Militia from Arizona. I'm Noah and this is Willie."

Burgmeyer looked them over. "We're not joining anyone's militia," he said, flat as stone.

"Gotcha," Noah said. "There's actually a drug cartel army, tens of thousands of men, with tanks, coming up the interstate and occupying Utah. They conquered Arizona last fall. We're what's left of the militia that opposed them. Salt Lake City formed another, bigger militia and we're heading north to join them."

"The cartel is coming up from the south? Mexican?" Burgmeyer said, as though he knew it would happen like this all along. He might've shot a withering glare at Willie, but it was hard to say. The guy's face was frozen in an expression that could've been anger, or maybe constipation.

"Not Mexican, exactly. They're cartel," Willie tried for a finer racial distinction, but the squinty stare on the man's face held fast.

He seemed to reach a conclusion. "Come in and tell me more." Burgmeyer turned and walked back through the berms. "Leave your weapons at the gate," he ordered without looking back. "And your radios, and any cameras."

Inside the fence, the place was like a doublewide wagon train, circled up for the night, with fifty trailers circled in concentric rings. The fence enclosed at least forty acres. It had the stylistic impact of a trailer park, pooped out on a dusty plain by whatever tornado monster ate trailer parks. It was decidedly ugly, but the inhabitants had survived. Rarely had Noah seen a group of people so untouched by the apocalypse. There were at least a hundred and fifty of them, including a dusty band of dash-about children.

Burgmeyer lead them to a nicer-looking motor home, up on permanent blocks, with its awning extended. Beneath the awning were a card table and four Costco chairs. Burgmeyer, apparently the leader of the compound, waved them each to a seat. He didn't offer drinks.

"Tell me about the Mexicans," he said.

"They're mostly criminal-types from the States, actually. Ex-drug dealers, organized by Gustavo Castillo, one of the big-wig drug lords from northern Mexico," Noah explained.

"I'd like to see them try to come at us," Burgmeyer huffed.

"Did we mention they have eighty M1 Abrams main battle tanks?" Willie asked.

Burgmeyer's face screwed up in a distasteful knot, but he didn't reply. Earth berms and chain-link would barely slow an Abrams.

"Are you ex-military?" Noah steered the conversation to safer waters.

"Army. '76 through '84. Germany, mostly. Lots of experience with tanks. Ours. Theirs."

Noah assumed he meant Russians. *Us and them.* It sounded familiar, like being home with Bill watching the news. Everything came down to the good guys versus the bad guys. But Bill wasn't ignorant like this guy. Bill was a renaissance man, really. *But then why would Bill choose the bad guys this time?*

Burgmeyer continued, "How did Mexicans get ahold of our tanks?" When he said "Mexicans" it sounded like *mexi-caans*.

"We don't exactly know," Noah answered. "We believe the tanks came out of El Paso, but we don't think the cartel overran Fort Bliss. We're not certain. But, for sure, they have them."

"They suck a lot of fuel," Burgmeyer said.

Noah saw an opening for his big pitch. "We're gathering patriot troops to oppose them. Can we count on your group to contribute men to the defense of liberty?"

Burgmeyer chuckled. "I fell for that bullshit back in my younger days. Cost me eight years of my life. Fool me once, bad on you. Fool me twice, bad on me."

"I'm sorry you feel that way," Noah said. "Would you mind if we put it to your people?"

"It wouldn't matter," Burgmeyer said, and leaned back in his chair. "You're not leaving here."

"Aw shit," Willie said. "I knew this place had a Deliverance vibe. You eat people, don't you?"

Burgmeyer ignored Willie. "We're like Hotel California," he

stood up from the card table. "You can check out any time you like, but you can never leave. It's how we survived the Big Crash. OPSEC. Operational Security. Look it up. You're staying."

"But the entire valley knows exactly where you are." Noah argued. "That's how we knew to come out here. Every man, woman and child within fifty miles can finger your compound on a map. Their gossip trumps your OPSEC, brother."

"Yeah, but nobody knows what we got inside. No one who's been inside ever left to tell about it."

"Yep. They're going to eat us. I knew it," Willie fretted.

Burgmeyer glared at him, but spoke to Noah. "We didn't build this place for every Tom, Dick and Harry to see. The only reason I let you in was because you had fresh intel. Now, you're here for good."

"So, you're not going to eat us?" Willie asked.

"As I told you before," Noah said. "We're with the Freeman Militia. My Cruiser is right out front. Our unit knows we came here to talk. By first light tomorrow, they'll be at your gate with hundreds of riflemen. Kidnapping us ain't an option."

"Eating us, neither," Willie added.

"They don't eat people," Noah said to Willie. "At least not white people."

"You need to take this seriously, dawg," Willie said. "These are some redneck muthafuckas right here."

Burgmeyer continued. "We have the entrenched, defended position. Your *militiamen* would lose twenty-to-one against us. We'll move your rig around back, and I'll tell them you came by, but then you left to the southwest. They'll have no choice but to believe me. Trust me, you're here for the long haul. This place stays secret, no matter the cost."

Noah decided that arguing with this guy made about as much sense as shouting at a goldfish. Once again, it reminded him of home, of Bill.

"Do I need to lock you up, or are you going to get with the program?" Burgmeyer waved another man over to their table. The guy looked a bit younger, thinner and carried a 1911 handgun on his hip. His hair was in perfect order, his face clean-shaven. Mister Clean-Shave hustled over to the boss.

"I'm doing you a favor," Burgmeyer said. "We'll ensure your survival. It's better than any deal you'll get out there." He pointed north. He turned to his helper. "Quarter these gentlemen in my old trailer. Get them toothbrushes, toothpaste, blankets, and a meal. They're our new arrivals. After lunch, put them on the work roster." He turned back to Noah and Will. "Nobody eats for free. Welcome to Falcon Base."

Burgmeyer headed off to other business. Noah suspected he'd expended his word budget for the day, like a grumpy, old man who would rather work on a carburetor than talk.

"Falcon Base?" Willie chortled. "What the hell's that? Is this an episode of G.I. Joe?"

"I'm Brad," the 1911 guy said. "Come with me, please." He steered Willie by the bicep and Willie allowed himself to be steered.

"What's with Burgmeyer?" Noah asked.

"Oh, he's a little rough around the edges, s'all," Brad explained. "But he's the reason we're still alive. He's the man with the plan." Brad barked a laugh. "You know, he put his entire inheritance into this place? Stacked Falcon Base to the rafters with beans, bullets, and band aids. We have enough dried food to last another year. After that, we'll go out and just pick up the pieces. It's okay. You won't be here for long. Just another year until everything out in the world dies back. Then we'll have everything we could possibly want: cars, land, and livestock. The world will be ours for the taking."

"Dude," Willie said, shaking his arm out of the guy's grip. "That stuff already happened. Most everyone's gone. The big cities, at least. You don't need to hide behind dirt piles. There's plenty of unclaimed land, man. Like, most of it. Any car you like, too. You gotta come up with the gas, but you can have a Lamborghini if you want."

"Burgmeyer does regular recon outside," Brad said. "He says town is still pretty much normal."

Noah clarified. "Sure. The town of Monroe is like you guys: hunkered down. They weren't overrun by refugees from the cities."

"But you were talking about a Mexican army..." Brad interrupted as he pointed toward a rundown, doublewide trailer.

"Cartel army," Noah said. "That much is true."

"That's why we have OPSEC," Brad explained. "We let all the fighting work itself out before we stick our necks out. Then, we move from *survive* to *thrive*."

"Hunh?" Willie grunted.

"It's a prepper mantra," Noah said. "First you survive, then you thrive."

"You were a prepper?" Willie asked.

"Yup," Noah answered. "My old man and I built a compound in the Arizona desert. A cattle ranch—a lot smaller than this. Just the two of us. It was literally the first place the cartel hit when they rolled across the border. Talk about shitty luck."

"That Burgmeyer dude reminds me of your dad, but not as funny," Willie said.

They stepped up into the musty trailer, passed through the flimsy aluminum door, and found themselves in a surprisingly tidy kitchenette. Brad followed them.

"The water from the tap's a little stinky, but it's fine to drink. Lunch is at noon at the center of the circle. It's easy to find. Just follow your nose."

"Thank you, but you guys don't really believe you're keeping us here, do you?" Noah asked.

"Why would you want to leave?" Brad asked rhetorically. "It's a living hell out there."

"Have you been out there?" Willie asked.

"You mean, have I left the circle? Well, no. Not since the collapse."

"There's hope outside," Willie said. "And your people can help rebuild. You *should* rebuild. It's your duty as survivors."

"We've been rebuilding this whole time," Brad argued. "Right here. We even had a baby two weeks ago. Look, I don't want to debate with you. You'll see what's what at lunch. You're not going to want to leave. Burg made it sound like you're stuck here, but it's really an invitation. You're the first ones he's invited since December. It's like you won the lottery."

They'd taken their firearms at the gate, but almost no effort was made to keep them from getting their hands on guns. At lunch, every adult member of the compound had a rifle nearby. Most of the guns were Chinese SKS rifles with folding bayonets and nylon shoulder slings.

Though Burgmeyer made it sound like they were prisoners, Noah and Willie weren't even watched. They wandered the sprawling complex with only a few double-takes from the residents.

Noah and Willie stood in line in front of a mobile home that'd been converted into a mess kitchen. Three smiling men and women served noodle soup into metal bowls, prison style.

"Pretty chill for a cannibal cult," Willie said. "Who do you think's in the soup?"

Noah barked a laugh. "As far as I can tell, it's only the guard towers preventing us from climbing the fence and walking to the Cruiser, and who knows if they'd even shoot."

They found Brad at a plastic table, the only person they knew, and sat down beside him.

Noah ladled a spoonful into his mouth. "Hm. Yeah. That's a

taste from childhood. Dried noodles and Textured Vegetable Protein. TVP. Just like mama used to make."

"You had a mama?" Willie asked.

"Until puberty, more or less. They sent me to live with Bill when I started getting into trouble. After that, Bill and I pretty much ate every meal out of a can. In the fundamentalist colonies where I grew up, rotating food storage was a twice-a-week religion. I was practically raised on TVP." Noah let his spoonful dribble back into the bowl.

"Tastes fine to me," Willie said. "For man-flesh, I mean."

"Wait till it comes out the other end," Noah said. "I'm praying for a fart fan over the crapper in our trailer."

"Your belly gets used to it," Brad promised.

Noah doubted they'd be there long enough to get used to the reconstituted food. "What's the deal? Nobody's going stir crazy? Everyone just does what the Burgmeyer guy says? Why?"

"He built this whole place with money from an uncle who passed away. He paid for most of the guns, the trailers, he drilled the well, and he made the earthworks with his own bulldozer. He even stocked the place with food. We're his guests, sort of."

"And you all just let him tell you what to do?" Willie asked.

"He doesn't order us around, if that's what you're asking. Burg doesn't come out much. Mostly, I'm in charge."

To Noah, it smacked of the Mormon fundamentalist colonies where he'd grown up in Juarez, Mexico. But his parents had been religious fanatics. These guys didn't have a Holy Roller groove to them.

"We're all from northern California, mostly," Brad continued. "Burg went to our church. He picked our families to come here. Once they started burning the cities, everyone wanted to go with him."

"What church?" Noah asked.

"Redeemer Lutheran. Fresno, California." Brad took a spoonful of soup.

That old Army guy, Burg, basically a fatter copy of his adopted father Bill, sunk inherited money into a dirt compound in the Middle Of Nowhere, Utah, and stocked it with prepper stuff. Then, he selected a bunch of Type B personalities from his church and caravanned here. Noah would've bet a thousand to one against the idea working. Yet here they were, a bunch of doe-eyed Lutherans, eating cheap, dried food storage, seven months after the balloon went up.

"How long ago did Burgmeyer build this?"

"Three or four years," Brad said. "I came out here with him and helped. I was one of the first. We kept it a secret, mostly, back then."

It wasn't the weirdest thing Noah had seen in the apocalypse, but it went on the list.

Noah finished his lunch. "Where's Burgmeyer?" He hadn't seen him at lunch.

"Burg usually takes his meals in his workshop," Brad said.

"Where is it?"

"Outer ring, northeast. He doesn't like to be disturbed."

"Well, I don't like being told I can't leave." Noah got up, carried his dish to the washing bin, washed it, stacked it and headed toward the outer ring. Willie followed.

The workshop was an old Quonset hut, and it was quiet when they arrived.

"Burgmeyer," Noah called out.

"In here," a voice growled from a dimly lit corner.

Noah's eyes adjusted and a massive, counter-top model appeared from the gloom: a rural valley in miniature detail. It occupied a full quarter of the Quonset hut, with walking paths on both sides. It was far too immense, and small-scale to be a model train set, but it resembled one. It had mountains, creeks, towns, fields, tiny homes, barns, and shops. It must've taken Burgmeyer hundreds, maybe a thousand, hours to build.

"Holy shit," Willie exclaimed.

"What's this?" Noah asked the man.

Burg grunted, but didn't look up from the tiny barn he was painting with a minuscule brush under a work lamp.

Realization dawned. "This is the valley," Noah said. "From Big Rock Candy Mountain in the south, all the way past Richfield in the north. There's Monroe, Joseph, Richfield, Sevier..."

"Don't touch," Burg grumbled. He was the damnedest cult leader Noah had ever seen, keeping somewhat isolated and slaving over meticulous models.

"But why?" Willie asked.

Burg answered anyway, "This is how we divide it up. Once everyone's wiped out."

"Once *who* is wiped out," Willie asked.

"Them. The sheep." Burg placed a tiny barn, no bigger than a Hershey's Kiss, in its place beside a farmhouse. "We'll give this homestead to the Baileys."

"A family already lives there, bro. I drove past that farm day before yesterday. Kids were playing in the yard," Noah said.

"Not for long," Burg wheezed. "When the shit really hits the fan, they'll be gone too."

"It wasn't a big enough apocalypse for you?" Noah asked with dawning realization. "You're holding out for something even more catastrophic than killing off ninety-five percent of everyone?"

"This is just the beginning," Burgmeyer said as he pawed through an immense tool chest. "This government will collapse too."

"What government?" Willie wondered out loud. "There's still a government?"

"Monroe."

"The town?"

Burgmeyer looked up from his work, finally interested enough to engage. "Yes. The mayor. The city council. They're still making rules. Setting up their welfare state. Levying taxes."

Noah understood what the old coot meant: the town of Monroe had unified and organized, and had survived the winter. Few died. They served one meal a day, late breakfast, at the city park. As far as Noah knew, nobody resented the little town government—except this guy.

"Burg, you don't need to wait around any longer," Noah reasoned with him. "Richfield got hit hard by the flu and dysentery. There are hundreds of farmsteads unclaimed right now, sitting fallow. If they don't get planted soon, they won't produce harvest in the fall. Your people could have all the land they could possibly want, right here in this valley. Right now. There's fresh food to be grown, animals to raise, and life to live. While your people choke down TVP and boiled wheat behind dirt walls, there's plenty of good, arable land. Free. It's just out of eyesight across the valley, literally everywhere."

"If we bow to the government now, we're doomed. We'll die like the rest of them when the shit hits the fan." Burgmeyer set down his work and his eyes burned with a mix of anger and raw stubbornness. Many a time, Noah had seen that look in his dad's eyes. He knew the futility of debating. Behind that face was an iron wall. "Us" and "them." A mere apocalypse wasn't enough to break down the breastwork in Burgmeyer's mind. In a way, the collapse had proven him right. It'd proved Bill McCallister right, too. They'd be more stubborn now than ever, more convinced they were right and that the "others" were incompetents, just sheep to be culled.

The massive, intricate model of the valley told the tale. This was a man who obsessed over strategies of battalions and regiments, but despised the soldiers. He fawned over the philosophies of constitutions, but abhorred the people who voted. He showered affection on a model of a town, but looked at the ground when he stepped foot outside. The "us and them" dogma protected him from human connection. The people inside these dirt berms were figurines to Burgmeyer. So, he took his lunch in a dusty, Quonset hut.

"Can I tell your people about the land that's available around Richfield?" Noah asked.

"*Hmph.*" Burgmeyer went back to looking through his tool chest. "I don't care what you tell them." Noah heard a tremor in his voice, the first breeze of doubt. "Just don't tell them lies, or you and I are going to have a problem." The threat could mean many things. Noah didn't ask for clarification.

───

NOAH AND WILLIE decided they'd at least wait until after dinner before they escaped the sulfur-smelling, prepper paradise.

At the center of the rings of trailers and outbuildings, the food area was open air, scores of folding tables and chairs, set up on a field of gravel and covered with an interlocking series of corrugated aluminum awnings.

"Heads up, friends," Willie trumpeted over the hubbub of dinner, once most of them had taken seats in the dining area. "We come bearing good news." The crowd hushed.

"The civil disorder outside has ended, and a few miles from here, on the other side of that fence, there are hundreds of farms, homes and parcels available at the low, low price of *FREE*. We can take you there in the morning, assuming the Burg-man—Burgmeyer—lets you go. You have him to thank for your survival. But now it's over and you can start growing food and raising livestock."

Noah nudged Willie's leg.

"Oh, and we could use some fighters for the war in the valley west of here."

Noah smacked him on the leg and gave him a wide-eyed "what the hell" look.

"What do you mean about a war?" a guy in overalls asked.

"There's an army up from Mexico and they want to take over Utah. They have tanks."

"That doesn't sound safe at all," the guy in overalls said.

"Yeah, but that's the only bad part, as far as we know," Willie attempted to recover. "It doesn't matter if you're inside here or not. The tanks will go right through your fence. So you might as well move out and start farming." Willie looked to Noah to save his ass.

"Dammit," Noah swore.

"Dawg. What was I supposed to say? The man asked a direct question." Willie hissed. "I don't claim to be no kind of orator."

"Maybe if you'd done it rap-style..." Noah said as he stood up.

"That will earn you a beatdown later." Willie sat on the bench seat. "After you fix this."

Noah bellowed, "What my friend means to say is that we're in a war with a small army of cartel, drug runners and Mexican Army deserters. We came here recruiting help. Aside from that, the state's safe. Many have died and there's a ton of open land. We need people to plant crops, tend animals and help the state recover. You can get outta here anytime you like and start a new life."

"Unless we're attacked by the cartel, like the black man said," a lady remarked, giving Willie the dirty eyeball. "No thank you."

"Yeah," another man agreed with her. "Why leave? We have a wall around us here." The dinner crowd grumbled.

"The big crash is still coming," another chimed in.

"Aren't you guys sick of this food?" Noah tried a different tac.

The crowd grumbled, but nobody replied.

"What else you got?" Willie chided him under his breath.

Noah gave up and sat down. He shrugged. "Tough audience."

Burgmeyer shouted from the side of the dining area. Noah hadn't noticed him arrive. "At eighteen hundred hours, gather at the shop. I have something to show you." He turned and walked away, back into the rings of trailers.

Noah and Willie followed the crowd to the workshop. It was hard to find one's way in streets shaped like rings. Noah didn't know if he needed to turn around and go back, or keep going around. But the crowd knew where to go. They'd lived inside the rings for seven months. They arrived at the dim Quonset hut and crowded under the blue-white dim of a half-dozen solar-powered LEDs.

Burgmeyer started his speech. "By the end of summer, the shit will hit the fan for real and we'll see once and for all how the government has failed us." He carefully plucked back a white sheet from over the valley model. Brad stepped forward and helped him, revealing the intricate houses, towns, and farms of the Sevier Valley. The crowd made hushed sounds of awe.

"When the big crash finally happens, we'll split up the valley among ourselves and this whole county will be the new Falcon Base." The crowd pressed in. Noah noticed that Burgmeyer had added little flags with family names over each ranch house from the town of Sevier north beyond Richfield. People whispered and pointed, helping one another find their future farmsteads. There were gasps and prattles of delight. It really was a beautiful model. "We'll barricade the highways here, and here. Across this side of the valley, we'll build an earth wall topped with barbed wire." Burgmeyer pointed to the inch-tall defensive fortifications with a yard-long dowel, after which more cooing ensued.

"That's never going to happen," Willie spoke up. "Y'all are on drugs or something. Those towns have lots of survivors. The big die-off is done. Most of those farms are empty already. I'm telling you the truth. I saw it with my own eyes."

"Yes, but the old boys' snakes-in-the-grass network remains standing," Burgmeyer shouted in a sudden, thunderous voice. "When we built this place, they wouldn't give us a permit to channel the hot springs, or to build the moat around Falcon Base, they lied and said we needed an environmental survey, that this place was wetlands, if you can imagine that! The judge was the city manager's cousin, and the county prosecutor was their grandfather's brother. They had it tied up like a hog, elected officials, hired bureaucrats, judges, and county men. The town of Monroe is just as corrupt as the federal government, and all corruption will fall! It must fall!"

"Aw shit," Noah mumbled. The more Burgmeyer talked, the more his shtick sounded familiar. It was just dinnertime with his adopted father, a rambling litany about lesser men who'd dragged Old Bill down.

"Until that snake pit is filled with gas and burned, we're doomed to repeat the fall, over and over!" Burgmeyer, the once quiet model maker, found his big boy voice, and the crowd ate it up.

"We're with you Burg," a guy shouted. Many agreed.

"Them guys in Monroe ain't going to just die," Willie's voice boomed back.

"Don't do it," Noah urged Willie. "This bacon's cooked, and it ain't going to get uncooked."

Either Willie didn't hear him or he didn't care. "Monroe and Richfield are rebuilding and planting crops as we speak. They're bouncing back. Y'all are nuts. God's honest truth."

"And as for these two," Burgmeyer roared, turning on Willie. "We don't really believe they came all this way from Arizona, do we? Nobody travels that far these days. They're the mayor's men from *Monroe*. They're spies and infiltrators. They were sent to inventory our supplies, to *socialize them up* into their town commune."

"Hunh?" Willie stammered.

"I've been listening to this," Burgmeyer held up one of the Baofeng radios they'd carried when they arrived. "It's chatter from town, how they're building a socialist utopia over there in Monroe. This is communist radio if I ever heard it."

"That's just farmers talking to each other, now that there're no phones..." Willie tried to explain but the crowd's rumblings drowned him out.

"We should go," Noah said emphatically. "They're taking a ride on the Crazy Train." He grabbed Willie's jacket and hauled him toward the door. Burgmeyer shouted for attention. Noah and Willie bailed out into fresh air.

"Run," Noah said. "Around back."

"Which way is *around back?*" Willie's head swiveled left and right. "Who the hell thought circle streets were a good idea?"

Noah steered his friend around to face the right direction. "The guard at the front has NVGs. I saw them on his helmet when we came in." Noah pushed Willie toward the back of the compound. Dark had fallen while they were inside the Quonset hut. Burgmeyer was still holding forth inside, booming a paranoid sermon about the "good ole boys" of Sevier county and their spies. Noah thought he knew the punchline already and it didn't bode well for him and Willie.

They ducked in and out of rings of trailers and headed toward the outside wall. The crowd must've spilled out of the Quonset hut in search of them, because anxious, scampering voices salted the night air. The people of Falcon Base probably thought the spies were heading to their granary or their armory.

"There." Noah pointed to a long stretch of chain-link between fence posts. In the back of the compound, something had bent the fence inward and created a coyote-sized gap at the bottom. Noah and Willie dug, scraped and twisted their way under the wire. Noah tore a ragged hole in his pants and gashed his calf on an errant finger of galvanized wire.

"Damn it to hell," Noah swore. "Tore my jeans and gave ma-self tetanus."

A guard must've heard the clanking fence because someone shouted the alarm.

"Good thing these paranoid white boys didn't get their permit for a moat or we'd be swimming for it," Willie said. There was no reason to be quiet now. It was time to run.

Noah and Willie stumbled down the dirt mound and broke into a hesitant run across the darkening sagebrush plain, bee-lining away from the prepper compound.

"Da'fuck was that?" Willie heaved as he kept easy pace with Noah's stumbling run.

Noah slammed to a stop. Directly in front of them Noah's Land Cruiser appeared out of the gloom. It had been driven around to the back of the compound and stashed in a gully.

Noah headed for the rear tire well where he kept a spare, magnetic key compartment.

"Let this be a lesson to you, William. This is how smart people step on their own dicks," Noah said. "It's mostly a white person thing, I guess. When we get everything we ever wanted, we go looking for something else to piss us off."

"That dude sounded like Bill."

Noah nodded in the dark. "He did indeed."

They climbed into the Cruiser, fired it up and picked their way through the sage in the twin cones of the headlights. Noah did his best to navigate away from the compound, heading west toward the last brushstrokes of orange on the horizon.

"Well that didn't go well." Willie understated the dangerous shit-show that had been their day. "We lost our guns *and* our radios."

Noah nodded.

Willie leaned toward the windshield, scanning for the next threat to pop out of the dark. "I wonder how long they'll hide in their dirt bunker waiting for the world to end. Again."

"Probably when their stale-ass food runs out," Noah said.

"Sometimes, I don't understand white folks at all," Willie bitched.

"It wasn't just white folks in there drinking the Kool-Aid."

Willie held up a finger. "*But* it was the white folks *slingin'* the bullshit."

"We do tend to get wrapped around the axle with our ideas," Noah agreed. He was struggling to understand how his dad could fight alongside shitbags like the cartel. "Sometimes it takes a helluva lot to talk us out of our latest scheme. A helluva lot."

―――

WHEN BILL MCCALLISTER returned to find Castillo, he had no blood on his hands. Bill had been right about Evan Hafer: he was ex-army. He'd been shot in the leg and was in a world of pain, but he didn't play games like the Navy SEAL. He didn't pretend to be a hero, either. He answered Bill's questions like a grownup.

"Did the Cedar City locals detonate the bombs?"

"No."

"Did they help?"

"Yes."

"Who?"

Hafer didn't know. Some locals set the bomb, built by Jeff Kirkham of the Utah Militia, and left a rifle on the roof. Kirkham had been there personally, detonated the bomb and must've escaped.

There was some back and forth about how Bill was a traitor to his country, blah, blah, blah, and then Bill ran out of questions. He wrapped up the interview and had the medics fix Hafer's leg. No broken bones, but infection would be certain. Bill went looking for Castillo to report what he'd learned.

Castillo wasn't at the cartel rally point. A street thug was waiting, though, with instructions to drive Bill up to the Mormon temple.

As they climbed the hill over Cedar City in a gun buggy, Bill's stomach seized up like a thrown rod. Cartel soldiers were going door-to-door rounding up people, clusters of people—families. They cried, wept and pled as they were goose-stepped up the residential boulevard toward the stately Mormon temple on the hilltop. This was not how Bill wanted America to face the music. Seeing Americans being rounded up, especially sun-drenched farm families, stuck in his craw.

The driver dropped Bill at Castillo's command Humvee.

"This isn't going to work, Gustavo. You know that," Bill shouted and his hands flew as he stormed up to his boss.

Castillo ignored him. Instead he opened a cream-colored pamphlet and showed Bill a page. "Check this out. They all have this little book in their scissor drawer that lists the church leaders and their addresses. Even the kids' Sunday School teachers are in here."

"If you shoot the locals, it'll only make them more committed. They'll go high order if you do this. I've seen it a dozen times in a dozen countries," Bill pled. He now understood the "surprise" Castillo had for him. It was a test of loyalty and a chance to play out Castillo's anger at losing the fuel depot.

"I'm not going to shoot anyone, Bill," Castillo said with cynical eyes. "What makes you think I'm going to shoot these fine people? Put them against the building," Castillo ordered. "I just want to talk to them," he said with a sideways wink at Bill.

"Don't do it," Bill whispered. "Don't do this, Gustavo."

"I'm General Castillo to you. Now shut the fuck up, unless you have something to tell me about who sabotaged our fuel depot."

"Yes. I got the information out of the prisoner."

"Then who did it?" Castillo asked.

"It was Utah Militia," Bill told half the truth.

Castillo laughed. "So, you're an American after all. And a liar. I know the locals set it up for the militia. I know that General Kirkham triggered the detonation. He was *here* in this city. *Our* city. The locals allowed it, and helped him." Castillo pointed at the men and women being lined up against the alabaster walls of the Mormon holy building.

"If you do this, the city will be hostile territory forever. We will never, not in a hundred years, pacify Cedar City. I saw it in the Philippines. I saw it in Botswana. I saw it in Afghanistan. Reprisals do not work. They bite you in the ass every, single—"

"Shut up, Bill, or I'll line you up with them," Castillo said, then grinned.

The gangland soldiers lined up a hundred people underneath gold-inlaid, engraved words on the wall that said, "Holiness to the Lord." The families of the doomed stood on the lawn facing them.

"If you comply, you have my word your families will live," Castillo shouted over the din of weeping and wailing. "If you do not, they die too." The threat cut the wailing in half.

Bill forced himself to watch as children clawed at their mothers, watching their fathers, sisters, and grandmothers standing against the big church. The children didn't understand what was happening, but they sensed imminent horror.

"Do it," Castillo said to one of his more hateful drug lackeys, a thin, acne-pocked Latino whose face was locked in an eternal sneer. The lackey waved at a troop of soldiers who trotted in front of the doomed hundred and stabbed two dozen claymores into the dry lawn between them and the crowd.

The soldiers backed away, stringing the control wires to safe distance.

"Paint the building," Castillo ordered with a chopping motion of his hand.

The claymores detonated in a ragged, arrhythmic order. The air filled with concussion, vaporized turf and red mist. The families shrieked, audible even over the explosions.

Two seconds later, the explosions ceased, and Bill found himself with his hands cupped over his ears, his mouth hanging loose.

The blood of the mangled, shredded bodies reached thirty feet up the side of the building. Their bodies slumped in an unrecognizable pile of offal. Limbs, heads, even hands were in the butcher's heap, but nothing else. Just scraps of clothing and raw meat. Tens of thousands of ball bearings, hurdled by the claymores, had chopped them as finely as an airplane propeller.

Bill gaped at the carnage, then at Castillo.

His boss shouted something at him, but Bill had forgotten to remove his hands from his ears.

"What?" he asked Castillo, numbly.

"Someday, you'll betray me," Castillo said with a smile. "I know it. But I'll know precisely when, and the moment before that happens... I'll kill you." Castillo flashed raised eyebrows at Bill. He pointed a finger gun at Bill's forehead. "Bang."

Bill had nothing clever to say in response. His brain sloshed inside his head. Castillo seemed perfectly composed.

He was a soul putrefied, the darkest type of monster. Bill had been wrong to think that Castillo's control could bring anything but suffering. There would be no ranch in Star Valley. There would be no fresh, efficient government. There would be no peace by the sword. There would only be atrocity under the rule of the madman.

Castillo turned back to Acne-boy. "Shoot them all." He waved his hands at the weeping, clutching families. "Shut them up."

Acne's squad of murderers spread out in a letter "C" behind the families and opened fire in full-auto. They dumped rounds, changed mags, and dumped more rounds until the families were nothing but a silent mound of blood and clothing on a yellow lawn.

Bill stumbled off the temple mount. It was all he could think to do. Castillo had broken him.

He staggered to the boulevard and wandered into the setting sun.

7

"That spring, after Black Autumn, four constitutional republics rose up like tulips. Each imagined it was America reborn and each had its own, distinct hue. Each of the early republics heard little more than rumors about the others.

"From northwestern Washington across the west half of Montana, a fiercely Christian republic formed in the "American Redoubt." In Colorado Springs, after quelling the threat of nuclear attack, Native Americans and U.S. military veterans formed a national government. In Little Rock, Arkansas, the Ku Klux Klan experienced a short-lived resurgence and formed a government under a schema of racial purity. That effort lost its footing in forever-long race skirmishes. In Jacksonville, North Carolina, almost the entire complement of U.S. Marines at Camp Lejeune survived, along with their dependents. They gathered local survivors from the East Coast, including a few congressmen, and elected a new congress, then a president. It would be many years before the several United States governments would learn of one another, and in that time, each calcified its ideals and predilections, setting the stage for future conflict."

— THE AMERICAN DARK AGES, BY WILLIAM BELLAHER, NORTH AMERICAN TEXTBOOKS, 2037

The Homestead
Oakwood, Utah

JENNA ROSS SHARED COFFEE WITH COLONEL ZHUKOV. IT'D BECOME A morning routine, as she intended when she'd conceived of it.

With over two hundred members within the Homestead, several hundred living outside, and a thousand Spetsnaz within a few blocks around the property, there was nowhere quiet on the Homestead grounds. Jenna and Zhukov met a few minutes each day after dawn on an iron bench in a stone alcove overlooking the valley below. As the morning mist curled away from the once-bustling towns of Bountiful, Layton, and Ogden, the handsome, middle-aged pair sipped coffee, chatted, and laughed. It was the most normal thing Jenna had done since the Black Autumn collapse. She could relax in Colonel Zhukov's gentlemanliness, and his easy-going air.

She hadn't asked him his first name. Until he said otherwise, his Russian family had possession of it. His wife and children would call him by that name, not an American woman in a land where he'd been abandoned.

The Colonel talked a lot about his family. They lived on the outskirts of a city called Saratov, and they enjoyed a small farm dacha three hours outside the city. The Zhukov family raised a small herd of goats, and vegetables, on their dacha plot.

The Homestead kept goats, too. They were minor celebrities among the survival collective.

Somewhere during the horrid winter after Black Autumn, it was discovered that a buck goat had gone undiscovered among the females in the Homestead goat paddock. In the middle of the terrifying month of November, amidst death, violence and the flu, several goat mamas gave birth. The Homestead was distracted, with the threat of the mob, and the nights were newly frigid. Two kid goats died within days. The women and children held a twin funeral for them. The children insisted on digging the graves themselves, with their tiny shovels. The sadness of it took Jenna's breath away, and she was spurred into action. She would not allow the three remaining kid goats to die, no matter the cost. There had been too much loss already. The children had already faced more death in the previous month than they should've in a lifetime. Jenna simply could not allow the three baby goats, spindly and rejected by their mothers, to die.

She poured over goat husbandry books in the Homestead library, bottle fed the baby goats three times a day and rallied a posse of women to make absolutely certain they survived the winter. One of the surviving kids was found dead in the kidding barn, probably stomped to death by a grumpy mother goat. That third funeral broke their hearts anew, but it annealed Jenna's will, made her almost mad with fervor to preserve the lives of the two, surviving sisters: Black Betty and Lucy.

Betty was entirely black, long-legged, and notoriously curious. She liked to jump on her mother's back and wobble about the pen in a balancing game that her mom barely tolerated.

Lucy had less spunk. Her mother had rejected her, for reasons known only to goat logic. When Lucy went to feed, her mother head-butted and kicked her away. She diminished while Betty gained weight. The circle of goat-tending women, formerly health spa regulars and Whole Foods shoppers, weighed the baby goats daily, held the mother still for teat feeding, and bottle fed the kid goats until their bellies were hard as cantaloupes. The women shot the goat mouths full of vitamin-rich Drench and tracked their weight on precious scraps of paper.

Both of the baby goats flourished under the ladies' ministrations. The winter abated. Souls began to heal. The flourishing goat herd became a symbol of new life, and the newly-calloused hands of the mothers of the Homestead held that hope in trust.

Jenna and Colonel Zhukov found common cause in stories of goats. As they recounted their antics, they relived more lighthearted days, with families that were all but lost. As the coffee mugs cooled each morning, and as the Homestead grounds buzzed with breakfast, the pair walked across the Great Lawn to the goat paddock, where the stars of Jenna's show bleated complaints at the morning cold. The pair of coffee drinkers prattled, cooed, and laughed at the Homestead goats, like children skipping school.

To call it a romance between Jenna and Colonel Zhukov would be to misunderstand the tidal pull between a man and a woman at middle age. Particularly in the face of all they'd lost, tender companionship and cheerful laughter was enough for the time being.

Zhukov rallied a platoon of his men, rummaged the Homestead grounds for mesh wire netting, and built Jenna a massive, two-acre goat enclosure, with four goat barns, a dedicated buck pasture, and a channeled goat run for veterinary checkups. The Spetsnaz troops cobbled together platforms, ramps and spiral obstacles for the goats to climb. The place became a favorite of the children, chasing goats and watching them scamper, hop, and leap in their hilarious acrobatics. It became the playground of the new, old world. Where once there had been a paintball field on the Homestead grounds, there was now a herd of tricksters.

"I have a gift for you," Zhukov said that morning over coffee. His eyes sparkled back the joy of her instant delight.

"You found a massage therapist!" she goofed at him. "Thank God."

"I don't know that word in English," he lied. She knew he knew it.

"Better than a massage," Zhukov laughed and raised his

eyebrows. "My men found a Great Pyrenees dog for your herd. Two dogs, actually. A boy and a girl."

"Oh my." Jenna clapped her hands together and squealed. After losing a herd of goats to a cougar two years before, she'd been terrified that another cougar would come and kill her Black Betty and Lucy Girl. Not only would the goat herd now have protection, but the Homestead might have puppies as well.

Jenna threw her arms around Zhukov and kissed him on the cheek.

"You're my hero," she said. "I'd like to personally thank the men that found the dogs."

"Of course," he promised. "They'll bring the dogs to you today."

Jenna clapped her hands again. "I'm going to sleep so much better knowing my babies are protected. Thank you." Physical protection was the ultimate gift these troublesome days.

She thought about her end game with the Colonel. The timing seemed right to move ahead. The signals coming from Zhukov leaned toward her in every way. They'd never discussed Jason Ross.

She took a risk. "You realize there's an army headed toward us. They have tanks, and a very bad man leads them," Jenna said.

"I have men watching and reporting on cartel movement," the Colonel said. His eyes narrowed slightly, and he used a sip from his coffee cup to cover his reaction.

"For this place to be safe, you must help General Kirkham." She cashed in the full sum of their friendship. "Or do you not see it that way?"

Zhukov bobbed back on his heels, very slightly, almost as though a breeze had moved him.

"I haven't figured out yet which course of action is in the best interest of my men ." His voice carried no metal, but the words were plain. She'd made a military suggestion and he'd replied as a military officer. She could either press or retreat; sally deeper onto the field, or demure to his light-handed reproach. She had informants of her own, and they told her that the cartel was preparing to leave Cedar City. They were within striking range of Jenna's home, of Jenna's adopted children, and her friends' children, and of the orphans and the goats. This was not romantic play. It was war, she reminded herself, and she was no less a duty-bound soldier than Zhukov. But he wasn't ready. Not yet.

There was always the nuclear option, offering herself, her deepest self. That would be an even greater risk, and it could easily backfire. She didn't have a firm sense of how he would respond. She wasn't even sure she could bring herself to do it. It would violate everything she had ever been. If the offer failed, she would be reduced in his eyes. It was a weapon to be used in battle only as a coup de grâce, because unless it was a killing blow, the blade would forever be dulled. And then there was the matter of her integrity.

Jenna looked to the ground. Her eyelids broke their gaze and drifted.

"I'm sorry. Of course, your first duty is to your country," she said in a gentle riposte. "That's the kind of man you are."

He scoffed, as she knew he would. "My country? No. They sent us here then forgot about us. I wonder if they even told our families we're still alive."

"I'm sorry. You deserve better," she said.

"Do we?" The Colonel hardened his eyes and belied his guilt. "You don't know what we've done. We didn't come here to help, Mrs. Ross. We came to destroy your country."

She already knew it. "It doesn't matter now," she said. "That old world has passed." She wanted to be the one to give him absolution. It was a gift that cost her nothing. "You're here with us now. You're part of this place now. Part of *our* family."

He nodded, obviously receiving it as more than a platitude. He absorbed it like a plunging blade, one that might lance a boil or excise a cancer. He was a man of battle, but he was a boy in this time and place. He was a man without a hearth, a soldier without a code, or a monk without faith.

She had offered him a home. The longing it answered might be even deeper than sex.

She meant it, too. No matter what demands her queendom placed on her, she would honor her word to him. He would have a home here.

He must've perceived her sincerity, because he nodded and looked toward the valley. A glistening gathered in the corner of his eye. She imagined that he was saying goodbye to his first home as he opened his heart to a new one.

"Thank you." He tossed the cold dregs of his coffee on the returning grass. "My name is Dimtriy, by the way." He nodded again, smiled awkwardly, then walked away to resume his duty.

―――

JASON ROSS UNLOADED the last of the re-purposed lumber from the bed of his OHV in the forest of the south fork of Bellamy Draw.

"Would you like me to send someone to help you build?" Jason offered Molly Beringer.

"No, thank you." She looked at the ground. "We can do it."

Whenever possible, she opted out of accepting his help. It was as though she counted the future cost of every favor, every scrap of wood and every bucket of wheat, in denominations of nakedness and hot breath on her shoulder.

Jason hadn't touched her, and neither had anyone else so far as he knew, but the debt of sex hung in the air.

The women were in their mid-thirties—Molly and Susan. Their skin was fresh despite the privations of the winter, and the Homestead's stolen wheat had preserved the padding around their hips.

They worked every day in the shady draw, building a new shelter closer to the Homestead. Jason had scrounged up a fresh tarp, still in the package. Yuri brought a hammer to lend them. The nails were pounded straight by the children after they pulled them from their last shelter at Turkey Springs, a mile away in the forest.

Jason left the women to their construction work and motored back across his land to the Homestead gate. It was late morning and the spring sun warmed the damp off the leaf litter of the forest. His heart lifted with the scent, new life, albeit in a world circled with danger.

His ex-wife manipulated his Russian allies. The women of the Homestead still despised him for the orphanage dispute, and Jeff Kirkham stood at the head of a belligerent militia, biding his time, no doubt eager to take Jason's head. But the forest air promised life and he accepted the open-handed gift.

He roared up to the outer gate and a Spetsnaz soldier swung it wide. The man's haircut marked him as Russian. It was short and clumpy as though cut by a knife, but he wore street clothes now. His camouflage had finally been traded for comfort.

As Jason drove up the cobblestone driveway, Jenna walked toward her office. He pulled up alongside her and cut the engine.

"Jenna. Do you have work for the two Beringer women, the mother and aunt of the little girl?"

"I was told you already found work for them," her eyes flashed with intensity.

"What work?" He had stepped into a cosmic posthole. His impulse was to stall for time. It was a well-worn pattern in his marriage: she was angry about something and he would ask meandering questions until he could gain an understanding of *what the hell was going on.*

She planted her hands on her hips. "Dimtriy told me."

"Who's Dimtriy?" he asked.

"Colonel Zhukov."

"He's 'Dimtriy' now?" Jason's voice strengthened. At first, it felt like he'd caught her in something she shouldn't have said, but then he wondered. *Was it really a slip?* He struggled to keep up, playing defense. He should've been playing offense. He was in charge of this place. He owned it. "Do you have a job for the Beringer ladies or not? We're feeding the family, they might as well work."

She stood on the sloping driveway, hands on her hips, and the silence stretched. "Send them to me. I'll take care of them," she finally said.

It sounded threatening, but he didn't quite understand how. He didn't want Molly and Susan to get a ration of shit from his ex-wife, but he felt like if he kept talking to her about it, the posthole he'd stepped in would somehow get deeper.

"Fine." He cranked the key and stomped on the gas. The OHV gunned around the corner toward the cook shed. He hoped the raging engine had set her back. He flicked a glance in the rearview mirror. She stood her ground, glaring in his direction.

Jacqueline Reynolds sat with Major Kvashnin at breakfast and they were obviously in love. Kvashnin laughed and played with her children, slipping into the father's role of poor, dead Tom Reynolds. Tom would be happy to see them cared for and protected, but their happiness felt like a noose tightening around Jason's neck. His allies were becoming the lovers of allies of Jeff Kirkham.

He hadn't exactly taken Jeff's family prisoner. Rather, he'd closed the Homestead gates to *anyone* leaving, and they'd remained closed for weeks. For the time being, Jason refused to negotiate the separation of any of the Homestead members. Separation would require careful division of food, resources, tools, guns, and ammo—a painstaking negotiation—to separate out the property they'd brought on the eve of Black Autumn. With every departing family, a sticky process of horse trading would be needed, like a divorce where the marital assets had been half consumed, half invested, and half given away to friends. Nobody could know for sure which of the three "halves" was which.

While the time of crisis persisted, Jason ordered everyone to stay put. It was not a popular decision. Homestead survivors hungered to leave, to find vacant land, to plant crops, and to raise livestock. With every day, their chances of surviving the next winter diminished.

Jason didn't much care that they were bothered. The old Homestead members had helped Kirkham steal his land. If they didn't like it, they shouldn't have stolen from him in the first place. They were lucky he didn't have them shot.

His Russians had taken over sentry duty on the inner wall and it would've been difficult for Tara and Jeff's boys to escape through chinks in the rubble wall. They would have to leave without anything they owned, but they could go whenever they wanted, technically. The Russians wouldn't shoot them if they fled.

Jason could guess how Jeff Kirkham felt about it: he'd be in a murderous rage. Kirkham hated to lose. He had an army of fifty thousand and his hands were currently full with the cartel, for now.

But Jason was being out-maneuvered *inside* the walls. The signs of a coordinated assault were all around him, as obvious as the salt shakers on the tables. The Spetsnaz were being taken in, befriended, and invited to bed. No force of arms could defend against such an attack. Whether it was sincere affection for the commandos or contrived manipulation didn't matter. He was being out-flanked. Soon, he would be encircled.

The tactical reaction to a flank was usually to counter-flank. Jason scanned the breakfast crowd for Colonel Zhukov and found him sitting with a few of his officers, enjoying eggs and fresh-baked wheat toast. Without collecting his meal, Jason made a bee-line for their table.

The men suddenly stopped talking, perhaps because it was rude to speak Russian, or perhaps because they didn't want Jason to know what they were discussing. He sat down with a strained smile.

"Good morning." He nodded to each officer. "Colonel, can we speak for a moment?"

The colonel gestured to a seat. The other officers stood, their breakfast finished. They left the two men to their meeting.

"Kirkham will attack soon. He hasn't forgotten about us. His family is still here," Jason said.

Zhukov's face betrayed nothing. He appeared to neither believe nor disbelieve the threat.

"Perhaps we should let his family go," Zhukov said. "They're a liability."

"They might be the only reason he doesn't attack us with mortars," Jason argued.

Zhukov nodded. It might be true.

Jason chose his next words carefully. He didn't know if he was talking to the man who was sleeping with his ex-wife. "There's a much easier way for Kirkham to take back this compound than mounting a direct attack."

"How?" Zhukov asked, his face an open question. He clearly had not seen the encirclement closing around him.

"If I were Kirkham," Jason said, "I would communicate secretly with my allies within the compound and have them convert people inside. I would flip officers of the occupiers into agents of my own. I would offer them what they wanted on a *personal level*." Jason stopped talking and lifted his chin in the direction of Major Kvashnin playing with the Reynolds kids, his one hand under the table, resting on Jacqueline Reynolds knee.

"Oh," Colonel Zhukov exhaled. Jason could see the implications dawn on him.

Zhukov turned troubled eyes back to the table. For him to even consider it, he wasn't likely sleeping with Jenna yet. If he'd taken her to bed, he'd be too far gone to entertain what Jason was saying. He'd be a rival, not an ally.

Jason quieted. Waiting was often the best play. The next person to talk would be the supplicant.

"Then what is our end game?" Zhukov asked. He had the look of a man who had lost the end of a spool of fishing line. "How do we defeat Kirkham and make this our home?"

Jason nodded and pretended to think it through. "We don't defeat him. Not us. Not directly."

Zhukov waited anxiously while Jason pretended to work it out. In truth, he had figured it out before he approached the table.

Jason shook his finger as though arriving at a strategy. "We give the Mexican cartel the key to total victory. We make ourselves critical to the outcome. We ally with the most powerful force in the region, more powerful than Kirkham."

"How do we do it?" Zhukov handed control to Jason Ross once again.

Jason painted his face with the satisfaction of a perfect plan, a perfect solution. He pointed at the valley, at the gleaming white tanks and spiral smokestacks of the Maverick Oil refinery.

"We give them *that*."

8

Shortwave Radio 7150kHz
3:00pm

"Today, I want to talk about 'ridiculous shit we used to fume over.' Call in on our sub-channel and Zach will collect your responses. 'Ridiculous shit we used to scream and howl at each other about.' Gimme yours.

"Tanya's surviving in Penobscot, Maine. I'm looking at the note Zach just handed me and it says, 'Ivermectin.' Holy shit, I'd totally forgotten that we argued about that for like a whole year. Funny story: our community raises goats, and the goats constantly get worms, ya know? We put out a call to the scavengers to find us some Ivermectin—to manage their worms. The scavengers came back with a **hundred and fifty pound crate** of the stuff, in little tubes, watermelon flavor. This guy, a dead guy, had a crate of Ivermectin in his garage taking up a parking spot. He didn't have livestock. He just lived in the city with a huge crate of Ivermectin. Must've cost him a thousand bucks. Let this be a lesson, Planet Shortwave: never fight the **last** war. Fight the one you haven't seen yet. We all thought the apocalypse would be COVID two-point-oh, and it turned out to be something totally different."

Interstate 15
Pintura, Utah

It was the hour before dawn, and a high desert wind whistled down from the snow-capped peaks and chilled Jeff's bones. He steeled himself for heavy losses.

The cartel had gotten smarter since the sabotage at KD Fuels in Cedar City. They'd dedicated fifteen Abrams tanks to security for the supply convoy. Jeff had hoped to face the normal escort of five. But he had no choice. If they didn't take this convoy down, the Maverick refinery would fall, maybe before sunset.

The night waxed icy-cold for spring. There'd be a sheath of crystal on the tender shoots of alfalfa come morning. The "X" of the ambush was a five mile stretch of freeway just south of the smudge on the map called Pintura, Utah. The canyon walls were steep. There was no way for the fuel trucks to escape, but the same went for his fighting trucks. They'd be trapped, too.

The map of southern Utah was, perhaps, the most serious hurdle to the enemy. West of the four lane interstate, a three hundred mile-wide band of featureless desert stretched all the way to Nevada, striped with lonely roads. A full armored division couldn't control that much open land. The Utah Militia was free to loop around the enemy and pop up anywhere to harass their supply lines.

The only protection for the Hood Rats was the Abrams. Wherever the tanks crouched, ready to pounce, the cartel was safe. Wherever the tanks weren't, Jeff could maneuver at will. To the west of the I-15 and the mountain spine that ran up the center of Utah, Jeff's force of a thousand gun trucks was like a German submarine wolf pack on the high seas of the Atlantic. He could surface and attack anywhere, anytime.

The cartel still hadn't pushed north of Cedar City. After losing the KD Fuels yard, they'd struggled to bring fuel forward.

Jeff was certain the Abrams were topped off, but defeating the militia fleet of pickup trucks required extensive maneuverability. If the Hoodies punched through to Salt Lake without securing the supply tether back to their fuel depot in St. George, they'd risk running the tanks out of gas. That would be the same as handing them to Jeff.

The cartel boss was too smart to rush north without a guaranteed resupply, so the battle for the Rocky Mountain West became a cat and mouse game down the length of the supply line from Cedar City to St. George.

The cartel controlled St. George, and they apparently had enough gas there to replace what Jeff had burned. This risky ambush at Pintura, the biggest in his career, would crush the Hoodie supply line and possibly deplete the St. George fuel bunkers.

But there were more tanks—far more tanks—than Jeff had predicted. And the cold nagged at him. His trucks were concealed in the nooks and crannies of the dirt roads around the valley. It was the perfect ambush location, with steep mountains on both sides and nowhere to run. But the Abrams came equipped with thermal optics. Jeff prayed the stolen Abrams hadn't been upgraded to the new Palomar thermal imager. The Palomar was scary-good. Anything warmer than an earthworm showed up in the targeting system as a burning white kernel on a blackened chalkboard.

Three hundred trucks were a lot of cats to herd. Jeff ordered them in withering terms to keep their asses behind dirt cover, but his troops weren't battle-hardened mechanized cavalry. They were bright-faced Mormons who relied more on the righteousness of their cause than on military discipline.

"Hotel Romeo Passing Alpha," Jeff's recon squad radio squawked. "Count two-five primaries, one-five secondaries, and five targets." *Twenty-five Abrams tanks, fifteen electric gun buggies and five fuel tanker trucks.* There were way too many tanks. The cartel knew it was an ambush.

This is war, Jeff reminded himself. *Men die. That's how it works.* He couldn't let this convoy pass. Even against twenty-five tanks, it was too late to retreat.

A forward security force appeared through the gap where the freeway emerged from Signal Mountain Pass; Jeff watched them through his night vision. The tanks trundled down the asphalt and the gun buggies darted ahead, probably to probe the town of Pintura and set security around a rally point. The cartel vehicles ran dark, probably operating with night vision.

Jeff sat above Ash Creek, on the far side of the interstate. It would be harder for his forces on this side of the valley to retreat, with the impassable Wasatch Mountains at their back, but the vantage gave him a good view of the ambush. Through his NVGs, Jeff could barely make out his pickup trucks down dirt roads. The enemy hadn't detected them yet.

Jeff stirred on his feet. What he saw coming down the freeway wasn't bush league gang bangers. It was a well-organized security force. The cartel was done dinking around. They'd found a commander who knew what he was doing and he'd stepped up their level of professionalism. The next slug of armor would be the main body of their fighting force, then set back a mile or two would be the fuel trucks, then rear security. Every element would be a mix of armor, mechanized infantry and ground infantry.

The main body of tanks and buggies crested the pass. Five fuel trucks appeared almost directly behind, under cover of the M1 Abrams' cannons.

Jeff exhaled. At least the Hoodies were bunched up, fearing the lone snipers Jeff had been using for weeks. If the Hoodies had prepared for a full-scale mechanized ambush, they would've set the fuel tracks back five miles to allow the main force to search and destroy before putting the thin-skinned tanker trucks at risk.

Jeff counted the fuel tankers cresting the rise in the interstate.
One, two...

He needed them all in the valley. If he was going toe-to-toe with twenty-five Abrams tanks, the cartel should pay for the privilege.

Three...four...five.

One of the Abrams in the forward security slammed on its brakes. The squeal carried across the black-lit valley. The Abrams engine roared in a fierce down-shift. Two seconds later, the tanks peeled off the roadbed and their turrets swiveled outward.

"Golf-Kilo, all-stations. We've been made. Execute, execute, execute," Jeff spoke into his radio, his voice as calm as he could make it. He knew this would be the last real control he would have over his fighting force. Attacking with three hundred pickup trucks with machine guns bolted to their beds was like throwing a hive of bees at the enemy. It was a lot easier to chuck the hive than to get it back in the box.

"May God help us," Jeff prayed aloud.

Boom! the first Abrams fired at a target. It must've missed because Jeff saw no secondary explosions.

"Concentrate fire on the fuel tanker trucks. Ignore the Abrams," Jeff hollered into his mic. He was repeating himself and he didn't like doing that over the radio. Every truck commander knew the mission. They'd been told a dozen times to forget about firing on the Abrams.

Kill the fuel tanker trucks then run. Don't stop for more than ten seconds at-a-time. If you're going to stop, get off the road so others can get past. Whatever happens, don't get blown up on a road. We need the roads clear for exfil.

That'd been the extent of Jeff's order of battle, and it was everything he could tell them to give even a gnat's chance against the flyswatter.

Boom-Boom-BOOM-BOOM-boom-boom!

The Abrams brought the tempest and the valley exploded in

lightning and thunder. The raw aggression of the tanks took Jeff's breath away. They lanced tremendous destruction down on his attack vehicles. The iron juggernauts fired, advanced, and then fired again. Twenty-five tanks hammered across the valley floor, closing the distance to Jeff's trucks. His pickups dashed across the foothills, seeking windows between the tanks to shoot at the fuel trucks, the only targets vulnerable to their machine guns.

A handful of trucks armed with TOW missiles darted into range, fired, then fled. Jeff saw one Abrams take a hit in the reactive armor, recover and continue fighting. Another lucky missile took the top off an Abrams. *One down.*

The smaller part of Jeff's army of trucks, near Pintura and in the belly of the valley, ran into the open. They were the bullet magnets, the distraction meant to pull the convoy deeper into the trap. They ran with their headlights on, guns blazing at nothing in particular. Their job was to draw fire. None were to stop for more than three seconds. Already, five of them were aflame, blazing like supernovas in Jeff's night vision.

Boom-Boom-BOOM-BOOM-boom-boom! Machine gun fire filled the air like static. Most of the trucks fired old M2 Ma Deuces, with every third or fourth round an incendiary round that burned with ferocious, implacable flame. Ropes, stingers, and garlands of burning machine gun fire criss-crossed the Pintura valley, and almost all of it slashed into the tail-end of the supply convoy where the fuel trucks crouched.

Jeff's trucks ignored the tanks and pounced. They paid dearly for their bravery. Secondary explosions filled the valley. The funeral pyres of his men and their trucks dotted the folds of the foothills, more burning trucks than Jeff could count. *Three dozen? Fifty?* The tanks devoured his trucks in flaming starbursts, as fast as they could fire. But by sheer numbers, Jeff's brave trucks overwhelmed them.

A shell growled overhead from a tank cannon and Jeff instinctively ducked. The cannon shot hadn't been aimed at him. He'd distanced himself from anything with a heat signature bigger than a refrigerator. His command post, Jeff, his adjutant and three radiomen, were alone on a pinnacle with a full view of the valley.

Another shell hurdled past and slammed into Jeff's command truck, parked a quarter mile away in a shielding fold. It exploded and bits of the Ford F-250 rained down on the cluster of men. Something that might have been the transmission, or half an engine block, thunked to earth ten feet from Jeff, on top of one of his radiomen. Wet flesh exploded in a sickening lotus, nearly knocking Jeff off of his feet with a blast of bone, muscle and guts. Where once there had been a man, now there was a lump of hissing metal.

"Stay on task," Jeff growled at his surviving men. He swiped away the gore from his face. "Ignore it. Hector," he shouted at his adjutant. "Take over for Simms. Get those units back online."

The accuracy of the fire that'd killed his vehicle proved the thermal capabilities of the Abrams. That tank had identified a sliver of a heat signature and destroyed it from over a mile away.

The death toll was staggering, but the mission seemed assured. Jeff counted the burning cartel tanker trucks. The smoke was invisible against the night sky, but the flames rose over five hundred feet in the air. The entire I-15 roadbed for half-a-mile was on fire, like a chasm in the valley floor where hell was trying to escape. The tear in the crust of the earth reached back almost to the mountain pass. The burning fuel trucks had dumped gas all along the interstate and conjoined in a single furrow of fire. Jeff couldn't count the annihilated trucks, as tens of thousands of gallons of diesel fuel rolled down the freeway in a flaming gash.

The Abrams on rear security were blocked from the valley by a wall of flame, but the forward security and main force didn't need any help. They murdered Jeff's trucks with impunity. With every two or three roars of cannon, another truck died—at least three good men vaporized in geysers of steel, fire and plastic. Jeff could no longer count them, the burning wrecks across the hills and folds of the hellish valley. *A hundred? A hundred and fifty?*

"This is Golf Kilo, all stations, withdraw immediately to the objective rally point," Jeff ordered over his radio. He repeated his orders, shouting over the shrieking, buzzing roar of the battlefield. "Mission complete. Get out of the valley now!" he said.

"Sir?" his adjutant shouted, yanking out his earbud. "We're in full retreat. How are we getting out? Us?"

"I don't fucking care about us," Jeff raged. "Get my men out of here!"

Every second, half a dozen new bonfires of men and machine erupted. Jeff watched as a burning truck on a dirt road blocked ten others. One-by-one, a greedy Abrams destroyed them all. It wasn't the only road blocked by burning wreckage. Jeff could see four others. The trucks escaping up those roads would be doomed to reverse course, then drive back into the face of near-certain death.

As the minutes ticked past, and his men struggled to escape Pintura valley like rats off a burning ship, Jeff was forced to face the cost. He'd traded two hundred gun trucks and more than three hundred men for just *five* fuel tankers.

"We're leaving," he bellowed at his staff, now on-foot. "Get ready to run."

It was going to be a long, exhausting night, if they survived. They'd have to cross the valley on foot, climb the western hills and, hopefully, reach the objective rally point in the small mountain town of Pine Valley, that was, if the Hood Rats didn't get there first and obliterate the survivors.

Three hundred men. He tried to picture them all in one spot. In a pile. In a row of graves. On a funeral pyre. He couldn't. It was too many. He'd never in his career lost even a fraction of that many men.

His rage needed something dry and grainy to feed upon. His

guilt and grief cried for gravel under his feet, and pain in his side. Jeff would embrace the pain and the thirst of the overland run.

Five fuel trucks in exchange for hundreds of men.

This was how wars were lost.

Interstate 15
Nephi, Utah

BY THE TIME Jeff reached Pine Valley, then hitched a ride with his survivors back to their base in the town of Nephi, the Utah Militia was already one-third disbanded. In his short absence, a lion's share of his men had decided to go home. Extraordinary defeat did that.

"Get me Thayer on the line," he shouted at his radiomen.

"Sir, these men drove up from Arizona to join," Jeff's adjutant interrupted his fury, herding forward a group of strangers.

"Colonel Withers of the Arizona Air National Guard, Tucson." A balding, Army officer shook Jeff's grimy hand. "And this is Corporal Noah Miller, Freeman Militia." Miller was thick of chest and rough of hand, more like a cowboy than a military officer. If he clamped a Stetson over the sandy blond hair, he'd be rodeo-ready.

Jeff shook hands with the cowboy. "I hope you brought a squadron of A-10s with you from Tucson."

"Unfortunately, no Warthogs," Withers said, "we had to cook all our jet fuel to keep it out of the hands of the cartel."

"If we sent a couple of tankers of JP8 south, could you fly Warthogs up? We control a good runway at Hill AFB and we have a maintenance crew," Jeff's said, his tattered hopes rising.

"We'd have to head all the way back down…it took us weeks to get here." Withers shook his head. "But it's possible. Our Warthogs need maintenance and parts, but we could cobble together at least a few of them from the airframes we have at AFB Davis. The cartel couldn't possibly have destroyed them all. I don't think they even tried."

"How many men do you command, Colonel?" Jeff asked.

"Three hundred and twelve."

"We lost over three hundred men in the last forty-eight hours," Jeff said. He put the bad news first, as was his style. He probably still had his radioman's gore on his face and clothes. The new arrivals deserved to know what they were up against.

The colonel blanched. "That must've been one hell of a battle."

"We're getting our asses kicked by Abrams main battle tanks."

"We know," Colonel Withers said. "We've been fighting those same bastards since before Christmas."

"You couldn't put A-10 Warthogs against them?" Jeff wanted to believe it was possible. There had to be a way of gutting the enemy, some tactic or technology that would cancel out the immense power of the armor.

"We put a few Warthogs in the air when they first invaded," Withers explained, "but Arizona isn't Utah. What's left of our militia is just a grab bag of random fighting men. By the time we organized, most of our survivors were clustered around four or five water holes in the desert. Any military force we once had dried up and blew away the moment the water supply died. The cartel went right through what was left of us."

"That's not entirely true, sir," the cowboy corporal interjected. "We are the reason you're facing eighty Abrams instead of a hundred Abrams."

Colonel Withers nodded agreement. "Miller and his men brought a refinery down around their ears. They killed twenty tanks outside of Las Vegas."

"Losses?" Jeff asked.

"Pretty much everyone," Noah Miller replied. "That win cost us almost the entire surviving complement of Nellis Air Force base. I couldn't even tell you how many died. I barely escaped."

That math sounded right to Jeff. Maybe that's what it would take: a thousand dead men per Abrams tank.

Even so, surrender wasn't an option. "You'd have to backtrack down Highway 89, then slip through cartel-controlled territory with fuel trucks, get to Tucson, put together a dozen aircraft, then fly them back to Hill AFB."

"Technically, it's possible," Withers said. "I doubt we could pull together more than a dozen planes, and we'd need luck on our side to dodge cartel patrols. They're climbing all over every route back to Monterrey, Mexico. It's their lifeline, and they defend it with Jeeps and those electric dune buggies."

Jeff nodded. It was good information. Bad news, but good intel. "Here in Utah, the Hoodies are concentrated in St. George and Cedar City," Jeff said. "Where are their bases south of the state line?" Jeff's intelligence didn't exist south of St. George. Nevada was a black hole on Jeff's map.

"Hoodies?" Noah Miller asked.

"Hood Rats, Hoodies, cartel..." Jeff said. "Drug runners. Shitbags, though we try to keep the language clean when we can, you know, because most of my soldiers are Mormon."

Colonel Withers looked around, probably for a map, but there wasn't one nearby. "We suspect their principal base is somewhere in the Nevada desert around Laughlin. There's a lot of dead ground and tumbleweeds outside of Vegas. Lots of solar, too." Colonel Withers scratched his chin. He'd shaved for this meeting, Jeff noticed. He was the only one. The cowboy, Noah Miller, ran operator-scruffy.

"Finding their home base is a luxury." Jeff shook his head. "Right now, I need to figure out why so many of my Mormon troops are packing up and heading home. I apologize, but you might have made this trip for nothing. We just got our asses kicked and I can't promise we'll still be a coherent fighting force by this time tomorrow. Stand by, if you would, Colonel, and I'll figure out what the hell's going on."

"Sir." Corporal Miller held up a finger. "If I may. My adoptive father's on staff with Gustavo Castillo, the cartel boss."

"Yeah?" Jeff knew the name Castillo. "Why the hell would your father do that?"

"He's playing both sides. He's former Green Beret, CIA, mercenary—a tiger-stripe-wearing, snake in the mud."

"I know the type," Jeff said. He knew the type because he was exactly that type.

"I'd like to volunteer to infiltrate the cartel and turn him," Miller said.

"No way," Jeff said, with a chop of his hand. "I've lost two officers and friends, and half-a-thousand men to the Hoodies in the last six hours. I'm just waiting to find my friends' heads on a fence post. I'd rather have you risk your life bringing me back a couple of Warthogs than send you to certain death. If you're asking, then I'm ordering: absolutely not."

"My father's been feeding us information about the cartel's plan to move up I-15, take your oil refinery and proceed toward Idaho."

"We already knew that," Jeff said. "How did he feed you information?"

"He's sent messages through refugees."

"Hmm," Jeff paused to consider the wrinkle. A war could turn on a scrap of paper. He'd seen it happen. "I'm still not sending you in there. You already know too much just from standing here now. If they torture you for information, any chance of us getting those Warthogs will go up in smoke. My answer is *no*...Colonel Withers: assemble a team. I'll have two tanker trucks with JP8 waiting for you in Salt Lake City. I suggest you take a hundred men and roll the rest of your troop into my militia."

Withers nodded. Miller didn't.

Jeff didn't have time to screw with an insubordinate newcomer, so he let it go. Miller wasn't his problem.

Jeff held up a hand. "Colonel Withers, a thousand Russian Spetsnaz commandos are barricaded in a stronghold north of Salt Lake City. They are to be considered enemy combatants."

"I'm afraid I don't understand," Withers said. "Russians?"

"I don't understand either." Jeff stared at him blank-faced. "Welcome to the apocalypse. Every black-hearted asshole on the planet has come to America. I won't be shocked if the damned Klingons land tomorrow."

"Russians?" Withers stammered. "From Russia?"

"As far as we can tell, yes," Jeff said. "Now, if you'll please excuse me, I need to get my army back."

Jeff did his best to keep the fury out of his voice. "President Thayer. Please tell me why my troops are abandoning the war."

Over the radio, the Mormon president's voice warbled, "I understand we lost over three hundred men outside of St. George?" Jeff stood by the ham radio array inside the local sheriff's station.

"Affirmative," Jeff replied.

"And was there a massacre of civilians in Cedar City in retaliation for an act of sabotage?"

"We believe so," Jeff answered.

There was a long pause. Jeff began to wonder if they'd lost the connection.

"Our LDS militia officers report some troubling…authority issues with your command, General Kirkham."

Jeff spat, "What the hell does that mean?" He inhaled. The words had flown out before he could stop them. Nobody spoke to a Mormon prophet like that.

"I apologize, General Kirkham," President Thayer said in a measured tone. "I should've put more thought into how I made that statement. Forgive me."

Blood rushed to Jeff's face. It wasn't the Mormon who should be asking forgiveness. If Jeff's father had heard him say what he'd just said to the LDS president, he would've beat Jeff's ass.

"Sir," Jeff spoke into the mic. "Are the officers having an issue with my leadership?" These were uncharted waters for Jeff. He'd never operated in an army where the soldiers could leave when they got their panties in a wad.

"Our men fight under the banner of God, General. Some feel that a certain…darkness…has crept into your command. You're aware that our people are sensitive to how *Heavenly Father* feels about our cause. If *He* is with us, we will prevail. If His spirit departs, then we will be defeated."

Jeff blurted, "And God's cool with whatever heinous torture befalls Utah?" It came out more harsh than Jeff would've liked, but he could scarcely check his anger. He'd sacrificed everything, left his family undefended, to be here fighting the cartel and protecting the Mormon homeland. Now those same people were pissing and moaning about his lack of a sunny disposition?

Thayer continued with perfect calm, as though Jeff were speaking to him like a professional, even though he wasn't. "God allows our freedom to be taken when we lose sight of Him. Yes. You've read the Bible, General Kirkham. That's how it works."

It was a subtle rebuke, but powerful. The Old Testament of the Bible was, essentially, the story of the Jews bailing on God, then getting their asses handed to them, then returning to humility. The Mormon's book was basically the same plot, in a different place. Thayer was telling Jeff that Mormons would pull back if he didn't clean up his act.

Jeff had no idea what that even meant. He was fighting a war. How was he supposed to kick ass without bringing the hate?

"Wait until they're under the boot of a homicidal drug lord. Then they'll know real evil," Jeff spat. "Let's see how your guys feel when their kids are being chopped up and sacrificed on pagan altars."

The radio went silent for several seconds. Then Thayer spoke. His tone gathered steel. "General Kirkham. Your enmity is driven by personal loss, and we grieve with you. You've lost friends and your family is in jeopardy. But the Lord doesn't choose the least wicked man in a struggle to lend him His hand. He strengthens the righteous, and that is all. Repent, Brother Kirkham, and be humbled." Jeff could scarcely believe what he'd just heard. "When is the last time you prayed?" the Mormon asked.

Jeff had spent his entire childhood in their church. His ear was attenuated to the words of President Thayer, but in his mind, it was galling gibberish. Wars were won by resolute armies, not by the fiat of some bearded dude in the clouds. Wars were not won by praying.

"Fine. I repent," Jeff said. "Would you please tell your guys that they need to resume their posts?"

"I can't do that," Thayer answered. "I'm not a politician. I'm a spiritual leader."

"Lead your people then, and order them to defend themselves. Either that or you're going to have a shitload of dead Mormons on your hands." Jeff knew, simultaneously, that he was right and that he was digging a deeper hole for himself. This was not how one spoke to a Mormon bigwig.

President Thayer responded with a sigh. "I'm sorry, General. I will not order them to fight. If I start down that path, I'll be the next tyrant you must dislodge. I will encourage them to stay, to call upon you to repent, and to pray for God to restore this army to the banner of goodwill and righteousness."

"Oh, spare me," Jeff said without keying the mic.

After a few moments, Thayer added, "I don't know what else to say, General."

"That'll do sir. Please talk to your men. Kirkham out."

The radioman shuffled back into the tent, acting as though he hadn't heard the whole, embarrassing conversation.

Jeff's radioman was a Mormon. Word of the rocky conversation with their prophet would circulate. Trust would be further eroded. Cowardice would masquerade as righteous indignation. More men would abandon the fight and go home.

Jeff needed to get his family back. He needed Tara.

He hadn't heard from her since Ross took down the Homestead. Thayer said she was okay and that the boys were fine. But they were being held ransom by a petty dictator and it ground under Jeff's saddle like a fistful of metal shavings.

He was losing the war. *War was work,* he often said. But war was people, too. Morale won wars as often as superior weaponry, and Jeff wasn't good at convincing people. He felt surrounded by strangers, betrayed by friends, and far, far from his wife. Not even on deployment had he ever felt so alone.

9

"Decades would pass before the truth about the Black Autumn flu virus was fully known. On a distant fringe of America, surrounded by the blue depths of the Pacific, Hawaii bore the terrible burden of that knowledge. The Chinese navy had infected Hawaii with the first weaponized version of the plague in order to cripple the American military response. The island natives who'd survived the virus rose up, and for four years after brought ferocious retribution against the invader."

— THE AMERICAN DARK AGES, BY WILLIAM BELLAHER, NORTH AMERICAN TEXTBOOKS, 2037

Interstate 80
Evanston, Wyoming

MAT'S VISION HAD WORSENED BY THE TIME HE AND GABRIEL CROSSED the Utah border at Evanston. He couldn't see anything in the center region of his right eye and his left eye was only maybe thirty percent better. If he swayed his head from side-to-side, like Stevie Wonder, he could see well enough out of his peripheral vision to keep from tripping over dead stuff on the ground, which was good, because these days, there was a lot of that.

He saw enough of the roadblock at the state line to be impressed. It was the first sign of government he'd seen since leaving Sheriff Morgan in McKenzie, Tennessee. At the Wyoming/Utah border, there were Humvees and soldiers in camouflage, and the camo actually matched. They climbed down out of Mat's truck and approached the roadblock on foot.

"Sergeant Gabriel Peña, Utah Militia," Mat's traveling companion snapped a salute at the border guards. "Returning with intel for General Kirkham."

"Welcome home, Sergeant," one of the men shook his hand. He turned and considered Mat.

Mat had to remind himself: he might be as blind as a bucket of goat piss, but he resembled an operator. He wore a chest rig bursting with mags, carried a Gucci AR-15 with a thousand dollar EOTech sight, and he stood ramrod straight like a career soldier. The fact that he was legally blind was invisible to everyone but him.

"This is Army Ranger Mat Best," Sergeant Peña announced him to the men. "He's with me."

"Roger that, Sergeant," the ranking guard replied.

"How's the war going, Corporal?" Gabriel asked.

The guard pursed his lips, held his hand out, and rocked it back and forth. "Win some, lose some. The Hoodies massacred a bunch of civvies at Cedar City in retaliation for blowing up their fuel depot. We still hit their supply lines regularly, and we lose a lot of men and trucks to Abrams tanks. We're holding them in Cedar, so that's good for now."

Mat didn't like the sound of it. Enlisted men were the last to get the memo when their side was losing. If they weren't pumped up and breathing fire, things were definitely not going well.

"We'll be proceeding directly to the front," Gabriel said to the guards. "Do you know where General Kirkham's headquartering?"

"Last I heard," the soldier thought out loud, "they were in Nephi. They might've gotten pushed back since then."

Gabriel and Mat said their goodbyes and climbed into the Raptor.

"That didn't sound encouraging," Mat said.

"No, it didn't. I was hoping Jeff would've figured out some trick to kill their tanks by now."

"You know him as 'Jeff?' Not 'General Kirkham?' "

"The general and I spent a few weeks together in a recovery room last fall." Gabriel chuckled. "That was before he was a general, right after the war with the Latinos."

"Latinos?" Mat squinted. "Sorry, but you look about as Latino as they come."

"I was on the other side for that one."

"And they rendered medical aid?" Mat asked.

"It's a long story. Ross' daughter did surgery on me and the Homestead sort of adopted me. Like a lost puppy with a broken leg."

"Emily, right? I trained her on weapons systems back when she was in med school."

"Trained her to do what?" By the tone of his voice, Mat had Gabriel's full attention.

"I taught her to shoot. How's she doing?"

Gabriel cocked his head, paused, and then started the truck with a rumble. It covered whatever weirdness was going on with him.

Soon, they rolled through the roadblock. Gabriel waved at the guards, then answered. "I'm sorry, but she passed away last winter."

"What?" Mat startled. Many had died, but the daughter of a guy who was as prepared as Ross shouldn't have been one of them. "Was she KIA?"

"No," Gabriel's voice gathered itself. Then he steadied. "She died from the flu." Mat could hear it in Gabriel's voice that she'd meant something to him.

"Mother fu—" Mat mumbled. "I'm sorry. She was a good one."

"She's the one who shot me and put me in the hospital, so I guess I have you to thank for that, too."

"You attacked their homestead and she shot you?" Mat couldn't imagine Gabriel on the wrong side of a fight.

Gabriel made a hand motion that Mat couldn't distinguish. "It's a long story. But essentially, yes."

They drove under a huge sign on the side of the freeway that said, *FIREWORKS. Pyro City. 50% to 60% off EVERYTHING.* Mat could barely make out the words if he rolled the sign around in his peripheral vision.

Apparently, Utahns once drove across the border to buy illegal fireworks, then smuggled them back in their underpants. Mat's mind turned to what he could've done with explosives back in McKenzie. Then he remembered the anthrax and mustard gas. He wondered how William, Candace, and Gladys were managing without him. He missed them—more than he thought he would. He hoped they were safe. Good memories mingled with the horror of people dying in muddy fields of hay stubble. As much terror as he'd experienced in McKenzie, it felt like home. Santa Barbara seemed like a pipe dream. His parents were ghosts from another lifetime.

"I hope Emily made good shots on you, then. When you're fighting for the bad guys, whatever happens next is on you."

"Word," Gabriel Peña agreed. "In my defense, I was fighting for family."

Mat nodded. He'd been on both sides of that equation. It got a lot more complicated when the fight was on home turf. When he factored the flag out of the equation, war was a black tar booger stuck to three fingers at once. You couldn't shake that baby free without getting it on your shirt and maybe in your eye. At least, as a badass operator...

Mat's mind quieted. If this eyesight thing didn't get better, he was nobody's operator, not anymore. When he looked through his EOTech sight, what he saw looked like a watercolor painted by a three-year-old.

"I'm sorry to ask," Gabriel said as they gained speed on the open road. The chunky tires of the Raptor picked up a low yowl as they rolled down the interstate. "Would you mind if we head directly to Nephi? I should report to General Kirkham as soon as possible. Our intel might effect decisions on the front line."

Mat waved him on down the road. "You're good. I don't even really know anyone in Salt Lake other than Emily." It wasn't the right way to say it.

"Thanks. We can cut through Heber and down Provo Canyon. It'll shave a couple of hours off our drive time."

Mat considered their "intel." The Sinclair refinery had been sabotaged, wiped out by one of the forces that'd come through. But the natural gas and crude pipelines looked intact. With the power grid down, they'd stopped pumping. If the powers that be in Salt Lake wanted to restore oil and natural gas to their refinery, it'd take a couple of months of generating supplemental power, opening valves and flipping switches. After that, Salt Lake might be the energy hub of the Western United States, or what was left of it.

Mat liked Gabriel. He was a good kid, and seemed to be a squared-away soldier. Mat couldn't allow himself, or his little eye problem, to be the reason Gabe shirked orders. Finding an eye doctor, if such a person even existed in Salt Lake City, would have to wait.

So Mat was on his way back to a war zone. This time, he was a cripple. He'd meet other warriors, this time as a broken has-been. They'd show him deference, just like he'd shown deference to blown-up, messed-up vets. They'd honor him as one of their own, but it would be different. He'd have all the same patches, but none of the ability. He'd be a gunfighter in name only. Mat was not looking forward to hearing the over-played consideration in their voices, like when a civilian said, "thank you for your service." From another warrior, it'd be like "thank you for being the guy who got fragged instead of me."

He'd get a spot around the campfire, and they'd still pass him the bottle, but when the real men went to battle, he'd be back in a tent somewhere, yanking on his baby maker.

For the first time in his life, Mat thought about offing himself. He wasn't serious, and he didn't dwell on it, but the thought came through clear as spring water: *if I'm not an operator, why am I even alive?*

Mat rubbed his face. He'd pitied the wounded warriors, even talked a few of them down from eating a gun barrel. He didn't think for a second he'd ever be *that guy*. Now, after a week of blurry vision, he already tasted the gun oil.

Everywhere Mat looked in his life, there were dead end roads. There was probably nothing for him in Santa Barbara but a burned-out house. He'd be useless to the war in Utah, and back in McKenzie, he was a liability, even before he lost his sight. There wasn't anywhere or any way he could create value, and without that, maybe a 9mm for breakfast would be best.

Mat had been silent for ten miles of blacktop. The open country of Wyoming descended into a tight canyon, with towering mountains on both sides of the freeway. There were dead cars on the eastbound side, Utahns, now long gone, who fled Salt Lake City into the badlands of Wyoming, and who hadn't made it more than halfway there before their gas tanks ran dry. Those cars had wintered here, and the personal belongings from the cast-open car doors and gaping trunks had long ago blown away. The deteriorating husks of vehicles would be the gravestones of refugee families. Their decaying bodies lay somewhere along the embankments. They were food for bacteria and fertilizer for the spring grasses.

Gabriel was wise enough to leave Mat to his thoughts.

Mat's vision problem wouldn't be obvious to the warriors he'd soon face. Mat needed to come up with a tight-and-tidy way of explaining that he wasn't battle ready, something that'd make this sound temporary, but that wouldn't mark him as a pansy. He didn't want to waste a bunch of time describing it, like an old man who had nothing better to discuss than his ailments.

He considered stripping off his battle rattle, his rifle and his gun belt, and leaving it all in the truck, but the question would remain: was he a soldier or not?

That's a damn good question, Mat thought.

With the vexing, circular thoughts, and the strain on his eyes, Mat drifted to sleep to the rumble of his truck's tires and the phantom taste of metal in his mouth.

―――

Jenna Ross had goat shit all over her hands and the sleeves of her coat. Maybelline had just taken a literal shit on her in protest of having her hooves trimmed. Just another day at the Homestead.

"Does this look a little watery to you?" she asked Jacqueline Reynolds, showing her the shit on her jacket.

Jacqueline barked a laugh. "It looks a little gross to me. But I think she's fine. You want me to finish her while you clean yourself up?"

Jenna shrugged. "I got this. Goat shit is sterile, right?" The ladies chuckled: Jenna, Jacqueline, Tara Kirkham, and Toshie Brooks. It was goat checkup day, as it was every six weeks, —and they all knew goat shit wasn't remotely sterile. Goat diseases transferred easily to humans, and the ladies sprayed disinfectant on their hands at every step of the process. They wore latex gloves up to the elbows.

Nobody messed around with pathogens these days. Not after what they'd gone through over the winter. Antibiotics were rare, when they worked at all.

Tara Kirkham had come out of hiding for "Goat Day." The four ladies made a minor tradition out of hoof trimming, pregnancy checking, and medically examining their beloved goat herd. Despite the threat Jason Ross and the Russians posed to the Kirkham family, Tara had come out of her suite on the far side of the Homestead "Big House" to care for the goats and get some fresh air. The Kirkham boys squealed and played with the other children, climbing the goat hurdles and chasing the goats around the new enclosure. Their favorite game was to get a fainting goat to keel over, a difficult feat, since the goats were having as much fun as the kids.

The ladies had chosen to bide their time with Tara's imprisonment. Jason Ross denied that the Kirkham family was being held captive. There was no guard in front of their suite nor were they restrained. But when Tara Kirkham and her boys attempted to leave the gates, they were always turned back on one pretext or another. It'd been a month since Jason Ross had seized control. Tara and her boys hadn't stepped foot outside the wall in all that time.

Jenna finished trimming Maybelline's hooves, disinfected the trimmers, doused her gloves in disinfectant, and moved forward on the examination stand to check the color of the eye membrane. Tara held the goat's neck and caressed her head while Jenna worked.

Jenna spoke in a low voice. "How're you holding up?"

Tara shrugged. "I don't think we're being watched anymore. But they still won't let us leave. The gate guard claims that we can't take supplies until everything's been inventoried and assessed."

"What were you carrying?" Jenna asked.

"Just our personal bags. No weapons or ammo. No med

supplies. The guard didn't even look in our backpacks. He just wouldn't let us through."

Jenna nodded. "I think Jason's afraid that Jeff will attack the Homestead if you're not inside."

"He might," Tara laughed. "I can only imagine how pissed he is right now. He doesn't do well without us."

Such a strange thing for her to say, but so common. Jeff was the general of an army, an experienced warrior. But he was vulnerable without the steadying voice of his wife and the calming prattle of his children. It made Jenna think of Jason, alone in the Homestead office, surrounded by people, but making decisions from a rusting, steel cage of isolation. It wasn't healthy for him, nor for the Homestead. It was how tyrants were made—lone men, unchecked by bustling family and female companionship.

The Russian men seemed to know this better than the Americans, which explained why they were so relentless in seeking female companionship among the single ladies of the compound. It wasn't just sex. It was the compulsion to stabilize, to rope themselves to family, and to pin themselves down to something that mattered for the long-term.

Jenna gently pressed on Maybelline's eyeball and examined the color of the flesh under her lower eyelid. It was glowing dark red, which was good, healthy.

"My Maybelline. Why can't you be true? My Maybelline. Why can't you be true. You done started back doing the things you want to do," Jenna sang in the goat's ear.

Tara laughed. All the female goats were named after women from classic rock songs. Jenna sang to each one before releasing them from the trimming stand. She butchered the lyrics, but she didn't care. Butchering lyrics was one of her things.

"Doing the things you *used* to do," Tara corrected her.

Jenna shrugged and grinned. "You have your way and I have mine."

"And Chuck Berry had his way," Tara joked.

"That's Chuck Berry?" Jenna asked as she lifted Maybelline down from the stand. She showed the goat back into the enclosure and swatted her on the rump. "I thought it was Social Distortion."

"Maybe it was. And maybe they made up their own lyrics when they sang it," Tara said.

The other ladies laughed as they shuffled a new goat down the chute and up onto the trimming stand.

"Is this Sarah Smiles?" Jenna asked. "Or Barbara Ann?"

She didn't wait for an answer. Jenna sang the Hall and Oates song, "It's you and me, together. Sarah Smi-iles. Come on and smile a while with me, Sarah."

"Oh Lord," Tara said. "Where do I even start with that mess?"

"*Hmpf*," Jenna smirked and repeated herself. "You have your lyrics and I have mine."

"I'm worried about Jeff," Tara said. "This isn't a deployment. He's not going to be in a headspace to make good decisions until he knows we're okay."

"I told President Thayer that you're fine," Jenna said. "He promised he'd get word to your husband."

"Jeff won't take that as gospel. He'll tear himself up with worry. I can *feel* him going dark."

Jenna nodded and the other girls quieted. Jenna understood what Tara meant. Jenna still sensed Jason's moods too, and his fears, even while separated by time, space, and Jason's awful choices.

The four ladies were the kind of women who mated for life, and it carried a twining of fates, an indelible tie, bound up in sex, family and God. It was a tenacious link, not easily broken, and it disregarded the politics of man. It was proof that this life was a fragment of a galaxy-spanning mansion of the soul. The tie was magic, supernatural. The same link across time and space shouted in Jenna's heart that Sage, Tristan, and Tessa were still alive, and it promised that Emily watched over them, and fretted over them from another realm. There was more to this life than the apocalypse. Taut strands between souls bound loved ones together.

"We need to get you out of here, Tara," Jenna concluded. "It's worth the risk."

Jacqueline Reynolds stepped up to Sarah Smiles and patted her flank. She whispered, "Ivan will do it for me. He commands the gate watch."

Major Kvashnin and Jacqueline were coming close to tying the knot. Jacqueline had lost her Tommy in the wars the previous fall, but the universe was making it up to her, little by little. Ivan Kvashnin was a good man, and the two of them would cobble together a beautiful family in the wake of all this heartbreak.

"We should be careful, then," Jenna said as she examined Sarah Smile's rear end. "If we make a mistake, they'll post a guard on Tara's suite."

"Where should we go once we're outside?" Tara asked. Her own family was presumed dead.

"President Thayer will find a place for you to wait for Jeff's return," Jacqueline said. "I'll talk to him when we meet tomorrow." As the pastor of the Homestead, Jacqueline was part of the Mormons' weekly meeting.

Jenna began trimming the front hoof. "It's settled then. I'll put together go bags for you and the boys. I'll bring them to your suite in three days."

Tara nodded. "Thank you," she sniffled. "I've never had sisters like you before."

Jenna's eyes brimmed. "Of course. We're family."

―――

JASON WASN'T sure if he could trust Zhukov. For one thing, he couldn't tell how far Jenna had her hooks into him. Their little coffee thing seemed to be limited to just that: coffee and friendship.

But in a flutter of eyelids and the pressing of bodies, Jenna might turn on the heat and Jason could lose his Spetsnaz. In a split-second of perfectly-choreographed passion, Jenna could take everything Jason had worked so hard to get back.

It'd been raining for two days when one of the old Homesteaders told Jason that the chickens had broken into the north slope paddock. The perennial greens in that area were coming on late because the hillside faced north and the snow had retreated later than the rest. The shoots were small and tender and the chickens could do serious damage to the eventual harvest. It was easier for Jason to head out and take care of the problem than to explain it to a Spetsnaz enlisted man.

In any case, he loved mornings on the Homestead. His beat-up Polaris Ranger already had his tools in the back, a brimming toolbox, a chainsaw, a sharpening kit, and several five-gallon buckets filled with the hardware from the latest fencing job. Despite the downcast glances from old Homesteaders, many of whom had betrayed him personally, Jason saw a few friendly faces as he roared around behind the Great Lawn, up the orchard hill to the North Slope orchard. Most of the friendlies were Russian but some of the old Homestead people had eventually welcomed him back.

He had to remind himself: he wasn't the villain his ex-wife or Jeff Kirkham made him out to be. This was his home, legally and morally, and he deserved to occupy it.

But it was hard to hold conflict in his heart with the smell of wet sod and fresh growth filling his nostrils. The powerful engine growled under his haunches and sang the song of honest work. Jason had dug the swales on these slopes with his own hands. He'd cut the post holes with his power auger. He'd strung fence and pruned the trees. This place was *his*, in more ways than deed and title. He'd started ten years before with a desolate pipeline easement across three hundred acres of mountainside and turned it into a dozen acre, edible forest, a hundred and fifty-tree orchard, and a perennial garden where bio-diverse topsoil reached down a full yard. He'd turned dead clay into worm-riven, black soil that crumbled merrily in his hands. After almost a decade of webbing bio-complementary trees, shrubs and herbaceous perennials together, and after stacking feet of decomposing wood chip over every square foot of arable space, the Homestead greeted the first spring of the apocalypse like a cornucopia of calories. Everything, including the nascent plants and churning life-web of soil, had been "baked into" his survival plan.

It was a good thing, because the place carried more human souls, by a factor of five, than he ever anticipated. They needed every apple tree, hazelnut bush, currant shrub, asparagus sprout, and sweetvetch herb to produce at maximum potential or the Homestead would go hungry in the winter. However packed with plenty the Homestead might be, the food situation was dire.

Jason passed a disgruntled Homesteader, a compatriot of Jeff Kirkham's. Jason raised a hand in a morning hello and the guy stared at the roadbed.

They didn't have time for this bullshit. The plants and animals demanded everyone's full attention. They didn't have the luxury of wasting calories on grudges and infighting. Humans really were fools. For every calorie spent planting seed or tending livestock, they wasted two calories competing with one another. With the wet wind in his hair and the morning sun just cracking through the maples, Jason couldn't remember why they did it. Why *he* did it.

He came over the rise. The pole barn jutted from the hill like a Viking longhouse, mighty and stout. He brought the OHV to a stop and shielded his eyes into the fresh sun, searching for the break in the fence the chickens had exploited.

Jason's ex-wife stood up straight from behind a clump of black currant and looked toward the sudden arrival of the machine. She carried a garden hod in one hand and a pair of pruning scissors in the other. She'd been foraging from his food forest, and clipping back spent limbs as she went. Years before, Jason had planted that currant field and seeded the mushrooms beneath. He'd knelt in the same ground and poked the tender shoots of the onions through wet, cardboard weed barrier. He'd sown, where she now reaped. He and Jenna were two halves of a blessed cycle.

A flood of emotions stormed his heart. The garden hod, filled with wine cap mushrooms and nodding onions. Her elegant form. The lamb skin gloves on her delicate hands. Her auburn hair, lilting in the breeze. The elegant curves of the fencing. The proud, leafing stands of elderberry along the sweep of the road. Her high cheeks, and the crow's feet just forming at the corner of her eyes, printed by a hundred thousand flashes of shared laughter.

This was his. All of it, his.

Not a possession. He'd never possessed any of it. It would remain long after his body decayed into the soil. Yet, it belonged to him and he belonged to it. They had co-created one another, the land, the soil, the plants, and trees.

The woman.

The hod hung on a crook in her arm, bursting with mushrooms. The wine caps erupted everywhere in this paddock where moisture prevailed in the field. Jason had, by his own hand, sprinkled the spores under the apples and pears, cherries and walnut. He sowed them many years before and Jenna now reaped the fruit of his labor. It washed over him like a sweet and succulent validation of his life. His eyes brimmed, and the tears barely held.

If he had died in the wars of the last half-year, this would've remained. His wife and friends would eat from his handiwork, still. Across these acres, in a way, he would live for centuries.

Jenna must've recognized him because she lowered herself back to the wood chip piled between the currant bushes and resumed harvesting. She twisted the wine caps up and away, as he'd taught her to do. Her hands were careful not to disturb the mycelia underneath, the living web that produced the fleshy, earthy, bounty.

She loved this land as much as he. Perhaps they belonged to one another too, this place and Jenna. He'd been a damned fool to think he could exile her from it. For the life of him, Jason could not recall why he would try to send her away.

She knew she was being watched now, but it changed nothing. Women bore domination more gracefully than men, Jason realized. Under the yoke of dominion, she bowed her back, faced Mother Earth and collected her bounty. If Jenna gave him any thought—her oppressor—it was only to plot the return of peace.

He realized the truth like a thunderclap: she'd been right all along. Right to save the orphan refugees. Right to stand with Jeff Kirkham. Righteous and patient, even against the torrent of his rage. Even in the drowning grief of the loss of their daughter, she had been a woman of peace.

With two fingers, Jenna swept back a lock of hair that'd escaped her ponytail. Her garden hods were full. She straightened and massaged her lower back with one, fine-fingered hand. She collected the hods and picked her way across the swales that were full of water after the rains of the last two days, and approached the OHV.

She held up a hod. "The fruit of your labor."

"I don't mind," he said.

"You used to call yourself 'the beast of burden,' " she reminded him.

"I wasn't complaining. It was a good gig."

She cocked her head. "When did it end? I don't remember firing you."

"I guess it ended when I left," he said. Hope rose in his belly, like the first stirrings of hunger.

"I made a vow," she said. "That's forever. The day to day may get a little wobbly. The other stuff might go away. But when I give my word, it's written in stone."

He didn't know what to say. "Is Colonel Zhukov aware of that?" Jason asked.

"Yes, he is."

Jenna had used just a handful of words, yet Jason's universe tilted on its axis. He swallowed hard against the knot in his throat.

"However," she lifted an eyebrow, "if you're screwing that Beringer woman, then it truly is over."

"I'm not," he blurted. "I mean, I haven't." He leaned against the steering wheel.

She plucked a particularly beautiful wine cap mushroom, reached over the passenger side door of the OHV and set it on the seat next to him.

"Well, then. Mr. Ross. Have a good morning." She turned and walked the foot path toward the kitchen shed.

Jason watched her go. Her hips glided in her jeans, as she disappeared into the forest.

"Damn," he whispered. He felt like a teenager.

He picked up the mushroom and smelled it, redolent of cut grass and perfectly-cooked seafood. So often, on the little farm, he found himself at the intersection of time, soil, and life-force energy. The aroma of the fungus, and the woman's fingers that'd lately touched it, wrapped him in a strange vortex, pregnant with meaning and bursting with *rightness*.

Suddenly, the reality of Jeff Kirkham intruded. At any moment, his war machine could pummel the Homestead with explosives and fierce men would trample the mushrooms underfoot. Jason would be driven out, again.

He shook his head, and forced himself to see her manipulation for what it was. Her seductive magic and the sweet rhythms of grass and field could carry him away to defeat. It was what she'd intended.

He had to be smarter than that.

Yet, as he continued down the north orchard road, unpacked his tools, and repaired the tear in the livestock fence, Jason smiled. Hope, like the spore of the wine cap, was nothing if not tenacious. Life begat life.

What vows had he made? Jason tried to remember.

———

"MAT," Gabriel Peña shouted and waved him to the Ford Raptor. "We need to go!"

Mat hustled toward his truck. "What's going on?"

They were in the parking lot of the Nephi Sheriff's office, the temporary headquarters of the Utah Militia. Mat had been introduced to General Kirkham, then ushered out while things heated up in the head shed. New, urgent intel had arrived, and nobody knew Mat well enough to have him around while they hashed it out.

"The cartel's moving, and we're displacing north. Gotta go," the kid said as he hopped into the driver's seat.

Mat climbed into the passenger side and slid onto the leather seat. He arranged his rifle between his legs. "The cartel is moving where?"

"Advancing," Gabriel said. "We don't want to be here when the tanks arrive."

"Where are they advancing to?" Mat asked. He didn't know Utah, but the map seemed pretty simple. Bounded by the Wasatch Mountains on one side and the vast desert on the other, the cartel could either go north or go south.

"They're going wherever they damn well please," Gabe said with his face scrunched up in worry—Mat imagined, without actually seeing. "We've got nothing that'll stop them. We're hoping they're low on fuel."

"Hoping?" Mat didn't like it. The M1 Abrams was practically unstoppable without aircraft built for that purpose. There were ground weapons that could hypothetically stop a tank, but the reactive armor on the Abrams, along with their god-like offensive weapons, made them very difficult to kill. The Abrams had invincibility honed to a fine art. If this thrown-together militia was *hoping* to stop tanks with machine guns bolted to pickup trucks, Mat didn't need a West Point education to predict the outcome. They'd get their asses kicked.

"Where are we making our stand?" Mat asked. There had to be some kind of plan.

"Um," Gabriel hesitated. "We're falling back to the Alamo. All we've got left is fighting them on our front porch in Salt Lake. We're slinging rocks at Goliath."

"Are you shitting me? You're in full retreat?" Mat asked. This might've been a bad time to join this militia, particularly for a blind man.

"Ha!" Gabe barked a laugh. "I'm in full retreat, Ray Charles, and you go where I go."

10

"You can run on for a long time
Run on for a long time
Run on for a long time
Sooner or later God'll cut you down
Sooner or later God'll cut you down."

—God's Gonna Cut You Down, Johnny Cash

Cedar City, Utah

The diesel fumes ruined Bill's morning ritual, but there was no hope, this morning, that he'd feel okay about anything. Not after the massacre of men, women, and children that he'd witnessed.

Eighty Abrams tanks fired up at once, then pulled a quarter-mile forward on Interstate 15 to organize into formation. A few stayed behind, struggling to start. Mechanics' vans raced to the stragglers.

Bill cranked up his music to drown out the tanks, but his old-school, foam headphones didn't cover the growl of the war machines. It didn't matter. Bill knew the words of the song by heart. He knew everything by Johnny Cash by heart.

Go tell that long tongue liar
Go and tell that midnight rider
Tell the rambler, the gambler, the back biter
Tell 'em that God's gonna cut 'em down

Bill was that long-tongue liar. *He* was that midnight rider. He was the man in black, the darkest stain of sinner. He stood up for the scythe of God, dried out and ramrod straight like the last-standing wheat of a stubble field. Old Bill was in the deep shit now.

Well you may throw your rock and hide your hand
Workin' in the dark against your fellow man
But as sure as God made black and white
What's done in the dark will be brought to the light.

The massacre at the Mormon temple obliterated all doubt in his mind. Bill was fighting for the bad guys, the chittering fiends, the gnawing chupacabras that preyed on children and devoured pregnant mothers. The cartel army wasn't an army. It was horror incarnate.

Bill could do the right thing, *right now*. He could escape and become another shooter for the partisan militia. Or...he could bide his time, keep false counsel with Castillo. He could wait for a pivotal moment and turncoat to flip this war upside down.

Bill's titanic force of will battled with his eternal soul. What he *wanted* wrestled against what was *right*. The roar of the tanks fought the music in his ears. The gravel-washed voice of Johnny Cash weighed in again.

God spoke to me in the voice so sweet

I thought I heard the shuffle of the angel's feet
He called my name and my heart stood still
When he said, "Bill, go do my will!"

The argument in his mind drowned out the music: he was worth more in the cartel inner circle than he was with the militia. He could rebuild Castillo's trust, convince him against all common sense that Bill was a loyal commander for the cartel. If Castillo hadn't put him to the sword yet, then he must *want* to believe that Bill could be useful. Bill could reinforce that belief, achieve victories for the cartel. It was the same game he'd been playing from the start. *Both ends against the middle.* It was right where he liked to be.

But advancing the tanks without a fuel reserve was nuts. Castillo was making a big mistake. They didn't have the fuel to maneuver and the Utah Militia was definitely going to force them to maneuver. Today they were making a run for Salt Lake City, and if Bill's intel was wrong, if Kirkham blew the refinery early, then the jig was up. Game over.

Bill had assured Castillo that the partisan militia wouldn't destroy the Salt Lake refinery so long as their tanks didn't cross the I-215 belt route that bisected Salt Lake City. Hafer and Wade, their highest-ranking prisoners, both said as much, that General Kirkham would have his men destroy the refinery with mortars if tanks came too close. Bill hoped that hadn't changed in the last two weeks. But even if the partisans didn't blow the refinery, running all the way to Salt Lake would dangle the Abrams at the end of a weakened supply line. It was an all-or-nothing gambit.

"Keep your eye on the prize," Bill told himself as he clicked off the music on his headphones and climbed into his Toyota Land Cruiser.

The dead Sunday School teachers in Cedar City weren't going to come back to life because of Bill's guilt. It served no purpose other than to slow him down. The game plan was the same either way, serve Castillo, bide his time, look for opportunity, and land on the winning side. He had to stop thinking about those murdered people. Nothing he could do would make them any less dead.

This is American soil, the hag in his head bitched. *We don't help drug dealers.*

He tried to see himself on the porch of a hewn-log ranch house, five years later, overlooking a pond where grandchildren played and cattle romped. He felt his old, weather-beaten hands, folded in his lap, tucked under a blanket. He pulled them out to see why they felt sticky. They were covered in blood.

Tsk, tsk, tsk, the hag in his head sounded a lot like his mother. *You know better, Billy. You're an American. The Lord blessed you to be born here, now you're acting like an evil foreigner.* It was definitely his mother, a nag and a shameless racist. She had died when he was sixteen.

"You wait until now to come haunt me?" he spoke into the empty cockpit of his Cruiser.

It gave Bill an idea. He dug around on the floorboards and found an old receipt for a truckload of straw, back from his days as a dirt rancher. He tore off the bottom quarter and wrote a note.

"Noah Miller. We're out of gas by the time we reach the 215. Send Grandpa Joe with a gas can or we'll die out here. Billy."

To the casual eye, the note would look like another last-ditch scribble in a sea of post-apocalyptic desperation. To Noah, it'd be a tip of the hand, a wink of an eye. Maybe his son's militia buddies could use the information to harass the cartel.

McCallisters do right. That's who we are, his mother chirruped in his ear.

"*I know. That's why I'm sending the damned note, Ma,*" he grumbled.

Bill cranked the engine, then U-turned down the on-ramp of the I-15. He drove to La Quinta Inn where his men were packing up captives to move them up to the front.

"Abuelo," Bill called to his right-hand man. Abuelo had a low-ranking prisoner by the arm.

"Gimme that guy," he pointed to the foot soldier in Abuelo's custody, now a half-tortured wreck. "I gotta have some fun too," Bill said.

Abuelo folded the flex-cuffed man into the front seat of the Land Cruiser.

"I'll meetcha in Spanish Fork," Bill hollered over the rumble of the motor.

Abuelo nodded and went back inside for another prisoner. Bill punched the gas and took off north to catch up with the rolling army.

After a couple of hours rumbling along behind the column of tanks at seventeen miles per hour, the absolute sweet spot for Abrams fuel efficiency, Bill peeled off at a small town exit. The prisoner said nothing the whole time, too terrified to even beg for his life. Bill was uncharacteristically quiet, too vexed by the nagging ghosts of his guilt to start a conversation that'd inevitably loop around to how the man had been tortured.

The Cruiser threaded a string of unimpressive mountains and bore west around the southern wetlands of Utah Lake. They came upon the half-starved town of Goshen. Bill pulled over at the outskirts. He dug around in his fatigue pockets and produced the note.

"This is for Noah Miller. If Noah Miller isn't there, give it to General Kirkham. Got it?"

The prisoner nodded. Bill stuffed the note in his front, pants pocket.

Bill popped the Cruiser in drive and rolled down the street until he found a driveway with a truck that looked to be in working order. He barreled up the gravel strip and slammed to a stop. The family tumbled out of the house. The father held a shotgun.

Bill reached across the flex-cuffed prisoner, opened the passenger side door and kicked him onto the lawn.

"Yo," Bill shouted at the confused alfalfa farmer. "Take this man to militia command. He has urgent intel. Do it now."

The man didn't point the shotgun at Bill. He just swayed back and forth with hunger and uncertainty.

Bill shouted, "Wakey-wakey, Brother Gomer Pyle, git over there and help him up. He's been a prisoner of the Mexicans." Bill searched for something that sounded Mormon-like to spur the local-yokel to action. "Take this guy to your bishop and get him to militia command in Salt Lake City. He has information about the war."

"We got no gas," the man finally sputtered.

"Well, shit," Bill swore. He yanked the parking break and jumped down. He dug around behind the driver's seat and pulled a five-gallon gas can free from the mess in the back. "Here. That'll get you around Utah Lake and to the Army of Righteousness."

"But who are you?" The man pointed the butt stock of his shotgun at Bill.

"I'm a God-fearing Mormon," Bill lied. "Name's Brother Kurtz."

The man didn't look convinced, probably because of all the swearing, but Bill had no time to weave a better story. He needed to get back to the convoy before Castillo noticed he was missing.

"Go!" He did a two-handed shooing motion at the gaping man. "May the Lord be with you. *Via con Díos*. The holy, almighty church needs you."

The mention of the church got the hayseed moving. He put the shotgun against the steps, walked over and hefted the gas can. As Bill pulled away, the pilgrim wife was cutting the flex-cuffs off the prisoner and the husband was filling the truck with gas.

"Half-starved idiots," Bill said to himself. The family had probably resorted to eating alfalfa root. He gave it fifty-fifty odds the note would even reach Noah.

Salt Lake International Airport
Salt Lake City, Utah

"They've got to be running on fumes," Jeff Kirkham growled. He stood atop the air traffic control tower at the Salt Lake International Airport, surrounded by a few of his men. His hands were balled into granite fists. He pounded on the railing. "Stop, you bastards," he coaxed the Abrams tanks as they rolled through his hometown.

The Utah Militia had retreated across half the state. With more than half his Mormons AWOL, his thousand pickup trucks were now three hundred. The Abrams tanks had pushed from Cedar City to Salt Lake City in a single day. They barely paused to shoot back at the militia gun trucks.

Jeff snatched the mic from his radioman and broadcast to his mortar crews ringing the Maverick refinery. "Standby for fire mission," he barked. They confirmed.

It was the death of hope—the refinery was the last remnant of the industrial world for a thousand miles. Without the fuel in the Maverick refinery, they'd tumble back into the Stone Age.

Jeff had a clear view across the valley. Dozens of plumes of black smoke and feathery dust rose from behind the phalanx of tanks. It was late afternoon, mid-May, and light rains brushed at the mountain rims on the snow-fissured lips of the valley.

"What happens next?" his radioman asked with a tremble in his voice.

"We destroy the refineries," Jeff said. "And then we run, all the way to Idaho Falls."

The plumes behind the tanks shortened, then curled in on themselves. They stopped.

"All stations, hold fire," Jeff radioed the mortar teams. "Repeat, hold fire."

"Why're they stopping?" the radioman begged.

"They know we'll blow the refinery," he guessed. Jeff had been praying they'd stop, but now that they had, his mind rushed to redefine the battlefield.

Reports rolled in over the radio, from the foot of the ski resorts on the east to the towering smokestacks on the west. The tanks had stopped, and shuffled into a rough skirmish line across the valley.

"Sir!" Another radioman interrupted. He was the Intel man who monitored the cartel channels. "The cartel is calling for a full stop. They're setting security."

The dust strokes dissipated. The valley settled. A new feather of rain swept across what had once been South Jordan.

Jeff exhaled. "Stalingrad."

"Sir?" the radioman asked.

"It's like the siege of Stalingrad. Our back's up against the Volga river. They have us half-surrounded."

Jeff's army was hemorrhaging men. With the front line advanced to Salt Lake, his Mormon soldiers would flee *en masse* to defend their families behind enemy lines. Terror had returned to the Utah heartland. In a single day, what little safe harbor they'd achieved across the fields of Utah was gone.

Jeff turned his binoculars to the west desert and spoke to himself. "We're cut off from the Tooele Army Depot. Whatever ammo we've got, that's all we'll ever get."

"Stalingrad?" the radioman muttered under his breath.

Jeff hardened his posture. The clouds thickened across the setting sun. Without the sun to warm the sky, the rain would fall dark and cold. There would be sleet in the foothills. The Homestead, where Jeff's family was imprisoned, would get snow tonight. The promised summer, the end of the apocalypse, retreated behind curtains of icy rain.

The devil had stolen their promised peace. The darkening

across the valley foretold a forever winter. America might never be restored. Jeff might never see his family again.

Jeff shook himself. He tried vainly to cast off the pall of defeat, but the Abrams tanks still stood out in the dusk, like a pack of hyenas around the encampment, waiting for wood to run out and the fire to die. Jeff's army quaked against their failures. The terrifying math of starvation confronted them.

He spoke his doubts to no one in particular. "We're screwed if this drags out longer than a few weeks. We aren't laying up winter stores while we're fighting. The Hoodies may not know it, but they're starving us right now, though we won't die until January." It was a dimension of war Jeff had never considered before—eventual starvation. "If they push, we blow the refinery." Jeff said. "It's the only card left to play."

"Sir," the radioman interrupted. "The mortar teams request orders."

"Tell them to stand down and stay frosty. This could go either way." The observation deck atop the tower had slowly filled with men from his command staff. They'd been drawn by the gravity of their plight.

The light of the setting sun filtered through the storm clouds and cast an orange-gray pallor over them, a tableau of spent men, staring into defeat. Jeff had no words of encouragement. He had never experienced the frayed end of the rope, after which there was only free fall.

"We're on the knife's edge now, boys," Jeff said. "This is when weak men fold."

Even as he said it, Jeff felt only weariness. He prayed that sometime during the night, God Almighty would give him strength.

JENNA SLIPPED through the dark and silent halls of the Homestead. She padded barefoot across the stone floor. Her shoulders hung with backpacks, loaded with food, water, flashlights, and medical supplies.

It was two o'clock in the morning, and the night had renewed the chill of winter, as sometimes befell the mountains in the second half of May. That afternoon, cartel tanks were seen in the distance, tightening the noose around the refinery.

When the cartel came, the militia would come too, and with the militia would come Jeff Kirkham. The Russian defenses hardened against a counter-attack by General Kirkham. Tonight was perhaps the last chance Jenna would have to free Tara and her boys.

Jenna thrummed her fingers lightly on the door of the Kirkham suite. Someone inside rustled. Tara Kirkham cracked the door, and pointed a shiny, black gun barrel in Jenna's face.

"It's me. You have to go now," Jenna whispered.

The gun barrel withdrew and Tara pulled her inside.

"Jeff's back. He's retreated to Salt Lake City. You have to go right now." Jenna sloughed the heavy packs to the floor and caught them with her foot so they wouldn't clatter against the tile. "They'll tighten security in the morning."

"Where do we go?" Tara went to work in the small kitchen of the suite, pulling odds and ends of survival gear from a cabinet. She'd been ready to run. The boys were stacked like firewood in a small sleeper couch just off the kitchen. The older boys woke the smaller ones. Tara must've prepared them for escape.

"Thayer said the Mormons will harbor you until Jeff comes. Here's a map to Thayer's house." Jenna handed Tara a folded scrap of paper. "It's a mile and a half across the neighborhood. Let's go," she urged.

"Come on," Tara hurried the groggy boys. "You can brush your teeth when we get where we're going. Take your bags."

They pulled on boots, and slid out the door into the hall. They climbed down the marble stairs, slipped out the patio door, skirted the pool, and descended through the steep landscaping down to the main drive.

Ivan and Jacqueline waited for them at the wrought iron gate.

"Hurry," Ivan said. "The night patrol just came past. Go."

Tara threw her arms around Jenna, kissed her on the cheek, and did the same to Jacqueline, then Ivan.

"Goodbye," she whispered. The Kirkhams disappeared into the black streets of the neighborhood. Jenna exhaled. A light snow began to fall.

"Thank you, Ivan," Jenna said.

"Of course," he smiled in the dark. "How could I say no to such beautiful ladies?"

"When this comes to light tomorrow," Jenna said, "It's crucial that I take the blame. Are we agreed?" She sensed them nodding in the dark. "I'll tell Jason that I showed them out through a gap in the wall. Nobody needs to know they went out through the gate."

"What will Jason do to you?" Jacqueline asked.

Jenna patted her hair in the dark. "I don't know, but it's time he decides what he's going to be, a warlord or my husband. This is the only second chance he's going to get."

"Time to put up or shut up," Jacqueline agreed.

"Wow," Ivan Kvashnin said in a thick, Russian accent, "Viking ladies. Warriors."

Jacqueline chuckled. "When your watch ends, come to my tent. I'll show you some Viking love." She grabbed him by the tactical vest, yanked him close and kissed him on the mouth.

"Dah," he laughed. "I come straight home."

JASON ROSS AWOKE with his stomach in knots. He'd tossed and turned all night, waking at three a.m. to fret about the return of Jeff Kirkham.

Any dream of getting back with Jenna had been swept aside by the return of the Utah Militia. Once the battle lines settled, Kirkham would turn his attention to the Homestead. Jason faced facts: the Russians' loyalty dangled by a thread. The Homestead women had plucked at the ties that bound them to him. He didn't believe they would stand firm if Kirkham attacked.

He launched out of bed at the first blush of dawn and went looking for Zhukov. The Russian colonel was in the cook shed, helping the early crew brew coffee.

"Colonel," Jason whispered with urgency, and pulled the Russian away from the women and toward the office wing of the mansion. "Kirkham's militia is back. We must move now."

Zhukov smacked the coffee grinds off of his hands. "How?"

"If we don't take the refinery now, the cartel might get it first, and we'll lose our bargaining chip."

"Today?" Zhukov's eyes darted about. "Now?"

"Kirkham will reinforce the refinery today, or the cartel will capture it, or one of them will destroy it. Now might be our last chance."

"How do we overcome the militia garrison?" Zhukov asked as they crossed the cobblestone driveway.

Kirkham had left a security force, probably armed with explosives to destroy the fuel tanks if capture seemed imminent. Jason knew this because a week earlier, he'd sent two men to recon the defenses in and around the Maverick. They'd seen what appeared to be reserve soldiers, mixed in with the original, corporate security officers. But they weren't looking north.

With the cartel at their doorstep, Kirkham's army would be tightened to protect the fuel storage. Jason had thought about it all night; the momentary confusion would be his last window of opportunity.

"Blitzkrieg," he said to Zhukov. "We hit the Maverick now and hit it hard, from the unprotected side. Are the BMD-3s fueled and operational?" He steered the Russian officer along the office colonnade to the best view of the valley.

"Yes. Eleven of them."

"Then we strike through that neighborhood." Jason pointed to the housing tract at the north end of the refinery. The homes would give the Russian tanks cover. They'd appear out of nowhere, unexpected and unidentified. Unless the self-destruct bombs were prepositioned with electronic triggers, they would overtake the facility within minutes. It was unlikely Kirkham had given the security force authorization to blow the facility without his direct command. The Russians must overrun the facility before that could happen.

"Are you sure?" Zhukov balked.

"Take three hundred men and go. Right now," Jason urged, hoping to overwhelm Zhukov's careful nature with raw urgency. "We capture it within seconds of being detected or they'll blow it sky-high. It's now or never."

Zhukov's head began to nod. Slowly, at first, then picking up speed. "I will command the assault," he concluded.

"I'm going with you," Jason said. "I can negotiate the hand-over of the refinery once we're inside. I cut the deal with the security forces back in January. They know me as their ally, more so than Kirkham. If I go in with you, we could take it without a fight."

Kirkham hadn't been in northern Utah for months. He'd gone south to oppose the cartel, and loyalty to him in the north had atrophied. Even the Mormons supposedly questioned his fitness to lead. Despite his assurances to Zhukov, Jason knew they risked being burned alive in a lake of liquid fire.

With the return of Kirkham, He faced death by firing squad or death in battle. Given the choice, he wouldn't go down without a fight.

THE ROAR of the Russian BMD-3 armored vehicles reverberated off the homes as they barreled through the neighborhood. The small tanks were fast and nimble, no match for the M1 Abrams, but devastating against anything less. The front armor would easily defeat the machine guns of Kirkham's fighting trucks, and the Russian 30mm autocannon would make short work of militia vehicles or gun emplacements.

Zhukov had placed Jason back from the front wave of BMDs in a command tank. The tank commander gave him an external loudspeaker. Three hundred infantrymen followed in assorted, Russian military trucks.

"I can't see a damn thing," Jason shouted at the Russian tank commander.

"Yah?" the commander poked his head back inside the cupola. He hadn't heard with the wind blasting in his face.

"I can't see anything," Jason repeated.

"The colonel ordered me to keep you safe until we're inside," the tank commander shouted over the roaring engine. "You stay inside."

The tank launched itself over some unseen obstacle and smashed through another. The tank commander shouted something in Russian to the driver and the tank banked off on another course. Small arms fire clattered against the hull, but the crew didn't return fire, just gunned the engine and smashed forward.

More bullets impacted the hull and the tank slammed through what Jason thought must be the perimeter fence of the refinery. The BMD slammed on the brakes and the men inside sloshed across the bench seat into a pile at the front of the troop compartment.

"Now, if you please," the tank commander shouted at Jason as he crouched below the cupola and sought protection from incoming small arms fire.

"This is Jason Ross of the Homestead with our Russian allies. Cease fire. Cease fire," Jason shouted into the hand-held microphone. "Don Tobler. Don Tobler," Jason called the name of the head of security over the P.A.. "Cease fire. This is Jason Ross with our Russian allies. Please cease fire."

Moments later, the gunfire tapered off.

"We are Utah Militia forces from the Homestead. This is Jason Ross, together with friendly forces. Please cease fire." Jason hoped the Russian tanks hadn't engaged the Maverick security men. There'd been no telltale concussion from their autocannons, so there was a chance they could do this without killing the security team and imperiling the fuel tanks. In any case, the refinery security forces had to be confused as hell.

A muffled reply resonated through the armored hull. Jason couldn't make it out.

"Again," the tank commander requested.

"Um. This is Jason Ross of the Homestead militia force together with our allied Russian forces. We have come to reinforce the Maverick refinery defenses. Please cease fire." The loudspeaker barked feedback, but the tank commander seemed satisfied, and the clackety-clack of rifle fire had completely stopped.

The tank commander ducked back inside. "You may dismount, sir. Please remain behind the vehicle for safety."

A soldier flung the rear doors of the BMD open and light poured inside. The smell of fuel filled the space. Jason didn't remember if the refinery always smelled like that or if one of the gasoline tanks had been hit. He climbed down out of the BMD and blinked back the stark light of mid-morning.

"This is Don Tobler of the Maverick refinery security force. Identify yourselves," a man shouted from behind a barricade.

Jason recognized the voice. Months before, he'd struck a deal with the security team, sealing a cooperative relationship between the refinery and the Homestead. Tobler had remained in the refinery in charge of security. Most of the refinery security force was on-loan from the Homestead. Of course, Tobler would know that Jason had retaken the Homestead, but he wouldn't know if Jason and Kirkham had ironed out their differences.

The curly cord of the handheld microphone stretched outside the tank. Jason peered around the corner of the armor. They were inside the first ring of fuel storage tanks. Nothing appeared to be on fire.

"Don, this is Jason Ross. We've come to reinforce your security with this armor. The cartel is within range." It was truth mixed with lies. He certainly hadn't come at the behest of the Utah Militia, and he had no idea of the cannon range of the cartel tanks. "Don...we're coming to you. Please order your men to secure their weapons."

"Good copy," Don Tobler replied over his loudspeaker. It was a noncommittal reply.

Jason followed on foot behind the BMD as it rolled down the gravel paths between the towering fuel storage bunkers. The machine gunner on his tank swiveled to cover threats from above, but nobody fired. Fighting this close, amidst thousands of gallons of gasoline, would be mutual suicide. The security men behind the machine guns had every reason to hold their fire.

Jason's tank rolled up to the mobile office where Tobler housed his HQ. The heavyset security man stood outside on the metal landing, clearly unhappy. He was generally an unhappy person, so the balled fists and the scowl on his face didn't mean much.

"What the fuck are you doing rolling up on us without proper warning? Crashing through our fence?" Tobler shouted.

Jason tossed the microphone back inside the BMD and rolled his AR-15 around on its sling from his back. He checked the breach, saw brass, then stepped around the corner of the tank. He pointed at Don Tobler's chest.

"Stow it, Don," Jason snapped, abandoning all pretext. "We're taking control of this facility. Tell your men to stand down."

Tobler's eyes darted left, then right. Jason guessed he was deciding if his life was worth making a Hail Mary attempt to destroy the refinery. Jason's gun barrel left little doubt. The next action could be Tobler's last.

Jason smiled. "Just be smart, Don. I have a dozen tanks inside your perimeter and three hundred men. This is over." The barrel narrowed on Don Tobler's heart as Jason walked up to the metal staircase of the refinery's mobile security office. "We're taking over."

"Yeah," Tobler objected. "For who?"

"Not your problem," Jason said. "Order your men to stand down and maybe this ends well for everyone."

Don Tobler wasn't the sharpest tool in the shed, but he knew when his possum was cooked.

"Stand down," he growled at his men. "Put your guns on the ground, you idiots. We're not going to fight Russian tanks."

"Where are the explosives?" Jason asked.

Don Tobler jerked a thumb behind him, in the office. So, they hadn't pre-positioned the explosives on the fuel bunkers after all, which made sense given the risk of catastrophic error.

"Commander," Jason spoke to the officer standing above the cupola, with his sidearm now drawn. "Please radio Colonel Zhukov and tell him to move up. We're secure. The refinery is ours."

"And here we are," Gustavo Castillo waved his arm around at the city of Salt Lake outside the hotel conference room, "and we still don't have the fuel to press our attack. How is this possible?"

Bill McCallister sat back in his chair and fingered his 1911 pistol.

When it came to his personal protection, Castillo had a very high opinion of himself. He figured he could out-draw any man alive, which might actually be true. Bill had seen him train, and Castillo was probably the fastest he'd ever witnessed. Castillo let his men keep their sidearms during meetings, which was beyond foolish for a homicidal maniac. If this meeting went like most others, Castillo would at some point threaten to kill someone, and they all had guns on their hips. It was a show of ludicrous confidence in his ability, as though Castillo was saying, "I'm not only the smartest man in the room, but I'm the best gunfighter."

Alejandro Muñoz sighed audibly. He'd been with Castillo since the beginning; those were the halcyon days when they were rich drug dealers, basking in their desert villas, drinking from the endless cup of brotherhood, and swimming in a bottomless pool of money.

Now, they were at war, and a very different version of Castillo had emerged: the emperor. The warlord. The fury. There was no lapping, tidal force of money to obscure mistakes and paper over their failures. In war, the enemy wanted you dead, not out of business.

Alejandro had failed to bring fuel forward to the battlefront. He had failed to find enough fuel trucks. He'd failed to get the fuel trucks he had through the militia wolf packs. Resupply from Mexico went through a gauntlet of partisan terrors, from Monterrey to St. George, then from St. George to Salt Lake. No fuel truck had made it in weeks.

"Tavo," Alejandro used his nickname. "We searched all of Las Vegas, all of Phoenix, Tucson, even Reno. We found *two* fuel trucks. Two." He held up two fingers. "All the rest have been burned up by psychos, or taken away by militia. You'd have an easier time finding a virgin in Tijuana than a fuel tanker in the west. The Utah Militia made sure to withdraw every single tanker truck in Salt Lake. I assume they're hiding them north of the refinery."

"And the two tankers you've got? They're on their way?" Castillo roared.

"Well, no." Alejandro shuffled a paper in front of him on the table, as though checking his list. "It didn't make sense to bring up just two trucks. We'd burn half the gas in their tanks just getting the convoy here. I can't send less than six Abrams in a convoy for them to survive. The militia trucks are almost kamikazes. They're willing to sacrifice a hundred trucks to kill one tanker truck. How can I defend against these suicide fighters?"

"Alejandro. *Hermano*," Gustavo's tone softened. "Look at me." Love filled the madman's eyes.

Bill considered unholstering his gun under the table, but even a slight shift of weight might draw a reaction from Castillo.

Alejandro looked up from his papers, too stupid to be alarmed.

Castillo's right hand flashed down on his holster, bounced the Glock 17 up, out, rotated and extended the gun in a blur.

BlamBlam.

Two rounds were fired before Castillo's arms were even fully extended. The bullets entered Alejandro's skull, almost right on top of one another, through the one-inch gap between his dark eyebrows.

Alejandro's expression froze in a mild state of confusion. His shoulders relaxed and his body slumped half an inch into his chair. He remained upright, eyes open, unaware that he was dead. A trickle of blood dribbled from the hole in his forehead.

Behind him, the lunch spread of celery, carrots, thin-sliced salami, and pickled artichoke hearts, was splattered in a chunky fan of Ale's blood and brains.

The others froze. Bill's hand clamped down on his 1911, but he dare not draw.

Gustavo's Glock was fully extended and steady as a post.

"Wrong answer," Gustavo said as he slid the Glock gently back into the Kydex holster on his belt. "Saúl. You take over the supply convoys. I expect a refuel within one week."

Saúl tipped his head in agreement. Both his hands were folded on the table like they were holding each other down. Saúl did an admirable job of masking his panic. His best friend of ten years had just been spread over the crudités, and his face displayed nothing but laser focus. Saúl was the smarter of the two.

"Our men will lose their shit, out there on the front lines. They're not going to like being cooped up inside the Abrams tanks, and they'll be under sniper fire when they go outside to take a piss. The clock is ticking. In thirty days or less, we *must* advance on the refinery. McCallister," he said, swiveling on his feet to face Bill, and again, Bill resisted the urge to draw his sidearm. "I expect you to find the window of opportunity we need to take the Maverick, intact, before that time comes."

Bill nodded.

"The clock is ticking," Castillo repeated. "In a month's time, we either take that refinery intact, or we burn it. If we have to burn it, we kill every man, woman and child in Utah, and head off to try our luck in Sinclair, Wyoming."

Bill had been afraid of that—that Castillo would invent a drop-dead date. It wasn't how sieges worked, but their psychotic boss was famous for making absurd deadlines and threats, then following up on them with ruthless precision.

Castillo was losing his shit now that his advance had outstripped his supply line. Like Hitler in Stalingrad, things were going to get medieval if Bill didn't find a way to take control of that refinery. Left to his own devices, Castillo would resolve the pressure on the supply chain by killing all of the civilian survivors, up and down the center of Utah, including everyone still alive in Salt Lake City. Castillo's drug dealer, psycho soldiers would be happy to do it.

Bill had, *maybe*, a month to avoid the biggest massacre since the Holocaust.

11

"The war for the American West, sandwiched between a coastal invasion by the Chinese and a grab for the nuclear arsenal by the Russians, teetered on the strangest of logistical logjams. At the outset of hostilities with the northern Mexican cartel, General Jeffery Kirkham ordered the search, collection, and consolidation of all trucks in the region capable of carrying liquid fuel. The single flash of prescience resulted in a cascade of missteps that nearly brought the cartel army to its knees."

— THE AMERICAN DARK AGES, BY WILLIAM BELLAHER, NORTH AMERICAN TEXTBOOKS, 2037

Hurricane, Utah

NOAH MILLER HAD ONE MISSION: TO RESCUE HIS ADOPTIVE FATHER and get him away from the cartel. They had positioned tanks across Salt Lake City, like a chain of one-bedroom, armored fortresses. He couldn't just slip through the battlefront and go door to door looking for his dad.

Excuse me. Have you seen a wiry, old man who swears a lot?

But if he did nothing, he feared his father would die an evil man. Bill McCallister possessed many of the seven deadly sins, had even invented a couple of new ones, but he wasn't evil.

But as Noah searched for a way to contact his father, Bill foundered on one of the worst decisions of his life, probably the game-ender. Even if he found him, Noah's confidence teetered like a ten-foot stack of pallets; Bill was nothing if not stubborn. But Noah had to try.

Noah and Willie attached themselves to Colonel Wither's expedition back to Tucson, returning south down Highway 89 to spin up a few A-10 "Warthog" tank-killers. It was a Hail Mary play. Twenty different things could screw their proverbial pooch and tank the mission. Air assets were notoriously finicky, and that was assuming they didn't run into cartel patrols on the road to Tucson, which they almost certainly would. The Hoodies relied on the corridor up the center of Arizona as their supply line back to Mother Mexico. Cartel sightings were a daily thing.

Since the Freeman Militia had recently made friends along the old Utah highway, they reached the state line in a day and a half. That was the easy part. Next, they'd be forced to follow the road that linked St. George to Phoenix, Tucson, Nogales, and Hermosillo, Mexico, aka, the Hoodie Highway.

Noah got permission to break away from the main force of a hundred and fifty Freemen, to reconnoiter St. George. He lied and said he wanted to scout new paths to ambush the enemy fuel convoys, but what he really sought was a way to reach his father.

They passed through the ghost town that'd once been Hurricane and looped south around Sand Hollow Reservoir. It'd once been a promising golf resort, overlooking a lake and the cottonwood and limestone valley of St. George. The Mormon temple fairly glowed in the pocket of green, framed in orange stone and pink sand foothills. One could almost forget the town had been hammered flat by the iron fist of the cartel.

Willie braced the spotting scope across the hood of the Land Cruiser and glassed the town. "Two tanks downtown, and two on the I-15 on the north edge." Willie had gotten pretty good at working the scope.

"There are two more Abrams at the mouth of Virgin River gorge," Noah added. "Look. There's a single Abrams on the airport bluff. That's overwatch. If that's all of them, they have five tanks securing St. George."

Willie swung the spotting scope around to the airport, almost directly across from their position, five miles on the other side of town.

"Yup. I would've missed that one," Willie admitted.

"You've got to think like the enemy. They're getting smarter," Noah said. Placing a unit on overwatch was something his dad would've done.

"If they were that smart, they wouldn't have left Warthogs in Tucson," Willie replied. It was true, and it hung in the back of Noah's mind. That wasn't something Bill would normally overlook. If the M1 Abrams main battle tank was the disease, the A-10 Warthog close air support aircraft was the cure. It was a mythical fighter plane, old, cheap, and tough. Even just a pair of A-10s would carve a hole in the Hoodie armored battalion.

The massive Davis-Monthan airbase in Tucson had hundreds of Warthogs, many of them still serviceable, plus thousands of mothballed airframes in the boneyard. The cartel controlled Arizona without any serious challengers, but they'd ignored Davis-Monthan. That made sense for Latin American ground fighters to ignore air power. They hadn't had much experience with combined arms and air support. But why would Bill have left threats to their armor, sitting like forgotten hand grenades in the middle of a playground? It gave Noah hope that Bill was still playing secret agent, still maneuvering on the side of justice.

The Freemen kept eyes on the Tucson airbase and it appeared

entirely bypassed by the cartel. The Mexican patrols passed within five miles of Davis-Monthan on their loop from Monterrey, Mexico and they didn't bother with the airfield. Maybe the sight of thousands of aircraft, moldering in the dust, convinced them that they were of no concern. It was an oversight Bill wouldn't make, not without some hidden motive. Noah took it as proof that his dad was still on their side.

"Bingo," Noah said, looking through the binoculars. "There's a fuel depot on the east side of the freeway in the industrial area north of town." A little fuel tanker truck pulled onto the freeway, heading toward the Walmart distribution yard to stage for the next attempted supply run into Salt Lake City. The two Abrams north of town stayed close, covering both the freeway and the fuel depot.

Militia gun trucks would hit the convoy somewhere between here and Salt Lake, and probably destroy it. They'd killed every convoy in the last three weeks, at a staggering cost of life to their gun truck crews. But not a drop of fuel had reached the Hoodie front line in all that time. If the militia could destroy the fuel depot in St. George, it'd send the cartel back to Mexico.

"Um, Noah," Willie stuttered. "We've got company."

Noah dropped his binos and looked up. His eyes adjusted to the waning light of late afternoon. Above them on the hill, a single dune buggy perched over them. Its belt-fed machine gun swiveled in their direction. Two gun buggies appeared on the hill to their south, and two more silently rolled up to the top of the dune. They were screwed, hemmed in.

"Damned electrics," Noah swore. They'd surrounded them without the slightest sound.

BILL MCCALLISTER WAS DRIVING SOUTH from the front line when his channel squawked on the manpack JTRS radio. They'd finally figured out how to get the newest U.S. military comms to work. The backpack radio took up Bill's whole front seat, but at least now he could communicate at a distance over fifty miles.

"Sir. There's a call from St. George. They have a Land Cruiser like yours pinned down near Sand Hollow. They were monitoring fuel and troop movements from an elevated position. Requesting permission to destroy."

Bill had reined in the bloodthirsty cartel troops for weeks. If they murdered everyone they saw, he'd have no one left to interrogate. He threatened to waterboard any team leader who didn't check in first before firing on a captured enemy.

"Negative. Hold for orders," Bill said into the handheld microphone. His comms man in Spanish Fork would relay the order back to St. George. "Repeat: negative on the attack."

His son, Noah, wasn't the only man with a Land Cruiser, but Bill wasn't taking any chances.

"Tell them to back off. Dispatch a team of two buggies to follow them at a distance. Figure out where they're going." Bill tossed the handset into the passenger seat and took off for Spanish Fork. He'd need the big radio for what he'd do next.

BILL CONSIDERED the strategic map as he flew through the towns of Lehi, Orem, and Provo. The streets were empty. The sun was setting. The surviving locals hid in their homes. The rural towns, unlike every other town they'd seen outside of Utah, had survived intact. Utah was a strategic gem in more ways than just its refinery. The wheels of civilization still turned here, in a 1950s sort of way.

As the intelligence chief for Gustavo Castillo, Bill had been given command over seven small teams of reconnaissance fighters.

Bill's teams of "campers" were given good ham radios, then upgraded to the Abrams' JTRS mobile radios. The four-man teams spread out with specific orders not to rape, pillage or murder. They were only to watch. Bill placed a team on I-70, west of Colorado. He dropped three teams on roads across Nevada. He had a team on the interstate from Las Vegas to St. George and two teams in the mountain wilderness over Highway 89. the back road into Salt Lake City from Arizona.

The Highway 89 teams had monitored a several hundred-man force that had moved slowly north from Arizona, then crossed over the Wasatch at the town of Levan. From there, Bill lost them, but they had likely joined the Utah Militia. Bill had delivered the information with dramatic flair to Gustavo Castillo, a chance to prove his worth as head of intelligence.

But then something fascinating occurred: that same small force from Arizona had turned around and headed back the way they came, past Levan, past Richfield—south, back into Arizona. Bill wondered if Jeff Kirkham had refused their help. Maybe the Arizonans didn't like Mormons. Maybe they'd asked to be paid to fight and had been turned down. Why would a militia cross Utah from stem to stern only to turn around and go back home to Arizona?

Had Kirkham given them a mission?

The thought dropped like a cold, hard turd in his bowels. With the nukes in Ellis AFB vaporized, Bill could imagine only one weapon worth the trouble.

Aircraft.

He'd seen a lot of tanks killed in Iraq, in the first Desert Storm. AH-64 Apaches did most of the work, but they were difficult to maintain and pilot, and their range wasn't sufficient to fly to Salt Lake City. Bill wasn't even sure there were Apache helicopters in Arizona.

But the A-10 Thunderbolt, the Warthog, didn't have any of those drawbacks. And he knew for sure there was a shit-ton of Warthogs in Tucson. Bill doubted the planes were ready for service, but they weren't scrapped, either. There'd been a big flap some years back when the air force decided to shit-can the Warthog in favor of fancier, close air support aircraft. Military aficionados went bonkers. The Warthog was a rare design that stood the test of time. It was the 1911 handgun of the skies. Why make it obsolete if it still killed tanks like squashing June bugs?

The A-10 was a simple plane, and could fly the apocalypse. It'd be the cartel's worst nightmare, the Achilles heel of an Abrams army. He'd heard rumor of A-10s hunting cartel forces early in the collapse, though none had ever engaged. If they could fly last fall, they could hypothetically fly again.

It was a weird oversight on the part of Gustavo's senior staff, but it figured. They were ground-pounders and gunslingers, including Castillo himself. To commandos, everything was a ground fight. They thought in terms of guns and grenades, tanks and technicals. Air power would be like the boogeyman, mystical and thankfully forgotten.

It was a wild guess, but Bill concluded that the Arizona Militia had gone back for Warthogs. It wasn't hard to imagine his son breaking off for a day or two from the convoy in order to get eyes on St. George. The Land Cruiser he had his men following could easily be Noah.

Once the picture got in his head, of the militia making a grab for Warthogs, it was hard to imagine any other way.

As Bill chewed through the big picture, he pushed the Land Cruiser to top speed. He flew off the freeway at the town of Spanish Fork and his tires chirped as he took the corner at full speed.

Did he even want to win this war?

Of course he wanted to win. He always wanted to win.

What did winning mean, this time?

He could let them go and give the Arizona militia free reign to get the Warthogs in the air. Or he could make a big deal out of stopping them. He could use this to gain back Castillo's trust. He needed trust if he was going to strike a decisive blow against Castillo. In any case, Bill would prefer not to die in the process of dethroning Castillo, and that meant proving himself irreplaceable until the very last second. Job One was for Bill to survive Castillo's suspicion. Job Two was assassination.

The Land Cruiser howled to a stop outside the Hampton Inn. Bill pocketed the keys and dove headlong for the communications room. A new antenna had been erected in the parking lot. A thick cable snaked through a cracked window. Bill blew into the room like a gust of wind.

"Get me our intelligence guy in St. George," he ordered the radioman. Bill couldn't remember the guy's name.

"Culbert-son," the radioman said with a Spanish accent as he turned dials on the military radio.

It clicked in Bill's head. The lieutenant in St. George was a white guy, a former street organizer from Omaha.

Bill followed his nose to the coffee machine, poured himself a cup and waited while the comms guy raised the mid-level, druggie manager in St. George.

"He's on, sir," the comms man called out and handed Bill the headphones.

"Culbertson," Bill spoke into the mic stand.

"Go ahead, sir," the radio crackled.

"Assemble a team of ten men; pull some from Alejandro's command if you need to. Assign four buggies, two empty trailers, and two solar recharge stations. Send them to the Hawthorne Army Depot and bring ten FIM-92 Stinger Missile Launchers to St. George. Tell the team that they have four days to be back or they'll answer to me. Repeat my last."

While the guy read back the orders, Bill considered the route. He'd left a garrison at Hawthorne Depot when they'd taken control of it last February. It would be smooth sailing for the team. Nothing but open desert between St. George and Hawthorne.

"Contact me the second they're back," Bill told Culbertson. "Don't make me beg for updates."

Culbertson acknowledged and signed off.

Fuck losing, Bill said to himself. *I'm going to end up in command of this beast.*

THE GUN BUGGIES around Noah and Willie withdrew as silently as they'd appeared.

As the last light faded from the western sky, Noah and Willie watched them go.

"Kinda creepy," Willie said.

"There's no way they didn't I.D. us as enemy combatants," he agreed. Noah and Willie had been watching supply movements through a damned spotting scope. They were obviously spies.

"So why didn't they smoke us?" Willie asked.

It would've been like whacking ducks in a kiddy pool with a whiffle ball bat. The buggies had them dead to rights.

"Maybe we have a guardian angel," Noah said, pointing to the sky.

"I ain't been that righteous," Willie said.

"Me neither."

They packed up their spotting scope and drove back the way they came.

"That felt a little like getting with the horny chick at the party," Willie said. "Ya know; the one that's *always* horny when she's drunk. It was a good time, all right, but I'm gonna be checking my junk for a month."

Noah nodded in the dark. That was how he felt too, like maybe his guardian angel had the clap.

WALI TASLEEM RUSHED into Jeff's tent in the middle of the night.

"Mr. Jeff. They have taken the Maverick refinery," he blurted in the dark.

Jeff jerked himself awake. "What? Wali? Is it on fire?"

"No. Mr. Tobler didn't blow it. He didn't have time. They used mechanized armor."

Jeff jumped to his feet with his sleeping bag still wrapped around his ankles. "They broke through our lines?"

Wali turned on his flashlight, as though more light would make it easier to understand him. "Not the Hoodies. It wasn't cartel. Mr. Jason and the Russians captured it."

"Ross?" The picture clarified in Jeff's mind. *That sonofabitch.*

"Mr. Jeff, your wife and sons are out. They're safe with the Mormon *sufi*."

Jeff's legs buckled and he slumped back onto the cot. "Oh, thank God," he said. They might lose Utah tonight, but he had his family back.

Mat Best stumbled into Jeff's tent. "What's going on?" They were camped beside the FAA control tower, on the lawns outside the air traffic control complex in the airport. Jeff wanted to be near the highest point in the valley where he would be able to see cartel movement with his own eyes the moment it happened.

"Ross took the refinery," Jeff explained. Mat Best had recently become a confidante, another special-forces operator. All Jeff's other SOF friends were either dead, captured, or harassing tanks on the front line.

"Our refinery fell? The Maverick?" Mat asked.

"Yes." Jeff turned back to Wali. "How'd they escape?" He meant his family.

"Mrs. Jenna helped them. They went out the front gate."

"And they're safe with President Thayer?" Jeff confirmed.

"Yes," Wali said.

"Who escaped?" Mat struggled to catch up.

"My family," Jeff said.

"Oh. That's good. But aren't we screwed?" Mat asked.

Jeff considered it. "Where's a lantern?" he asked Ryan, his adjutant, as he staggered into the tent behind Mat. "We need coffee. We gotta figure out how screwed we are. There might still be a play to run. Get me a map of the whole valley." The adjutant nodded and rushed out. "Coffee first!" Jeff yelled after him.

"Why are we in tents?" Mat asked as they stumbled around in the dark, opening folding chairs and setting them around the plastic table in the middle. "There are buildings right next door."

"They still smell like dead people," Jeff said. "We don't have the manpower to clean them. We'll be lucky if there's anyone to make us breakfast."

Even in light of the fallen refinery, Jeff felt a thousand pound weight lifted off of his shoulders. His family had escaped. Ross had been like jock itch that spread from the balls, to the inside of the thighs, to the nether regions in between. He was the sticky spot on the floor when barefoot, the man who absolutely, positively needed to die. *It's all fun and games until a man snatches your family,* the gunfighter in Jeff's chest thundered. *Then it's a fight to the death, at the earliest, possible opportunity.*

The tent exploded with light. The adjutant entered behind a burning lantern and a big thermos. "There's more on its way," he said.

Jeff didn't know if he meant the map or the coffee. He felt the absence of Evan Hafer, lost somewhere to the cartel, maybe with his head on a spike. For now, the war council would be Jeff, Wali, and Mat Best.

"Is Jason Ross working for the cartel?" Mat asked as they settled around the table.

Jeff shrugged. "That's the big question, isn't it?"

Wali interjected. "Mr. Jason wouldn't do that."

"He kidnapped my family," Jeff snapped, then reigned in his tone. "We have to admit it's a possibility." .

"He won't give us over to the drug dealers. He isn't a traitor," Wali said in halting English.

It was uncharacteristic of Wali to argue with Jeff, but Afghans thought of loyalty differently than Americans, and they were frequently screwed over as a result. Wali and his sprawling family had been guests in Ross' Homestead from the beginning of the collapse. They'd dined at his table and eaten his bread. An Afghan wouldn't forget that hospitality, even in the middle of a war.

What was Ross thinking? Jeff tried to imagine. If Ross had taken the refinery in some secret deal with the cartel, they'd know soon enough. The Hoodies would roll over the militia in the morning and crush them beneath their tank treads. There'd be nothing to stop them.

"If the Hoodie tanks advance in the morning, we run for Idaho," Jeff concluded. "If they don't, we bottle up that refinery tighter than a hot sister's hoochie on Mardi Gras."

"Hoochie?" Wali asked.

"We can't let Ross communicate with the Hoodies," Jeff said.

The adjutant handed Jeff a big, flapping map. Jeff lifted the lantern and slid the map underneath it. He rotated the map pointing north. "The Hoodie line is here." Jeff ran his finger along the 215 until it merged into Interstate 80 and stretched off toward Nevada. "The Maverick refinery is here." He poked the location about ten miles in front of their line. "If we can keep the bastard from cutting a deal, we can cut the balls off Ross' plan to defect. It's our only hope."

"Can we hit the refinery with mortars?" Mat asked. He wasn't really looking at the map, Jeff noticed, which was weird. They were all staring at the map, even his adjutant. But not Mat. Something was wrong with him.

"No," Wali said. "They have Russian tanks in a circle around it. Ten or eleven of them."

Jeff knew he meant BMDs. He still didn't know for sure why the Russians were in America, and why they were meddling in the affairs of Utah. There was nothing strategic about this place from a global perspective. Jeff felt like he was missing critical pieces of information. He needed to see his wife. Without her, he felt like he had only half of the picture.

"What do the Russians get out of all of this?" he wondered aloud.

"In Cheyenne," Mat said, "the local refugees talked about the Russians taking control of the ICBM fields. An army of American Indians ran them off."

"Okay, that's weird." Jeff massaged his chin. "What brings them here? Why take the Homestead, and then the refinery? Are more Russians coming? Why are they mucking around with Ross?"

Nobody answered.

"Indians from where?" Jeff added. "Why aren't they rushing in to save our asses? Why didn't they stop the cartel down in Navajo country?"

To Jeff, this felt like medieval warfare, particularly the sketchy intel. Like a flock of sparrows hopping from branch to branch, reliable news bounced around in tittering bits. If he knew what the hell was going on, he might form a plan that had a reasonable chance of success.

He felt like he understood the cartel. They wanted gasoline and wanted to control the region. It was a land grab.

But what did the Russians want? And what were the Native Americans doing? Were they even real, or just another post-apocalyptic rumor?

The world was full of weird rumors, especially over the radio waves. If the radio was to be believed, a dozen tinfoil hat conspiracies had come together all at once. The Chinese had taken over

Hawaii. Sinatra was back alive and performing in Las Vegas. The President was a sniper-commando. Canada had invaded Michigan. The U.S. government had reformed itself in Colorado Springs. Elvis was the new mayor of San Francisco. Daily, Jeff was passed some new, absurd tidbit of national gossip.

He could imagine the Russians sending Spetsnaz to take and hold American nukes. That made sense. Nobody wanted hundreds of nukes flapping in the wind for history to sort out later. Maybe the Russians were here as peacekeepers, as much as Jeff doubted their good intentions. But if that were true, why did they take over a Utah oil refinery?

Messengers and spy networks had been crucial in medieval warfare, and Jeff could see why. He wished he'd put more effort into building high-power HF towers—or carrier pigeons, or smoke signals, or any damn thing to know what was going on outside of the valley.

When he had a chance, and more men, he would send men to conduct long-range recon. Knowing what was happening on the other side of the Rockies, and the California High Sierras, could be life or death for the Utah Militia. The Russians had come from the east of the Rocky Mountains, and now they had flipped this war on its head. Out of sight was not out of mind. Recon mattered. He'd always known it, but he'd been set back on his heels, reacting to the enemy. This react-to-contact bullshit needed to end. Jeff had to get out ahead. He hadn't been doing his best thinking. He'd let mysteries accumulate without answers. He'd been pissed about his family and it occurred to him just now that he'd been playing catch-up for weeks.

"Mat, what the hell is wrong with you, anyway?" Jeff asked.

"Um. Yeah. My eyes don't work very well," Mat admitted.

"Like, just now?" Jeff drilled down.

"No. It's been this way for a couple of weeks."

"Okay. That sucks, but I need you to figure it out later. Right now, I need you on the road, recruiting more men. Go north to Idaho and recruit 10,000 men. Get back fast. The cartel is coming for Idaho too. Send messengers from each town. Keep me informed of *everything* you learn. Can you do that? Sorry about your eyes, bro. Maybe you'll find a doctor or your eyes will heal themselves. I'm worried about our heads getting stuck on T-posts at the moment. Your brain works fine, your mouth works fine and you're a Ranger. Get me 10,000 Idaho infantrymen, preferably with pickup trucks."

"Copy that," Mat agreed.

"Now, if you please," Jeff added.

Mat bumbled about for a second, apparently found his legs and moved with purpose out the tent flap and into the night.

Jeff turned to Hector. "Get me Pete, Sam Sparks, Oliver what's-his-name, and Mike Conti. Tell them they're going on a road trip. Tonight."

The lantern had turned the air in the Springbar tent stale. Jeff left Wali, stepped outside the tent and inhaled. With the coming of dawn, they might be on the run, but Jeff felt a hell of a lot better now that he was taking action and making half-way intelligent moves. It was like a hood over his head had been lifted. Tara and the boys were safe now. Instead of seeing only black, he saw the first streaks of light.

"It's like Kabul," Wali said as he stepped up beside him.

Jeff didn't know if he meant the crystal sky and the snow-capped mountains, or if he meant the shifting loyalties and marauding warlords.

"I hoped never to see that again," Jeff said, meaning the brutality of the Afghan war.

"Me too," Wali agreed.

12

Shortwave Radio 7150kHz
3:00pm

> *"From the refugees out of the Big Apple, we hear that it got real bad—like Snake Plissken bad. If you've got a story of escape from a big city like New York, Chicago or Los Angeles, Zach is putting together a history book so we don't forget our once-great megalopolises."*

Snowville, Utah, on the Idaho border

MAT BEST AND GABRIEL PEÑA DROVE NORTH THROUGH IDAHO, toward the headwaters of the Snake River, warning towns and putting out the call for fighting men. When they reached La Grande, Oregon seven days later, they reversed course and mustered a second batch of freedom fighters. East Oregon and Idaho did not disappoint. Thousands of men and women strapped on rifles and marshaled in town squares, church lawns, and Walmart parking lots. Mat hoped Jeff Kirkham and the Utah Militia would still be there when they got back.

In Snowville, on the Idaho/Utah border, a dark-haired young man with a lever-action rifle grabbed Mat by the arm.

"Sir. A question, if I may?" The blurry form swam in the center of Mat's vision.

"Sure," Mat replied. He'd been on his way to Mollie's Cafe, the town diner that'd exploded out into the street to serve more than three thousand Idaho irregulars.

"Do you have any news about the Ross family in Oakwood? Utah, I mean."

Mat was about to answer that he'd only been in Utah a few days and didn't know anyone other than Gabe and General Kirkham, but he hesitated. "Jason and Jenna Ross?"

"Yes sir," the dark-haired young man answered.

"Yes, actually. They're alive and well, but..." Mat didn't know what else to say. Their story was complicated, and what he knew was hearsay. "You should really talk to Gabriel Peña. He's close to the Ross family. He's a Latino guy wearing multicam with...a gun." Mat had never properly seen Gabriel. "Ask around for Gabe Peña from Utah." Mat motioned toward the sea of people wearing camouflage that was milling about.

"Thank you, sir." The young man drifted away toward a knot of people, and carried on with his search.

———

Salt Lake City, Utah

JEFF DIDN'T DIE the next morning. Nor the next. A week later, the Utah militia was still standing, and still holding the international airport. The cartel hadn't moved from their skirmish line bisecting Salt Lake Valley. The Maverick refinery still stood, under mysterious, new management. But all was not quiet on the western front.

Whoever controlled the Maverick refinery had no interest in

speaking to Jeff's envoys. Every man he sent to talk to them got turned around and sent packing at the point of an AK-47. The same occurred when Jeff sent messengers up the hill to the Homestead. The old barricades, the one's he'd originally erected to stop the gangbanger army, were now manned by Russian commandos and they refused any offer of parlay. Jeff concluded that they were negotiating a deal with the cartel. Deals like that, between passing rattlesnakes, took time.

A hammer hung over his head, set to crush his skull the moment the Russians finalized a deal with the Hoodies. Given the thousand routes in and out of cartel-controlled territory, Jeff was forced to surrender to the reality that he couldn't stop them from talking.

"General Kirkham," Hector said, interrupting his reverie. "It's Master Sergeant Best on the horn from Idaho for you."

Jeff followed Hector into the radio tent outside the admin building of the FAA tower. "Go for Kirkham," he said into the radio mic.

"Good news from Idaho," Mat began over the speakers. "We have over four thousand recruits, now."

"Thanks. We could use good news," Jeff replied. "When's your ETA?"

"We'll arrive tomorrow morning."

"Good."

"Even better news: I think I've found a solution to the winter famine," Mat said.

It was Jeff's biggest worry, second to losing the war. They could win the war and still all die a slow, miserable death. Medieval history was full of victory in battle, then starvation the next season.

"Go ahead," Jeff said.

"The Idahoans have a lot of potatoes in the ground. Many of the families planted in the spring, apocalypse or not. Also, entire valleys managed to over-winter their cattle. There's a hundred times more food growing in the ground than Idaho can eat. Everyone I've talked to swears they'd trade food for gasoline, all day long and twice on Sunday. A gallon of gasoline for their tractors and cars buys a helluva lot of taters and beef. The Maverick refinery is the key to it all. We're sitting on a gold mine."

Jeff wanted to say, "*the Russians are sitting on a gold mine,*" but he didn't want that over the airwaves. Still, it was good news. If he could win the war, they might not starve.

Check that, he said to himself. He had to win the war AND preserve the Maverick refinery.

"Hold on that thought," Jeff ordered Mat. They'd already said more over the open frequency than they should've. "We'll talk about it when you get here. Come see me immediately."

"Roger. Best out."

Jeff nodded to Hector. His adjutant was smiling. Jeff wasn't the only person sweating bullets over winter famine. Everyone had it in the back of their minds. They'd all just witnessed hundreds of thousands starve and perish from disease, and nobody wanted to relive that hell. At last, there was a ray of hope. Just a few hundred miles north of Salt Lake, there was food for everyone: potatoes rich in carbohydrates and beef cattle heavy in fats and proteins. They had the makings of a new trade network. Utah would refine gasoline and grow hay. Idaho would plant potatoes and raise cattle. With population numbers down at least eighty percent in the big cities of the Rocky Mountain West, it could work. They could form an economy with those building blocks.

Other than the Maverick, there wasn't another surviving refinery for a thousand miles. With the Sinclair refinery in Wyoming gone, Jeff couldn't think of a refinery this side of New Mexico or Texas. California refineries, on the far side of the High Sierras, might have once existed, but they were almost certainly destroyed by mayhem.

"Could we send horses and wagons over to Idaho?" Hector asked, reading Jeff's mind.

Jeff huffed. "That's probably a two week trip, and impossible once it snows. What would we trade them?"

"Hay?" Hector wondered.

"They probably have enough hay to get by with what they grow in Idaho already. Gasoline is our thing. We simply can't lose the Maverick. It's our only hope of getting the pipeline going again. Without that refinery, it'll take us years to get the energy sector primed and running again."

"It won't matter at that point," Hector pointed out. "We'll all starve."

"Why should we be any different than the rest of the country." Jeff scratched his head. "We've been lucky, so far. If we lived on the eastern seaboard, we would've died months ago."

That was what they'd heard all winter on the ham radio: death, death and more death. Starvation. Flu. Utah had been blessed on many fronts, none more than its access to gasoline. Salt Lake City had eighty percent die-off instead of ninety-nine percent like other cities. But that good fortune had drawn flies. And the flies, in this case, drove tanks.

———

IN JUST HIS UNDERWEAR, Bill McCallister looked out the balcony of his room on the twenty-fourth floor of the Grand America hotel in Salt Lake City. His intelligence sources, mostly captured militiamen, revealed that General Jeff Kirkham set his headquarters at the base of the air traffic control tower of the Salt Lake International Airport, three miles across the valley from Bill's room. He could see it as clearly as the Oquirrh Mountains to the west, just giving up their last glint of a snowy bonnet.

In his dark tower against the backdrop of the Great Salt Lake,

General Jeff Kirkham must be looking over the same battlefield, dotted with smoke pockmarks where Abrams tanks formed a wide necklace of burning buildings, spent ordnance, and smoldering vehicles around the ultimate prize: the Maverick refinery. Its smokestacks peeked between the multi-story office buildings of downtown, bristling at the foot of the hills that bounded the farthest edge of the city proper. The necklace would encircle a little each day, wrapping to the north, inching closer to the refinery, becoming a garrote.

Until the cartel resupplied fuel, the necklace would be open in the back, little more than a curving battlefront, confounded in the west by the brackish waters of the Great Salt Lake and bounded in the east by the Wasatch mountains.

The route around the lake through Nevada was a staggering 380 miles—almost two tanks of gas in an Abrams. Going up and around the Wasatch mountains was shorter, under a hundred miles, but it transited numerous mountain passes, some still choked with snow.

Circumnavigating the refinery to cut off the militia's northern supply and reinforcement routes would require weeks. Once the cartel got the militia fully encircled, their own supply lines would stretch around vast and dangerous miles of mountain territory.

Bill couldn't see it happening. Castillo had bit off more than he could chew. This was the same sort of boondoggle Stalingrad had been for Hitler.

Along the 215 Freeway and Interstate 80 in Salt Lake City, militia gun trucks tangled with M1 Abrams tanks in a game of mouse versus lion. The outside range of the M1 Abrams main cannon was 3,000 meters, but the tank gunners had to see a target to shoot it.

The buildings of Salt Lake rarely offered more than a hundred yard line of sight, so the machine guns mounted on top of the tank turrets, surrounded by a clear, bullet-proof shielding, did most of the fighting.

Militia gun trucks would whip around the corner of a building, fire a string of rounds, reverse course, and disappear before a tank's cannon could come to bear. Castillo's tanks rarely scored hits. They held ground, and denied the militia access to more than half of Utah's agricultural land, but the skirmish line had become a stalemate.

The sniping, day and night, penned the cartel troops into their armored boxes. As the siege wore on, it became apparent that living in cramped, metal shoeboxes was a form of torture. Almost a hundred cartel soldiers were killed in the first week of the siege as they stepped outside the tank to take a piss, cook a meal, or smoke a cigarette. Their armor was impregnable, but no place for human habitation.

As Bill listened, an Abrams thundered below, then kicked in with the burr of machine gun fire. Another concussion.

More machine gunning.

Silence.

Smoke.

Bill concluded that it was another hit-and-run attack, perhaps two miles away. Smoke drifted up from where the urbanscape melted into squat, industrial buildings. Maybe the tank had killed a militia gun truck. Maybe it'd set a building on fire. Maybe men died. But certainly, nothing had been accomplished.

Every tree of any size downtown had been felled for firewood during the long winter after Black Autumn. Salt Lake City had been denuded by her survivors. Still, the greening had taken firm hold, in the park strips, the planter boxes on the boulevards, and the mountain slopes. It cast strips of emerald along the grayscape of homes, businesses, offices, and factories. The stone planters along main street, below Bill's hotel room, burst with tulips planted the year before, the dying year, before anyone knew just how doomed they were.

There was a knock at his door. A summons.

"McCallister. Gustavo has called a meeting," a soldier yelled from the hallway.

Castillo had lately been given to unscheduled, rage-filled staff meetings. He'd yelled and screamed about advancing again today. But the intel hadn't changed. Captured militiamen all said the same thing: if the cartel progressed beyond Interstate 80 or the 215 freeway, Kirkham would blow the refinery.

There was a thin rumor that Russian Spetsnaz had taken control of the refinery. It was just the kind of nonsense captives said to avoid another bout of waterboarding. Bill hadn't passed that bit of information up to Gustavo Castillo. The maniac might take it seriously.

There'd been another thread of scuttlebutt, now validated by four men under interrogation: Jeff Kirkham did have a rival. A man named Jason Ross.

Ross controlled a hard-point defensive fortification in the mountains north of town. Kirkham had captured it from him, then lost it during the last few weeks. If Bill could make contact with Ross, he might dig up a weakness in Kirkham's plan to destroy the refinery.

Bill pulled on his black, Crye multicam pants. Half his survivability in this criminal's army was due to a manicured, dark mystique, the black camo pants, lean muscle, and legendary commando status made the men fear him almost as much as Gustavo Castillo himself. Rumors of cutting off tongues and waterboarding prisoners didn't hurt his mystique. Bill had to "fake it to make it," but that approach wasn't new to him. He'd been playing this game a long time.

Bill had several bits of intelligence to share with Castillo today, the key to keeping himself alive long enough to pull off his broader plan.

He'd reveal the rumors of Jason Ross, and a trickle of hope that Bill's intelligence network could break the aching stalemate in the Salt Lake Valley. Then he'd add a splash of terror, dropping intelligence he'd kept to himself for over a week: that the Arizona section of the insurgent militia was preparing to attack with A-10 Warthogs, flying from the old airbase in Tucson. Simultaneously, Bill would reveal that he'd already taken action to order a unit to Tucson bristling with surface-to-air missiles. Again, Bill would be the bearer of horrifying news and the one-man solution to the nightmare. It was how he kept himself germane and alive, surrounded by those who would have him dragged before a firing squad.

Castillo would send a half-assed force out of St. George, or maybe Nevada, to destroy the airbase. With most of their tanks committed to Salt Lake, and with the remaining gun buggies rushing around, failing to protect the fuel convoys, Castillo would flounder. Bill and his Stingers would be his only hope.

Bill pulled on a T-shirt, one of his favorites from before the crash. It read: *Nobody Cares. Work Harder.* This was a good day for a brash challenge to Castillo's other lieutenants. Bill had been saving up the Warthog intelligence for a day like today, when Castillo's frustration would reach its apex.

Bill would look like the salty, old hero. The other lieutenants, struggling against vast supply lines and cavitating against a stalemate, would look like fumbling boys. More than half the job of being the intelligence chief was manipulating Castillo, but it was the easier part.

The hard part was keeping those balls up in the air. He needed to produce just enough victory to keep Castillo hopeful, but not so much that Bill became obsolete. If his psycho boss ever found his footing, Bill was a dead man.

The flying Warthogs weren't the only bit of intelligence Bill had been hoarding. He grabbed a hotel pad and wrote his name and one of his titles across the top.

Bill McCallister, Green Beret, retired.

This bit of intelligence wasn't for Castillo, though. This bit would keep Bill relevant on the *other* side of the war.

He drew a diagram that only another Green Beret would likely understand, then folded the paper in half, then in quarters. He held the paper in the palm of his hand instead of slipping it in a pocket. It felt like carrying an envelope full of ricin, except the toxin would kill only him if someone opened it and saw what it contained.

Bill walked down the twenty-four sets of stairs to the ground floor of the hotel. He liked his room being that high. Fewer people walked up all those stairs to bother him, or to catch him betraying his boss.

He looped through the hotel kitchen, where a gang of locals had been pressed into service cooking meals. At the moment, they were hustling to prepare lunch. Bill swooped around the back of the stainless steel tables where wary cooks worked, wide-eyed and afraid. Bill stooped over and smelled a steaming pot.

"This isn't poisoned, is it?" he asked a terrified cook. He knew for a fact that this particular man was a spy for the militia.

"Give this note to General Kirkham," Bill whispered as he pressed the folded paper into the man's hand. Bill grabbed a wooden spoon and tasted the cream-of-something white soup. He curled a lip as though it tasted like stewed donkey balls.

The cook's eyes grew big as saucers. He was too dumb to play the game and too easy to read.

"This is shit! Don't come back tomorrow. Don't come back ever," Bill snarled in the cook's face. "Just leave." Bill kicked him hard in his ass. The inept spy scuttled out the back door of the kitchen.

"Someone else, get over here and remake this soup," Bill shouted. "Do it fast. It's disgusting."

―――――

Colorado City, Arizona

Noah Miller had a case of the crawlies.

He and Willie had stopped in the burned-out town of Juniper Creek for a week, once a polygamist enclave, while they conducted counter-surveillance to shake off a possible tail. The cartel didn't practice "catch and release." Yet they'd caught them, then let them go. Something was wrong, and Noah and Willie both agreed that they shouldn't bring bad juju with them to their unit in Tucson. So, they held up in Juniper Creek and searched for a tail.

They'd seen no movement, no followers, but it was a big world, full of fallow hillsides and unspoiled plain. There was no sign of chase vehicles, nor anyone on foot, but that didn't mean they weren't there, watching.

The wildlife had come back strong in this post-apocalyptic wilderness. Noah had never considered the degree to which mankind hampered the wild things, but as he spent two days behind his binoculars, looking for a cartel tail, he saw hundreds of coyotes, rabbits, and mountain lions. Once, he even thought he saw a bear. In a single, unchecked springtime, mammals flooded back to the American West. Noah wondered how once-domesticated animals were doing: cattle, horses, goats, and sheep. A big part of nature's flux could've been the millions of decaying bodies of mankind; that much carrion might've pulled the attention of predators, allowing herbivore numbers to explode. It complicated Noah's surveillance. His binoculars were repeatedly dragged away to follow the motion of deer, elk, cougar, and coyote.

"We should move on," Willie said. "Colonel Withers will wonder what happened to us. They might organize a rescue mission."

"Doubtful," Noah said. That wasn't the deal in the Freeman Militia. The world was still too unsafe to wander around looking for a couple of missing men. "They probably assume we got captured by the Hoodies."

Willie huffed. "Well, we've delayed long enough for them to get to Tucson."

That was true. The fuel tanker trucks, full of JP-8, would've been soft targets for Hoodie gun buggies, and if the cartel knew what they were meant to fuel, they'd come looking to kill them. The convoy had either made it to Davis-Monthan airbase or they hadn't. If the militia had been interdicted, it wasn't because Noah and Willie led the Hoodies to them.

"Let's head for Tucson, then," Noah agreed.

"How 'bout a quick bootie call in Flagstaff?" Willie raised his eyebrows up and down, up and down, like a black Groucho Marx.

Noah laughed. "I guess we can stop over at your place for a few hours."

Willie's wife and kids were set up in a house on the fancy golf course on the outskirts of Flagstaff. She had a huge garden growing over top of the grass on the sixth fairway, watered by a series of ponds that once swallowed golf balls. Willie hadn't seen his family in weeks, not since he and Noah set off to link up with the Utah Militia. Noah had no wife and kids—they were killed a couple of years before the collapse.

"Aren't you worried about dropping in unannounced?" Noah asked. "Noel might've found herself another beau while you were off at war. A fine woman like that—with gardening skills and all. I wouldn't leave her alone on the homestead if it were me," Noah joked. "Nope. I'd stay right close."

"I'm not worried," Willie bragged. "I loved her up so good before we left, it'll keep for a month."

"If you say so, Hoss. What kinda fresh veggies will she have?"

"Bro, it's May still," Willie gave Noah the dumbshit stare.

"Yeah, I know. Some stuff's ready by then."

"Maybe garlic, snow peas and radishes," Willie said. "Nothing good. Lettuce, mayhap."

"Look who's Farmer John now. Talking like he knows a thing or two."

"I told you," Willie said, "Noel's turned into a regular green thumb. Most of her pillow talk is about greenhouses, fertilizer, and vegetable starts. Even my pecker knows shit about gardening."

"Well then, we should get your pecker back to plowing the field." Noah stowed his binoculars and hopped into the Cruiser. They'd already packed their camping gear.

"Amen to that, Brother Miller," Willie said, after taking a last look around. "Then after that, let's get some ass-kicking airplanes into this fight."

Davis-Monthan Air Force Base
Tucson, Arizona

TWENTY-FOUR HOURS LATER, Noah and Willie reconnected with their unit in Tucson.

"We got over a hundred good aircraft," Colonel Withers patted the turbo fan engine as he walked around the plane on the tarmac of the airbase. "That's not the problem. So far, we've only located three pilots who know how to fly them. We're looking for more, and training up others as fast as we can."

"I heard they're easy to fly," Noah said about the Warthog.

"To fly?" Withers shrugged. "Sure. But to fly on a combat mission? That's a ton more difficult. We don't have any working simulators. We have no heat-seeking missiles. We don't have training munitions, or defensive flares. We have a couple truck loads of 30mm combat mix for the Avenger cannon. We got that from McAlester last winter after you and your dad scouted the place for us."

Withers was being kind not to mention that Noah's dad had intentionally destroyed the first load of 30mm to stay in good graces with the cartel. The militia had gone back for a second load, but by the time they'd returned to Tucson, the cartel had disappeared into the Nevada desert. That was in February, before Castillo re-emerged to take St. George.

"We're lucky you had the ammo. What about missiles or bombs?" Noah asked.

"That'd be peachy if we had some, but we have no idea where they're kept stateside. Could be Hawthorne. Maybe Sierra Depot in Northern California. We don't have a single hot missile on site."

"So you have ammo for the gun, but only three pilots," Noah summed it up.

"We've got two guys who know the combat system. We've got another guy who fought in the A-10 way back in Desert Storm. Those three pilots are trying to teach a dozen guys with pilot's licenses how to shoot and kill tanks. So far, nobody's crashed, and that's the sum total of the good news."

"They're flying already?"

"Yeah, but even I can tell they suck." Withers ran his fingers through his hair. "None of the new guys can hit a damn thing, even with the targeting systems. Back in the day, A-10 pilots did a lot of training. Hundreds of hours of combat simulations and live fire practice. You can't stick a guy with a Cessna license in the cockpit and cut him loose on tanks. There's like a hundred switches in there." He pointed toward the bulbous canopy over the Warthog cockpit. "It's like trying to bang your old lady while you cut your hair."

"What do you need me to do?" Noah said. "I'm no pilot."

"We need to get out of here," Withers said. "I'm seeing more cartel activity than ever before. They know something's up. More patrols. Fewer convoys. It doesn't smell right."

Noah nodded. "The cartel caught Will and me with our pants down above St. George. They let us go."

"No bueno," Withers agreed. "I don't like it when they fight smart."

"Yeah, I liked it better when they were a bunch of gangbangers."

"I hate to say it," Withers said, "but it makes me think of your dad."

"It's possible he's involved," Noah agreed. "I'm trying to reach him. I think we can turn him. That's why I took the side trip to St. George."

"That's why I let you go. But you need to be prepared for the possibility that he doesn't want to be turned." Noah could tell he took no pleasure in saying it.

Noah had come to respect Withers. He was an officer who cared about his men. His deference for Noah went beyond him being "famous" as one of the earliest freedom fighters against the cartel. Withers shared Noah's concern for Bill, traitor or not.

Withers looked at his burly wristwatch. "I gotta go. I have training in ten minutes."

"You're flying?" Noah asked.

"Yeah." Withers winked. "I have my pilot's license, so I train. Those were the orders: everyone with a pilot's license learns to fly the 'Hog.'" Withers had issued those orders.

Noah smiled. "You any good?"

The colonel demurred. "Better than some. Worse than others," but he was obviously proud of himself. "Put together an anti-surveillance team and a defensive plan for this base. Get ready for a fight. We're doing our best to fly out over the east desert to run training sorties, but it's impossible to hide jets taking off and landing. If the cartel doesn't know what we're doing yet, they will soon. We're the only planes in the sky."

As if to illustrate his point, a taxiing Warthog heated up its engines, sped down the runway, then lifted into the skies with a screech that could be heard for twenty miles. It made Noah feel very vulnerable. They'd been running and hiding from the cartel for half a year and the planes painted them into a corner. They'd ride or die with their backs against this runway. Luckily for them, most of the cartel tanks were 600 miles away.

"Screw flying out over the desert to train," Noah followed Colonel Withers toward his flight lesson. "The cat's out of the bag. Fly your training missions over the interstate and burn anyone coming this way. Use those practice rounds on live targets."

"Good point. You set up the ground defense," Withers ordered as he walked away. "You've got the town. The planes will cover the ground in and out."

———

Two hours later, Noah and Willie had reconned a five mile circle around the Air Force base, and had sent out the warning order for the few infantrymen to support the new mission.

"Covering town" would be a pipe dream, even with a thousand men, and he only had a tenth that number. Noah knew nothing about surface-to-air missiles, but with even a mile of deadly range, a man with a SAM could sit in a swing set in any one of thirty thousand homes and shoot down a Warthog as it took off or landed. The city of Tucson had functionally surrounded the airbase with tract homes, and both sides of the runway pointed like gun barrels down the middle of neighborhoods.

Why had people built homes under the howling flight patterns of military jets? For a guy who'd grown up in the sticks, it made no sense. City people were a breed he'd never understand. He might never have to. They were mostly gone.

But the corpse of their stucco beehive remained, and the enemy would use it as cover to shoot down their warplanes and their few pilots. How was he supposed to cover them?

If Noah were the enemy, he'd come under the cover of darkness, armed with a DeWalt saber saw, cut a big hole in the roof of any one of fifty thousand homes, and fire his surface-to-air missile at the next Warthog to fly by. Splash one pilot.

Willie was with Noah when they turned in a circle, in the

middle of a cookie-cutter neighborhood, taking in the magnitude of the challenge.

Willie rubbed his chin. "Do the Warthogs have those burny-flashy things that shoot out their butts as they take off and land. I think I saw them doing that in and out of Kabul airport on a YouTube video."

Noah shrugged. "Who knows? It'd be just our luck if the Air Force stored flares in a depot in South ButtScrew, Arkansas."

"You know the Hoodies followed us, right?" Willie said. "It ain't felt right since we left Flagstaff."

"Yep," Noah agreed. It'd felt like they were being watched since the day they arrived.

"I'm not even sure how to think about a tactical situation where we're the defenders," Willie said, then chuckled. "I'm so used to hit and run. I don't even know how to set up a security perimeter."

Noah nodded and realized that Willie wasn't just a sidekick anymore. He'd become a hardened soldier. Now, he had more gritty, combat experience than most military operators.

Noah handed him a map of Tucson. "Why don't you command this side of the runway and I'll handle the north side? I'll put fifty men in your command, and fifty in mine," Noah said. "I'll put up a perimeter about a quarter-mile from my end of the runway, in a semicircle. I don't know if that's far enough to push a missile out of range, but I'll only have twenty-five, two-man teams. They'll have about a block between them, and they'll only be one team deep."

Willie whistled. "When you put it that way, fifty men sounds like nothing. If I had my way, I'd have a surveillance team in every third house," he remarked.

"And if pigs had wings, they'd be wingshooting bacon in North Dakota," Noah answered. It would require at least 5,000 men to accomplish what Willie suggested.

"We need to get these planes the hell out of here," Willie concluded. "They'd be safer in Utah."

"For a minute or two, until Old Bill realizes what's going on. Then they'll attack Hill Air Force Base."

"Okay. But," Willie held up a finger, "won't they eventually run out of tanks to cover all that ground? They won't be able to put a cannon over every piece of critical real estate."

Noah nodded. "They're probably past that point already. I hope my old man can feel it in his bones. Given enough time, the ants eat the elephant. Maybe that's all we got going for us."

13

"As America awoke the spring after Black Autumn, with only six percent of the previous summer's population still alive and with manufacturing entirely destroyed, modern agriculture was an impossibility. There was very little of any fuel, fertilizer, chemical herbicide, or disease-resistant seeds. There was no gas, and no parts for modern farming equipment, nor anyone to finance the new year's crop. Cash money was still used for trade, but nobody knew quite what a dollar was worth."

— THE AMERICAN DARK AGES, BY WILLIAM BELLAHER, NORTH AMERICAN TEXTBOOKS, 2037

Ross Homestead
Oakwood, Utah

THE NIGHT CHILL HAD FINALLY CEASED TO THREATEN THE YOUNGLING plants, and the Homestead garden was in full swing. Soon, they would harvest the garlic from between the tender cucumbers, and the snap peas would ripen. The brief time of fresh food would come.

It amazed Jenna Ross at how much food colored her world. She'd eaten mostly dried food storage since after the Black Autumn collapse, and her soul echoed her gut: heavy and sullen.

As she ran her fingers across the bright, green pea vines, curling up the circle garden trellises, fresh vitality danced in her heart. Tiny, white blossoms nodded at her touch. Baby peas, almost transparent, were so delicate; they drooped with sweet promise.

She would never think of vegetable sugars the same way, nor would she ever take fresh meat for granted again. Her heart broke at the thought of harvesting some of her lovely goat-children, but her tummy smiled and the bittersweet truth of man's survival sang a melancholy tune in her ear.

Jenna served this clan of beloved people, as did the goats, as did the rabbits, as did the snap peas. They all held hands, man, beast, and plant, in a great, year-round circle. Each gave itself to fortify the whole. The life-bound guild passed in lockstep from one year to the next, some creatures overwintering, and others not.

It made her think of her Emily, her body now rejoining the soil. Jenna's breath hitched, and her eyes softened.

How had she persisted fifty years on this planet without knowing the quiet cycles beneath her feet? She'd been entirely blind to them, wrapped in the miniature, tinkling dramas of Yelp reviews, Facebook rants, and her friends' petty squabbles with their husbands. All that time, the living planet had thrummed its melody, mighty yet ignorable; it had been forgotten under the tires of her Tesla.

"Remember that year when we grew Cherokee Purple tomatoes?" Jason startled her. He chuckled when she squealed. "I'm sorry I scared you. I just thought, with so many people around—"

"It's fine. I'm fine," she said. "You're back."

"I'm back," he agreed.

"So, you and Zhukov took control of the refinery by force," she said, wading straight into her concern.

"Are you missing your colonel for coffee?"

"It's not that. What are your intentions?" she asked.

He stalled. "With the refinery?"

"You know what I mean, Jason."

He pursed his lips and examined the broadening leaf of a young squash plant. He lifted it and looked under it, probably checking for squash bug eggs. "Why do you concern yourself with the big picture? Why do you care? Are you hoping for Jeff to come save you again?"

Jenna knew they didn't have the luxury of jealousy, but here it was, front and center, with lives hanging in the balance. Worries about food and starvation were swept aside while the men wrestled with their pettiness.

Jenna stabbed her fists on her hips. "Of course I care about the outcome of the war. I don't want our family and friends under the boot of a murdering thug," she said.

"You'd rather they be under the boot of a murdering, gorilla-necked commando."

"Jeff's no murderer," she argued.

"He's a thief, and a tyrant. He disbanded the Homestead committee after he stole my land. He took control for himself. What do you call that?"

"You mean, after he stole *our* land?" she fired back. "I offered him my vote after you tried to have me thrown out."

Jason inhaled and shuffled around a planter bed. She'd outmaneuvered him, so he went silent. She might've left it at that, an argument won, but she couldn't leave the refinery alone. She needed Jason to know that her favor relied on him doing the right thing.

"Please give control of the refinery back to the church and the militia," she said.

He laughed, dark and rueful. "You mean, give the refinery back to Jeff Kirkham, your champion? I'm afraid he's going to have to take it from me, and this time, he's not the only one with a gun."

"There are too many lives at stake for you to play this game," she said. "If we waste any more time infighting, we're not going to survive next winter."

"Oh really?" he laughed again. "So I'm supposed do whatever you want whenever you bat your eyes? Is that the game that saves lives? You helped Tara escape." His brows knitted together in the middle. "You betrayed me and you used my Russians to do it."

"Was she imprisoned?" Jenna countered. "If so, that's the first I've heard of it."

"Don't play coy. You know she was supposed to stay in the Homestead as a guarantee against Kirkham's next attempt to steal this place."

"If you want to clear things up with Jeff Kirkham, holding his wife and kids hostage was a stupid way to do it."

"Who said I wanted to clear things up?" Jason raised his voice. "I want him dead. I want him in a gunfight, man to man, not hiding behind women, as he obviously prefers."

"Look around you, Jason," Jenna attempted to dial back his anger. "Look at the life that's roaring back. We have this *one chance* to create instead of destroy. We have this *one season* to restock, restore, and come together. We can't afford rutting bulls trampling everything underfoot as they fight out delusions of dominance." She knew she'd gone too far. She'd been too straightforward, and it'd push him away, which was the opposite of what she wanted.

Jason tossed the old tomato stalk he'd been twiddling in his fingers. "And you're playing me like a young, all dick-and-drool buck. Well, surprise! I'm too long in the tooth for that game. I've been around the block enough times to know when a woman's using me. You act like you and I still have a chance, then you betray me. And now you imagine you can talk your way back into controlling me. You'll have to work your mojo on someone younger and dumber. Sorry to disappoint you." He turned and stormed out of the circle garden.

"Damn it," Jenna swore under her breath. She'd blown it.

JEFF KIRKHAM STARED at the sweat-stained, tightly-folded, piece of paper in his hand. Supposedly, it was from a former Green Beret named McCallister. He'd written his name across the top of the page.

Bill McCallister, Green Beret, retired.

The Freeman militia guy, Noah, must've been adopted, Jeff figured. The Special Forces dad would've been late Viet Nam, or maybe early 1970s.

Still, a Green Beret was a Green Beret. Jeff had no great difficulty imagining an SF guy batting for the cartel. War was a job, and a lot of guys were in it for the action. The flag-waving patriotism wore thin, especially after slinging hot rocks for the kind of shitheads America used to sponsor. Joining a drug lord's lineup was no big shock. Jeff had seen a lot of good guys work for bad dudes.

The grimy piece of paper in his hands implied that the old commando was, at the very least, batting for both sides. Other than the Green Beret's name, there was no writing on the page, just a diagram.

It was a stick figure tanker truck in a valley, then a hill with a stick figure pickup truck on the other side. The dotted line from the gun truck to the fuel truck went up and over the hill and into the tanker truck. A mushroom cloud hung over the fuel tanker.

"I'll be damned," Jeff said. It was something he should've thought of himself, but he'd been too wrapped up about his family and too busy hating Jason Ross.

He looked at the back of the page. Nothing. He studied the front again. There were no instructions about how to reply to the sender. It was a one-way letter.

"Okay, Bill McCallister. Let's see if you're with us or against us," Jeff mumbled.

───

JASON ROSS VISITED the refinery for the first time since the takeover. It was time to bring the colonel up to speed on current affairs and to check his temperature. He'd been away from Jenna for four days.

"I went on a motorcycle ride and did a bit of in-person recon." Jason pulled a map out of his assault pack and spread it out on the table beside the colonel's BMD-3.

"You traveled in the open? Were you not concerned that the militia would pick you up?" Zhukov asked. He'd been bunkered up inside the refinery since they seized it, worried the Utah Militia might try to take it back.

Jason played that risk up. He didn't want Zhukov thinking he could go back to the Homestead when he felt like having coffee with Jenna. "Yeah. It's a risk. If the militia recognized me, they'd capture me for sure. Fortunately, I speak perfect English." Jason grinned.

Zhukov's accent was thick as borscht. The implication was clear: if you go out, you'll get rolled up.

Jason explained how he'd done it. "I kept to the hills, mostly. I could see the militia front from Ensign Peak." Jason pointed to a spot on the map overlooking downtown. "The cartel tanks are stretched across the valley along the 215 and the I-80. I couldn't see their deployment out past the Kennecott copper mine, here. The militia is concentrated in the middle, around the airport. I buzzed the battle line, here, by Sugarhouse and the entrance to Parleys Canyon. I think that's the best spot to make contact with the cartel. There's tons of cover in the these neighborhoods and there's local civilian traffic crossing the cartel lines on the bridge at 1300 East. The cartel's covering that bridge with two tanks, but they're letting unarmed vehicles pass."

"*Hmm*," the colonel examined the map while Jason drew little squares along the south side of the freeway where he'd seen Abrams tanks. The colonel scratched his short sideburns. "Are we sure we want to make a deal with the cartel? Why not make a deal with the Utah Militia? The cartel has the tanks, but they look spread out to me. I have doubts they can hold this much ground. Where's their resupply? How much local resistance do they face?"

They were good questions. Jason had almost forgotten that Zhukov was no fool. He was a Spetsnaz officer and he'd experienced a great deal of war: Afghanistan, Chechnya, Syria, and Ukraine. It would not be easy to keep Zhukov from growing his own opinion, even without Jenna pouring poison in his ear.

"The cartel looks well supplied," Jason lied. "They have supply convoys coming up from the south. I'm not sure where they're getting their resupply, maybe Las Vegas or Phoenix. There are Army supply depots in California. Gasoline wells and refineries too. They could be getting gas from the Mexican government. I need to make contact with them to find out."

Zhukov seemed to buy it. "It doesn't hurt to talk. To collect more intelligence."

Good, Jason thought. Zhukov was on the hook. Once they started horse trading with the cartel, the Utah Militia option would fade to nothing.

Jason slapped the hood, as if an agreement had been struck. "I'll make contact with the cartel at 1300 South. I'll go in alone, in case things go south. We can't have you at-risk," he said, pretending Zhukov was in command. "I'll cross tomorrow morning at 1000 hours. If I'm not back by nightfall, consider the cartel our enemy. If I don't come back, you should negotiate the best terms you can with the militia." Jason didn't really care what Zhukov did if he didn't come back. If he was captured or killed, Zhukov could turn himself over to the Mormon Tabernacle Choir for all that he cared.

"Yah," Zhukov agreed. "Gather all the intel you can and then we'll decide what's best for the men."

"Fair enough." Jason folded the map.

He still had a chip in the big game. He owned a refinery. The *only* refinery. He'd walk up to the cartel boss and plunk that chip down, then play it for all it was worth.

This time, Kirkham would be the one packing his bags and marching off into the wasteland. That or he'd hang from a lamppost.

———

WHEREVER JEFF FOUND himself in militia HQ, between the air traffic control tower, the cluster of tents, and the communications array that'd sprung up in a Delta Airlines hangar, his eyes circled back, like leaves down a storm drain, to the Maverick Refinery.

How could he have ignored such a cataclysmic threat at his back? His personal fury with Jason Ross had blinded him to the military realities: Ross and the Russians had good reason and ample opportunity to snatch the strategic prize of the valley. Jeff hadn't thought of it because he couldn't see around Ross holding his family hostage. He hadn't considered what other belligerent acts Ross might commit. The obesity of Jeff's fury had blotted out the lean inventory he should've made of the threat. He'd been so fixated on the risk to his family that he'd lost control of the entire state. *How could he have been so emotional?*

"Jeff," the voice shook his self-condemnation. It was Tara's voice. His wife. "Jeff. It's me."

He whipped his head away from the Maverick to see her striding toward him. She threw her arms around his thick shoulders, pulled him into her chest, and kissed him hard on the lips.

"You're okay," he said.

She leaned back from the embrace but kept hold. "You look like shit. You missed me, didn't you?"

"You will never know..." Jeff stammered.

Tara chuckled. "Oh, I have a pretty good idea."

"No, I mean...I've fucked things up royally."

"Um yes. Yeah, you have." Tara had never been one to bullshit. "But I'm here now and we can un-fuck this. Sit down and tell me everything."

"Yes, ma'am." Jeff pulled her toward the command tent. What he really needed was to get naked with her, connect, and put all the separation behind him. He needed to *feel* her safe and back in his arms. But there was no time for that. "The boys are okay?" He asked, already knowing the answer from his call earlier with the Mormon president.

"Leif's stump has finally healed. The boys are fine. But they're not going to be fine if we don't win this war. So, let's focus on winning. I'm sorry I climbed up your ass before. I was wrong. You were right. We can't afford to lose to the cartel. Focus up and tell me everything that's happened."

Jeff sat down on a stack of ammo crates in his command tent and briefed her up to the current moment, up to the part where Jason and the Russians were probably trading the Maverick refinery to the cartel.

"He won't do it," Tara said, flat as stone and twice as hard. "Jason Ross will not betray Jenna, not again."

"He's a piece-of-shit sonofabitch," Jeff started into a tirade.

"Hey!" Tara snapped her fingers two inches in front of his face. "No time for that. Hold fast. I was his captive. He never so much as said a cross word to me or the boys. He didn't lock us in a room or even post a guard. He's a prick, for sure, but he will stop himself before the point of no return."

"You're wrong, Tara. You have Stockholm Syndrome or something. Remember, Jason Ross was going to send his own wife into exile, to die. He was going to send her out into the flu and the winter. He crossed the point of no return months ago."

Tara shook her head vigorously. "No, no, no. He *said* he was going to send her into exile and you intervened. He wouldn't have gone through with it. You've got to see around your hate and see him for who he is."

"He's a shitbag, that's who he is."

"Just stop, Jeff. You're painted into a corner where everything's black and white. But things are never black and white in the real world. Besides, we don't have a choice. You have to trust that Jenna can turn him."

"She thinks she can bring him and the Russians to our side?" Jeff said, but he didn't believe it.

"Not every war is won with bombs and bullets," she argued against the doubt in his voice. "I never spoke to Jason, but I spoke to Jenna. I spoke to her a lot. She has this under control. You've got to believe in her."

Jeff found himself really wanting to, if just for Tara.

"Jeff. Believe in her. Believe in us."

He didn't know if she meant he should believe in their marriage or believe in the women of the Homestead. He didn't ask, so strong was his desire to blend into Tara, to be one with her again, to be healthy again. The impulse was so powerful, he almost did believe.

14

Shortwave Radio 7150kHz
3:00pm

"Let's get back to our game, 'where would you rather be?' Zach took answers on our receiving channel for three days. Here are your answers, Planet Shortwave.

"Tom in Fort Meyers, Florida, wants to be 'wherever the soil doesn't suck so bad.' Britt in Everett, Georgia, said the same thing. 'I wanna be where the ground ain't so sandy.' He says, 'We have to mix in our own poop to grow anything.' Sounds lovely, Britt.

"Glenda in Smithfield, Virginia, says she wants to be anywhere there's not so many rats." The pig farms went to rot and now there's a pneumonic plague outbreak.

"Sandy soil, poop fertilizer and rats. Maybe we should've named this segment, 'Things I Should've Considered Before Moving There.'"

Grand America Hotel
Salt Lake City, Utah

Jason had to knock on the steel shell of a cartel tank to get someone from the cartel to talk to him. After a storm of heavily-accented questions and two-way radio calls, an electric gun buggy whizzed up to the security outpost on the 1300 East bridge and picked him up. They took him to the Grand America hotel in downtown Salt Lake, where he and Jenna used to go for one night "staycations."

A thin, grizzled white man met him in the lobby.

"Jason Ross, as I live and breath," the old man said as he greeted him with a handshake.

"Have we met before?" Jason asked.

"No," he pumped Jason's hand as he spoke, "but I'm aware that you're a local legend. You're the ultimate prepper who built a mountain stronghold and held out against the apocalypse. I've been known to put aside a few MREs myself. Name's Bill McCallister, Master Sergeant, Special Forces, retired."

"And you're cartel?" Jason asked with a cock of his head.

"Army of Southern Liberation," McCallister corrected. "We're a combination of Mexican and American forces."

Jason noticed he hadn't said "Mexican and American military." They were cartel, but McCallister was being cute about it. "What brings you here?" He made it sound like Jason was visiting the church across the street from his regular church, not flirting with defection.

"My allies and I are the hottest girl in school and we're shopping for Homecoming dates."

"*Ahh.*" Bill tapped the side of his nose with a finger. "That ole game. Whatcha got under your brassiere, if I may be so bold?"

"Two million gallons of gasoline, give or take."

Bill sucked air through his front teeth. "And what do you want for it?"

"Jeff Kirkham on a spit, for starters."

"So it's like that." Bill said, nodding.

"We want safety for our families and a seat at the table. Is your boss capable of remembering who his friends are when this is all over?" Jason didn't know how to guarantee the answer, but he could ask the question.

A shadow flitted across Bill's face. Jason couldn't determine if it was a tell or if the man meant to give him a peek behind the curtain.

"He's a good enough chap."

So he wasn't.

"All right," Jason said, but he was unnerved. He hadn't thought through what he'd do if the cartel turned out to be a reckless band of thieves. "I've got some questions about your ability to project force, and to govern. I need to lay eyes on your supply chain, and the depth of your bench. I have allies and they have questions."

"Allies?" Bill raised an eyebrow.

"I represent a consortium of interests," Jason said. "We have tanks, thousands of commandos, and the ability to project force. That's how we've come into possession of the Maverick refinery."

Bill's eyes widened.

The part about controlling the Maverick needed to be crystal clear. It might be the thing that guaranteed that Jason would make it out of there alive. The conversation was amicable enough so far, but he could be imprisoned as a spy for the militia or executed on the spot. If the rumors were to be believed, the cartel tortured, maimed and sometimes defiled their prisoners. "And I need to meet your boss, personally," Jason added.

"I can arrange that," Bill said. "Do you have proof that you actually control the refinery? I only ask because I know my boss will ask."

"If I could get my radio back..." Jason began. The guards who'd brought him here had relieved him of all weapons and comms.

"Certainly." Bill smiled. In his eyes, Jason could see his mind going a million miles a minute.

"McCallister tells me you control the refinery." The tall, handsome drug kingpin handed Jason a glass of brown liquor. Dinner was on its way, but the sun still had a long path across the southern sky.

"My allies and I control it," Jason corrected and sat the glass down. The man before him had movie star good looks, but his mangled right ear told another, more sinister story. Jason needed the drug lord to know that he was not without recourse should anything happen to him.

"Can you prove that?" Castillo smiled, but the muscles around his eyes remained impassive.

Jason held up his radio for permission.

Castillo nodded.

"White One, this is Oracle."

"Good copy, Oracle," the radio replied within seconds.

"Initiate dirty burn," Jason said.

"Initiating."

Jason pointed the radio antenna north, toward the white smokestacks at the base of the foothills, eight miles away from the balcony of their banquet room. One of the stacks loosed a thick, black column of smoke. After a few moments, it ceased.

Castillo nodded again. "I see," he said. "So they're Russian? Your allies?"

The slight accent over the radio had been enough for Castillo to deduce the truth, or maybe he already knew. The fact that Jason's allies were Spetsnaz was information Jason was ready to divulge, but Castillo's perceptiveness was unnerving. He picked up the glass and sipped to hide his face. This whole setup, the fancy Mexican food, the tour of the main battle tanks, the stealthy gun buggies, and the salt-and-pepper demigod straight out of central casting, with the livid scar around his neck, it was too much like meeting Lucifer.

He was committed now. In it for "all the marbles" as they say. Jason plowed ahead. "They're Spetsnaz. They were deployed here to secure the American ICBMs."

"And now?" Castillo asked.

"And now, it appears that their Motherland has bigger fish to fry. They're stranded, but still a battle-capable unit, complete with armor."

Castillo sipped his glass while Jason rattled his saber.

"Guatemalan sipping rum." Castillo pointed his chin at the glass. "It used to cost three hundred a bottle. Now, it's priceless, like gasoline," he chuckled. "Only gasoline goes bad in a year. How long has that gas been sitting in those storage tanks?" He tipped his glass at the refinery.

"Since the collapse," Jason said, suddenly on the defensive. He didn't actually know how long the gas had been in the storage tanks. It was important information, but there was no record of it they could find. The computer networks at the refinery all died with the electricity.

"Lucky for you, my tanks could probably run on my piss after I drink this," Castillo held his glass up, amusing himself. "Even your degraded fuel might do."

Jason hadn't foreseen a negotiation. He'd thought he'd be the one holding all the cards and naming his price.

"Well that's good," Jason sputtered.

"So if we push through to the Maverick tomorrow, you'll secure the refinery for us. You'll hold it in trust?" Castillo pushed.

It was moving too fast. Jason shuffled his feet. He looked around the room. Bill McCallister had left but Jason hadn't noticed. He was alone with this man, this dark demigod.

"I have to speak to my...partners. At present, they're prepared to destroy the refinery in case of any attack." Jason was lying. Jason hoped it was obvious to Zhukov that he should destroy the refinery if threatened, but the Russians were more likely to simply withdraw if faced with a superior force. They had no reason to set the storage tanks on fire. Jason did his best to hide his recalculations behind a mask of feigned disinterest. "I have to get back before sundown or they'll open negotiations with the Utah Militia." That part was almost true.

"Oh really?" Castillo smiled. "Then we better get you back. I'm sorry you won't get to enjoy dinner."

Jason set his glass down, half full. He couldn't remember the taste of the expensive liquor. It could've been stale beer for all he'd noticed. He wanted out of there, away from this man and his penetrating, green eyes.

"It's good to finally meet you," Jason said reflexively.

Castillo cast an amused grin. "Indeed."

Jason fled the banquet room without shaking hands with the devil.

IT'D BEEN days since Ross and his Russians had taken control of the Maverick, and the Hoodies had still not advanced. Jeff Kirkham stood outside his tent sipping afternoon coffee and wondering how he was still alive. He had a vastly inferior force and posed no credible threat to his enemy. Why hadn't they swept him from the valley?

The snow had finally drawn back from the Oquirrh mountains. The brimming valley sage and spindly tamarack had fully awoken from winter. They pumped new color, blues and salted greens, across the marshes from the airport to the smokestacks of the old copper mine fifteen miles away. White crags stippled the angular Wasatch mountain range to the east. The stubborn snow at the top of the ski resorts might last half the summer.

Jeff's Mormons were trickling back. He'd lost 15,000 men behind battle lines when the Hoodies surged up to the 215 freeway, but many of his men had filtered back, many without their trucks. Another wave of 3,000 militiamen accompanied Mat Best out of Idaho and western Washington State. His troop numbers swelled; it wasn't enough to stop armor, but enough to keep them pinned in their metal crates by sniper fire. Jeff thought of the cartel street soldiers, steeping in the sweet vapor of one another's MRE farts.

He'd sent Tara and the boys away to an army buddy's home in Tremonton, seventy miles north of Salt Lake. With his family outside the reach of immediate harm, he could breathe again. His hatred for Ross had settled to a low simmer and he could see the waking world more clearly. Things made more sense. The battlefield arrayed before him like a sand table with little, metal tanks and tiny, painted soldiers.

Jeff couldn't afford to hope that Ross meant well, though Jenna Ross swore that he could be contained. Jason Ross had taken the refinery by force of arms, and the Maverick refinery was still a gun pointed at Jeff's balls. Ross couldn't possibly be dealing in the best interests of Utah. Yet as every day passed, hope crawled up from the pit of his restless gut. It filled his belly and made his head fizz with unearned promise. Something invisible held the Hood Rats at the 215 freeway, and it wasn't Jeff's gun trucks.

With each passing day, it became more likely that the cartel knew the militia had lost control of the refinery. They stood nose-to-nose in this valley, sipping from the same streams and breathing the same air. Locals darted back and forth across the battle lines, carrying food, firewood and rumors. The Hoodies had to know, but still they waited.

Were the Hoodies entirely out of gas? Impossible. They had enough fuel to advance five miles to the refinery. No tanker truck had crossed between St. George and Salt Lake City since the surge, but they could shuffle fuel between the Abrams. They could mount an assault even if most of the Abrams were on "empty."

Was Ross negotiating with them? Was that why they waited?

Maybe. In that case, Jeff was at their mercy. He heard a familiar whine, a shriek in the sky. Then a low growl.

Burrrrr. Burrrrr. Burrrr. Burrrrrrrrrrr.

The ground vibrated under his feet. The sky ripped open with a feral snarl and two A-10 Thunderbolt "Warthogs" rocketed past the air traffic control tower, peeled apart and banked over the foothills to line up, again, down the length of the 215 freeway. Jeff shielded his eyes against the morning sun and saw a new column of black smoke on the cartel lines. Something exploded and shook the ground. An Abrams tank had died. Smoke braided skyward.

"Die, you motherfuckers," Jeff bristled. His smile broke new lines on his face. "Burn, baby, burn."

The pair of Warthogs lined up down Parley's Canyon, one behind the other, and cruised low and slow along the freeway, directly in line with the airport and Jeff's vantage. The Avenger cannons roared.

Burrrrr. Burrrrr. Burrrr. Burr... Burrrrr. Burrrrr. Burrrr. Burr.

Another concussion, this one farther away, rumbled underfoot. A new, black bundle of threads curled from the ground. A secondary explosion sent an orange mushroom cloud churning against the backdrop of city and mountains.

The jets tore over Jeff, wagging their wingtips, one after the other. They banked north over the Great Salt Lake, heading for Hill Air Force Base in Ogden. The Warthogs had finally arrived.

"Eat dick, Castillo," Jeff swore. He plowed back into his command tent to await the incoming report from Hill AFB.

"Why only two?" Jeff barked into the radio.

"They have three combat-ready pilots and one of them had to stay in Tucson to train more," JT Taylor reported over the radio.

"Get those two back in the sky for another sortie," Jeff ordered.

"No can," JT said. "We're still trying to figure out how to load the damn guns. Nobody at Hill has ever done it before and the pilots don't know how to either. It requires a special loading truck and we don't know if there's one on the base. We're looking for a manual, or something."

Jeff had transferred all the 30mm ammo from Tooele Army Depot to Hill last March before it got overrun by Hoodies. But when it came to modern weapon platforms, especially air assets, the devil was most certainly in the details. Stupid shit like a missing, purpose-built loading trolley could shut down an entire wing of attack aircraft.

"Figure it out. Work all night. Do whatever it takes," Jeff ordered into his mic. At the same time, he knew JT couldn't cut corners. Arming an aircraft was nothing like loading a rifle or hucking a grenade. There were six hundred ways to do it wrong, some of which could damage the airframe. Complex weapons were never designed to be operated by knuckleheaded militiamen in an apocalypse. They depended on months of training, and an expert crew. Chucking stuff against the wall to see what stuck wasn't in the design process. The Chair Force hadn't even known what the word "improvisation" meant.

Previous to Black Autumn, Hill AFB, a dozen miles from Salt Lake City, had a dozen F-35 Lightning fighter jets, but the jets had been redeployed elsewhere during the collapse. There'd been no fighter planes at Hill when Jeff occupied the base in February and no pilots to fly them. Most of the servicemen stationed at Hill had vanished, some of them to their homes in Ogden, and many to their families sprinkled across the U.S. The spotty skeleton crew now at Hill would do the best they could, but Warthogs hadn't been the air base's main gig, even when they were fully staffed.

Jeff needed the guys from Davis-Monthan to withdraw to Utah. Tucson was a dedicated Warthog airbase, and there'd be lots of men and women trained on the weapons system there. But like everything else in this godforsaken place, getting personnel to Ogden would take time, and he still didn't have comms with his people in Tucson. Jeff hadn't even known these two planes were coming.

Now, the cat was out of the proverbial bag. Castillo had gotten his first lesson in how every weapons system, even a main battle tank, had an evil twin in the arsenal, a weapon that could render it as helpless as a wet kitten. With the arrival of the Warthogs, Castillo would have a fire under his ass. The odds of him making a grab for the Maverick refinery had just gone up five hundred percent.

If Jeff had actual control over this three-ringed donkey show, he would've held the Warthogs back until they could mount a definitive strike. He would've pre-positioned enough planes and ammo, so that it'd give the Hoodies no time to assemble a counter-attack.

Instead, they'd just blown their wad on killing two damn tanks.

———

JASON RETURNED to the Homestead after dark. He'd crossed the battlefront at dusk, under the shadow of the cartel's Abrams at the 1300 East bridge. Jason drove directly to Zhukov at the Maverick refinery. He had to make sure the colonel didn't jump the gun and begin talks with Kirkham or the Mormons.

Zhukov was waiting patiently. He poured Jason a finger of vodka. The Russians seemed to have brought an inexhaustible supply with them.

Jason cut straight to what little he knew. "The cartel wants the refinery. They say they'll give us whatever we ask."

"How do we know this *Castillo* will keep his word?" Zhukov

asked.

Jason shrugged, feigning ambivalence. In truth, Castillo scared him shitless. With his sinister poise and grotesque scars, Castillo could've walked onto the set of any spaghetti western movie and played the evil land baron.

"This is a negotiation, and it's going to take several meetings to work it out," Jason explained with more confidence than he felt. "It's up to us to come up with a deal where our future is guaranteed and secure."

"How can we guarantee that?"

Jason poured himself another splash of vodka. "I have some ideas. None of them are watertight, but layered together, they should be enough."

Jason and Zhukov talked for another hour, devising an interlocking stack of carrots and sticks that should keep the cartel in check once they gave them the fuel. As the bottle drew down, the two men ran out of things to say, and Jason saw himself out.

He drove the short distance between the refinery and the Homestead, wary of militia eyes. It probably wasn't the best idea to take his own car, a black BMW sport utility, but getting another car fueled up would've been a pain in the ass, so he risked it. Driving his old car, from the good old days, lent him an air of confidence he sorely needed. Driving drunk felt even better. There was no one on the street to hit. He was like a diplomat who met with foreign dignitaries and flouted the law.

The Spetsnaz guard at the Homestead gate saluted him, though it was a weird thing to do, given that he was neither an officer nor Russian.

Jason pulled around to the office entrance and parked in his regular spot on the cobblestone drive. He unlocked the office wing and groped around to the minibar. He didn't want to turn on the lights for fear of attracting anyone who might disturb his peace now that he'd gotten his drink on.

It was 11:30 at night and most everyone would be asleep. The Homesteaders kept farmer's hours these lengthening days of spring; they were up at dawn and back to bed not long after sundown. But someone might still see his light and come nagging for answers about sewage treatment, allocation of fuel for the rototiller, or some other piece of daily minutiae. He poured a glass of cheap whiskey by braille.

The full moon poured through the French doors and lit the heavy wood table of the conference room.

"Hi, Dad," someone said from a chair in a dark corner of the office.

Jason nearly dropped his drink to draw his gun. The liquor sloshed and splashed on the stone floor.

A figure stood from the shadows. "It's me. Sage."

"*Sage?*" Jason knew the name, but struggled to retrieve it.

He reached for the switch and flicked on the light. His son stood before him, dressed in camouflage, wearing a warrior's chest rig and a gun belt. A full, brown beard wrapped his chin, but his eyes were those of his seventeen-year-old boy.

Jason had accepted that his son was dead, but here he stood. A man. He felt his face flush. His legs went weak. His heart broke. He tossed his glass on the desk and wrapped his arms around his son.

"You're alive."

"Yeah," Sage said, his words smothered against his father's neck. "I'm married. I have a baby on the way."

Jason held him at arm's length to see if he was serious. "You're just eighteen. Barely old enough to vote."

Sage laughed. "It was a really, really long year. I'm a lawman and a rancher now. Wallowa County Sheriff's Deputy. A soldier too, now, I guess." He looked at the sleeves of his camo jacket.

"How'd you make it through the winter?"

"I learned how to survive. Then I crossed the mountains into Union County on my way home. That's where I met my wife and her family. They needed me and I needed them. We tended cattle and hunted elk. That's how we survived. Ranching."

"And you're married?"

"I married Katie Lathrop, daughter of the county commissioner over in Wallowa. I work their ranch. Our ranch now, I guess. We're having a baby end of summer."

"I'll be damned." Jason snagged another tumbler and poured one for his son. They touched glasses. "To life," Jason said.

"To fathers who teach their sons how to handle themselves," Sage said.

"Did you talk to your mother yet?" Jason asked with barely-concealed trepidation.

"Yeah. We spent most of the afternoon catching up. I'm on leave from the Utah Militia today and tomorrow."

Jason shifted in his chair. "What'd she tell you?"

"Everything, I think."

"About Emily?"

Sage's head drooped, and he looked into his glass and nodded.

"Did she tell you about the orphanage?"

Sage looked him straight in his eyes. "You got on the wrong side of right on that one. I'm not judging; I got myself there too a time or two. Luckily, some good people showed me grace and forgave me. You know she still loves you, right?"

"Who?"

Sage laughed. "Mom, of course."

Jason didn't know that. Not at all. "What makes you think so?" he asked.

"She told me. And she said you're on the verge of making a dumpster-load of bad decisions. She said you hold the refinery and you might be doing a deal with the cartel to give it to them."

Jason didn't bother denying it. "You don't understand. It's one tyrant or the other, here. There are no good guys or bad guys, just bad guys and bad guys."

Sage nursed the whiskey. "Do you remember last year when you asked me what I thought the word 'honor' meant?"

It might as well have been a thousand years ago. Jason had to really think, to reassemble the old world in his mind before he could remember something he'd said back then.

Sage paused, then continued speaking, "I was running around town getting it on with all the high school girls from down the hill. You pulled me up short and asked me what I thought the word 'honor' meant."

Jason didn't exactly remember, but it sounded like something the old version of himself would've asked. "Yes. I remember," he said. He didn't like where this was going.

"You told me, 'honor is doing what's good for everyone, even when it's not good for you.' "

Jason set his tumbler down hard on the desk. "You make it sound like you know what's good for everyone. You don't understand how complicated it's become. That sonofabitch who leads your militia…he stole our land. He ran me off my property. He took our *house!*" The burst of rage, combined with the booze, caused him to sway a little on his feet.

Sage sighed. "It's late," he said. He polished off the last of the whiskey in his own glass.

Jason regretted slamming the glass. He didn't want to drive a wedge between him and his son. He didn't want him to go to war on that note.

"Hold on, Sage." Jason held up a hand. "Sincerely, how do you know what's honorable? Especially now, when we've all done all these things we regret. Everyone here is a half-baked warlord and we are *real* enemies. Real, *no-bullshit,* shoot-each-other-on-sight enemies. How does your honor fit into that world?"

"It's not *my honor*, Dad. It's your honor. You planted it in my heart, and that damn question ran me up one side of the mountain and down the other this last winter. That question is the reason I survived. You're not the only one who's been wrapped around the axle during the apocalypse, trying to do what's right." Sage set his glass down next to his father's and smiled. "It's a bitch, but it's the only way."

"So how do you know what's honorable?" Jason surrendered.

"You do what *she* thinks is right. Simple as beef stew."

Jason didn't need to ask his son who he meant by "she."

"See you in the morning, Dad," Sage said. The boy, who had become a man, hugged his father, picked up his rifle, and headed out to find a place to sleep.

———

JASON SWIRLED his glass and drank alone for another hour.

If he gave up the Homestead and the refinery to the militia, Kirkham would kill him or exile him. If he gave the refinery to the cartel, Jenna would refuse to take him back. He could only see one way where he got both: Kirkham needed to die.

If Jason gave the cartel the refinery, they'd go through Jeff Kirkham like a knife through a bag of shit. Kirkham would be gone and Jason would be governor of Utah, if not king.

Jenna had already turned Jason's son against him. If he gave her what she wanted this time, she'd control him until the day he died. She'd bleed him for her every desire. If she won this, he'd be a pawn in her game forever. She had only to withdraw her affection, and he'd crumble. She'd use it every time he didn't give her what she wanted.

Could he really live like that?

He left his glass and walked out of the office and into the night. The air was chill and wet, but it felt good against the skin of his arms. He could just keep walking, down to the Beringer women's shelter. He could bring them back to his room. Then it would be over. His course would be set, his marriage finally done.

It was just the booze talking.

Honor, his son had reminded him, like a scene from a movie that'd stirred him, but it'd been an old movie, even before the collapse. Honor had been a big deal to him, like the several religions he'd passed through.

But a woman like Jenna would never stop, his booze-addled brain argued. He would never be "good enough." The rest of their lives, she would wrangle him, cajole him, threaten him into becoming the servant of her will. If he didn't stand up for himself now, he would die a dim projection of a relentless woman.

As bad as Castillo appeared, at least he was just passing through to another place. He didn't insist on taking up residence in Jason's soul. Castillo would reward him, then move on to Idaho, or Montana, or Colorado. Castillo felt like a predictable wind when compared to Jenna.

Jason was too old, and too world weary to subject his will to a woman again, certainly not to a beautiful woman with decades of bending men to her will.

She had betrayed him. Once, with the orphanage. Twice, when she'd helped Kirkham steal his home. Three times, when she'd freed Tara Kirkham. Now, for her grand finale, she would turn his last, surviving son against him. Jason had been a fool to think she would ever love him like a person should. She could never bind to him as mate and companion. To her, he was horseflesh. He was harnessed to the plow, to furrow the ground ahead of her implacable, endless desires.

Jenna moved through the world like a shadow, quiet and fine. Nothing rattled or shook as she passed, but still, she might be the ultimate tyrant of all.

He would not surrender himself to her hand, no matter how much he burned for her.

Castillo would get his refinery.

15

"The summer after the collapse, the first legal crises erupted in small towns where survival rates had been high. The critical question was: who owned the land? Families had perished up and down entire lines of inheritance. Where one died, often all died. The county courthouses that hadn't burned were full of titles and deeds attributed to people who no longer existed. Corporations were nothing more than dusty paper in forgotten file drawers. Federal and state governments, in many states the largest landowners, were reduced to ashes. Even as people peeked out of their shelters to survey a tenuous future, they perceived an opportunity to squat on unclaimed land and add it to their family lineage. Neighbors objected. Clans argued theories of ownership. The few surviving lawyers had forever-conflicting ideas. An estimated ninety-eight percent of American land was unclaimed—a legal keg full of dynamite, surrounded by a pool of gasoline."

— THE AMERICAN DARK AGES, BY WILLIAM BELLAHER, NORTH AMERICAN TEXTBOOKS, 2037

Somerset Place Apartments

Tucson, Arizona

NOAH MILLER HAD NEVER BEEN IN THE MILITARY, BUT HE WAS GETTING his fill of house-to-house door kicking. They called it "pop goes the weasel," and it was a lot less fun than it sounded. Door kicking reminded Noah of stories his dad told of going house to house in Fallujah, which was ironic since his dad might've been the one who ordered these shitheads to sneak into Tucson to blast him in the face.

Noah climbed the stairs of the Somerset Place apartments and peeked around the corner of a hallway. The wall exploded in chunks of wood, sheetrock, and paint. Noah threw himself back onto his buddies, causing a domino effect of five men tumbling down half a flight of stairs.

"Crew-served! Bring up the SAW," Noah called his own belt-fed machine gun forward.

"I think it's jammed between my ass cheeks, sir," one of the men buried in the pile yelled back. "Standby."

They'd been taking sporadic small arms fire, presumably from cartel forces that'd moved into the neighborhoods surrounding the Davis-Monthan airbase the day before. Yesterday, they'd come across enemy gunmen in the ruins of Tucson, but this was the first time they'd faced a crew-served machine gun.

Noah's team was on the second floor of a three-story apartment building. There were twenty-six buildings in the Somerset Place complex.

Noah pointed his rifle at the top of the stairs, but the enemy machine gun position had gone quiet, no thunder of bootsteps down the hallway. The Hoodies were probably in the same boat as he and his men, undermanned and spread out across a dozen neighborhoods surrounding the airfield. Like an army of badgers fighting an army of raccoons, nobody had the upper hand.

Noah hefted a hand grenade from his chest rig and tried to

guess the physics of bouncing it off the wall at the top of the stairs and sending it at a forty-five degree angle down the hallway. He'd caught a glimpse of the gun emplacement at the end of the corridor, at least forty feet away and surrounded by what looked like refrigerators tipped on their sides. A grenade wasn't going to conform to that funky geometry.

Longhair motioned for Noah's attention. He dug through his backpack with an eager grin. Noah's ears were ringing like a train whistle. He had no idea what Longhair was trying to tell him.

"Forget the SAW. We're heading upstairs," Noah gesticulated with his gloved hand. "One flight up. We're not the only ones here with grenades." Longhair threw his pack back over his shoulder and flashed a thumbs up. The team rushed to the third floor. Sal from Anaheim cleared the hallway and gave the hand sign for all clear. Longhair shouted something.

"What?" Noah yelled back at Longhair.

Longhair held up a finger, then pulled a long, yellow power tool out of his pack. It was a battery-powered saber saw with a mean-looking blade.

"You've been carrying that this whole time?" Noah shouted.

Longhair nodded vigorously and showed his teeth.

"Well, okay then." Noah moved forward and doubled up on Sal covering the hallway.

Sal bounded forward to the first apartment on the left, booted the door and rushed inside. Noah flowed behind him and broke left to Sal's right buttonhook. Their thundering boots triggered a barrage from the 240D on the floor below, splintering the floor of the hallway and forcing the others back to the stairwell.

Noah flowed through the apartment, clearing as much of each room as possible from outside each doorway, then rushing inside to seize the point of dominance. After two rooms, he came face-to-face with Sal, clearing counter-clockwise back toward him.

"Clear," Sal hissed.

"Clear," Noah agreed. "Come up!" he yelled back to the stairwell.

Longhair ducked into the apartment and moved forward, clearing the space ahead of him with the saber saw in his hands, his rifle slung. Noah glared at him and Longhair triggered the reciprocating blade. It buzzed like a three-pound hornet. Some moments in war were so jacked, you had to laugh.

Longhair's tool opened up new possibilities that everyone instantly understood—better ones than a frontal assault on a machine gun. They'd cut down from this floor to the floor below, where the Hoodies were bunkered up, and flank their asses.

Sal carved up the corner of the carpet with his folding knife, got ahold of it, then ripped it back, revealing the pad and plywood underneath. Noah helped peel the pad back, exposing half the bedroom floor. Another guy tipped the bed and mattress up and out of the way. Stacks of dusty Playboy and Hustler magazines tumbled into the light of day.

"Sweet!" Longhair exulted. "Grab me that one with the redhead," he pointed the saber saw at a Hustler cover with a buxom girl.

Noah swept the magazines aside with his boot and yanked on the carpet again, exposing a seam in the plywood. Longhair went to work, buzzing the seam open into a big, circular hole. The crew-served machine gun answered the DeWalt by chewing up the floor in the hallway.

Behind their refrigerator barricade, on the floor below, the Hoodies wouldn't have had a clue what the tool noise meant. They were well protected, but blind, and cornered.

Longhair pried the circle of plywood up with the screeching of nails, and started in on the floor joists. He cut them away in chunks, then kicked a hole in the ceiling of the second-story room below. A ragged chunk of drywall dropped free into a space that appeared to be the kitchen of an apartment. Longhair tossed the saber saw aside, threw himself on the floor and poked his head through the hole in the floor.

"All clear," he gasped for breath as he resurfaced. He pointed at Noah's chest. "Gimme that grenade."

Noah unclipped the grenade and handed it over. Longhair jammed it into his pocket, breech-checked his rifle and dropped through the hole in the floor, landing with a thunderous clap on top of a linoleum countertop.

At the sound of the crash, the enemy crew-served machine gunned through the apartment like a scythe. The hailstorm of .308 rounds blew bits of wood, cabinet and sheetrock around like confetti. Longhair had dropped to the floor and lay curled into a ball behind the counter.

Noah rushed back into the hallway and emptied a mag down into the floor, approximately over where he'd seen the machine gun nest. The shooting stopped.

Noah ran back into the apartment while he swapped out mags. "You alive down there?" he shouted to Longhair.

Longhair uncurled from the fetal position, raised a thumb and crawled out of sight.

With Longhair sneaking around on the second floor, the team needed to keep the machine gunner's attention.

"Back down. Back down." Noah flashed a knife hand back down the stairwell. The team *trump-trump-trumped* down the stairs. Now, everyone was back on the second floor, but Longhair was perpendicular to the machine gun nest, though blinded by thin walls.

Noah got to the corner first and turkey-peeked around. The 240D swiveled toward him, but he ducked back before it roared a barrage into the corner.

"Keep their attention here," he ordered the man behind him, then Noah ran back up the stairs to the third floor. They were slowly but surely surrounding the machine gun nest; Longhair and the team on the second floor and Noah back on the third, looking for an angle down into the fridge bunker.

Noah snaked through the rooms of the third floor apartment until he figured that he was perpendicular to the machine gun nest, then he kicked through the wall with his heel until he busted between studs and re-entered the hallway, directly over the machine gunners. They'd have to detach the gun from the pintle mount to shoot up at him. Noah opened fire into the floor with his AR. His men on the floor below fired down the hallway. Longhair went to town from the room below Noah. After who-knows-how-many mags, all went quiet.

"Clear," Longhair shouted up through the floor.

"Clear," the men in the hall echoed.

Noah changed his mag, breech checked, and returned to the second floor. His men milled around like bored puppies.

"Two dead Hoodies," Longhair said as he heaved for air, bleeding off adrenaline. He had half a pound of sheetrock dust in his hair.

Noah glanced behind the fridges. Two shredded bodies lay on top of each other like bloody ducks on a waterfowl pile. One of them had taken a round through the top of his head and out the neck.

"Leave the machine gun," Noah said. The 240D required two men to manage it.

"Hah! And y'all said I was dumb for carrying power tools in my backpack!" Longhair triumphed.

"You're an idiot." Noah grabbed him by the shoulder. "A very brave idiot."

Swooosh! Swoosh!

Twin rockets fired outside the apartment building.

"Oh, shit," Noah shouted. "To the roof! To the roof!" He'd been so caught up with the machine gun that he hadn't noticed the whine of jet engines on approach.

Boom! Boom!

They rushed up the stairs and burst onto the roof. Two apartment buildings over, three strange men stared at the sky, one of them with a Stinger missile launcher on his shoulder. Noah opened fire across the void. The men dropped out of sight behind the low wall around the building's roof.

The scream of the jet engine warbled. Noah dropped to his knees and searched the sky. One Warthog bled black smoke from an engine. It flipped on its side, then cartwheeled into a gray hill at two hundred miles an hour.

Ka-whomp! The concussion felt like it might sweep Noah off of the roof. His men scrambled to line up on the roof's edge, searching for targets, but seeing nothing.

Another Warthog came in high over the apartment complex, trying to keep as much distance as possible from the SAM threat. It looked like he might try to dive-bomb the runway from high altitude. At the last minute, the pilot reconsidered and pulled up, swooping around to the west to make another run. Then, the plane righted itself and changed course, probably landing on the downwind side of the airfield.

They were pilot trainees, Noah realized. And they'd taken SAM missile fire while learning how to land.

Another Stinger launched, ten buildings over.

Pop! Swoosh! A contrail streaked across the sky, corkscrewing toward the fleeing Warthog.

The buildings were all on the same level and Noah couldn't see anything to shoot. Another Stinger fired from yet another building.

He watched helplessly as the jet slowly banked away. The first Stinger ran out of range and it exploded harmlessly in naked sky with a *ka-thump*. The second sought the hot engines of the Warthog. A quarter-mile short of its target, it too burst into a fireball. The Warthog ran clear, alive and free over the southern desert.

A black column of smoke rose from where the first 'hog had plowed into the ground.

"Let's go." Noah waved his men down from the roof. "Let's clear these other buildings." It was all they could do, too little, too late.

―――

FOUR HOURS LATER, it was dark. Noah's team finally cleared Somerset Place, just twenty buildings of the thousands of residential structures that surrounded the airbase. They failed to encounter any enemy, save the two they'd killed behind the 240D. The Hoodies had fired their Stingers and dipped into the sprawl of Tucson. They only had to hunt the sky, where a Warthog stood out like a raven for all the world to see. Noah had thousands of homes, offices and apartments to search, and even after he cleared a building, the Hoodies could move right back in the next day.

Nobody knew how many Stingers the Hoodies fielded in Tucson, the missile system was entirely man-portable, weighing little more than a machine gun. Wherever the Hoodies had dug up the Stinger missiles, there were probably hundreds more.

When the collapse occurred last October, dozens of army depots were filled with weaponry. With enough time and heavy equipment, men would crack open the bunkers and all those potent, military weapons would pass into general circulation.

Noah heard it over the radio: the pilot who'd gone down in the doomed Warthog had been Colonel Withers. Not only had they lost a pilot, but their leader.

"Fuck this," Noah said to Longhair as they drug their asses back to the airbase. "We need to burn it all down."

"The world?" Longhair asked.

"No, dipshit. Tucson. We need to burn these neighborhoods back at least a mile. Burn them to rubble. It's the only way we're going to get planes outta here safely."

"Sheesh. How're we going to stop the fire once we start it?" Longhair wondered.

"Maybe we won't."

"What about the people?" Longhair asked. They'd encountered pockets of survivors while they cleared. The remainders of Tucson lived like vermin in the dead city.

"They're going to have to get the hell out of the way. If they've survived this long, they probably have enough common sense to smell smoke and leave."

"Probably," Longhair muttered, not sounding convinced. The people they'd seen looked more like starving coyotes than humans. Arizona was not a good place for survivors. Utahns were a thousand times better off. They had more food and water, and less crime.

"Boss." Sal ran up to Noah. "Airbase folks are calling for you on the comms. They say you're in charge now."

"Well, that's fan-fucking-tastic," Noah cursed. "Just what this petting zoo needed: a jackass to run it."

The Homestead
Oakwood, Utah

JENNA ROSS DIDN'T OWN a rifle, but she had trained a lot with a Glock. She retrieved one from the shoebox-sized biometric safe in the house's gym. It'd been forgotten in the months of survival, and she'd kept it in mind, like a backup plan of sorts. Not a soul had used the gym in all that time, daily life being workout enough.

She'd exhausted all of her influence as a woman and mother, and now, she would risk her life. She simply could not allow her husband to follow through with the plan she feared he harbored in his heart, an alliance with the Mexican cartel.

Jenna didn't know how the gun might factor into her gambit.

She'd need it for protection to cross the few miles of residential streets between the Homestead and the refinery. Would she need it for anything else? Something more sinister and final? Jenna avoided thinking about it—side-stepping the mental picture of drawing the gun on her husband of thirty years and ending his life. To even imagine it caused her breath to seize in her throat. Was she even capable of it?

She had no proof that Jason planned on turning to the cartel; nevertheless, she knew it in her gut. Like water seeking the low point as it broke through the dike, Jason Ross had been drawn toward ever-greater evil. Step by faltering step, his ego and the decaying world had pulled him into a quagmire where his soul hopelessly foundered. She could not allow it. Her son would fight and perhaps die to stop it, and now, so would she.

Jenna stuffed the gun in one pocket and the extra mag in the other. She cinched her belt to keep her pants up, then walked across the house to the garage. Her Tesla awaited it had a residual charge left over from the good times. She hadn't driven it since last fall, but it lit up as though happy to see her.

"Maybe one last trip," she said, caressing the door. It bumped open at her touch.

Jenna pulled on the red cord and lifted the garage door. She slid behind the wheel of her car and rumbled into the cobblestone courtyard, then drove toward the gate. The sound of tires on pavement harkened to a world now lost, and a crashing wave of sadness nearly caused her to pull over and weep.

Jenna pulled up to the gate and smiled a wet-eyed greeting at the Russian gate guard. Her obvious emotion flustered him and he waved her through.

"Boys. Am I right?" she chuckled to her Tesla.

She had no idea how to get to the Maverick refinery, though she knew exactly where it was. It'd occupied a pie wedge of her view of the valley for ten years, but she didn't know which direction the entrance faced, or which road approached it. She circled the perimeter fence until she found a road that turned toward the squat, rusting tanks and towering smokestacks. A white-splotched, Russian tank and several armed men stopped her.

"I'm Jenna Ross here to see Colonel Zhukov," she explained. She didn't know if Jason was there or elsewhere, but she'd calculated that her best chance of getting inside was to ask for Dimtriy.

After a long wait, they waved her in.

"The colonel waits for you at the office," a man explained in a thick Russian accent. He pointed toward the thickest tangle of pipes and tanks. She pulled forward with the window down and the gravel grumbled under the wheels of her car.

Dimtriy waited for her at the foot of a metal staircase.

"Jenna," he greeted her, confused, but smiling. She stepped out of her car and his eyes took in the handle of the Glock poking out of her jeans pocket.

She hugged him. "Can we talk?"

"Certainly," Dimtriy showed her up the steps and into a boxy office trailer.

He swept aside a pile of papers from a chair and offered her a seat. "I have no coffee. I apologize," he said.

"Thank you. I'm fine." She sat and folded her hands in her lap. The gun dug into her hip. The office was a mess, with boxes piled everywhere. "My son Sage came home," she caught him up. "He lives in Idaho, north of here, and he's married. He has a baby on the way."

Colonel Zhukov's face lit up, and his eyes wrinkled with genuine joy at her good fortune. "I'm so pleased for you."

"Dimtriy, are you thinking of offering this refinery to the cartel?" she asked. She'd crossed town, alone, with a gun poking out of her pants, so he must already know this was about more than catching up.

"It is one possibility," he admitted.

"Oh, Colonel. Please don't," she went straight to the point.

His face twisted. He'd been struggling with the question. Dimtriy Zhukov was responsible for a thousand men in a strange country, surrounded by enemies. He'd been too humbled to play games with her.

"I must do what's best for my men," he said.

She nodded. "Of course. But they will not be safe under the boot of a murderer. The leader of the cartel is an evil man."

She could see the wheels turning in his mind. He'd been born during Communist rule. They were quite nearly the same age, she and Dimtriy, and the Berlin Wall had fallen when she was twenty years old. He understood the rule of evil men, from oligarchs and gangsters, to Putin. He was probably more comfortable than she thinking in terms of the lesser of two evils. In his eyes, she saw her political innocence reflected. He didn't see the world the same way she did. He likely believed her naive in the ways of realpolitik, and that much was probably true.

She tried another tac. "Where is Jason?"

"I don't know," Zhukov answered.

"Has he started negotiations with the cartel?"

Zhukov stared at a blank wall of the temporary office. He looked miserable, weighing his allegiances.

"He's had one conversation with the cartel leader. They reached no agreement yet."

"We have to stop this," Jenna pleaded.

"Jenna." Dimtriy held up his hands for her to slow down. "He is your husband. You are a loyal wife." His eyes betrayed his misgivings. He loved her. It was as clear on his face as any affliction.

She could have the refinery. She could end the threat. In one word, she could remove the strategic resource from the game board and hand it to Jeff Kirkham. All she would have to do was betray her word of honor. *Until death do us part.* She need only leave her troubled, treacherous husband and give herself to this handsome, humble man.

"I'm a married woman, Dimtriy," she said. It was a denial. An apology. A salve to the thundering undercurrent of heartbreak that rose up and crashed around them. The vast sadness of her words rang in her ears.

She was terribly fond of him, and she hoped it was written on her face. She'd caused this moment of reckoning by sharing coffee with him. She'd encouraged this friendship to protect the Homestead. It was her fault that he suffered. She reached out and rested her hand on his. "You will find someone perfect. You're a good man."

He slid his hand gently out from under hers. His eyes stilled like blue pools of regret.

"Dimtriy, Jeff Kirkham is not your enemy. He's a good man too. He's like you. Jason is confused. He's lost his way." She saw a flicker in his eyes. "You know he has." His eyes flicked again, then the warrior returned.

"I am responsible for the fate of a thousand men, Jenna. I cannot wager their lives without certainty. We will wait and see what guarantees the Mexicans can provide, then we will decide."

"Let me talk to Jeff Kirkham. Let me negotiate with him for your men," she begged.

"But how can he win? The cartel has so many tanks?"

"You have tanks too," she said, but she could tell right away that it was the wrong thing to say.

"They are not the same. We have light tanks; they have main battle tanks, several dozen of them."

"But Jeff Kirkham has airplanes." She knew she was out of her depth, but she couldn't give up.

"We have seen *two* airplanes."

She re-gathered. "Let me talk to Jeff Kirkham on your behalf," she said again.

"Okay," the colonel relented. "I cannot guarantee we will agree to his terms. He must defeat the cartel for his word to mean anything to us."

"I understand. That's all I can ask." Jenna stood. "Thank you." She kissed him on the cheek and left him, deflated, in his cluttered office.

The Grand America Hotel
Salt Lake City, Utah

"*How did they get airplanes!*" Castillo shrieked at his staff.

"Tucson airbase," Bill McCallister answered, deadpan.

"How do you know that?!" Castillo shouted in McCallister's face.

"I had two of their men followed to Tucson, then I sent Stinger missiles. I had a feeling they'd try and put tank killers in the air. I shot one of their planes down this morning," McCallister said. He was precisely, perfectly, meticulously arranged for this conversation. Castillo was a snarling beast, but Bill had the cattle prod.

"When were you planning on telling me all this?" Castillo's voice softened slightly, but he still shouted.

"Today, when the other Stingers arrived in Salt Lake City."

"And have they arrived?" Castillo stood across the table and glared.

Bill sauntered to the door of the banquet room. He projected insouciance but inside, he prayed that Abuelo had followed his instructions. Bill cracked the door, leaned outside, and hefted the bulky, shoulder-fired missile with one hand. He swung into the room and pendulumed it to his shoulder. He pointed it at Castillo.

"Pow." Bill leaned out from behind the aiming reticle and smiled. "The A-10 Thunderbolt is the disease, and this is the cure, Tavo. FIM-92 Stinger missile. Heat-seeking. Fire-and-forget. Two kilometer range. We have to get close, but that shouldn't be a problem against CAS aircraft."

"CAS?" Castillo asked.

"Close Air Support."

Castillo's face tripped through a train of emotions: alarm, ferocity, cunning, and then revenge. "How many do we have?" he asked.

Bill rolled the launcher off his shoulder and dropped it on the table with a messy crash of dishes and toppled wine. "A shitload, give or take. Thirty launchers here and another thirty in Tucson."

Castillo stalked around the table. "So you had militiamen followed and they led you to Tucson. And you deduced that they were spinning up A-10s?"

"It was an educated guess." Bill preened. "That's what I would've done," he bragged. "I'd go for the Warthogs."

"What is that valley you wanted?" Castillo stroked the gray-speckled stubble on his chin. "Star Valley?"

A chill dribbled down Bill's spine. He hadn't told anyone about that. Not that he could remember. *Had he mentioned it to Abuelo?*

"It's in Wyoming, actually. Star Valley would be nice," Bill muttered.

"It's yours," Castillo said. "That's what I do for my people who bust their ass for me. They get everything they ever wanted." He returned to his seat, picked up his goblet of wine and sipped. "Of course, first we have to destroy the Utah Militia and take the refinery."

―――――

WHEN JENNA RETURNED to the Homestead, it was dark outside. She saw a light in Jason's office. He was drinking, as was his custom. Secretly, she preferred him that way, loose and a little maudlin. He was less scary when he was drunk.

Their son had come home, and there was only one person for

her to share that with. She'd made it clear to Colonel Zhukov that she was utterly unavailable, and it'd been a revelation to her as well. The war simmered, some few miles from the Homestead, but war and love ran on entirely separate tracks.

She had chosen, and now she would topple into her choice, with all the agony of a fall into new snow. Jenna returned to her quarters, cleaned up, let her hair down, touched up her makeup, and slipped into a white sleep camisole. She watched herself in the mirror. She was mature and graceful, trim and medium-breasted. The camisole hung straight down from her nipples, betraying the chill in the house, or maybe her surrender to her husband.

She slid into slippers and went to him. She found him drinking alone behind his heavy desk.

"Jenna. To what do I owe the honor?" he slurred the last word.

"Shhh." She touched her lips and came around the desk. She took the drink from his hand and sipped. She hated whiskey, but the sip was a bridge between them. An opening. Her long armed reached around and caressed the short hair on the back of his head.

"Have you been with anyone else?" she asked in a whisper as she lowered herself onto his lap.

"No," he answered. "No one." A husky tone intruded on his voice.

She felt him harden through her camisole.

She stood up. "Come," she pulled his hand and he rose from the chair, then followed her through the halls of what had once been their home.

16

"In ancient history, civilization took shape around fresh waterways. The irrigation and soils prompted mankind to plant, harvest, and then work together in cooperative communities. It's where the Rule of Law began. After the great collapse of Black Autumn, civilization first re-rooted around fragments of the old, modern world: oil refineries, nuclear power plants, hydro-electric plants, large orchards, and fields of remnant grain. Cooperation rose again, not as a means of agriculture but as a way to defend beneficial resources."

— THE AMERICAN DARK AGES, BY WILLIAM BELLAHER, NORTH AMERICAN TEXTBOOKS, 2037

Outside Davis-Monthan Air Force Base
Tucson, Arizona

THE TRUCK SPRAYED GASOLINE ON THE HOMES AND NOAH'S MEN ignited it with tracer fire. Whole neighborhoods went up in a handful of minutes. Dogs, cats, rats, and sometimes people scampered from the hungry flames. Hunch-backed and shifty-eyed, they fled into the shambles of Tucson and disappeared. Noah's men hadn't found any charred bodies, but they weren't looking very hard for them, either.

Noah had seen this before, had learned how to do it from Gustavo Castillo himself. In Artesia, New Mexico, Castillo had massacred an entire town with gasoline and flames to punish them for destroying a refinery. Now, the southern third of Tucson burned at Noah's own hand, a desperate ploy to push back the SAM snipers who'd shot down his commanding officer.

Noah's plan was to burn two miles of the city surrounding Davis-Monthan airbase, and then crush the cinders flat with Caterpillar D9 bulldozers. They'd been at it all day and had destroyed thousands of homes, yet hadn't engaged a single cartel hunter-killer team.

It felt so *final* to burn neighborhoods, like an admission that civilization would never come back, would never use these strip malls and stoplights again. The massive cloud of smoke and soot hung over Tucson like a shroud. Mankind had massacred itself.

A sound jerked Noah's attention to the sky. A low rumble, then a whine. Two A-10 Thunderbolts split the smoky, cumulous clouds and banked wide around the airbase.

"Who are they?" Longhair shouted against the roar of the jets.

Noah shouted back, "From Salt Lake." It had to be the two they'd sent north. All other Warthogs were grounded in Tucson until Noah and Willie's team could secure the buffer around the landing strip.

Someone at the airbase must've made comms with the Warthogs, because they circled again, then lined up over the deepest patch of razed homes. A Stinger launched from deep within Tucson, but it corkscrewed early and sluiced away.

"Out of range," Longhair said. "It's working." He grinned like a boy playing with matches. His face was covered in soot. The smile cut flesh-colored furrows in the filth.

The A-10s landed, one behind the other.

"You're in command," Noah said to Longhair. "I'm going to find out what's up."

Noah jumped into his Land Cruiser and sped toward the runway.

SOMEONE POINTED the lead pilot toward Noah's incoming Cruiser and he stormed toward him like a man on a mission. Noah jumped out and met him on the tarmac.

"General Kirkham orders all A-10s deployed immediately to Hill Air Force Base."

Noah shook his head. "No can do. Our pilots are still bullshit on ground strikes. They're learning, but we've been taking SAM fire around the base, so I grounded them. That's how we lost Colonel Withers."

"Understood. We took missile fire on approach, but it's now or never in Salt Lake City. General Kirkham wants all our planes armed up and flown immediately to Hill AFB in Ogden, no matter how trained. They expect a final attack any moment. Maybe it's happened already. You still don't have comms with Salt Lake?"

"Nope. We've been busy flushing out the cartel. We haven't put together the right transceiver, generator, and antenna. It's next on our list," Noah explained.

"Don't bother. You're pulling chocks. Everyone's out of here. The Freeman Militia's ordered north with all the AP 30mm you can load on trucks."

"Roger that," Noah said. "Reyes!" he shouted over the A-10 engines as they winded down. "Scramble all pilots and planes. We're heading to Hill AFB. Leaving in thirty minutes."

Reyes saluted and dashed away.

Noah climbed back in his Cruiser. "The planes are all armed

and gassed. You get your birds refueled and rearmed, and get them in the air. We only have ten planes, including yours. You're in command of the air wing. I'll get the south end of the runway cleared safe, then I'll load up the trucks and get on the road right behind you."

The major saluted as Noah drove away to complete the burning of Tucson.

The Homestead
Oakwood, Utah

AT MIDDAY, Jason couldn't find Jenna anywhere in the Homestead. In a world where there was nowhere to run errands, her absence could only mean treachery. She wasn't getting her hair done or her back massaged. She was with Kirkham or Zhukov. In the hard light of day, Jason counted himself the fool for trusting her, for sleeping with her.

He could tell from her lovemaking, she had not been with Zhukov, not with her body, at least. She had betrayed him several times, though not in the one way that mattered most. All her other betrayals had been in perfect keeping with the woman he'd known her to be. She remained the woman he loved, though also his enemy.

Jason hadn't seen his son, Sage, since the day after he arrived home. His son was a soldier now and he'd been on short leave. He imagined Sage on hit-and-run missions against Castillo's tank crews. It was a futile gesture, with little risk to the tank crews and enormous risk to the partisans, like tossing live grenades at the clouds.

Jason poured cheap whiskey in with his coffee. It was coming up on lunchtime and he had a date with Castillo downtown. It'd be their fourth meeting, and probably the last. They'd nearly completed their negotiations, and Zhukov was antsy for a final package so he could present it to his men.

Tension rose between the belligerent forces, the cartel and the Utah Militia, with occasional jet planes screaming overhead and increased guerrilla strikes against the Abrams crews. Soon, something would set it all off, like a hungry wolf pack circling an old buffalo. At some moment, the buffalo stumbles and the alpha wolf lunges. After that, further negotiations would be written in blood.

Jason needed to get the deal done today. He climbed into his BMW and pulled away from the Homestead. He drove the back roads to the 1300 East overpass. If the militia knew what he was doing, negotiating with the enemy, they'd ambush him. If Jenna had observed him, and told Kirkham, Jason would die this morning in his BMW. But he had to go. He was out of time.

This route took him around Ensign Peak, up on the bench escarpment of what'd once been the shoreline of ancient Lake Bonneville. From high on Victory Road, the strategic map opened up to him in the valley below. The I-80 and the 215 demarcated the rough line between clustered residences and industrial flatlands. If the cartel tanks advanced any farther north of their current line, they'd pass into open country. They were bounded by the marshes and shallow waters of the Great Salt Lake to the west, and a twenty-mile long, primeval rock slide to the east. The next battle would be fought across dry salt marshes, twenty miles wide, between residential Salt Lake City and the refinery in North Salt Lake. It was a flat, open no-man's land where tanks would rule once they committed to a thrust.

Jason and his Russian friends would see the cartel advance coming, five miles away, and they could destroy the cartel's prize with the flick of a switch, if Castillo played him false.

Jason was the key that could unlock the entire region, with its oil reserves, agriculture, and mountain defenses. He was the pivot on which everything turned. Castillo was a pit bull on a chain, but Jason was the iron piling in the ground, pinning him in place. Jason would need that confidence as he faced Castillo and finalized their deal.

He drove down out of "The Avenues" and circled the valley along the rim of what had once been the University of Utah. Dead vehicles had been pushed to the side of the road, but none had been removed. All of the cars had been ransacked, but most of the flotsam had blown away on the wind. The place looked like a flea market, but at least now there were no dead bodies on the sidewalk.

Jason made the final turn south and the number of people working in the streets, yards, and park strips, most planting food or corralling livestock, thinned out. He was coming close to the line between the militia and the cartel, and people had relocated to get away from the sniping and skirmishing. A Chevy truck with a machine gun in the back raced down the other side of the street, maybe rushing wounded to medical care. Jason tensed. They didn't recognize him and sped away.

By the time he reached the 1300 East overpass, all was quiet. He drove slowly over the freeway under the swiveling gun of the Abrams on sentry. They recognized his SUV and let him roll past.

The last three times he'd come, they hadn't accompanied him to the Grand America. They'd allowed him to drive himself right up to cartel headquarters. He supposed it was a show of trust, allowing him that close to their headquarters, but what could he really do? One man in a luxury SUV? Nobody, he supposed, would think of him as a potential suicide bomber.

That thought bothered him; it burrowed like a tick.

Why wouldn't they think him capable of sacrificing his life? Was he really that mercenary? He imagined himself as the cartel must see him: a local collaborator, wheedling concessions from them to win advantage for himself and his friends. Then, he imagined himself as Jenna must see him: an angry, confused, middle-aged man clinging to control. He imagined himself as Sage must see him: untethered from honor and greedy for power.

The tick burrowed deeper.

The deal he was about to strike made sense, and it carried guarantees of future performance from Castillo. Jason and the Russian Spetsnaz would act as Castillo's regents when the cartel pressed north. Jason would maintain order in Salt Lake City. He would do more than just providing the Maverick refinery; he would pacify the state. Someone had to do it for Castillo. It was a win-win, and Jason thought he could see that realization in Castillo's eyes as they dickered through the details of command and control.

That was the proverbial carrot: the refinery and a regency. Jason had worked in the "stick" as well. The Russians would maintain a garrison on the grounds of the Maverick, and their network of destructive devices, designed by the Spetsnaz demolitions expert, would remain in place. If Castillo violated the terms of their deal, the Maverick would go up in a fireball.

Jason would keep the Homestead. Zhukov and his men would get homes of their choice, entire neighborhoods, really. The Russians would be re-armed from the local army depot. As a kicker, Jason would get title to the entire Heber Valley.

It was a solid deal, perhaps one of the best of his career. He'd looked at it from every angle and couldn't see a way for Castillo to screw him. This deal would set up him and the Russians for life, for generations.

Jason drove past a burned-out Wendy's fast food restaurant. He remembered the Wendy's because he'd had "the talk" with Sage, passing through that very drive-thru, while ordering lunch.

"Are you having sex with your girlfriend?" Jason had asked his son, already knowing full well he was.

"Yes," Sage admitted.

"Is she on birth control? Are you using protection?"

Sage had hesitated. "No. I mean, I don't know. That's her thing."

"So, if she gets pregnant, do you plan on doing the honorable thing and marrying her?" Jason had asked.

"What? No. I'm not getting married. Geez. I'm only sixteen."

Jason had accepted the bag of burgers and fries from the girl at the drive-up window. "Yeah, but if she gets pregnant, what will honor require of you? What does honor even mean to you?" That'd been the question he'd been angling toward for the whole drive, the question he was setting up to ask his son.

"What?" Sage floundered. "What does honor mean? Um. I don't know...but isn't she supposed to handle the birth control thing with her mother, or something?"

"Has she?" Jason pushed the question back.

"Has she handled birth control with her mother?" Sage set the bag down on the floor. "I don't know. I never asked."

"Well, just so you know," Jason then dropped the bomb, "I've spoken to her mom and her dad and they definitely *have not* handled birth control. They don't even think she's having sex. So if she gets pregnant, and if you're a man of honor, you're heading toward a very big life change."

"YOU TOLD THEM WE WERE HAVING SEX?" Sage panicked.

"Yep."

"How did you know?" Sage asked with a tone of accusation.

"Because I have common sense. Because it's obvious. Her parents didn't believe me."

"Oh." Sage had stared absently into the bag, like he'd left something in there but had forgotten what it was.

"So *you* get to tell them," Jason finished.

Sage looked up with eyes the size of baseballs. "No way. I can't do that." The Ross family had known the girl's dad for many years. He was a dive buddy of Jason's, and they'd gone to Alaska together. They'd gone shooting, and fishing. "There's no way I'm telling him that we're having sex."

Jason had nodded. Then asked, "So what does honor mean to

you, Sage?"

Three, long years after that question, Jason smiled as he rolled past the burned-out Wendy's and remembered that day.

Sage had immediately called the girl, and insisted she talk to her mother about birth control, to tell her they were having sex. Jason heard back the next day from his buddy. The dad and Sage had a conversation. Sage decided to be a stand-up guy, after all. He might not have known what honor meant before, but he got a crash course that day.

Now, an apocalypse later, Sage was a man. He was married and expecting a child. Jason got the impression that surviving the winter had been another course in honor for his son. Survival and Mother Nature had their own way of teaching the hard lessons.

Jason rolled up to a cartel checkpoint, a block away from the Grand America. They waved him through.

What was Mother Nature telling him? While he was away in Wyoming, his land had abided, with him or without him. It had sustained his wife and friends while he wandered the Wyoming plain.

"Dad, you got on the wrong side of right...you know she still loves you, right?" That was what Sage had said to him. Had Jenna told Sage that, in so many words?

He pulled under the awning of the Grand America. A cartel valet approached.

Bullshit, he said out loud, to himself, as he got out and handed his car keys to the boy. The kid looked at him, confused. He was no gangbanger. He was probably a Salt Lake local who took the job to help feed his family.

Jason walked into the hotel and across the white marble floor, wrapped in gray marble walls, sparkling under glass chandeliers. The cartel didn't have enough electricity to run the elevators, but they had enough to light the room. Maybe they were doing it for his benefit, as a demonstration of power.

Today he'd close this deal, Jason reminded himself. It was a good deal. A great deal, actually. A win-win for everyone, especially for Utah. This was how peace was made. Everyone gave up something and the world moved on. *Who knew?* Castillo could be dead from venereal disease in a year and none of this would matter. It was an uncertain world. The best he could do now was to cut a sensible deal with this psychopath, then do his best to run interference for the locals. He could be the voice of reason in the chaos.

*"It's easy, Dad. You do what **she** thinks is right."*

That's what Sage had said. He wanted Jason to follow Jenna's lead. Jenna had allowed the flu into their home; her bad judgment had killed their daughter. *What did an eighteen year-old know about life?*

He remembered Jenna's body the night before, warm and supple against his. Her backside and legs pressed against his belly. The orange blossom-smell of her skin.

Jason entered the banquet room of the Grand America. Castillo sat on the edge of a corner booth, nursing a cocktail. Bill McCallister sat opposite him with what looked like a Bloody Mary.

"Well," Castillo stood up with a sweep of his arm. "Are we doing this deal or not?"

"Yeah..." Jason mumbled. He stuffed a hand in the pocket of his slacks as he pushed aside a slight erection at the memory of his wife's naked body.

Jason had always worn dress clothes to these meetings. At first, he told himself it was because the slacks and tie put Castillo at ease.

In truth, the dress clothes made him feel modern, powerful, and important.

Why wasn't there security in the room? Jason looked around. It was only him, Castillo, and McCallister. There were no men with guns.

Why hadn't they patted him down when he arrived? He'd walked straight into the banquet room where the men were drinking their aperitifs.

When had he ceased being a dangerous man?

Jason paused halfway to the booth. *They didn't think he was dangerous.* That was why there was no security.

"What's the problem?" Castillo read Jason's body language.

"Nothing," Jason lied.

He thought back to sipping whiskey with his son, the boy who'd become a man. The boy who had married and would soon have a child. The boy who was, right now, fighting in pickup trucks against Abrams tanks.

"I forgot something," Jason stammered.

"No you didn't," Castillo thundered. "Sit down and get this done. I'm running out of patience."

Jason took two steps toward the booth and stopped again. He pulled his hands out of his slacks. He looked around, then settled his eyes on Castillo.

"No deal," Jason said.

Castillo laughed, then quieted. "Are you fucking serious?" he seethed. "You're bending me over for more concessions at this point in the game?" Castillo shouted.

"I'm not bending you over," Jason said. "There's no deal. Not under any terms."

A breath he'd been holding in his belly released. His back loosened. His shoulders settled. Finally, in that moment, Jason returned home. Home to his wife. Home to his land. Home to himself.

"Get in here!" Castillo shouted. Half a second later, men burst through doors. They came with guns drawn.

"Him!" Castillo pointed at Jason. "Take him to the same room where you took that Mormon guy last week. This *pinché cabrón* and I are going to have some private time." Castillo picked up his cocktail and tossed it back it with an angry gulp. "Looks like we're doing this the hard way."

17

"By default, the largest organized group of people, whether it was Masons, Mormons, or a motorcycle club, dominated any given region. With governments and militaries swept aside, what remained were churches, clubs and ad hoc clans. These formed the core of new government and culture, which explains the personality of states and communities that formed the first year after the collapse: The State of Zion; NASCAR County; John Deere City; Bible Country. Micro-governments formed around any surviving passion."

— THE AMERICAN DARK AGES, BY WILLIAM BELLAHER, NORTH AMERICAN TEXTBOOKS, 2037

Highway 89
Panguitch, Utah

NOAH MILLER RODE SHOTGUN IN THE LAND CRUISER WHILE WILLIE Lloyd drove. They ran third car back in a scout element ahead of the semi trucks that carried ammo and the remainder of the gasoline Jeff Kirkham had sent to Tucson. For the third time that month, they passed the hick towns of central Utah: Marysvale, Panguitch, and Mount Carmel Junction. By now, they knew the small town mayors by name and by sight. The convoy plowed north, rushing to join the brewing battle between the patriots and the cartel. The hundred men of the Freeman Militia would help a little, but the armor-piercing ammunition for the Warthogs could be the difference between winning and losing.

But the convoy had a long way to go, and rushing meant risking an ambush. If the cartel had any idea of the cargo they carried, they'd send everything and the kitchen sink to end them, to turn the convoy into a burned-oil stain on the highway. If they knew...

If his father knew...

"I don't get all the stop and go," Willie complained. "I thought we were in a hurry to get this ammo up to Ogden."

The drive from Phoenix to Salt Lake City used to be a half-day's drive. But they traveled under security, and that was a helluva lot slower.

"We're definitely in a hurry." Noah glassed out the window across the soil-and-sprout valley carved through the mountains by the Sevier River. Some enterprising farmer was running broadcast sprinklers across what Noah assumed was a field of alfalfa. He wondered how the guy got the water pressure for sprinklers. Gasoline generator? Gas powered pump? Some kind of solar rig? It was only nine months since the Black Autumn collapse and already farmers and ranchers were bouncing back. This rancher would likely rotate his hundred head of cattle onto the sprinkled field soon after the growth kicked in. Gone were the days of sending cows to a finishing lot to be stuffed with corn then sent to fast food joints in the city. These cattle would be fattened on home-grown alfalfa and clover, then they'd be turned into steaks and stew for local families. The people of Panguitch, Utah would probably be happier than they'd ever been, happier with less, closer to their families, with more work and more enjoyment.

"Happiness is a weird word, isn't it?" Noah said from behind his binoculars.

Willie chortled. "You're going to have to bust off a few more words for me to know what the hell you're talking about."

"I mean, our society chased this 'happiness' thing, and the more we chased it, the further away it got. Then, we pitched right off into the ditch, and most people died horrible deaths. And we did it chasing happiness. Hell, that probably caused it."

"*Hmph*," Willie made the sound he always made when he needed a second to think about something. "Noel's like a thousand times happier growing beets and tomatoes than she ever was painting ladies' nails."

"Why was it so hard for me to make a living raising cattle?" Noah continued. "That doesn't make sense. What's better than eating beef? Cattlemen shoulda' been rich."

"Amen to that. I could use a burger about now."

Noah shifted in his seat and glassed up the road. He saw nothing.

"Paul Revere to Road Runner," Noah radioed back to the convoy. They called him Paul Revere from his days riding out ahead of the cartel, warning people to militia-up.

"Go ahead, Paul."

"You look good through Panguitch. We'll bump forward to where Highway 20 goes up into the mountains. Hold three miles outside of town until next check-in."

"Roger, moving through town, then holding three miles north of the junction," Longhair replied. He drove the semi with the "precious cargo" of 30mm.

The stop and go, stop and go, of secure movement really was a pain in the ass. The trucks spent half their day waiting for the scout element to clear the road ahead and for overwatch to get into position. There was no way to rush it. Any less caution left them vulnerable to an ambush.

The militias had absolute shit for communications. They'd never achieved proper comms with Salt Lake. Now, on the move, they had only their vehicle radio rigs.

Worst of all, they had no encryption. At all times, they had to assume that the cartel was listening.

The enemy had somehow anticipated that they were spinning up the Warthogs, and they'd figured it out fast enough to deploy SAM missiles to Tucson. It made Noah very nervous. Someone was reading their mail, and the 30mm they carried made that perilous in the extreme.

Noah picked up a glint on the west mountains from a homestead. According to the map, a canal ran across a string of farms and supplied them with water from Panguitch Lake. He shifted his binos to the homestead and watched, braced on the dashboard. He saw no movement, which struck him as odd. Very few of the locals up and down the old highway had fled during the crash. Most of the homesteads were still occupied by their original owners. It was late morning and he should've seen the farmer and his family conducting the endless chores of farm life. Instead, he saw nothing, no movement at all. It was weird, but not weird enough to gum up the already-sticky works.

"Move them on up to the 20," Noah said to Willie. "This section's clear."

―――

Hampton Inn
Spanish Fork, Utah

BILL MCCALLISTER HAD BEEN CALLED BACK for an alert from one of his recon units on Highway 89. It wasn't unexpected. His hunter/killer teams in Tucson had reported that the Davis-Monthan airfield sent its CAS planes north, packed up their shit, and bailed. Bill predicted they'd head back the same way they came, which was shitty OPSEC, but probably unavoidable. There was only one way north, aside from the cartel's own supply corridor along the I-15 interstate.

"Gimme," Bill motioned to the radio-head behind the controls. The man adjusted a dial and nodded for Bill to transmit. He picked up the mic and called his recon team. "This is Actual, go ahead."

"We got another militia scout element heading north," the recon man said over the JTRS military comms.

"Describe them," Bill ordered.

"A late model Toyota Land Cruiser has conducted surveillance for thirty minutes. They just pulled out, then a convoy passed with sixteen other vehicles, including one fuel tanker and one semi truck and trailer, running heavy. Also eight technicals and five passenger vehicles. Vans, mostly."

"Good copy. Continue Mission. Actual out."

Bill's surveillance team occupied a farmhouse south of the town of Panguitch, Utah. Bill was supposed to be the only person with this information, but that was questionable. Castillo took pride in hacking Bill's intel networks. It'd taken Bill ten minutes to get back to his radioman. Castillo might already know about the militia convoy.

The Land Cruiser they'd just reported was Noah's. Bill could feel it in his bones. His son was returning to Salt Lake from Tucson, and he had cargo. The last time they'd escorted cargo, he and his son, it was TOW missiles and 30mm ammo from an army depot in Oklahoma. It was almost certain that's what Noah carried now, 30mm to kill cartel tanks.

If Bill didn't clear that ammo off the board, he was a dead man and no good to anyone. Noah's convoy would have to loop a hundred miles to the east, then around the Wasatch and the Uinta mountains. Bill still had time to do this in a way that didn't get Noah killed.

Was Abuelo secretly reporting to Castillo? Was Radio-head? Bill had no choice but to report it to Castillo, but he'd add the right topspin. For all his omniscience, Castillo still couldn't possibly know that Bill's son was fighting for the Utah Militia.

Bill scrawled out a note and handed it to Radio-head.

"Transmit this to Salt Lake, Castillo's eyes only."

The note read:

Supply convoy transiting north on Highway 89. Likely ammo and fuel from Phoenix/Tucson. Estimated five days to reach Salt Lake City. Route around mountain ranges uncertain. Could be any one of ten possibilities, all of them hundreds of miles from your position. Recommend we ignore. By the time they arrive in Salt Lake, militia encirclement should be complete.

Long range reconnaissance was Bill's job. Encirclement of the Utah Militia position was Saúl's job. Unless Castillo gave Bill a direct order to interdict the convoy, he could throw the thing back in Saúl's lap.

But the cartel encirclement around Ogden had stalled out. They didn't have the fuel to send a force up Parleys Canyon, over and around to Ogden. It was a hundred miles of uphill, at minimum. The mountains made things difficult. Every time Saúl sent a probe to suss out routes, they got chewed up by gun trucks that infested the logging and hunting roads. The hick towns of Heber, Coalville, and Kamas took great pleasure in fielding .50 BMG pickup trucks to destroy cartel scouts.

It required at least a dozen tanks to secure the mountain passes, and that'd pull fuel from the Abrams they needed to take down the Maverick refinery. Saúl did not have the armor to complete the encirclement.

Bill needed to slow roll an interdiction against Noah's convoy. As long as it didn't get his ass in a sling, he was fine with the 30mm reaching Hill AFB. Bill dropped the radio headphones on the table and walked out of the Hampton Inn, back to his Land Cruiser.

"Hold up, sir." The radioman chased behind Bill through the propped-open sliding door of the hotel. "Incoming reply from command."

Shit. Castillo must've been hovering over the radio console. Bill followed the radioman back inside.

"McCallister," Castillo's voice boomed over the speakers. "*You ambush that convoy. Do it now.*"

"Are you giving me an Abrams?"

Castillo paused, probably thinking it over. "Pull an Abrams off the blocking force holding the south end of Salt Lake county. Siphon gas from the other Abrams at that position."

It'd leave the other Abrams empty, unable to maneuver. Things were getting lean in the cartel army.

"You go personally," Castillo repeated. "Leave now. Hit them in Gunnison. Castillo out."

He hadn't given Bill any wiggle room. Bill would be in Gunnison, setting up the ambush before dark, and Castillo would have comms with Bill's Abrams over the JTRS radio, which was probably why he'd given him an Abrams in the first place, to keep him on a short leash.

Castillo had to know more than he let on. He sensed that this convoy was personal for Bill. Things had just gotten a *lot* more dangerous.

"Defcon One," Bill said to himself, as he got back into his Cruiser.

If he bailed out now, his son would surely die.

———

Gunnison, Utah

A THREE MILE stretch of highway descended into the desert town of Gunnison. The state penitentiary sat to the east, bristling with guard towers and barbed wire. The city park sat on the west, shady and green under the monolithic, green cottonwoods. Someone had mowed the grass of the city park, which was, perhaps, the most amazing thing Bill had seen in months. Who had time and energy to water grass, and to mow it?

The town must've known the cartel had come because the streets were completely empty. Bill ordered his tank to pull in behind the towering trees, then back into an alleyway behind the Valley Furniture store.

The militia convoy would send a scout ahead to the top of the hill alongside the prison. It was the logical place to conduct surveillance and overwatch. They'd pass the Abrams, hidden behind the store, observe for a short time, then call the convoy forward.

Bill commanded the Abrams tank, three gun buggies and thirty infantrymen, but all he really needed was the tank. He could control where that one weapon pointed. He couldn't control three dozen eager guns. Bill parked his Land Cruiser behind the Abrams and climbed up on the turret and looked down into the open hatch.

"You." He pointed at the tank commander. "Climb up on top of that furniture store and radio down when the scout vehicle comes through town. Don't let them see you." Bill let the tank commander climb past him, then lowered himself down into the belly of the beast.

"All stations: withdraw to the town of Fayette and hold there as QRF," Bill ordered over his personal radio. When he received no reply, he climbed out of the turret where reception would improve. "Hold at the town of Fayette until ordered."

The infantrymen and gun buggies acknowledged and withdrew ten miles away to the next town. It was a suspicious move, to pull most of his force away from the fight, but Bill wasn't going to allow men to go "weapons hot" with his son in the middle. He needed this to go down like spine surgery. He'd take out just the semi truck with the ammo, pluck it out of the convoy like a bulging disc.

It wouldn't matter in the end. He had a growing, churning, growl in his gut; it wouldn't be the Warthogs that ended Castillo. It'd be Bill.

"THE SCOUT *ES PASANDO*," the tank commander radioed from the roof. Bill hated that, when the men spoke in half-Spanish, half-English.

"What kind of vehicle?" Bill asked

"I dunno. Some kind of Jeep but not a Jeep."

"Okay. Radio when you see the semi truck." It was Noah in that scout car, just three blocks away. It had to be.

Time passed slowly, like listening to a fire and brimstone sermon at church. The ventilation system in the Abrams was good, but he could smell every fart, and every whiff of cheap Mexican laundry detergent. He stifled in the smell of the gunner who used too much cologne. He'd trade this whole, shitty army straight across for one man like Noah.

Why was he even here? The game had worn thin, like the last season of Happy Days when the Fonz got put on dialysis, or got married, or went to work for Terminix. Bill couldn't remember the last season of Happy Days. He just remembered it being a letdown. *Why the fuck had he agreed to fight for Castillo?* His plan had gone rancid and now he was being forced to put his son in grave danger, the only person in the world he actually gave a shit about.

"Da trucks *entraron en* town," the spotter reported.

The tank driver looked up from the controls for orders.

"Hold," Bill said. "Wait."

If Bill had any chance of moving to the next round of this shitty game, he needed to destroy the ammo supply truck. It was the only way Noah could go free and Bill not end up in the torture seat.

The town was about two miles end to end, and there was only one main road, right down the middle.

Time slowed down when the enemy got near the "X," so Bill counted down an extra thirty seconds in his head.

"Go," he ordered the driver. "Load," he ordered the loader. "Drive onto the main road and prepare to fire." Bill took control of the cannon.

———

From three blocks away, atop the hill just above the penitentiary, Noah Miller heard an engine roar to life and he knew instantly that it was an Abrams tank.

"Ambush, ambush, ambush!" he shouted into the radio.

Longhair was driving the lead semi, the 30mm ammo truck. He slammed on the brakes and even halfway across the town, the heavy-laden truck howled like an air raid siren. The fuel truck behind it shuttered to a halt.

The Abrams tank gunned past the city park and into the middle of the main road. The turret was already pointing straight down the throat of the convoy.

"Get out!" Noah screamed.

Ba-doom! the Abrams fired its main gun. The semi truck, with Longhair in it, took a cannon round from stem to stern and erupted in a ball of flame. The cab bucked like an arch-backed bronco. Crates of 30mm, some on fire, launched into the blue sky. They clattered down on the town like a vengeful storm, crushing homes, shops, garages and churches. The fuel truck roared in protest as the driver threw it in reverse.

Ba-doom! the Abrams fired again and the fuel truck imploded in a *ka-whomping* thunder of high explosives and aerosolized gasoline.

"Drive!" Noah shouted. Willie blinked back his amazement and horror, threw the Cruiser in gear and sped away from the town of Gunnison. "Get out of here!"

They fled north down the backslope of Highway 89 while Noah tried desperately to make comms with the survivors of his convoy.

The Land Cruiser raced blindly north, away from Gunnison, rolling up and over a series of desert rises. They flew past a farmhouse on a hilltop, crested another, and found themselves nose-to-nose with a cartel roadblock: two trucks and six gun buggies, all with belt-fed machine guns pointed at the Cruiser's windshield. Willie stood on the brakes.

They jerked to a stop. Noah swiveled around in his chair. Another three gun buggies raced out of a barn and blocked their retreat.

"Keep your hands on the wheel," Noah said to Willie. He dropped his own AR to the floor. "I don't know why, but we're not already dead. Let's keep it that way."

The gun buggies waited, poised to shred them. Seconds passed. Then a minute. A cow lowed beyond the farmhouse.

An old man in camouflage stepped out from behind one of the trucks and walked, unarmed, to the driver's side of the Land Cruiser. He leaned in the open window and regarded Willie and then Noah.

"Buenos dias, *chavalos*. I'm Abuelo. Why don't you hop down and come with me."

18

Shortwave Radio 7150kHz
3:00pm

> "I recognize that not many Mormons south of Salt Lake tune into my show. Too many durn curse words. I get it. Even so, Salt Lake's under siege by the cartel and we need you back on the double. We're going to lose this war, and Gustavo Castillo is not the man you want as your new prophet."

Scipio, Utah

JEFF KIRKHAM SLIPPED OUT OF SALT LAKE CITY AND RACED INTO THE west desert for a final, desperate attempt to starve out the cartel.

JT Taylor had organized a civilian air patrol out of North Salt Lake Regional Airport. A band of half-licensed, half-stoned, fixed-wing pilots overflew the state of Utah, hunting for cartel movement. JT insisted they call it C.R.A.P.—Civilian Regional Air Patrol. The day before, a "C.R.A.P." pilot called in a cartel fuel convoy pulling out of St. George, heading toward Salt Lake City. Jeff Kirkham threw together a hundred trucks and flew around the cartel battle line across the salt flats, sped through no-man's land, Nevada, then barreled east into a blocking position by the napkin-sized town of Scipio, Utah.

Six Abrams tanks flanked six fuel trucks, and eight electric gun buggies traveled with them, three in front and three behind, with two in the middle to act as a quick reaction force. The fuel convoy was like the Atlantic Fleet in World War Two, a cluster of supply ships surrounded by destroyers and battleships. Jeff's swarming gun trucks would fight like a daring wolf pack of a hundred German U-boats.

But the comparison to ship-to-ship battles ended there. The Abrams tanks were not only indestructible, they had godlike powers of detection. The thermal imaging gunsights on the Abrams would seek and destroy any attacker with even the slightest heat exposure. The cartel fuel convoy was the hardest target Jeff had ever faced.

He would've preferred to send Warthogs after the convoy, but he wasn't going to make the same mistake twice. He wouldn't shoot his wad on a fuel convoy when he had a whole refinery to defend.

Jeff could call in the ten A-10 Warthogs that'd just come in from Tucson. They'd be over the battlefield in minutes and they would shake and bake the fuel trucks for sure. But that would be it for them, one and done. After that strike, the birds would have no talons. They'd be out of ammo.

The Air Force PUDS still hadn't figured out how to re-arm the Warthogs. The 30mm they had at Hill from Tooele Army Depot had been the wrong kind, high explosive, antipersonnel rounds instead of armor-piercing, tank-killing rounds. All ten Warthogs had landed in Ogden and were ready to fly, but after they blew through their one load of armor-piercing ammo, they'd be shooting rounds that couldn't penetrate the tanks.

Jeff had no comms with the Freeman Militia convoy coming up from Tucson. The 30mm armor-piercing ammo they were bringing might never arrive, so he decided to hit the fuel convoy with gun trucks alone.

The Hoodie fuel convoy had overnighted in Cedar City, and that'd given Jeff's trucks just enough time to get out in front of them. As the morning dawned, Jeff looked across the broad valley bowl, five miles wide. The town sat in the center, and the I-15 freeway sliced down the middle. There were more than a hundred gun trucks lying in wait for the convoy, but Jeff couldn't locate a single one in his binoculars. That was good, exactly as planned.

All of his trucks carried Ma Deuce heavy machine guns, bolted to the floor of their beds, each with a mix of ball and tracer ammo. Jeff had run out of TOW missiles. This ambush had a single objective anyway: destroy the fuel trucks, not the tanks.

Jeff was convinced the cartel was running on empty. They hadn't attempted an assault on Hill Air Force base, despite the fact that the airbase harbored the tank-killing Warthogs. The only explanation Jeff could think of was that they hadn't the fuel to do it.

If the militia destroyed these tanker trucks, it'd push the stalemate even deeper into Stalingrad territory—force the enemy to confront the agony of their long supply lines and hostile local citizenry. They'd finally feel the pain of being the occupier, a misery that would never let up so long as they tried to enslave Utah.

The battle plan for the coming ambush had come straight off the grimy paper passed to Jeff by "Bill McCallister, Green Beret retired." Jeff had given his gun trucks simple instructions.

Hide your truck behind a hill so you can't see the interstate or the mountain pass. Put a spotter on the hilltop, covered with a space blanket. Have the spotter walk your shots onto a fuel truck. Once you splash a truck, don't stop firing until you run out of ammo.

It was called "plunging fire" in the parlance of machine gunners and it should cancel out the Abrams' thermal sights. If the gunner couldn't see the target, then the target couldn't see the gunner. All the thermal imaging in the world couldn't see through a hill. The tanks would see a rope of white-hot fifty caliber streaking across the sky from behind a hill, out of thin air, and falling on their tanker trucks. The Abrams would have to break formation and chase the gun trucks, one-at-a-time. By then, Jeff's boys should be out of ammo and hauling ass back to the rally point.

The concept took advantage of simple physics: what went up would eventually come down. Even big bullets arched back to earth given enough distance. Jeff's men would be shooting two or three miles across the Scipio valley, within lethal range of the massive .50 BMG machine guns, but in a steeply plunging trajectory, like fast, rock-hard mortar shells.

This was no "sniper" shooting. It would be a barrage of tens of thousands of rounds, one-third of which would be wobbly tracers, burning with the greedy fury of phosphorous. The old Green Beret on the other end of the smudgy diagram understood smash-mouth war: extreme violence with blunt objects, preferably very fast blunt objects.

The sun strengthened in the east as Jeff's forward observers called in first contact.

"The herd's just leaving Holden. Grandpa Rex is coming up in front of them."

The militia comms were totally un-secure. They employed cheap-o radios they could get in quantity, the ones stacked up in the Walmart distribution centers: FRS family radios, designed for keeping track of the kids at Disneyland. They had a "privacy tone" but that did nothing whatsoever to keep the enemy from hearing their comms traffic. The best Jeff could do was employ a ridiculous array of "pro words;" code language that made the militia sound like local yokels, which wasn't far from the truth. Using replacement words was confusing as hell, and the words had to be changed every week lest the Hoodies figure out their code. It was a horrible work-around, and pretty easy for the enemy to figure out. But as far as he could tell, the Hoodies still hadn't caught on.

Holden was a small town at the top of the mountain pass. Grandpa Rex was code for the electric gun buggies that would crest the hilltop to glass for threats. Jeff prayed the buggies didn't venture too wide of the interstate. The farther out they spread out on the mountaintop, the more likely they'd be to spot a gun truck.

Jeff saw the sparkle of chrome around a juniper bush, one of his trucks getting too eager. He pawed angrily at the notebook with his code words. "Uncle Steve, you've got a bull screwing a cow. Back him up, now," Jeff snarled into his radio. He hated code words with a passion.

"Um. Uncle Steve says good copy."

To Jeff's ear, it still sounded like military communication and not farmers using radios to talk about livestock.

Minutes later, the silver truck bumper backed up and disappeared. Jeff scanned the valley, hunting for any telltale signs of his men. If the cartel saw even a glint of metal, or heard a suspicious radio call, it would screw the whole deal. The Hoodies would hold up until the tanks hunted down the threat.

"Grandpa Rex is on top of Williams Pass," his forward observer reported.

Jeff held his breath.

Five minutes later, the observer reported again. Jeff wished he'd shut up.

"Um. Grandpa is still in motion."

Gawd, Jeff worried furiously. *Could the pro words be any more obvious?*

Two of the three electric buggies appeared on the ridge, gleaming in the fresh sunlight. Jeff prayed for luck.

Jeff keyed his radio. "Breakfast is ready," he said. It was code for *stay dead still. They're coming.*

The first two Abrams tanks crested the pass and clanked down into the valley. They didn't pause. The Abrams took advantage of gravity, sped up going down the hill and clattered down the road until they reached the bottom of the slope where the off-ramp emptied into Scipio. There, they fanned out and seized the points of dominance.

Perfectly timed, the next Abrams appeared, immediately in front of the first fuel tanker truck. The cartel was leaving nothing to chance, executing a perfect security maneuver, only nothing was perfect in war, and tight security meant "the best defense we can mount given the circumstances."

The Hoodies couldn't protect against a buried, semi-suicidal enemy willing to throw themselves in front of the cannons of the Abrams.

The next part would require precision, and the biggest thing Jeff had going for him was that none of his pickup truck gunners could actually *see* their targets. They would be shooting blind, which meant that nobody could get a morning hard-on and start blasting too early.

Jeff wrapped the space blanket tightly around him and nestled close against the trunk of a juniper. He was four miles away, and Jeff's position was so deep in the valley that the tanks' thermal imagers would barely measure a blip, no more than the heat signature of a rabbit.

Another tanker truck appeared in the gap. Then another. They were rolling just thirty yards apart. If it'd been Jeff in charge of the tankers, he would've spaced them a football field apart, but the Hoodies had opted for increased cover under the Abrams' cannons.

Three more tanker trucks appeared, then the final one. They were all six in the valley, now, but not yet on the "X." Jeff wouldn't trigger the ambush until all six tanker trucks hit the flat.

They descended into the valley. The guns of the Abrams sat silent, but poised. The gun buggies loitered on overwatch. The clanking of the main battle tanks on rear security rattled the morning calm. A mist hung over the Scipio valley. It carried the dirty pine-pitch scent of juniper.

The brakes of the convoy howled across the distance. The fuel trucks shuddered to a stop; the Abrams downshifted to a stop. Jeff's blood froze.

They weren't far enough into the envelope of the ambush. *But did he really have a choice?*

Jeff tucked the M240 SAW machine gun into his shoulder and he let the space blanket slide off his back. He clicked the safety off and aimed in the direction of the six tanker trucks as their idling engines barely mumbled. Jeff couldn't hit them with a 7.62 machine gun from four miles away, but that would be the trigger for the ambush: Jeff's machine gun opening up.

The engines growled and whined afresh. Jeff backed off the trigger. The first fuel tanker resumed rolling, then the next, then the next. He lifted his finger from the trigger and placed it alongside the trigger guard. The tanks picked up speed. Whatever had caused them to hesitate had gone away. It took a full two minutes for the convoy to resume travel.

The first tanker truck reached the off-ramp, the "X." Jeff's finger gravitated back to the trigger and rested on the pad. He let out a slow exhale and gently squeezed.

The machine gun shattered the morning silence. Bullets flew out into the light, cool air between Jeff and his enemy. They streaked into the void, hopeless to kill, but waking the militia wolf pack. A moment later, the Scipio valley went berserk. The sledgehammer violence of a hundred Ma Deuce belt-fed machine guns detonated across the valley. Bullets the heft of a ball-peen hammer spiraled up into the sky faster than a fighter jet, then down toward the crossroads. Countless streams of tracer, emanating from dozens of pockets of sand and sage, splashed the off-ramp, surprisingly accurate, right from the start. Within three seconds, one of the tanker trucks exploded in an orange fireball. The other drivers panicked, but the trucks were too close to one another to back out of the sudden maelstrom.

The Abrams on the off-ramps were the first to respond, and Jeff's light machine gun had been the first hot target.

A cannon round shattered a juniper tree just twenty yards from Jeff's position. Bark and splinters showered down. Jeff abandoned the machine gun and ran for his life. Another cannon round shrieked overhead and he hunched. It exploded in the sand nearby and covered Jeff in a thick rain of rock and rubble.

He ducked onto a roadbed behind a hill and sprinted at top speed toward his truck. His adjutant, Hector, who'd been hiding behind a stack of boulders, dodged in behind him, running in terror. They were out of sight of the Abrams, but it didn't stop the cannonade. Another six high explosive rounds gnawed at the hillside and peppered them with frag as they bolted for cover.

Jeff reached the pickup truck first, threw open the door and jumped inside, eager to escape the rockfall. Hector dove into the passenger seat.

"Go, go, go," Hector screamed, forgetting himself for a moment.

"Calm yourself," Jeff said. "Get on the radio. Do your job."

The fusillade turned elsewhere and the cab of the truck quieted. The war raged across the valley, a steady storm of violence.

Jeff pulled the notepad from his vest and blinked back the sand in his eyes to read the dog-eared page.

"Papa Bob," he radioed. "This is Grandma. How are the sheep?"

It was foolish, at this point, to use pro words, but when war was at its worst, Jeff stuck to the plan.

"Hunh?" someone screamed into their radio.

"Bob." Jeff raised his voice. "How many tankers are on fire?"

"What?" someone else interrupted. Everyone was under heavy cannon fire and surrounded by ear-splitting machine guns. Getting a straight answer would be impossible, and it hardly mattered now. They killed whatever they killed. His men would shoot all their ammo and run. Sometimes the simplest plans were the *only* plans.

Jeff started the truck, threw it into gear and spun out in the gravel. He shot up the dirt road until the hills parted and he could see the valley floor below. He slammed on the brakes, threw the truck into park and grabbed his binos.

He didn't need them. The overpass and the interstate leading up to it was an utter wall of fire. He couldn't count tanker trucks because they were a single, hundred-yard-long pyre. The blistering heat must've swallowed the two Abrams tanks too, because their guns had gone silent. The other four Abrams fired, one cannon shot after another, but their targets were moving—a scrambled tangle of pickup trucks fleeing the valley.

Jeff jumped back into the driver's seat, threw it in gear and tore out of Scipio valley, heading west over the foothills.

"Did we win?" Hector begged.

Hunched over the steering wheel, Jeff laughed like a man possessed. He squinted his eyes at his adjutant, and laughed some more. Eventually, Hector joined him.

Gunnison, Utah

BILL MCCALLISTER DIDN'T HAVE time to investigate his heebie-jeebies, but they rumbled in his gut like too much taco and tequila. He'd accomplished his mission. It was the morning after and they were mopping up. But something was off.

The militia semi trucks were blown completely to shit, splattered across the town of Gunnison, as though a boot had smashed a roach and shot the guts across the floor. Bill had his men collecting the 30mm crates, stacking them in a church parking lot, and burning them in a ginormous, snap-crackle-pop bonfire. It never ceased to amaze Bill just how definitively homicidal an ambush could be.

His son had made it out alive, and that was all that really mattered.

Noah had been in one of the scout cars, and other than the now-blackened hulks of the semi trucks, the militia convoy had scattered to the four corners of the Earth. They hadn't even tried to return fire. Bill's QRF stayed tucked in the town of Fayette and they reported no shots fired. His strike team reunited around the Abrams in Gunnison and maintained perimeter security while the others policed up the 30mm.

Bill wandered the north end of town looking for answers to his unease. "Americana" they would've called the style, a three-block row of flat-front Main Street stores with just enough awning to keep the rain off Saturday evening strollers. Lila Lee Apparel had a blooming pear tree in front. Dorius Law Office looked as boring as it sounded, with gilded letters on the door and black-on-gold scales of justice. The Casino Star theater boasted a six-foot wide, old-timey, marquis. Matinees had been at five o'clock, apparently.

Bill drifted north across to the park. There was a tiny, wood cabin with a plaque; it was probably the first building in town. At the other corner of the park he came upon a gray-painted anti-aircraft gun from a World War Two warship.

Again, it was the trim, green grass that pulled him up short. Somebody cared here. Maybe somebody cared everywhere. Maybe America wasn't the piece of shit he'd led himself to believe. Maybe people did things for reasons other than selfishness or political expediency. Maybe they loved liberty, so they mowed the grass.

Beyond the tiny cabin was a playground, and in the jungle gym hung some bit of rags, or maybe wreckage from one of the blown-up semis. Bill stepped closer out of curiosity, and the knot of twisted cloth clarified into the body of a man. The poor, shredded corpse had hung in the playground all night.

Bill tilted his head as he came closer, deciphering the twisted face and singed, black drapery around it.

It wasn't cloth. It was long, black hair. The explosion had thrown the body a block and a half from the truck, probably up and over the Main Street shops and into the park. The broken legs tangled in a playground amusement that resembled a ladder suspended between posts. Bill remembered playing "chicken" on one of those as a kid, back when playgrounds were places of minor, elementary school combat.

The dead guy's head dangled at a downward angle, but Bill could see how that half of the long, black hair had burned down to the scalp. The man had dark skin, like a Latino or an Asian. He had a Fu Manchu mustache.

The eyes dribbled open and the dead man regarded Bill.

"American," the broken man whispered. His right hand moved, as if to reach for his handgun, unsurprisingly absent from the holster, given how far he'd been thrown. The motion caused the body to untangle from the jungle gym and slide to the chip-wood litter of the playground.

One brown eye stared up at Bill. The man's back was broken, and the head was unable to turn.

"American," the voice exhaled again. Bill couldn't tell if he was asking, telling or self-identifying. To Bill's ears, it sounded like an accusation.

The one open eye flickered, then closed.

American, he said. A warrior's dying words. Perhaps, the final dedication of his life.

Bill's head was still cocked, looking into the eye. A wave of dizziness flashed over him.

He stood straight and struggled to locate himself on the planet. Green, trim grass. Tall cottonwoods. A tiny cabin and a cement-filled AA gun. An Abrams tank was parked on the street. The top hatch clanked open.

"Sir," the tank driver shouted for him from atop the Abrams. "Castillo is on the horn for you."

Bill returned to the here and now, crossed the park, and climbed up the treads and onto the skirt of the tank. He took the handset, stretching the curly-cue cord.

"McCallister here," Bill said. They'd dropped speaking in call signs and code when they got the military-grade comms running.

Castillo replied. "Come back to Salt Lake now. We're prosecuting our attack."

"Now?" Bill's sense of doom jumped a notch.

"They wiped out our fuel convoy this morning. Time to shit or get off the pot," Castillo said. He liked using American colloquialisms, probably because they made him sound impressively bilingual. Castillo rarely missed a chance to show off his brains.

"We destroyed their convoy," Bill reported, stalling for time.

Castillo had moved up his timeline for attacking the refinery, which didn't make sense. He'd given them three weeks to find a workaround to a high-risk frontal assault. But Ross had screwed them on the deal to hand over the refinery. And the Utah Militia had destroyed their last fuel trucks. None of those data points improved the cartel's shitty odds of taking the refinery intact. So why was Castillo moving up the attack?

"We destroyed their ammo shipment," Bill said. Things were moving too fast. Maybe that's what he'd felt coming, impending doom.

The psychopathic drug lord answered over the radio, "Good, but that doesn't cut shit now. Return to base. Castillo out."

The line went dead. Bill tapped the handset against his bump helmet. He couldn't shake the feeling that he'd missed something.

Dealing with Castillo was often a white knuckle poker game. But before now, Bill always knew his odds of making the "nut"—the best possible hand. But out here in the sticks, he felt too far from headquarters, in the middle of bum-screw, Utah, and he couldn't get a read on the cards Castillo was holding. Radio communications were useless for reading nuances. Bill needed to get back and get a handle on things.

Hopefully, Castillo wasn't serious about attacking the refinery. Hopefully, he was just angry. Hopefully, Bill could find a way to buy them more time.

American, the dying man had said.

Bill's son was American, and the thought suddenly made him proud, not just of the man, but of the dream, the old dream, old as the town of Gunnison.

This is American soil, the ghost of his mother in his head repeated. *We don't help evil men.*

"Yeah. So you say, Ma." Bill argued with the dead woman, "Life ain't that simple." But in his gut, Bill knew it probably was.

19

"Three hundred and ten million Americans died from violence, flu, starvation, and dysentery, leaving behind three hundred and ninety-eight million firearms. It's estimated that the United States military had over five billion bullets in storage in twelve military depots, and there were sixteen billion bullets in private hands. After the first year of the apocalypse, there were twenty guns and a thousand bullets for every man, woman, and child. It'd been commonly assumed by pop culture that the ubiquitousness of American guns and ammo would result in a melee of violence after a collapse of government. On the contrary, guns and ammo were traded almost as frequently as greenback dollars. Every adult and capable child carried a loaded firearm at all times. It is perhaps unsurprising that courtesy between strangers became *de rigueur,* and politeness returned as a fixture in American culture."

— THE AMERICAN DARK AGES, BY WILLIAM BELLAHER, NORTH AMERICAN TEXTBOOKS, 2037

The Homestead
Oakwood, Utah

JASON HADN'T COME HOME FOR DAYS AND JENNA ROSS WAS WORRIED. She hiked out to the Beringer women's hut to see if her husband had "broken bad," but the Beringer women said they hadn't seen him in weeks and Jenna believed them.

She feared something had gone wrong. Maybe he'd been kidnapped by the cartel or killed by Jeff Kirkham. Jason had played a dangerous game. There were many ways harm could've come to him.

She grabbed her Glock and jumped into her Tesla, then raced out to the airport to confront Jeff Kirkham.

When she inquired, Jeff said, "I haven't seen him, but I just walked through the door from an operation in central Utah." His command tent was a swirl of activity. "I can't talk right now. The Hoodies are getting ready to do something. *Get those birds in the air!*" he shouted to a man sitting behind an oven-sized radio console. He turned back to Jenna. "It's likely that your husband just handed the drug cartel our refinery with a ribbon on top, so if you can talk him out of that, we might not all die today."

"He didn't do that," Jenna said.

"You're sure?" Jeff looked at her askance.

"Mostly." She exhaled. "Pretty sure."

"Not good enough." He waved her behind him and barked orders. "Consolidate platoons one through thirty-six on the wetlands between here and the Maverick refinery," Jeff ordered. "Tell them to break off harassment operations and use the trucks as a blocking force between the cartel and the Maverick refinery."

"Against tanks?" the adjutant asked. "In the open?"

"Yes. That's an order," Jeff said, then turned to her, pressing two thick fingers against his temples. "Jenna. You shouldn't be here, but if you're going to be here, find out what the hell is going on at the Maverick if you can. Here's a radio." He grabbed one off a charging rack. "Call me on this if you come up with any concrete information. I need to know if my men are going to get shot in the back by your husband or your Russians."

"I will." Jenna grabbed the radio, turned, and ran toward her car.

"They're on the move!" a spotter shouted in the tent flap. "The Abrams are all crossing the 215 freeway from Highland to Sugarhouse."

Jeff had anticipated this as the first move in a full advance: the Hoodie tanks would push through residential Salt Lake City. They would close out the east flank in a pincer movement around the refinery. Once the formation wrapped the open flatlands, the entire Hoodie line would advance the final five miles to the Maverick. The militia had fifteen minutes before a frontal assault.

"Pack it up!" Jeff shouted to the command team. "We're pulling back."

Jason Ross stared at the stump that'd lately been his left hand. It seemed so strange, now that the white lightning pain had receded to a thrumming roar. He would spend the rest of his life without that hand. He could scarcely bear the sadness of it, despite his rational mind telling him that he would soon be executed soon with or without it.

The uproar in the Grand America bespoke upheaval. Battle, perhaps. Rescue, unlikely.

They'd screwed Jason's left forearm down to the arm of a heavy, oak chair with galvanized straps, then Castillo had carved off his hand with a knife, like whittling a root ball down to a serving spoon. He'd taken each joint apart, one at a time with a razor-sharp blade, while Jason shrieked.

The drug lord had worked the hand down to a nub, carefully separating the ligaments, cartilage, and tiny muscles of the fingers with the same focus as if he was repairing a watch. Jason's screams didn't even cause Castillo's hand to shake. He cut a bit, stopped, and then seared leaky vessels with a battery-powered soldering iron. Then he cut a little bit more. Jason's hours-long agony might as well have been opera music for all it ruffled Castillo.

Now, the stump of his hand ended at the wrist, crafted by a true obsessive-compulsive. Every ragged tip of flesh had been nipped away. The radius and ulna were exposed, shiny and drying, exposed to air. Castillo had carved and seared the flesh into a perfect skirt around the bulbous ends of the bone. The shriveling bits and bloody pieces of what had once been his left hand were stuck to the sides of a white trash bag in a small plastic trash can at his feet.

Castillo had left to attend to other business, and the hustle and bustle outside the hotel room implied big things afoot. Anything would be better, Jason thought, than having his other hand removed.

Still, his broken mind returned to one thought, like a gnat drifting back to the honeysuckle: he had come home to his family. He had returned to his wife. Nobody but he might ever know, but it was enough. Castillo had his repulsive revenge. But Jason had taken back the only thing that mattered.

―――

"NO, NO, NO, NO!" Bill McCallister pounded on the dashboard. New columns of smoke rose from downtown Salt Lake City. The chatter from the radio in his passenger seat told the age-old tale of war unfolding. The cartel was making their move on the Maverick refinery.

Castillo had called Bill back, but he hadn't consulted him before prosecuting the attack. That wasn't good, not for Bill and not for his personal sell-by date in the cartel army.

Over the radio, on his way back from Gunnison, Bill got caught up on the full story of the cartel fuel convoy getting its ass handed to it. Kirkham had obviously received Bill's note. He'd used plunging fire to destroy the fuel tankers. Bill chuckled at the thought. He loved it when a plan came together.

"You go, girl," he whispered to Jeff Kirkham through his windscreen. A Green Beret was a Green Beret. Bill could just as easily be sitting where Jeff Kirkham was sitting right now, running a partisan militia.

"*American,*" Bill whispered to himself in the cab of his Cruiser. He was surprised by the sound of the word, hopeful, clean and bright. He remembered the shredded man hanging from the monkey bars in a green, mowed park, in the center of a town in the heartland of his country.

If Bill had half a brain, he would turn his car around and drive off into the sunset. Returning to Salt Lake was foolish in the extreme. But he hungered to know how the story would end. He couldn't shake the feeling that he had one, fat poker hand left, bulging with aces. On this last round, he'd catch the river and play Castillo for every chip in the pile.

Into the wild gusts of wind through the window of the Cruiser, Bill muttered a missive to Castillo: "I'm all in, you sonofabitch."

It was how he'd played his life, and he wasn't about to quit now.

WITH ONE HAND pressed against the roof of the bouncing truck, half-blind Mat Best shouted at Gabriel Peña. "But why is Kirkham putting us *in front* of the refinery?"

"We're the blocking force," Gabe replied as he swerved around a marshy spot. "*Oof!*" Gabe grunted as his front tire smashed into a boulder behind a clump of marsh grass. "Isn't that basic defense? Get in front of the enemy?"

"Maybe..." The word hung in the air of the jostling truck cab. Their unit, twenty pickup trucks with machine guns bolted to the back, poured into the gap between the advancing Abrams tanks and the Maverick refinery.

Mat couldn't see a damn thing except for the blue-gray blur of sagebrush whipping past the windshield. Because he couldn't see, his brain pieced together an image of the battlefield from what he'd been told.

The dry salt marshes of the Great Salt Lake opened up into a skirt between the mountains and the lake. The airport was on one end of the marshland and the Maverick was on the other, with five miles of open land in-between. Jeff Kirkham had ordered all Utah Militia forces into that gap, between the skirmish line of tanks and the Maverick refinery. It was their last stand.

"If the refinery's shot full of holes, it's no good to anyone, right?" Mat asked the obvious. "So the Maverick is NOT like any other defended structure. It's more like a hostage."

"What?" Gabriel yelped as they bounced over a derelict roadbed. The dust of the other, flying trucks surrounded them in a gritty haze.

Mat gathered certainty as he considered the map in his head, but since he couldn't see, he pondered instead. He shouted his doubts. "The refinery isn't a defensive objective. It's a VIP hostage. You get *behind* a hostage, not in front of one." With the words hanging in the air, he became sure. Mat groped the rattling cab of the truck. "Where's my radio?"

His hands located the Baofeng. He held the radio three inches from his face and punched in the number for Jeff Kirkham's command link.

"Jeff Kirkham, this is Best."

"Go for Kirkham."

Mat shouted over the truck noise. "Send the trucks *behind* the Maverick, not in front of it. Over."

Silence hung over the channel for a full minute. Mat checked the frequency again. It was correct.

He was about to transmit again when Jeff replied. "Mat. This is Kirkham. You're right. Standby."

The other radio, Gabriel's, blasted with Jeff's voice. "Frag-o: all units. Redeploy truck squads to the *north* of the Maverick. I repeat: redeploy to the NORTH side of the Maverick. Make them fight through the objective. Destroy the refinery with your .50s if the Hood Rats overrun it. Kirkham out."

Mat slumped back in his seat as their wolf pack of trucks veered off to circle around the refinery. They passed within a half-mile of the fuel tanks and smokestacks.

"What the hell?" Gabe exclaimed. "The refinery's surrounded by little tanks."

"Are they white?" Mat asked.

"Yeah. They are."

"Russians," Mat said. "At least they're not shooting at us."

"They can't beat Abrams tanks with those mini tanks, can they?" Gabriel asked.

"Not really. The Abrams will go through them like rain through wet paper."

JEFF NEEDED TO *THINK*, now more than ever. Mat Best had just called him out on an absolute blunder. He'd ordered his fighters in between the objective and the enemy, but this wasn't *that* kind of objective. Jeff *wanted* the refinery destroyed if the cartel reached it. Why sacrifice men to protect it? He must force Castillo to shoot *through* the refinery to score hits on the militia. It'd taken a blind man to see what Jeff had been missing.

What else was he not seeing? What were the Russians going to do? Had Jenna pulled a rabbit out of the hat?

The Russians were the wild card, but what could a thousand men and a dozen light tanks do against main battle tanks? If the Russians surrendered the refinery to the cartel, Jeff's trucks would shred it with their .50s, then light it on fire with tracer rounds. But that wasn't the only tool on Jeff's tool belt.

Jeff's command Humvee bounced off the end of the runway of the airport and charged through the outer fence. With his gun trucks circling behind the refinery, he would take up a command overwatch in the marshes north of the Maverick.

"JT, are the Warthogs in the air?" Jeff radioed Hill Air Force Base.

"They're lining up on the runway, boss," JT replied. Jeff could hear the jets powering up in the background on JT's radio. "Don't forget, we've got only one load of ammo. The 30mm from Tucson never showed up."

"Copy," Jeff answered. He had ten planes with a little over a thousand rounds each, flown by half-trained pilots. The A-10 Warthog was a fantastic weapon, but it wasn't the master of the battlefield. It required hundreds of bullets to kill a single tank. The Avenger cannon fired in two second bursts with a hundred and fifty bullets each burst, ideally "chewing" through the tank's armor. The gun fired very fast, from seven, spinning barrels. A single bullet would have marginal effect. To kill an Abrams, and to overcome its reactive armor, it required a well-aimed, concentrated burst of armor-piercing rounds through the thinnest portion of the Abram's plating. A ten plane squadron, with a single load of bullets, would not destroy fifty-three Abrams. Not even close.

"Logan, this is Kirkham. Report." Jeff swapped to his reconnaissance channel. He'd sent Logan, his dedicated marksman, to the top of Ensign Peak, out of the fight, but a critical eye over the battlefield.

"Kirkham, Stark. Hoodie tanks are passing outside of downtown and rolling under the I-15 interstate. Tanks along the I-80 are on the move toward your position. Over."

The attack on the refinery had begun. The Warthogs were lifting off. Jeff's gun trucks were in position. Things would happen very fast, now.

———

JENNA ROSS WAVED at the gate guard at the Maverick. Luckily, she knew him from the Homestead. Leonid *something-or-other*. He waved her Tesla through.

The facility was in chaos. Men and machines darted every which way, and they paid little attention to the Tesla Model S weaving toward the security office. She parked and jumped out of her car, with her hand over her Glock to keep it from bobbling out of the holster.

She scaled the stairs and burst into Colonel Zhukov's command post. He was surrounded by men hovering over a map.

"Jenna. Why're you here?" He looked up, confused. "We're pulling out."

"Where would you go?" she asked.

"North," Zhukov said. "We'll retreat into the mountains."

"Please don't," she begged.

"We might have an alliance with the cartel. We don't know. We lost comms with your husband. Do you know where Jason is?"

"I can't find him. I just came from Utah Militia headquarters and they haven't seen him."

Zhukov groaned. "Then, we must retreat. If we fire on the cartel, all deals are off. Our best bet is to fire on the Utah Militia. They're the weaker force."

"They can still win," Jenna said with a desperate air. "The militia can win with your help."

"I don't see how." Zhukov shook his head. "The cartel has dozens of main battle tanks. Our Arkan rockets might disable a few if we get lucky shots, but we have nothing that can stop this many tanks."

Jet airplanes screamed over the refinery, and everyone rushed outside to see.

"How about those?" Jenna shouted over the howl of jet engines. "Can we win with those?"

Zhukov stared into the sky and scratched at his beard stubble.

———

"*Yee-haw!*" JT Taylor whooped in the cockpit of the Warthog. He had no idea what he was doing, but he was betting it all on being a fast learner. He'd flown an A-10 years before in a video game, so he had that going for him.

"Buzzard Three, return to formation, and refrain from screaming into the mic. You're on VOX."

JT had been wagging his wingtips in ecstasy. He'd flown in the buddy-seat of a jet fighter once over Las Vegas on one of those "fly a jet fighter" experiences. This was way better than that.

There was only one seat in the Warthog, and it was all his. The guy from Tucson who was supposed to fly this bird was back at Hill AFB puking his guts out. He'd drunk some stank water or eaten a bad taquito. JT had jumped into the guy's pilot seat. Somehow, he'd gotten the jet rolling, off the ground and now he was in the air. He felt like the drunk crop duster in the movie Independence Day.

"I picked a helluva day to quit drinking," JT mumbled, quoting the movie.

"Buzzard Three. We can still hear you."

"Apologies, gents." JT grinned and wobbled his Warthog back into formation.

The jets flew across Interstate 80, then south over the once-bustling industrial parks of Salt Lake. A ten-mile-long row of tanks was crossing the freeway and rolling onto the runways of the international airport.

"Contact front," JT barked into the radio.

"Yep, we see them Buzzard Three. Line up last. We'll make our turn around the smokestack at the tip of the mountain and come at 'em from the west. You copy?"

"I sure do, Buzzard One." JT lifted out of formation so he could see the others line up. He had no clue how they were supposed to do this, so he moved out of the way. The plane wobbled in the slipstream and JT fought for control. He got the plane's wings to stop pitching up and down and exhaled.

He couldn't help but say it, "Lead, follow, or get out of the way."

"Still on voice-activated, Buzzard Three."

JT scanned the hundred buttons and switches on the jet's console and couldn't find the one that'd take his microphone off VOX. In that split-second, he almost crashed into the other planes.

"Sorry. Can't fix the VOX," JT apologized. "Sorry, not sorry." *He was flying a freaking jet into battle!*

A couple of the other pilots laughed. They banked around the big smokestack and lined up for their attack run.

"Focus up, ladies," the flight leader said. "Remember: just two second bursts on the Avenger cannons."

"Good to know," JT whispered. He had been planning on dumping his whole load on the first tank he got in his gunsights. "Just press the trigger, right?"

"Put the little green dot in the middle of your HUD display on the tank in front of you and press the trigger. Then disengage and regain altitude."

"Which dot?" JT leaned forward as though leaning forward

would make the heads up display more clear. There were two dots, a circle, and a circle inside that circle, with tons of glowing tic marks and three different sets of numbers floating in the gun reticle.

"The top pip's your armor piercing impact point," Buzzard One answered. "Put that one on the tank."

Sounded easy enough.

"Which pip—" JT almost asked, but he was interrupted by screaming.

"—Contrails! Bearing four o'clock. Another at two o'clock..."

"One o'clock."

"Two more, dead ahead..."

Contrails. The cartel must be firing surface-to-air missiles. JT had no idea what to do about it, so he filed it under "Don't Know/Don't Care" and went back to searching for tanks on the ground.

And there they were, lined up in a ragged line across the flats, with plumes of dust behind them. They didn't look very organized, more like a bunch of roaches running across the kitchen floor. He chose a tank in the distance and followed the guy in front of him as he descended toward the hard deck.

A missile streaked into the engine of the Warthog in front of him.

BOOM!

The plane slewed right and tipped out of formation, bleeding a thick cable of smoke that blinded JT for a second.

Other missile strikes followed, but JT couldn't afford to pay them any mind. He was almost on the tank he'd chosen. He dropped lower, steadied his approach, inhaled and guided the little green dot in his HUD onto the tank. Just before the dot covered the Abrams, JT held down the trigger.

BRRRRRRRRRRR! The plane shook and roared. It felt like he had a Gatlin gun for a pecker. The plane had been built around the gun, like a bun around a frankfurter.

"I say DAMN!" JT yelled.

As he rocketed past the tank, the black smoke of burning oil billowed up from under the turret and the trail of dust behind the tank ceased. "Dead Tank, bitches!" He slapped the stick and the plane wobbled viciously.

"Buzzard Three pull up and shut up. We have incoming." JT didn't know who had called, but the Warthogs in front of him peeled to all corners of the compass, half of them dodging thin trails of smoke. JT yanked up on his stick and gained altitude, building a buffer of "big sky, little bullet" between his bird and the swarm of heat-seekers.

"Buzzard Squadron: regroup around the smokestack and line up for another run."

JT banked north, then back west. He locked in on the stark runways of the airport, and slid into a line of Warthogs. He didn't have time to count them.

He prayed it took longer than a couple of minutes for the Stinger crews to find more missiles.

———

JENNA, Zhukov and the Russian officers stared in awe as Warthogs killed tanks, and missiles killed Warthogs. At least two planes fell from the sky in the first sortie. It was impossible to tell how many Abrams had died. A half-dozen snarled, black snakes twisted up into the air, caught the breeze and bent to the south. The horizon still bristled with the squat menace of armor, kicking up dust and making the ground tremble. Way too many tanks were still coming at them.

The Warthogs banked into another attack line and bore down on the Abrams. This time, fewer missiles rose to meet them. One Warthog took a hit next to the cockpit, cut in half and dropped from the sky.

"They cannot win," Zhukov said. "If they had five times as many planes and half the missiles against them, maybe. Like this, never."

"Dimtriy..." Jenna took his face in her hands and forced him to look at her instead of the battle. "They will not win. Today. Next month. Next year. *We* will win. *They* will lose. This is *our* home."

Something in her words caused a flicker in his eyes, her confidence overcoming his doubt, the partisan's righteousness against the evil of tyranny. She could see it in his eyes: Zhukov understood the compelling power of *home*.

"Yes," he said. "But what do we do now?"

Jenna drew her Glock and faced the incoming tanks. "We fight."

───

"RELOAD and get them back in the air!" Jeff radioed JT.

JT was on-approach to Hill Air Force Base. He needed to focus on flying. "Roger, but it's going to take time. We only have two of the reloading machine-thingers, and we just burned through the last of our combat mix ammo. All we've got now is anti-personnel rounds."

"The cartel doesn't know it's the wrong ammo. Get loaded and in the air as quickly as possible. Jeff out."

JT didn't know how many of the planes had survived. He'd killed three tanks, and missed two others. He'd seen three planes go down and three more were flying, but full of holes.

It sure as hell didn't look like they were winning.

───

BILL MCCALLISTER RETURNED to cartel headquarters just in time to see the galactic disaster play out. It was like watching their armored beast die by a thousand paper cuts.

They were getting chewed up by Warthogs, fuel issues and mechanical breakdowns. In one Abrams, the tank commander vomited all over the controls in sheer terror and fatigue. His men couldn't hack the smell and they bailed out, one Abrams killed by tummy issues.

In the banquet room of the Little America, an enterprising gangbanger had set up a dry erase board with every tank listed in a column and a horizontal bar extending across the width of the board until each tank stopped communicating with HQ. Then he drew an "X" across that line. Dead tanks filled the board.

It came down to addition and subtraction. They'd begun the battle with fifty-three main battle tanks. Bill had returned with one more. The six that'd been on convoy security were just now rolling into the south end of the Salt Lake valley. Fifty-three, plus one, plus six. Sixty tanks.

As best he could tell, four tanks had suffered mechanical failure from the start. One was rendered combat ineffective due to Commander Puke Face. Six had run out of fuel within the first couple of miles. Bill's tank, and the six from convoy duty, were running on empty, and were behind the main battle line. Eighteen tanks hadn't joined due to the equivalent of erectile dysfunction.

Of the forty-two that went to battle, thirty-six had taken rounds from the Warthogs. At least fourteen were dead and burning; the comms group was still trying to make contact with several of them. Another ten were out of action, but might be repairable. That left twenty-four Abrams still in the fight.

Gustavo Castillo paced the floor, pulling out his hair.

"We're taking rocket fire...from somewhere," a commo guy screamed. "We're down two more."

Twenty-two.

Bill shouted over the din, "It's laser-guided missiles from the Russians. Arkans. Tell the tank crews to focus fire on the Russian light tanks." Bill didn't even know why he'd said that. He shouldn't have. He wanted to snatch the words from the air and pull them back. He couldn't help his impulse to win.

Damn my big mouth, he swore to himself.

"Tanks 52 and 34 confirmed killed," the dry erase board guy put red "Xs" at the end of two horizontal bars. Probably Warthog casualties.

"Getting reports of a fuel storage tank hit at the refinery. Maybe from our own cannons."

"Another storage tank hit," a comms guy yelled. A distant rumble shook the hotel windows.

Castillo began mewling and growling. He glared at the floor, then stomped his foot.

"Sir," McCallister sensed an opening to make up for his bad judgment, so he lied like a sonofabitch. "My long range recon patrol reports that the Utah Militia has set fire to the Sinclair, Wyoming oil refinery. Sir—they're burning down our backup plan." Bill had no long range recon patrol in Wyoming. He had no idea what was up with the Sinclair refinery. He just wanted to add to the confusion and make up for all he'd done to help these bastards.

"STOP!" Castillo screamed. "Stop the tanks. Stop them now. STOP SHOOTING AT OUR FUEL!"

The communications room flipped into chaos as five radiomen tried to take incoming intelligence and to issue new orders at the same time.

"We have the refinery half-surrounded. We're two kilometers out. Holding position, sir."

"Reports of aircraft overhead. More A-10s out of Hill AFB."

"Castillo!" Bill yelled, trying to penetrate the confusion and rage. "Gustavo! Do you have a white flag? Some way to call a truce?"

The drug lord looked at him with feverish eyes, his hair pulled out of its coif in all directions. Castillo's eyes burned with rage and sudden, molten uncertainty.

"Here's what we do now!" Bill leaped, feet-first, into the confusion.

"Jeff, Hoodie tanks are holding two clicks from your position," JT radioed from the sky. "They look stopped."

JT hadn't re-armed his plane. The line had been too long. He'd refueled then jumped back in the sky with only the three hundred rounds of combat mix left over from the first sortie. If he'd waited for the stupid reloading truck, he would've spent half the day on the tarmac.

JT was on his own, without a wingman or flight leader to tell him what to do. He searched the sky anxiously, more afraid of a mid-air collision than getting hit with a SAM.

"JT, Jeff. Why are they stopped?"

"I don't know. But there are like twenty tanks in a two-mile semi-circle with the Maverick refinery in the middle. No dust clouds. No movement. And you've got four storage tanks on fire, bro." JT used the massive columns of smoke as a navigation beacon. He circled them in a five-mile donut. Four storage tanks out of thirty or forty were burning. Hopefully, the fire wouldn't spread.

"Copy," was all Jeff said in reply.

The Stinger missile fire had stopped. Maybe he was too far from the Hoodie ground troops for them to get target lock on his plane. It'd been an armored blitzkrieg, and it looked like the Hoodies had won. They had at least twenty tanks still alive.

But the tanks had stopped, and JT couldn't tell why. As he circled the burning refinery, a missile snaked out from one of the small tanks tucked around the refinery and struck an Abrams in the turret. Chunks flew off in the fireball, but there were no secondary explosions. The tank didn't return fire. It just took the hit on the chin.

"Jeff, I think they might be waiting to talk." JT said on his radio.

Hundreds of gun trucks jockeyed to the north of the refinery. JT couldn't tell if they were shooting at the tanks or not, but from over three miles away, against armor, it would've been pointless.

"Who's shooting rockets at them?" JT asked.

"Jenna Ross," Jeff replied.

"Bad ass," JT mumbled. The Russian Spetsnaz had finally chosen a side.

On his next turn, JT lined up on a tank and burned through all but sixty rounds in his Avenger cannon. The tank took the hits like a punching bag. No smoke. No secondaries.

"Buzzard Three," the earphone still clamped over one of his ears warbled. "Buzzard Six and Nine lining up on you."

"Um, how about I line up on you, instead," JT said.

He really had no idea what the hell he was doing.

———

JEFF HAD six A-10 Warthogs in the air, now, but he was reluctant to use them. They were armed with anti-personnel rounds, and he was pretty sure those rounds would ping off the Abrams like bottle rockets. If they fired on the tanks, eventually the Hoodies would figure out they were shooting blanks.

The Abrams were stopped, at present, arrayed around the refinery at lethal range. It was a Mexican stand off against real life Mexicans.

The Russians must've figured out the fire suppression systems at the refinery because the flames and smoke from the Maverick were tapering. Jeff still hadn't heard from Jenna Ross, but it dawned on him that he hadn't given her his main command channel. He'd handed her the radio reserved for his field guys, buddies like Evan or Logan who might call in with asymmetrical intel. Jeff dug around on the table for the right radio, marked with big, white "B" for "Bros."

"Jenna, this is Kirkham. Come in."

"Jeff!" she gasped. "Finally. I've been trying to reach you."

She addressed the recriminations first. Apparently, that was a thing women did even in the middle of a tank battle.

"I've been busy," he said. "Report."

"Um. Nice to hear that you're okay." On the other end of the radio, she waited. For the life of him, Jeff had no idea what she wanted him to say.

"Jenna, can you please tell me what's going on at the refinery?"

"We have injured people. Some men were killed. Eleven, I think. We're fighting the fires right now. We think we can get them put out because the fuel overflowed into safety tubs dug around the storage tanks. We're out of rockets, though. We lost four of our armored vehicles."

"So the Russians are on our side?"

"Yes," she said. "Have you heard from Jason?"

"I'm sorry. I haven't."

She sniffled into the radio. "What do you want us to do now?" she asked.

"Hold steady. Prepare for another attack." Jeff paused to get his head around the tactical map. The Russians were on the front line, essentially embedded in the refinery.

"I recommend the Russians pull their armor and gun emplacements deeper into the refinery. Give the Hoodies no clear target. They're obviously reluctant to put rounds into the Maverick. Let's use that to our advantage. Should I be talking to the Russian officer in charge?" he asked.

"No. It's better that you talk to me," Jenna answered. "I'll let you know what we end up doing here. Bye."

20

Shortwave Radio 7150kHz
3:00pm

"JT Taylor, your radio host here. I'm not saying that I'm Top Gun or anything, but I did earn myself a jet fighter pilot call sign. That's all I'm saying. I'm a self-taught fighter ace. I killed a bunch of Abrams tanks. If the ladies chucked panties at me, I wouldn't blame them."
"So, what's your call sign?" Zach asks over the airwaves.
"That's not important. I'm just letting Planet Shortwave know that anything's possible—even teaching yourself to fly a jet fighter in the middle of a battle and racking up a bunch of kills on your first try. But maybe that's because I'm unbelievably talented and had already trained extensively on video games."
"What's your call sign, though?" Zach asks again.
"It's not important."
"Yeah, but what is it?"
"Chatterbox. My call sign's Chatterbox," JT blurts.
"Cool," Zach says. "Chatterbox. That's awesome. Tell us how you got that name."
"Could you please get off my show and go find something else to do?"

Flying J Travel Center
North Salt Lake City, Utah

JEFF HAD NEVER FELT LESS LIKE A STRATEGIC GENIUS, BUT IN THIS moment, he had no choice. It was the biggest, scrambled-egg mess of a battle he'd ever seen. His staff grabbed armloads of junk from the ransacked quickie-mart and with a bright orange spray can, Jeff sprayed out a twenty-foot wide map on a blank spot in the parking lot. His people used empty ice cream vats to mock up the Maverick refinery. They placed empty beer bottles for tanks and sprinkled hundreds of cigarette butts behind the refinery to represent militia gun trucks.

Twenty-six Abrams Main Battle Tanks held the southern approach to the Maverick. Two kilometers ways, the defending Russians had eight surviving armored trucks and a thousand men. They were supposedly on the militia's side.

Maybe the cartel had stopped short of their objective to negotiate the militia's surrender. Maybe there'd been a coup in their leadership. Maybe stopping two clicks out had been their plan all along. The tanks were in position to destroy the refinery for a day, now, and yet no attempt had been made to parlay.

"Is that General Kirkham? I can see that it's either a man without a neck or a fire hydrant with arms," Mat Best said as he approached.

"Master Sergeant Best. That was a good call on the redeployment behind the refinery. You saved a lot of lives." Jeff gave credit where credit was due.

"I can't fight, but I can still yap," Mat said. "My own ass benefitted, which is always good. I'm happy with my ass in its current state."

"Any thoughts about what the enemy's up to? Jeff asked.

Mat looked at the sky. "I think they set their mission objective on fire and it gave them pause."

"General Kirkham," Hector waved a hand and hurried across the parking lot to where the two men stood in the middle of the enormous sand table map. "I think you should hear this." Hector had a notepad, but he didn't look at it, just waved it around like a prop. "Our border outpost into Wyoming at Evanston just interrogated two suspicious, *umm,* Latino travelers heading east out of the state. Our men might've gone a little overboard with their interrogation, and the captives confessed they were going to *Sinclair, Wyoming* to check out the oil refinery, to see if it was still intact. Get this: they were doing it secretly for *Gustavo Castillo.*"

"It's still intact?" Mat asked. "The Sinclair refinery?"

"Someone burned it down." Hector shrugged. "You're the one who reported it. You and Gabriel Peña saw it."

"Oh, yeah. *That* refinery," Mat said. "It's leveled."

Jeff looked hard at the beer bottle tanks at his feet. "If the spies were sent recently, it implies Castillo's making tactical decisions *fast*, like a bull dumped in with the cows."

"Maybe the tanks ran out of gas?" Mat suggested.

"All at once?" Jeff doubted it. They'd sacrificed a lot of lives to deprive the cartel of fuel, but there was no way to know precisely how much gas they had left. It was hard to imagine fuel becoming that big of an issue.

"Have any of the tank crews bailed out?" Mat asked.

"A few," Jeff replied. "But those might just be the ones disabled by the 'hogs' or the Russians. Most of the Abrams are still sound. They're just sitting, waiting for us to flinch or something."

"Should we send someone to knock on the door and ask to borrow a cup of sugar?" Mat asked.

Jeff rubbed his bald head. "How long does it take for a main battle tank to rust out?"

Mat laughed and shook his head. "I wouldn't get too comfortable. Any minute, someone, somewhere is going to make a decision. This is us, standing up against the wall while the firing line chooses the best background music. My advice: don't worry about tactics. Get ready to run."

Salt Lake Water Reclamation Facility
North Salt Lake City, Utah

BILL MCCALLISTER HAD SMELLED his share of human waste, in the gutters of Africa, Haiti, the Philippines, and the Middle East, but this went beyond anything he could recall. This was the fifth circle of sickly-sweet hell. The cartel had decamped forward to the only cover near the Maverick refinery: the county sewage treatment plant.

The collective poop of Salt Lake City had been swilled, stagnated, partially frozen, thawed, and then allowed to ferment for three months of spring. Now that the blazing heat of summer approached, the off-gassing smelled capable of evolving new forms of life. The facility was easily as big as the Maverick refinery, and it produced a fuel of its own, though hardly useful.

The smell permeated everything, including their mood. Castillo had made himself scarce, hiding in the Airstream trailer he towed around as his personal quarters. He seemed to be waiting for something, some piece of information that might unlock the stalemate that had arisen from his ill-advised and suddenly-abandoned charge on the refinery.

Bill would've been more concerned for his own skin if Castillo weren't also refusing to talk to Saúl. Both of the lieutenants were either on the chopping block together, or they were being ignored. Nonetheless, the peril to them was immense. The entire army teetered on the edge of oblivion, though the enemy had no way of knowing.

In the last twenty-four hours, six more tanks had idled their fuel tanks down to empty. Castillo had learned the hard way that the Abrams tank, even sitting still, consumed quite a lot of fuel to keep its hydraulic pumps cycling and it's defenses active. Saúl had resorted to shuffling tanks on and off, shutting down most of them to save fuel while a few idled, and occasionally moving their turrets just too look alive. With the climate control off on the idling tanks, the atmosphere inside must've been foul. Only the threat of a thousand enemy machine guns must have kept the tank crews from running away on foot.

At least the Warthogs had stopped shooting at them. Bill's Stingers had downed at least four of the ten planes. The other six planes circled over the refinery on a rotation. The enormous wasp nest of gun trucks flitted around behind Maverick to the north, ready to pounce.

Saúl discussed pulling gas from the reserve tanks and sending a small fuel truck out to the tanks in the field, protected by the seven Abrams they now had in reserve, but they were both concerned that any suspicious activity might spur another round of attacks by the Warthogs, and any single bullet could destroy the fuel truck.

And was it really worth upsetting the applecart while Castillo brooded? A mistake could get them both lined up in front of a firing squad. Keeping their heads down and waiting seemed the most prudent path.

"Saúl," Bill approached with a map curled in his hand. He needed to look like he was doing something. He'd always been the guy with the Big Plan, and he needed to keep up that appearance. Otherwise, Saúl would sense his shift in allegiance. "Should we send three tanks to flank around here, behind the refinery?" Bill knew it was a bad idea. "We could push back those gun trucks and maybe clear more dead space for a refueling mission." His finger ran a line across the salt flats in a flanking move that could push the militia back another mile. It'd clear the left flank enough that they could get a fuel bowser out to the tanks.

"The Russians could still hit us from the refinery," Saúl stated the obvious. He looked like shit, with bags around his eyes and his hair unwashed for days. He pointed at the refinery on the map. "My forward observation post says the Russians set up heavy machine guns on top of the big storage tanks. DShKs. They'll waste anything we send out into no-man's land. Do you want to be the one to tell Tavo that we lost more fuel?"

"Nope," Bill said. "Has he been out of his trailer today?" Bill changed the subject and folded up the map.

"Yeah. He got breakfast and had conversations with two guys I don't know."

"Who?" Bill asked, suddenly guarded. There wasn't supposed to be anyone he didn't know. He was in charge of intelligence. If Castillo was meeting with new guys, that could be the end of Old Bill.

He needed to get out of this army. It wasn't just the horrible smell, the writing was on the wall. *Death is Nigh. The End is Near.* The cartel had played their hand and now their juggernaut of tanks was down to a quarter of its former heft, and most of them were running on fumes.

In the heat of the moment, Bill had straight-up lied to his boss about the Sinclair refinery being burned down, and that lie would eventually land him in the torture seat.

Yet, that was the hitch, the tiny, barbed hook that held him twisting in this foul-smelling, wind. He had been at the right place at the right time to fight for his country, to confuse Castillo just enough to get him in a bind. Just like the long–haired, dead man said. *America.* He stuck around because he knew in his bones, before that psycho killed him, he'd be in the right place at the right time. Again. And maybe he'd save some important shred of his long-gone country.

With a few words tossed out to the breeze during the confusion of battle, Bill had blunted the cartel advance. He'd saved the refinery, and set the clock running on a time bomb that would also, probably be the end of him. Castillo would eventually find out that the Sinclair refinery wasn't destroyed. Bill would probably get his dick chopped off or something worse, but in the end, he'd begun to feel like this country was worth saving, even after it was trashed.

He could feel it, even see it on the snow-laced mountains that towered over them all. *America the beautiful.*

Bill closed his eyes and groaned. He despised those words and all the vacuous, flag-waving bullshit they stirred up among the masses. But in this moment of great peril, he believed them. Only now, at the end, he'd come back home, and knew the place for the first time.

Now that America was gone, he wanted it back. It was a terrible time to discover sentimentality and patriotism, but here he was, pining for John Wayne movies, Main Street parades, and Grandma's farm. Bill had seen it in the cut grass of Gunnison and the dying eye of a broken warrior. America wasn't dead. It hadn't been forfeited. His son had been fighting for it all along, and it was worthy of both of their lives.

"Well, damn it all to hell," Bill cursed at himself.

So this is what regret feels like...

"McCallister," someone shouted, jerking him out of his reverie. It was Castillo, coming down out of his Airstream. "Make contact with the militia. We're withdrawing, and THEY are going to give us the gas to do it."

Bill looked up at the mountains and they gave him strength. He didn't know if he actually felt his balls drop or if he only imagined it, but his belly warmed. Shit was about to get real.

Showtime.

"Jenna, this is Jeff." Her radio was on full-blast and it woke her with a terrible fright. She'd been asleep on the couch in Zhukov's office. The colonel had stayed away from the mobile office while she'd slept off her scorching migraine. Jenna could hear men bustling outside, probably re-organizing and re-arming.

They knew they were a sacrificial force, sitting on top of a firebomb, daring the enemy to commit mutual suicide. Jenna stayed, and somehow, it meant everything to the Russians. They'd even moved their command headquarters while she dealt with her headache. They were true, old school gentlemen, and she was proud to fight alongside them.

There had been a moment in the battle, as the tanks rushed across miles of wasteland, that she'd fired her handgun dry, flinging 9mm bullets across miles of nothing, against armor that could stop a missile. As silly as it seemed now, her head buried in a pile of throw pillows to block out the light, it hadn't seemed silly then. For a moment, the Russian paratroopers had gaped at her moxie, then dashed to their gun emplacements.

Her little ones waited for her at the Homestead, but she was right where she belonged.

"Jenna, come in. This is Jeff Kirkham."

She sat up. "Yes. Jeff. This is Jenna." The light coming through the gaps in the blinds dragged her migraine back. Her hand hunted for water and found a water bottle on the floor beneath the sofa. She unscrewed the cap and took a long drag.

"The cartel wants to talk. You and your friends should be represented at the meeting."

She smiled. "That's a good thing, right?" she said. *They might not all die today.*

"Don't count on it," Jeff grumbled. "These are not the kind of people who give up."

"Oh." She paused, not knowing what else to say. "When's the meeting?"

"In an hour. Come to my headquarters at the Flying J truck stop and we'll go out together. Bring a Russian officer. It'll be good optics for us. Kirkham out."

Jenna didn't know what that meant, "good optics," but she couldn't speak for the Russians anyway. Not in military negotiations. She got up, arranged herself, and went looking for Dimtriy.

AN HOUR LATER, Jeff Kirkham drove into the gap between the circled Abrams and the Maverick refinery. He sat in the cab of a Humvee with Mat Best, Jenna Ross, and the Russian Colonel Zhukov. Nobody spoke. The cabin noise of the Humvee, clattering over salt-crusted bowls and criss-crossing vehicle tracks, was insurmountable save for shouting. They were headed into the unknown, to face an enemy they'd never met, to discuss terms they couldn't predict.

Jeff had never been a negotiator, or a diplomat. He'd been a weapons specialist in the army, the furthest thing from a peacemaker. He'd never even been an officer, but he did know the history of war. Nothing about the conflict of these past months had been modern warfare. It'd been savage, ancient, and more than a little medieval.

The Battle of Hastings, the Siege of Orléans, The Blitzkrieg of Poland, and Stalingrad—all those historical battles harkened to the War of the Wasatch. Jeff considered the similarities and differences as he piloted the Humvee to the mid-point in the battle lines.

Nobody waited for them and Jeff worried that it might be a trap. But two minutes later, a dust plume appeared between the distant Abrams and a black SUV approached.

"That might be Jason's car," Jenna shouted over the engine noise.

The Hoodies stopped thirty yards out, nose-to-nose with Jeff's Humvee. Four men stepped out of the black SUV.

Jeff knew instantly which man was McCallister. He had the wiry look of an old mercenary. This was the man who'd sent Jeff the diagram of plunging fire, the architect of his successful ambush.

Jeff didn't allow his gaze to linger on McCallister. He read the body language of the other three. Gustavo Castillo was obviously the tall one striding forward, good-looking and feigning confidence.

"Checkmate," Jeff said to the drug lord, behind a face of stone.

The Mexican stood a head taller than Jeff, and he straightened his back taller still. "I think you mean 'check,' don't you? And, I'm still not clear. Whose move is it?"

As planned, six Warthogs overflew their meeting. The jet engines drowned out any argument.

Castillo chuckled. "I see. Should I shoot one down?" He toyed with a radio clipped to his belt.

"You called this meeting," Jeff replied. "How about you move it along?"

"Okay." Castillo nodded. "We would like to disengage…"

"Then disengage," Jeff snapped.

"We require fuel to withdraw." Castillo's eyes sharpened, as though glaring might fortify the weakness of his position. "If you don't give us fuel willingly, our best bet is to try our luck against the refinery. Surely, not all of the storage tanks will burn."

This scenario hadn't been on Jeff's list. He hadn't thought they'd ask him to *give* them fuel, but he could see the logic in it. They couldn't retreat without it.

"Leave the Abrams and go," Jeff said. "I grant you safe passage out of the state."

"No, no, no." Castillo wagged a finger. "Where I go, they go." He held up a palm.

"I'll send you a thousand gallons. Good riddance," Jeff said.

"*Psh.*" Castillo sniffed. "That wouldn't get us out of Salt Lake county. It's going to take a lot more fuel than that to reach the state line."

"If I give you any more fuel than that, you'll attack. I'm not topping off my enemy's gas tank."

"Be reasonable, General Kirkham," Castillo cooed. "Give us a thousand gallons now, and another two thousand at the county line. Then another thousand gallons every twenty miles, back to the state line."

"You'll withdraw completely?" Jeff asked. "To where?"

"We'll pull back to central Nevada," Castillo offered. "*If* you provide the fuel."

Just two days before, Jeff figured himself for a dead man. Suddenly, he felt like he had this ass clown on the ropes. One good ambush and ten Warthogs had tipped the fighting octagon on its side. But this was far from over. If he gave them fuel, at any point, the Hoodies could double back and hit them again. Or, they could tap another source of fuel in Mexico, California, or Texas and come raging back, like a fiery case of the clap. Jeff could not, under any circumstances, allow the Abrams tanks to leave Utah. If he did, they would hang over them all like a guillotine.

Once the tanks got underway, they'd go farther and farther out from under the cover of the Warthogs, not that the Warthogs did him much good without armor piercing rounds in their cannons, but Castillo would know that he was getting out of range, and he could concentrate SAMs around his retreating convoy. The Warthogs would have their horns clipped if he let Castillo go.

"I'm going to need certain assurances," Castillo continued. "I want hostages to guarantee our safety."

The Russian colonel huffed at the unexpected turn. There hadn't been hostages exchanged in battle for a thousand years. It was an artifact from the days of royal blood—a preposterous ask.

Jeff considered torching the refinery right then, while the Hoodies ran on fumes. If he destroyed their gasoline, they'd be good-and-proper fucked. His gun trucks would wait them out until each tank crew finally ran for cover, then they'd mow them down.

They'd hunt Castillo and his gangbangers like jackrabbits, and every one of them would die, with Utah dirt clotting their wounds.

But without the refinery, it'd be almost impossible for Utahns to restart the oil fields, the pipelines and the transportation system. Instead of making it happen that summer, as they'd planned, it'd be five years, maybe more. Five years of starvation. It'd be another bitch of a winter. The flu would come raging back, stoked by the hunger.

The people of Utah had stabilized, grown hopeful, even, with the plan to use the Maverick refinery to trade with Idaho, power farm equipment, and get the local power plants back online. If Jeff set fire to the Maverick, that hope would go up in smoke. They'd be starting over from nothing. They'd be set back to horse-drawn carriages, and it'd take years to breed enough horses even for that.

"Mat, can you get the folding chairs out of the back of the Humvee? And the map?" Jeff asked. "This is going to take some time to pencil out." Jeff turned to Castillo. "Let's talk specifics."

―――

"And for the hostages, I'll take the blind guy and your wife," Castillo said to Jeff. "Aside from those I already have in my possession."

Jenna Ross sat up straight.

"You're not getting my wife," Jeff blurted out.

Jenna spoke for the first time. "What Jeff means to say is that his wife isn't in the state. She left with their children some weeks ago," Jenna lied.

"What about you then?" Castillo asked. "All hostages and prisoners will be returned to General Kirkham at the state line. Why not you as a hostage?"

"I'm a mother, not a warrior," she declined, though that was exactly what she wanted. She understood men like Castillo, men who wanted what they couldn't have. She knew that Castillo might have her husband prisoner, and she needed to go to him even if that meant giving herself as a hostage.

"Who else have you taken prisoner?" Jeff was probably thinking the same thing.

"Chad Wade, the Navy SEAL. Evan Hafer. Jason Ross. A few Mormon bishops and stake presidents."

Jenna covered her shock.

"What is their condition?" Jeff asked.

"They are more or less intact."

Jeff shook his head emphatically, probably guessing what Jenna wanted to do. "We're not giving you anyone else. You have your prisoners. Release them at the border. I'll agree to that."

Castillo observed, then reached a conclusion. "Either I get her and the blind man as hostages, or there's no deal."

"I'll go." Jenna stood, unclipped her holster and set her handgun on the table. Mat Best did the same.

"Then it's settled," Castillo said. "Bring the first thousand gallons to the sewage treatment plant and we'll begin our withdrawal immediately." He motioned for Mat and Jenna to follow. He got a few steps, then turned back to Jeff. "I don't have to tell you what happens to them if you deviate from the conditions of our deal, do I? When I'm angry, I can be rather…surgical."

Jeff glared, but said nothing.

21

"Without a power grid, the American Southwest became a land of nomads. Small oases persisted along the shores of reservoirs and in valleys anciently occupied by Native Americans, such as Walnut Canyon and Wupatki Pueblo. Nomadic Native American tribes took up their old ways and followed ancient cycles of gathering. The Paiute, Goshute, Shoshone, Ute, Washoe, Apache, and some Navajo eschewed land ownership and followed the harvest of fish, bird, animal, and plants in circular patterns across vast tracts of America. They went where the food grew naturally, harvested it, and then moved to the next bounty. Non-native, usually white, survivors filtered into these nomadic clans, intermarried, and eventually erased the racial distinctions between them. The concept of 'race' in the Southwest and Great Basin moved from skin color, lineage, and even religion, and focused on how a person, family, and clan conducted food acquisition. Farmers looked down on foragers. Foragers disdained permaculturists. Permaculturists despised farmers. But there was plenty of land, too much really, and each practitioner of agriculture practiced their lifestyle without infringing on the other—for a time. Eventually, communities and governments formed around the dominant agriculture of each region, passing laws and arbitrating land disputes in favor of the 'most moral' method. Even agriculture could serve as the basis of division. Old prejudices realigned around how a person fed their family, and those prejudices hardened. Rather than race, religion or nationality, the new lines of hatred between a man and his neighbor were set between monoculture, permaculture, hunting, and gathering. It would not take long for that hatred to manifest in violence."

— THE AMERICAN DARK AGES, BY WILLIAM BELLAHER, NORTH AMERICAN TEXTBOOKS, 2037

Sun River Parkway Interchange
St. George, Utah

FOR THREE DAYS, JEFF TWISTED AT THE END OF AN OVER-SPUN ROPE. He could not allow the twenty-seven surviving Abrams tanks to leave the state. And yet, he could not let his friends die.

It'd been a grueling three days, fueling forty gallons per Abrams at each stop, and resetting overwatch in case the Hoodies decided to double back and counter-attack. Then they did it all over again twenty miles south. Inch-by-inch the cartels shuffled out of Utah, and inch-by-inch they moved closer to the death of his closest friends.

It was as though Jeff himself was the executioner, with the days ticking down to the final day, the day he would be responsible for putting his friends in front of a firing squad. Castillo would not hesitate to kill his hostages at the slightest provocation. He might kill them anyway.

Jeff's left hand shook with palsy. He suffered from headaches, day and night.

Tara had rushed from Tremonton to stand by his side during the cartel's retreat, but she could do nothing for him. The slow, clanking march of a confrontation with his sins, a lifetime of war-making, bore down on Jeff as the red rock walls of the Utah/Nevada border approached.

"I can't," Jeff mumbled to his wife. The time had come to order his fuel tanker trucks forward to meet the Hoodie army at the port of entry, where they'd receive the final top-off. It'd be enough gas to get them to Las Vegas. It'd also be enough for them to turn around, wipe out Jeff's militia and retake St. George.

Jeff wished the cartel would do it. He wished they'd break the treaty. Then, at least, it'd be *war* that consumed his friends, and not his own ruthlessness. He'd made his peace with many decisions to kill. There would be no peace after this one.

"I'm sorry, Jeff." Tara was, for the first time ever, at a loss for words. She repeated back what Jeff knew already. "You can't let those tanks leave. They'll come back. You know that. This is your only chance to end it. At any price, you have to end it. Evan, Jenna, Mat, and Chad, they'd say the same thing if they were here. It's worth the cost."

"They're our friends," he repeated. "We fought to protect *them*. What's the point of it all if they die?"

"Sir," Hector called from the Humvee, monitoring the radio. "The Hoodies are at the port of entry awaiting refueling."

Think! Jeff forced his aching brain to work harder and better. *Find the key that unlocks this mess! Thread the needle.*

He'd failed at so many turns in this war. He'd lost Evan by taking unnecessary risks. Hundreds of men had died on missions he still wasn't sure were critical. He'd missed huge opportunities, failed to think of the Warthogs earlier. He'd failed to foresee the thermal ability of the Abrams and to conduct proper recon. All those mistakes added upon one another, mistake after mistake, until this massive, shitstorm bore down upon him and forced him to make this last, fateful, unavoidable decision. He had to sacrifice them. There was no other way.

"You must," Tara said, reading his mind. She touched his forearm and his skin stung where she touched him.

His entire army, almost a thousand gun trucks, was marshaled and ready, two miles north of St. George. They were prepared to swoop in and strike. It would be a bloody, chaotic melee that would last for days, but it would be final. When the last Abrams ran out of fuel, this war would end. His friends would almost certainly die. But Castillo would die too. Jeff would have the Abrams tanks and the war would be over, forever.

Hundreds had died. A few more would not sway the math. This was the right choice.

Jeff walked away from his wife and into the desert wilderness.

———

IT WAS the end of the line for Bill McCallister. He wouldn't be crossing the border with Castillo and his band of merry murderers. He pictured himself going down, guns blazing and he was fine with that. Happy even.

Then he saw his son, Noah, being frog-marched forward with the other hostages. Bill's mouth went dry as driftwood.

Abuelo dragged Noah and Willie to the edge of the blacktop of the Nevada port of entry. A dozen riflemen followed. They lined up in a firing line facing Bill's son, his friend and five others.

Gustavo Castillo seized Bill by the shoulder from behind and whispered in his ear. "So many secrets." He spun Bill around, but left the 1911 handgun in Bill's holster. "Am I right?" Castillo grinned, but his eyes cut twin gashes across his face. His smile formed a hard line that matched the red weal across his throat. "So many lies," he whispered dramatically.

They'd done enough shooting together, Bill and Castillo, during the winter in the Nevada desert, for both men to know how they stacked up against each other. Gustavo Castillo was very fast. Much faster than Bill. He *wanted* Bill to draw his gun. Castillo had a hard-on to kill.

Their army was in full retreat and it was anyone's guess if the Utah Militia would keep their end of the bargain and let them leave the state. A good, old fashion gunfight would probably make Castillo feel better about getting schooled by a bunch of hayseeds.

Castillo had been working Abuelo as an asset, probably right from the beginning. Abuelo had picked up Bill's son back in Gunnison, and that left Bill as helpless as a puppy with a nine pound tail.

Noah was on the execution line, hands zip-tied together, his face a mask of defiance. It was Castillo's favorite kind of theater, the kind where he played Shakespeare and Brutus. The playwright and showman. The smartest guy in the room with everyone scrambling to catch up. It was Castillo's superpower—thinking ahead and predicting every act of disloyalty, every turn of the worm.

But Bill had a superpower too. It wasn't sexy, but it'd have to do.

―――

JEFF STUMBLED down a hill and into a sandy ravine. He needed to be alone. If he was going to kill his friends, he wanted one, final moment to think it through.

When was the last time you prayed?

The Mormon president had asked him that question, weeks before, and the words had stuck in Jeff's gob, like a nagging bit of flank steak between the molars. He couldn't take a breath without smelling it. Finally, the thought busted through, fully-formed and insidious.

When was the last time you prayed?

He pictured himself, on his knees, reciting the Mormon-style rhetoric he'd learned in Sunday School.

Dear Heavenly Father, we're thankful for this day…

"Screw that," Jeff said out loud. It was just so *lame*. Embarrassing. Demeaning.

Then it hit him like a shockwave from the cobalt-blue skies: how prideful he'd become. How stoic he was in the face of suffering, how self-contained and certain. He held the lives of his friends, slipping through his hands, and *still* he refused to kneel.

The shock softened his muscles. His legs wobbled. He dropped to his knees in the bottom of the dry wash, next to the sage tumblers and salt cedar spires. Jeff knelt down in the sand, on a planet orbiting a star, circling a galaxy, awash in a universe of a billion galaxies. He was a small, self-obsessed man in a massive, outstretching eternity, a man about to commit his friends to death. He held precious lives: Jenna. Evan. Chad. Even Jason Ross.

His unworthiness drenched him. Saturated him. Why was it *he* who would live and they who would die?

A sob wracked his chest, and he spoke. "God. This is Jeff Kirkham. I don't know what to do. I'm out of options. You call the play and I'll run it..."

A warm, invisible arm wrapped around him and pulled him into the heart of the vast universe. His throat clamped shut, yet he sobbed. His eyes overflowed, yet he could finally see. Never in his life had he felt more loved than in that moment. It almost drowned him, the love was so deep, so wide, and so everlasting.

Let them go. The words rumbled in his ears. *They're not yours. They're mine. Let them go.*

Jeff's taut, hard back went loose. His throat opened, and he wept, loud and unashamed. He cried like a boy. The sadness of losing Evan overwhelmed him. All his dead men cried with him. The suffering of the winter flooded the wash around him, rocking him from side to side.

The vivid dreams of the last year, and the strange turns of fate—the thoughts that had come to him unbidden, those weird bits of the supernatural hit him all at once at this lonely crossroads. He would send his friends to their deaths, and it would be okay.

He could feel it now: all the invisible currents flowing around him, filling the space between this galaxy and the next. In that warm, compassion-steeped vastness, it was *okay* for them to die. They would die into something, or someone, that Jeff could not hope to understand, but he could, for this one, fleeting moment, *feel*. Jeff lingered in that warm bathwater, despite the impending doom. It was too good and too real to rush.

Eventually, he pulled himself to his feet and wiped the copious snot from his nose with the camouflaged sleeve of his shirt. Then he walked back to his wife and his soldiers, his face an utter mess.

"Well, boys. Get your game face on," Evan trumped on the execution line. "Time to die. Jeff must be late with the gas. *Sumbitch* is always late."

Jenna Ross couldn't join them in their gallows humor. The sight of her husband's wretched wrist, with his hand so carefully removed, the bone withering in the sun, broke her heart completely. She knew these were her last moments, yet she could not climb on top of the sadness. Jason's stump, and his broken, hanging shoulders bespoke the finality of it. This man—her man—had finally been shattered. The world must be ending, at least for them, their love affair, their family. She didn't know if it was defeat, but it was the end. The rest of the world, and her beloved little ones, must now go on without her, and without him. Like his dead hand, Jason and Jenna were being carved away from this life.

Mat Best was shoved alongside her. Jason was at the far end of the line and his head hung to his chest. Evan, Chad and two men she didn't know stood with them. They were lined up on the edge of the blacktop in a place that was some kind of weigh station for truckers. She'd seen it before, driving to Las Vegas, but she hadn't known what it was until now.

"Do I get a cigarette?" Evan chortled. "You got your asses kicked by a bunch of Mormons and a general who wears socks with sandals. What kind of morons zip-tie a prisoner with their hands out front?" Evan held out his hands to prove the point.

"Don't listen to that guy. He's an idiot." Chad called out. "A cigar for me, please."

"Make him stop." Castillo flicked a hand at one of the soldiers.

A camo-clad rifleman walked out of the firing line and hammered Evan in the gut with the butt of his rifle.

He let out a woof, doubled over, then straightened. "Now I gotta crap," he said. "Do we get a crap stop before you shoot us? Trust me, it's in your best interests. We won't be here to clean up the mess."

Gustavo Castillo looked at his watch, a hefty, expensive-looking timepiece. Jenna used to love it when Jason wore a big watch like that. She thought it was sexy. She looked down the line at him. His arm hung at his side and he panted with pain and probably fever. He'd never wear a watch on that arm again.

The drug lord glanced around at the orange and pink mountains that towered over the parking lot in the middle of nowhere. The far end of the asphalt strip was crammed with rows of tanks. Most of the cartel army was there too, standing back as though the executions were a disease that might spread to them if they came too close. This was an army adrift in uncharted waters. Even the men in the firing line glanced around like nervous kittens in a room full of stomping children.

The drug lord was waiting for something. This was a show. Six men and one woman had been lined up in open view, in an obvious firing line. It was meant to elicit a reaction of some kind, probably from Jeff Kirkham.

"God help him," she prayed.

NOAH MILLER HAD ALWAYS WONDERED what he'd do if he faced execution. He rolled his shoulders and spoke to Willie out of the side of his mouth.

"Get ready," he said, apropos of nothing.

"Huh?" Willie replied.

Noah took in the whole scene and grinned. There were two kinds of people in this world. McCallisters and everyone else, and nobody understood McCallisters but McCallisters. Noah would bet it all that his dad was about to fuck some shit up.

"Saddle up, brother," he said to Willie. "It's about to go down."

THE FIRST MOVER had the advantage, and Bill always made damned sure he was the first mover. But Castillo had played him. He'd set the table, loaded the deck, marked the cards, and paid off the dealer. But there was the matter of Bill's superpower.

Little did Castillo know, Bill had already been shot, a shit-load of times. He'd been shot in the bicep once, in the legs twice, in the ass, both cheeks by the same bullet. He'd been shot through the left ear and twice in the belly. One time, a 7.62 had just missed his pecker. When he was a kid, his little brother bounced a .22 round off of his skull.

Some guys could take a punch. Bill McCallister could take a bullet.

Twelve soldiers shuffled into a firing line. Abuelo stood behind them. Castillo was turned away, but his right hand hung free. The show was apparently meant for Jeff Kirkham, who was now officially late with his last delivery of gas. He'd never been late before, so this was it. The balloon was about to go up. Time to dance.

Without fanfare, Bill went for it.

His hand snatched the 1911 from his holster, but he could tell right away, by the smile flashing across Castillo's face, that the move was expected. Castillo's hand flickered, like it'd dipped into another dimension, and his Glock magically drove toward Bill's chest.

Bill let a knee go skeewampus, as planned. He pitched sideways to the left. As Bill's own pistol cleared the holster, Castillo fired the first round. It plowed through the fleshy flank of Bill's chest like a bolt of lightning. But his next round went wide, where Bill's falling body had just been.

Bill's .45 thundered as he fell, into Castillo's legs or the ground, he couldn't tell.

Bill didn't even try to catch himself from falling. His senior citizen's legs weren't going to recover, and he didn't care. All he wanted was bullets in the air. His finger slapped at the trigger of his .45, sending rounds in a wild frenzy.

Another bullet from Castillo punched a flaming channel through his shoulder. Bill fell as his gun thundered. Castillo's face did a little spasm, a jump in the eyebrows and a drop in his cheek. His shoulder twisted, yanked by an invisible fishing line. Castillo kept shooting. His follow-on shots rattled like a snare drum. Bill hit the blacktop and bounced.

Castillo hit the ground too, and twisted to the side like a writhing snake. He pawed at the hot blacktop. Somehow, in the flash of gunfire, Castillo had dropped his gun.

Bill scrambled like a stomped lizard. The 1911 was in one hand and the other was full of hot blood. He scaled Castillo's expensive combat boots, up his shins—one shin shattered by Bill's bullet— climbed up the body, snatched Castillo's groping arm, pulled himself up to Castillo's chest, shoved the 1911 under his chin, and pulled the trigger.

The top of Castillo's head spattered across the asphalt. His hand hung a few inches off the ground, then slowly lowered, palm up, until it rested on the pavement, still.

Bill collapsed onto Castillo's deflating chest and gasped for air.

He'd just beat the world's fastest dickwad by shooting him in the shin. Bill couldn't decide if it was the dumbest gunfight ever, or the coolest.

In any case, Bill passed out.

THE OLD WHITE guy drew his gun, but the Latino guy drew faster.

Chad Wade launched himself into the fight, pirouetted in the air as one of the executioners brought an AR-15 around to his face. The bullet buzzed past Chad's cheek.

A second bullet hit Chad's head like a wrecking ball and punched him over backward. Before he hit the ground, Chad's world flicked out like a busted light bulb.

EVAN HAFER RUSHED the firing line behind Chad. They covered twenty yards, half the distance, before the first wave of bullets dropped Chad like a laundry sack.

Evan jinked left and bounced off the running black dude like a cue ball. The black guy took a round in the hip and crumpled.

Evan dipped his head and hit the first soldier in the gut with his shoulder. An errant bullet from the guy's own buddy chipped a chunk off the guy's skull, like a golf club hacking a piece of turf. The soldier went over backward with Evan on top of him.

Evan snagged the dead guy's fatigue jacket with his flex-tied hands and rolled him on his side, like a meat sandbag. The body shuddered from the impact of bullets meant for Evan. Then a bullet passed through and hit Evan hard in the groin. He felt the bullet rattling loose in his jockeys. It must've come through the body sideways. Evan's junk felt like it was bleeding and it hurt like a bitch.

The dead guy's AR was pinned under him. Evan levered the body up. Just then, one of the firing squad dudes came straight at him, hot to punch his ticket. Evan swiveled the trapped AR and shot the guy in the foot, point-blank. The bullet ripped from toe-to-heel and dropped the dude like a baseball bat to the head. Evan put three more rounds into him on the ground.

Evan prairie dogged over the dead guy and grabbed the other guy's dropped rifle.

Safety off, Evan went to work. He shot three confused guys still standing in the firing line.

Boom-boom-boom-diddey-boom.

The other soldiers fled like scattered chickens. Hoodies at the far end of the tarmac decided to join the fight. Their rifles barked like a pack of wild dogs.

The Ross lady, who'd been in the execution line too, was blasting at targets with a found rifle. Some militia dude Evan didn't know laid on top of her like a turtle shell.

Another white guy that Evan had never met was on the ground in a strangling contest with a Hoodie from the firing line. The white guy had a gigantic bloom of blood on his lower back. Evan thought about helping him, but didn't want to crawl out from behind his stack of dead bodies. Rounds were falling around them like hailstones.

On second thought, *screw it.*

"Moving," Evan yelled, jumped up and ran for the cover of a shiny, black SUV—probably King Drug Dealer's pimpin' ride.

The gangbanger army opened up on him from the far end of the parking lot and he took a round in the fleshy part of his thigh. Evan stutter-stepped, then kept running. He hit the SUV hard, denting the door, and rolled around to the back. Bullets smashed into the BMW, shattering plastic and glass, and sending red tail light fragments in a fan onto the blacktop.

Mat Best saw a milky, flurry of action and heard the rattle of close gunfire. He sprang left, knocked the Ross woman to the ground and spread his body over hers.

She shrieked, but he kept her pinned. A dozen rifles joined the fight. They popped off at close quarters. Men screamed and roared. A bullet hit Mat in the back. Another went in the top of his thigh, a raging, cable of pain through muscle and bone. He gathered the woman tighter by wrapping his muscled arms around her shoulders. Another guy from the firing line, shooting and running, tripped over Mat and went down with a clatter. Bullets pounded the ground around them.

The woman writhed under Mat, squirmed half out of his grasp and grabbed the dropped gun. She steadied, and Mat's gut pounded with the compressed concussion of a rifle blasting between his belly and the ground.

The Ross chick had grabbed a gun and was going to town. Mat tried to make space for her to work, but his leg went into flaming spasms when he tried.

"Get...off...me!" she shouted. He managed to roll half off of her torso.

She fired at targets he couldn't see until her mag ran dry, then she belly-crawled out from under him toward a body on the ground. She pawed at a dead guy's vest. She produced a magazine, then flipped the rifle, one way, then the other, like she was trying to decide where to put the mag.

"How do you do this?" she shouted at Mat over the gunfight.

"Gimme," he reached for the gun and the mag. In a flash, his hands dropped the dead mag, reloaded the freshie and smacked the bolt home. "Safety's on." He threw the gun back to her. The AR clattered on the asphalt. She snatched it, rolled back onto her stomach and returned to shooting.

Another wave of bullets and frag *pock-pock-pocked* at the pavement around them.

Mat crawled over to a dead man and clawed at his body, seeking the hard, angular shape of another magazine. He found one in the thigh pocket, dug it out and weighed it in his palm. It felt full.

He scrambled back to the Ross woman, keeping his dick tight to the ground and waited for her gun to run dry.

"Give," he said and reloaded her AK-47, then handed it back.

She must've run out of targets, because she stopped shooting.

"What's happening?" he asked through clenched teeth.

"I have no idea," she said.

"Are you shot?"

"I think so. How about you?" she asked.

"Definitely," he answered.

Mat slid off into a world of pain.

———

JASON ROSS WENT STRAIGHT for Gustavo Castillo when the shooting started. He didn't care if he got shot. But within two steps, Castillo was down. Within two more, his brains were blown across the tidy, painted blacktop.

McCallister eighty-sixed his boss, then he fell.

Jason half ran, half stumbled to the bodies, dropped to the ground and scooped up Castillo's Glock. He would've checked the chamber, but he had only one hand.

The gunfight swirled around him like a tornado wrapped inside a meteor shower. There was no rhyme or reason to it. The firing squad hadn't been prepared for a shootout and they'd been overrun by the condemned.

The old man they called "Abuelo" scampered off into the desert. *Exit, stage right.*

"Ross," Bill McCallister gasped.

Drug Kingpin Number Two wasn't dead after all.

"What?"

"Go help him." The old, shot-up man pointed his hulking, silver .45 at a man taking cover behind the toll booth. McCallister sluggishly dug around in his pocket and changed out his magazine. "I can't get up."

A wave of incoming rifle fire fell around them.

"Go help him," McCallister repeated. "Get your ass behind cover."

Evan Hafer darted across the tarmac and ducked behind Jason's BMW, lately driven by Castillo. Bullets carved off bits and pieces of the SUV while Evan crouched behind the quarter panel.

Jason pushed back the fever that addled his brain, and looked at each body on the ground. There were at least twenty, but he recognized Jenna's right away: a fan of auburn hair, lying in a pool of blood.

"Go help him," McCallister repeated.

Jason ran for his wife instead.

―――

"Grrr!" Evan yowled. "Motherfu..." His leg burned like it was getting worked over with a blowtorch.

He leaned around the corner of the SUV. A fresh wave of bullets poinked into the metal like a flock of angry woodpeckers. Another window shattered.

Evan did a quick inventory: Chad was dead for sure. The black dude was twisting around on the ground with a pelvic hit. The other white guy, the one who had choked out the Hoodie, had found himself a rifle and was hiding behind a little building.

Jenna Ross was face down on the firing line with another militia dude. They lay in twin pools of blood, and neither was moving.

He didn't see Jason Ross, but that guy had been a mess right from the start, missing a hand and obviously in a world of hurt. They'd overcome the firing squad, but that was when good luck drove off the proverbial cliff. A shit-ton of pissed off Hoodies were sorting themselves out at the far end of the weigh station. The whirlwind bore down upon Evan and his remaining friends.

Evan hoped Jeff was watching because it was high time for the cavalry to come to the rescue. They'd killed or severely wounded the firing squad, and the Big Boss was dead. His own lieutenant, the white guy, had shot him in the leg, and then blasted him in the melon for the win.

But now, the whole damn Hoodie army was shooting at them. As soon as they un-boogered their leadership, it'd go bad for Evan and his shot-up pals. Confusion was their only friend, but confusion was a fickle bitch. The Hoodies would get sorted out very soon, and they had tanks.

Jason Ross levered himself up off the pavement, then loped toward Jenna Ross. His motion attracted another spat of gunfire. Evan returned fire and drew rounds to the SUV.

Ross scooped his wife off the ground with his good hand, and she actually helped get her feet under her. She wasn't dead after all. Ross steered her toward the cover behind the toll booth.

They stumbled behind the shack, then up the off-ramp toward the interstate. Ross was getting his wife the hell outta there, using the cover of the toll booth for all it was worth.

"Run, Forrest, run," Evan mumbled. He fired his last few rounds at the Hoodies, still three hundred meters away.

Evan had wounded men down, like that black feller, and the guy behind the toll booth. Evan didn't know them personally, but they fought for the same flag.

He sprinted from behind the SUV, snagged another AR off the ground, and made a galloping, uneven run to the toll booth. The Hoodie rifles crackled in the distance. A machine gun opened up from on top of an Abrams.

The toll booth came apart in chunks. Evan and the other guy flattened themselves to the pavement.

"I'm Evan. Good to meetcha," he shouted and waved. His face stayed glued to the road.

"Noah Miller," the guy responded. "Arizona Freeman Militia."

The belt-fed paused. The dust twinkled in the air like fairy farts. Jason and Jenna Ross ran north. They made it to the interstate and kept going in the direction of St. George.

"Should we run?" Noah Miller asked.

"Not with a crew-served dialed in on us," Evan said.

"Good point. So now what?"

"I was thinking Butch Cassidy and the Sundance Kid," Evan said.

"We go out in a blaze of glory?" Miller asked. "I'm totally down with that."

That was what Evan was going to suggest, but getting shot again wasn't sounding as cool as it had a second ago. He was bleeding a lot and it was making him dizzy. Plus, he wasn't keen on getting shot with a .50 BMG.

"I need ammo," Evan hesitated. "I can't go out dry firing."

"I only got what's in this mag," Miller tapped his gun.

They both lay face down on the blacktop. The machine gun probably thought they were dead. In the distance, another Abrams fired up its engine. In a moment, it would roll down the parking lot, with a stack of infantrymen behind it.

"So do we just stay here while they run over us?" Miller asked.

"Nobody would fault me for it," Evan said. "I'm shot in the ass."

"Bro. We're all shot. That's no excuse."

The RPMs of the tank engine roared and shrieked and the clanking began. The Hoodies were coming.

"Wasn't there a movie where a dude shot a tank down the barrel and it exploded?" Evan asked.

"I dunno," Miller said. "We only had Netflix. But I think you should try that."

"I told you: I'm out of ammo."

They both laughed and couldn't stop. The tank rattled toward them. They laughed until they cried. *When shit gets supremely screwed up, you have to laugh.* It was something Evan's old man said.

"So." Miller flipped on his back so he could look at Evan. "Do you have any idea what the hell's going on?"

"No. Not a clue. I've been locked in a motel room for two months and they let me out for this. Story of my life: they keep me in a box until they need me for janky shit."

The clanking of the treads got closer. Miller flipped back around to watch the tank.

"Hold up. Hold up," a disembodied voice echoed across the pavement. It was one of the cartel. "*Hijos de puta,* STOP!"

The clanking stopped.

Miller scooched out from behind the toll booth and peered around the corner. "Oh shit. That's my dad."

The drawling voice continued. "It's over. *Terminado.* Put your guns back in your jalapeño-holders. Hold onto your chorizos."

"That's your *dad*?" Evan asked as he belly-crawled around to take a look.

"Yeah."

"He's, like, a total racist, isn't he?"

"Yep."

"Will they listen to him?"

Miller gave him a "how-the-hell-should-I-know" look.

"A sniper shot the boss," the old dude shouted to the Hoodie soldiers. "Got 'em right in the melon. It's over, boys. Pack it in. Where's Saúl?"

Evan and Miller crawled up off the ground to their knees.

"Time for *cerveza*," the old man crowed. "War's over. *Dos Equis* for everyone."

"Can you get him to shut up?" Evan asked Miller.

"Not usually."

Evan checked the chamber of his rifle, then dropped it on the tarmac. "You handle your dad and I'll render aid to our guys."

"Roger that," Miller said.

Evan limped over to the bloodbath and sorted through bodies. From the north, he heard a rumbling. Hundreds of pickup trucks from the direction of St. George cut the heat mirage on the freeway like gleaming warships.

The cavalry had arrived.

EPILOGUE

The Homestead

JENNA ROSS LAY BESIDE HER HUSBAND IN THEIR BED. HE SLEPT AWAY the agony of the last surgery, the one that'd taken his arm up to the elbow. She prayed the stump was healing clean under the bandages. They were stained by iodine and blood like they'd been dipped in dark tea. The doctor had assured her it was normal. Her primary concern was infection. She checked his cheek for elevated temperature at the thought.

Jason lay face up, his mouth slightly open. His breath swooshed in and out like the tearing of paper. His shadow-ringed eyes had aged with sun and worry. His hair was fading to gray-streaked, muddy brown, instead of the rich chestnut he'd had into his fifties. She thought about touching it up with her hair dye. Or maybe she'd let them both, finally, go gray.

Jason had told her about his aborted negotiation with Castillo, when he'd chosen their family over his pride. He'd endured torture and sacrificed his hand, and he'd done it for her and for honor. A chapter of her life closed with his fateful decision. In a way, it was a last chapter. She would never leave his side.

There was a knock at the door. Their son Sage stepped into the room.

"How's he doing?" Sage whispered.

Jason woke. "I'm good. I think this surgery's going to stick," he held up his shortened arm and closed his eyes in pain.

Sage came to the bedside. "I've got to get back to Wallowa. Katie's pregnancy must be getting pretty close now. I'm running a tanker truck of unleaded up to Union County to trade for cattle and spuds. I'll be back in a couple of weeks for another visit. I'll come bearing burgers." Sage smiled.

Jason reached out across the bed to shake his son's hand. "Thank you," he said.

"For what?" Sage laughed.

"You got me around the bend. You reminded me who I am."

Sage nodded. "That honor thing. It's a butt-kicker. Am I right?"

"Yeah. It's a hard way," Jason said.

"We're together." Jenna took both of their hands in hers, like a bridge between men. "No matter how bad the world gets, we're family. We grind things out."

Jason looked at her like a travel-weary boy with dark crescents under his eyes and creases across his forehead. When he smiled, the young man who married her broke through and smoothed the troubled waters on his face.

"I barely made it back," he said. "I lost myself. My results snowballed and it got harder and harder to see a way home."

"You don't have to explain," Sage said. "We've all been there."

"You weren't the only one who made mistakes," Jenna agreed.

Jason's face belied his sins, and his guilt. "I got started down a path of killing for expediency."

"We all had to...do things," Sage interrupted. Jenna realized that she had no idea what her son had been forced to do to survive.

"It's not the same." Jason propped himself up in bed with his good hand. "There were men I killed to protect this place, but I also shot the neighbor with my hunting rifle—Tim Masterson. And I killed LeGrand Moore from Mill County for trying to steal our food with a tax scheme. Once killing became a solution to my problems, it changed me."

Jenna hadn't known any of that. She hoped the shock she felt wasn't stamped across her face. She needed time to process. *Could she be with a man who had murdered?* Jason settled back, exhausted from the wounds to his soul.

Jenna had been the beneficiary of his sins, knowingly or not. He'd killed to preserve their home. This Homestead had cost him more than they ever had imagined. Before all this, they thought of it as a refuge from the storm of apocalypse. Instead, it'd become the eye of that storm, a swirling tempest that drew evil into their family. Maybe murder hadn't been the only way, she would never know, but Jason had murdered for *her*. She couldn't claim to have clean hands. Tim Masterson had been rallying the neighbors to take the Homestead's food storage and divide it among them. The Mill County men had come to rob them under the pretext of government. The gangbangers Jason had killed were a raiding army. Everyone he'd killed had been a threat. He'd hoarded the guilt to himself and it rotted his heart. He'd even protected her from the secret.

Jenna spoke. "If you'd told me, I would've agreed to every one of those killings." When she heard herself say it, she knew it was true. "I'm with you, no matter the consequences." In this world of death and violence, the consequences for murder were unknown, maybe nothing, but whatever the consequences were she would bear them with her husband.

Sage stirred, interrupting the spell. Jason's confession had tilted her world asunder, and she was surprised how quickly she found her feet. She'd become a solid woman, a woman who knew where she stood.

"My vote," Sage said, "is that you keep this between the two of you. I get it: confession's good for the soul and all that, but the neighbors don't need to know. Don't give them any reason to try to take this place from you again."

It sounded like wise counsel, and by keeping the secrets, she really would be complicit. It once again sealed their calloused union.

Jason had drifted off, exhausted. His eyes were closed. "Ain't love grand?" Jenna said to her son.

Sage chuckled. "And here I was, thinking you two had life all figured out."

Lakeview Hospital
Oakwood, Utah

MAT BEST COULD FINALLY WALK around his hospital bed, then shuffle the loop of the hospital floor. The air conditioner didn't work and it was stuffy as balls, but at least it was a proper hospital.

"I'm going out." Mat hailed the floor nurse. She looked up from her reading and waved acknowledgement. He was dressed in the same, blood-stained clothes he'd been wearing when they admitted him a month before and his eyes were no better than before. He thought maybe they'd gotten worse. "Can I get a ride from someone?"

That was another thing about the new world: people expected you to exercise common sense. Nobody tried to do it for you. If Mat thought he could leave the hospital, the nurse wasn't going to stop him.

Mat climbed into the passenger seat of the OHV in the parking lot. A few minutes later, a young attendant trotted out of the emergency room sliding doors to drive him.

The doctor had given Mat some eye drops for cataracts, but the world was still a milky blur. He'd begun to accept it.

He and the attendant chatted in wind-buffeted shouts as they motored up the foothills toward the address taped to the dashboard. They pulled up to the only house with a Humvee in the driveway.

Jeff Kirkham came out the front door with a Doberman Pinscher and a battle rifle. When he saw Mat, he lowered the rifle and smiled.

"They let you out?" Jeff asked.

"Not really." Mat climbed down out of the OHV, careful not to pop his many stitches. "I'll be in the hospital a bit longer, but the doc told me to get some exercise. So I thought I'd come visit."

Jeff nodded. "Come in."

The Kirkhams had taken up residence in a little mansion on the hillside not far from the Mormon temple. Mat drifted toward the picture window at the back of Jeff's new home. He imagined that the view over the valley must be amazing, but he could only see thick brushstrokes of green and brown, set under the ultra-blue sky.

"Utah's prettier than I imagined," he said.

Jeff steered one of Mat's hands onto a mug of coffee. "Are you staying in Utah?"

"No. My home's Tennessee. That's where my son lives," Mat said. "And I promised to put him through Ranger School."

Jeff chuckled. "All wars end."

"Thank you for giving me a chance," Mat said. "You made me feel useful again."

"You saved our asses," Jeff replied. "I'm glad you gave *yourself* a chance."

"What will you do about Jason Ross?" Mat asked.

"Hmm," Jeff drew a long breath before answering. "He held my family captive. I can't forgive that."

Mat nodded. "But are you letting it go?"

Jeff sipped his coffee. "I suppose he goes his way and I go mine."

Mat stared at the panorama he couldn't really see. The colors were as vibrant as ever, but the details were gone. It was all rays and swirls. In a way, the view was even prettier like this.

"In the end, we are the dragons we slayed. Aren't we?" Mat asked Jeff. "The dragons define us. They're the white skulls of our past…But even a dragon slayer becomes a legend at some point, then maybe a sage, a priest, or maybe a wise king. It's the warrior who refuses the inevitable who becomes the drunk, the hermit, or the fumbling fool." Mat wanted to give Jeff advice, and he hoped to cover it in philosophy. "We've both seen the warrior thing go south. A warrior's got to know not only who he is, but where's he's at on his journey, when it's done. He has to pass the sword while his hands are still warm."

Jeff sipped his coffee and nodded slowly, thoughtfully. "I never told you how I made the decision to let Castillo execute the hostages."

"No," Mat replied. It was a question a lot of people were asking. *Why had Jeff refused the last refueling? Why did he violate the agreement and put his friends in jeopardy?* On the grapevine, Mat heard that the Mormon Church sidelined Jeff for it, stripped him of his commission. He was no longer their general. Apparently, they couldn't trust a man who would send his friends to their death rather than hand over fuel. Jeff Kirkham had refused to defend his decision. He resigned.

Jeff paused with the coffee a centimeter from his lips, as though struggling to find the words. "Has God ever told you what to do—told you like He was standing next to you?"

"Not exactly," Mat said. But the truth was, he often wondered if it hadn't been God that stayed his hand back in McKenzie, Tennessee, when he considered using chem-bio weapons. Mat thought that maybe his soul, and the town's soul, had been saved by divine intervention. Instead of sharing that tidbit, he covered his awkwardness with a joke.

"God and I aren't really on speaking terms. I haven't always been a Ten Commandments kinda guy, particularly not with the ladies."

Jeff didn't take the bait. He nodded, as though he knew Mat was bullshitting, but it was none of his business.

Outside, in the backyard, Jeff's boys ran across the lawn, howling at the clouds. They pounced on the trampoline and jumped in a jumble, caroming off each other.

Jeff set his coffee mug on the glass tabletop with a clack. "People don't understand what I did and I don't blame them. I don't understand what I did. But I don't *need* to understand. God prodded me along for months after the collapse, with dreams, weird coincidences, and with the perfectly-timed words of my friends. It all came down to that single decision on the Nevada border. God told me to let you guys go and I did."

"God told you?" Mat said, bewildered.

Jeff nodded. "Yep."

It was the weirdest thing Mat had ever heard an officer say, and he'd heard some doozies. But it wasn't nonsensical. Mat wasn't terribly interested in the existence of God, but he found himself unsurprised by the idea of God intervening that day. So much life and death surrounded war, and so much history teetered on the trajectory of each bullet, it was a wonder that the creator didn't take more naked interest. If the Almighty was ever going to throw His weight around, battle would be the right time to do it.

Mat understood why Jeff wasn't talking about it, though, why he'd let the Mormons shit-can him without defending his decision. Men had died. Chad Wade was killed on the spot. Willie Lloyd lost a leg. Evan Hafer would probably limp for the rest of his life. Jenna Ross, Noah Miller and Mat spent a lot of time under the knife, patching up bullet holes and cleaning out pockets of infection.

Jason Ross hadn't been shot, but there was no replacing his lost hand. The doctors had cut it back to the elbow.

But the Utah Militia was now in possession of thirty-seven fully-operational Abrams main battle tanks, a thousand gun trucks, and a full wing of A-10 Thunderbolt Warthogs. Nobody was going to screw with them anytime soon. Their sacrifices had secured the Intermountain West.

"It was quite the thing," Jeff said to himself.

With his jacked-up eyes, Mat couldn't see the lines on Jeff's face, or even read his expression, but he could perceive it, like he perceived the hope strung across the yearning, Utah sky. The war was over and losing his rank couldn't have mattered less to the general.

They would survive the next winter. They would restore their city. And, someday, they would thrive again.

Even without sight, Mat could see; Jeff Kirkham was a warrior at peace.

AFTERWORD

The American Dark Ages,
by William Bellaher, North American Textbooks, 2037

"With the salvation of the Maverick refinery in Salt Lake, the city became the nexus of commerce from the California High Sierras to the Mississippi River. Within a year, the flow of crude oil and natural gas resumed down the Kern River pipeline, from Wyoming to Salt Lake City. Electrical power was restored to the Wasatch Front eighteen months after the Black Autumn collapse—the first major city to restore power. Motorized transportation of food, fuel, and goods commenced within weeks of the defeat of the Army of Southern Liberation, and their trade network extended north into Washington, Oregon, Idaho, and western Montana. A year after 'Blood Spring,' the first industrial manufacturing plant powered up in Salt Lake City. The region's first corporation, Ross Industries, manufactured chemical fertilizers for farms stretching from Cedar City, Utah to Spokane, Washington.

"Salt Lake City became a hub for fuel, agricultural consumables, food, and the first manufactured goods in the re-born United States. Former General Jeff Kirkham revived once obsolete, industrial methods and built a minor manufacturing empire that cast metal irrigation fittings out of molten, recycled steel. He applied the 1920s technology of sand cast molding to everything from engine pistons to tractor hitches.

"Bill McCallister and his son, Noah Miller, disappeared from history after the defeat of Gustavo Castillo. They were said to have ridden off into the sunset, headed for Texas, in a quest to locate a shaman known as 'The Nuge.' Father and son never returned to Utah.

"Evan Hafer left Salt Lake with his wife, children, and a band of misfit warriors, and headed south toward Guatemala in an expedition to restore their depleted stock of green coffee beans. They never came back to Salt Lake City, but shortwave radio rumored them to be farming coffee on the south slope of Volcán de Fuego and inciting revolución against the local oligarchs.

"While the Intermountain West flourished as a semi-Mormon epicenter of trade, another empire solidified on the opposite side of the Rocky Mountains, in Colorado Springs, Colorado, and that empire held claim to the constitutional succession of the government of the United States of America. The President of the United States had blessed the new government before his death, and unwittingly set them on a collision course with Utah and the newly formed State of Zion. Religious faith and legal authority, as often happened throughout history, squared off in a moral struggle to rule a nation."

THE END OF THE BLACK AUTUMN SERIES

With the defeat of Gustavo Castillo, the Black Autumn series concludes. There are nine novels and one anthology of short stories in the series. It was our great pleasure to craft them for you.

Next in the Black Autumn universe, we are pleased to announce three new series by Jason Ross: Fallen Sons, Blood of the Father and ReUnited States.

Fallen Sons (To be published in 2023) Terry Frampton is a liberal, an Ivy League genius and an internet troll. He makes his lonely life worth living by tearing down others and lapping up his own self-righteousness. He's called away to a barely-inhabited Hawaiian island to place final touches on a complicated solar power system for a Native eco-community. As he arrives on the remote island of Kaho'olawe, an apocalyptic virus slams the islands, locking down travel and marooning him on a bald rock in the Pacific. Frampton's the furthest thing from a rugged outdoorsman and he quickly comes to despise his rural, Hawaiian hosts. The islanders punish his arrogance with a ritual beating that sends him fleeing for his life along the beach to nurse his wounds and restore his devastated pride. Without food or water, Terry must either learn to survive or die. Between predatorial waters and parched land, with each life-or-death challenge, the Hawaiian gods shred his technocrat soul. But their plans run deeper and wider than one man's fragile ego. Unbeknownst to all, the mainland United States is reeling from its own apocalypse, and the island of Kaho'olawe has drifted to the center of an ominous, global power struggle. The roiling hatred between Terry Frampton and the Hawaiians could be the tipping point for all mankind, and perhaps a do-or-die test from the stone-crusted, ancient gods, evoking the question, is modern man even worth saving?

Blood of the Father *(To be published in 2023)* As Bridger Callahan promotes the hell out of his veteran-owned survival goods company on social media, he hasn't a clue that he's wandering into a doxxing trap set by ISIS and executed by the Mexican cartel. As Bridger takes his nine year-old son and best friend to Southeastern Alaska on an "Alone-style" wilderness survival challenge, sprinkled among his online fans, an assault team of *sicarios* tracks his every move. In the middle of their challenge, the forest erupts in gunfire and Bridger flees with his child and precious few supplies. What begins as a lark turns into a deadly game of predator and prey with a starving boy caught in the middle. Without guns or police backup, Bridger fights with nothing but a recurve bow and his Special Forces training, but the raw vulnerability of having his son beside him bores holes in his confidence, robs him of sleep and shatters his battle plans. How can a man make war on his enemies without unleashing the demons that could end his family? Bridger Callahan must either find the answer in the moss and cedar rainforest or lose it all.

ReUnited States *(publication date to be determined)* Five years after Mika McAdams is elected President of the United States (*President Partisan*, 2021), tectonic conflict seizes America along the fault lines of agriculture, religion, and foreign invasion. The Chinese army presses east from seized ports along the West Coast, Christian fundamentalists hold their ground in the American Redoubt, the State of Zion flexes its economic muscles, and bands of eco-gatherers and permaculturists battle everyone in a religious fervor to protect the environment from the mistakes of the past. The Dutch McAdams family and their allies navigate a churning tempest of conflict in the ruins of America, relying on secret prophecies and a band of religious zealots controlled by a shadowy artificial intelligence. Will America devolve into a five hundred year dark age, ravaged by war and hatred, or will they find a new path—one that leads the nation back to faithfulness to its founding principles?

ALSO BY JEFF KIRKHAM AND JASON ROSS

The first five books of the *Black Autumn series* rampage through the seventeen days of the Black Autumn collapse, chronicled coast-to-coast through the eyes of thirty-one desperate survivors.

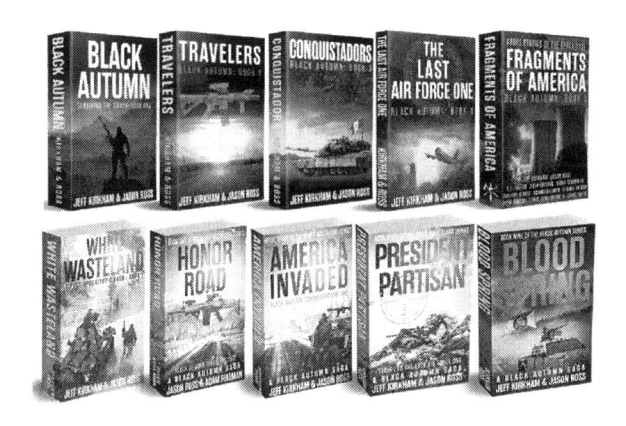

Series in order:

1. Black Autumn

2. Black Autumn Travelers

3. Black Autumn Conquistadors

4. The Last Air Force One

5. White Wasteland (same characters as Black Autumn)

6. Honor Road (same characters as Travelers)

7. America Invaded (same characters as Conquistadors)

8. President Partisan (same characters as The Last Air Force One.)

9. Blood Spring (all characters from all books.)

10. Fragments of America (short stories)

While the unique book order can be a bit confusing, it helps to think of the five "black cover" books as a single, epic novel covering the same seventeen days of collapse, then the four "white cover" novels telling the story of the following, impossible winter. Then, Blood Spring culminates all storylines and characters. Like *Game of Thrones*, or *The Stand*, the Black Autumn series breaks down an epic tale with dozens of characters, fighting for their survival.

Our apologies for any head-scratching that may ensue. We couldn't think of a better way to tell the massive, 2,000 page tale bouncing around in our brain buckets. As usual, I blame it all on Jeff.

— Jason

ABOUT THE AUTHORS

Jeff Kirkham (right) served almost 29 years as a Green Beret doing multiple classified operations for the US government. He is the proverbial brains behind ReadyMan's survival tools and products and is also the inventor of the Rapid Application Tourniquet (RATS). Jeff has graduated from numerous training schools and accumulated over 8 years "boots on the ground" in combat zones, making him an expert in surviving in war torn environments. He spent the majority of the last decade as a member of a counter terrorist unit, working in combat zones doing a wide variety of operations in support of the global war on terror. Jeff spends his time, tinkering, inventing, writing and helping his immigrant

Afghan friends, who fought side by side with Jeff. His true passion is his family and spending quality time with his wife and three children.

Jason Ross (left) has been a hunter, fisherman, shooter and preparedness aficionado since childhood and has spent tens of thousands of hours roughing it in the great American outdoors. He's an accomplished big game hunter, fly fisherman, an Ironman triathlete, SCUBA instructor, and frequent business mentor to U.S. military veterans. He retired from a career in entrepreneurialism at forty-one years of age after founding and selling several successful business ventures.

After being raised by his dad as a metal fabricator, machinist and mechanic, Jason dedicated twenty years to mastering preparedness tech such as gardening, composting, shooting, small squad tactics, solar power and animal husbandry. Today, Jason splits his time between writing, international humanitarian work and his wife and seven children.

Check out the Readyman lifestyle...search Facebook for ReadyMan group and join Jeff, Jason and thousands of other readers in their pursuit of preparedness and survival.

Blood Spring

Black Autumn
Book Nine

by Jason Ross & Jeff Kirkham

© copyright 2022

Created with Vellum

Made in the USA
Columbia, SC
10 April 2024